QPB COLLECTIBLE EDITIONS

Dear QPB Reader:

Several years ago I was on a panel discussion with several writers about "Women and Literature." At one point the moderator said, "All women writers at some point write about adultery. Why is this?" My first response was not, *Is that true?* but, *Do I have to?* The moderator's question stayed with me and I found myself thinking about adultery stories, most of which conclude with the woman either punished for all time, or dead. But what, I wondered, is the story of a woman who is not ostracized, who doesn't end up under a train? Typically, in the adultery story, the spouse finds out about the indiscretion. What happens, I considered, if, in my obligatory adultery story, the child finds out? I thought about my favorite kinds of stories, the naughty schoolgirl story, in which the heroine is plucky, curious, and sensitive; she breaks the rules and ends up wiser to the world and sadder. The adultery story, it seemed to me, was an extension into adulthood of the naughty schoolgirl story. Too, by the time a woman is wife and mother, good daughter and wage earner, she might very well long for the girl she had once been, that unbridled girl who was alive to herself, alive to the world. How about, I asked myself, a woman in middle age itching to fall in love, to have her own self back? Give her a high-spirited daughter, a distracted husband, and, most important, give her a wry, observant son who is a born storyteller, a boy whose favorite poem from childhood is A. A. Milne's thrilling and frightening poem, "Disobedience." It's a funny and astonishing thing, that one question to a group years ago sets a course that ends in paper and ink, and now this edition in your hands.

Best,

Jane Hamilton

Disobedience

Jane Hamilton

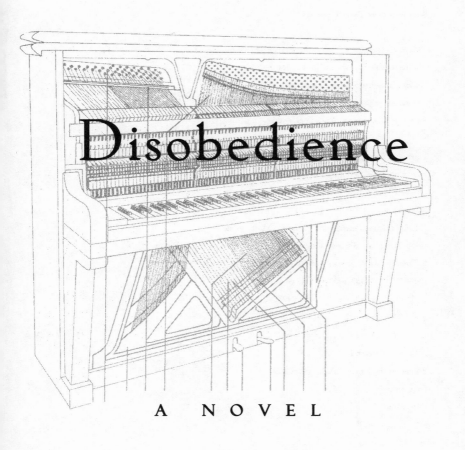

Disobedience

A NOVEL

PUBLISHED BY DOUBLEDAY

a division of Random House, Inc.

1540 Broadway, New York, New York 10036

DOUBLEDAY and the portrayal of an anchor
with a dolphin are trademarks of Doubleday,
a division of Random House, Inc.

BOOK DESIGN BY TERRY KARYDES

Library of Congress Cataloging-in-Publication Data

Hamilton, Jane, 1957 July 13–

Disobedience: a novel / by Jane Hamilton.—1st ed.

p. cm.

1. Electronic mail messages—Fiction. 2. Mothers and
sons—Fiction. 3. Women musicians—Fiction. 4. Chicago (Ill.)—Fiction.
5. Teenage boys—Fiction. 6. Adultery—Fiction. I. Title.

PS3558.A4428 D57 2000

813'.54—dc21   00-029504

ISBN 0-385-50117-X

Printed in the United States of America

October 2000

First Edition

10 9 8 7 6 5 4 3 2 1

ALSO BY JANE HAMILTON

THE SHORT HISTORY OF A PRINCE

A MAP OF THE WORLD

THE BOOK OF RUTH

DOUBLEDAY

New York

London

Toronto

Sydney

Auckland

Disobedience

Reading someone else's e-mail is a quiet, clean enterprise. There is no pitter-pattering around the room, no opening and closing the desk drawers, no percussive creasing as you draw the paper from the envelope and unfold it. There is no sound but the melody of the dial-up, the purity of the following Gregorian tones, and the sweet nihilistic measure of static. The brief elemental vibration that means contact. And then nothing. No smudge of ink, no greasy thumbprint left behind. In and out of the files, no trace. It could be the work of a ghost, this electronic eavesdropping.

I was the boy in the family and therefore, statistically, the person most likely to seize upon the computer culture, the child to wire the household, tune it into our century, keep the two systems, one for me, the other for the rest of the Shaws, up and running. Elvira, my sister, was detail oriented and analytical and could have easily outdistanced me if only she'd had the desire. She had the intelligence, certainly, to learn complex languages, to program, to hack. But through most of the time I was living at home she was scornful of technology, stuck, as she was, in 1862 with her Civil War infantry regiment, the 11th Illinois. At a young age, much to my mother's sorrow, Elvira became a hardcore Civil War reenactor.

It was I who begged and moped a little and pleaded for some kind of computer, a dud, a two- or three-year-old dinosaur—anything would do. I built myself a cardboard replica of the first Macintosh model, and for a good half hour at a stretch I lay on my bed typing on the paper keys, pretending to write programs that would win me fame and fortune. When I was nine, I appealed to my grandmother in a simple poor-boy letter: my grandmother, the one money bag we all in our particular ways went to, again and again, a source that seemed inexhaustible and at the ready. When the box arrived on our doorstep, I sat patiently with my parents showing them the fundamental maneuvers—dragging the mouse, clicking the mouse, see Mommy and Daddy double-click the mouse—as if the two of them were babies being prodded through an ordinary developmental stage.

Several years later with my own money, I seriously upgraded. I had to lure my mother to her own e-mail account with the promise that she'd have satisfaction and even happiness. It was still early days for the kind of communication we now take for granted. Wizard that I was, I guaranteed her pleasure. I provided the password for her so she could commune with her musician friends, the hip ones, so she could have her circle of intimates right in front of her without having to go down to the end of the town. For her screen name I did away with her flat, no-crackle name, Beth, and from the full Elizabeth plucked the zippy Liza, attached her age to it, Liza38. I told her it sounded like the code name of a blond spy with a sizable bust, someone operating out of what used to be East Germany. When I was fourteen and fifteen, I liked to think that what was surely my sophisticated sense of humor had blossomed into its fullest dark and ironic potential. But big-busted-floozy spy jokes were not my mother's style. She was not herself well endowed, and from my point of view she was no seductress. She smiled at my attempt at wit: Nice try, Henry. Although she would but of course retain her dear perfection no matter what name she used, Richard Polloco, the lover, took to the pizzazz of her screen self and often called her Liza38.

When I first stumbled into her e-mail file, I didn't mean to. It was accidental. It was about as easy to type in her password as mine. I wasn't even thinking. I had no plan, nothing premeditated, no scheme in place. I realized my error as the icons slowly formed before me in their beamy pleased way. It was through my fingers that I understood the misstep. "Welcome," our provider said. My hands froze above the keys. And again the voice. "You've got mail." *You've* got mail. What was the old girl up to? I suppose that thought went through my mind.

I can't say for certain what the first message revealed, or even whom she had written. Because it was not only messages from Richard Polloco and messages meant for Richard Polloco that I read during that time, but others too, e-mails that my mother wrote to her friend Jane, hundreds, thousands of words, to explain, to justify, to excuse herself. What I do remember is the letter, a real United States Postal Service letter that I found in the box in the hall, the place we put outgoing mail. I noticed it because it was addressed to him, to Richard Polloco, in Tribbey, Wisconsin. My mother was in the kitchen making up a shopping list, and she must have set it there for just a minute. Richard Polloco. I already knew enough to think, *I shouldn't pick this up,* and *I don't want to pick this up,* and *How can I keep from picking this up?* I held it to the light, and I could see the scrap of paper inside. I could see the scrap, the size of a stamp, so small you couldn't write more than a single word on it. That's what I thought: What did she write that could be more than a single word? I held the envelope up in part because it was seemingly empty. At the angle, with the aid of the lamp, it was impossible not to see that single word on the slip of paper. *You.* That's all she had written. But that single word had weight. I knew enough by then to understand, to feel, if I'd wanted to, the ache in that short word.

It is true that the subject of love, generally, is exhausted, but a person can still go on for a good long time about the specifics of a love scene, including the setting and then who said what and why, and how it made the listener feel. One of the first e-mails I read, and perhaps the very first one, was my mother's message to her friend Jane, back in Vermont. "This is an old story," she began. "There is nothing new in it." What she was doing, she said, was hardly noteworthy because it had been acted and reenacted countless times before. For me, during that year, the story had no elements that felt in any way worn.

I don't believe that everything a person has seen and done is stored in the brain, there to retrieve if only you can pick the right lock. In fact, I blame the brain for making us as selective as we are, for editing out what we don't want to hear, for refusing to take hold of what could be the important detail. Still, if I have forgotten the first message, I have the sense of what it could have been. "This is an old story," my mother began. "There is nothing new in it." The seemingly shopworn tale my mother inhabited did not stop her from recounting, through the year, at great length, her feelings, her guilt, her despair, as well as the particulars—terrible in their vividness—of her journeys to see Richard Polloco in Wisconsin. Rpoll, he was, at luge.com.

This is how our family was back then, not so long ago, less than a decade ago: Elvira Shaw, thirteen; myself, Henry Shaw, seventeen; Beth Gardener Shaw, thirty-eight; Kevin Shaw, forty-three. We had moved from a small town in Vermont to Chicago when I was four-teen. My parents seemed to feel that the upheaval, the trauma, of moving from one culture to another, from Mercury to Pluto, in effect, was worth it for all of our educations. I still ask myself regularly what it was, actually, that they were thinking. My father is a high school history teacher, a job that combines the skills of preaching, mudsling-ing, acting, and arm-twisting. You take his American history survey course and you can never again celebrate a holiday such as Colum-bus Day or Memorial Day or Presidents' Day with any sense of na-tional pride. After my father has done his song and dance, you know more than you wanted to about the roughly 9 million Native Ameri-cans who died between 1642 and 1800. You are filled with disgust, dismay, and self-loathing because a complex civilization, a creative and by and large generous civilization, was wiped out. My father was offered a position at the Jesse Layton School in the tony Lincoln Park neighborhood in Chicago. At the time I didn't catch the detail that he'd been fired from his job in Vermont, probably because too many of his students felt disgust, dismay, and self-loathing after learning about their heritage.

No problem, to move from the Northfield mountains, pure gran-ite, from a town of 317, to a Midwestern city of 7 million built on a swamp. *What, really, were they thinking?* If we were going to go urban, my parents figured we might as well bypass the suburbs and do it up right. Without much discussion, as was her way, my grandmother purchased a brownstone for us on the upscale block of Roslyn Place near the Jesse Layton School. Minty, we called my grandmother, dollar signs blinking in our eyes. It was I, as a toddler, who parsed Grandmother Gardener down to the essential component. It goes without saying that we all wanted to be as close as we could to the aging matriarch, she who ruled with her iron hand from Lake Bluff, Illinois.

As far as the Jesse Layton parents went, the school was basically a front for the Democratic Party, for rich bleeding-heart liberals. If Kevin Shaw couldn't live on a racially balanced street, at least he was given free reign to teach as he pleased, to turn out little socialists from his class to his heart's desire, with the understanding, of course, that the firebrands would someday settle down and become responsible Democrats. Although his salary was modest, he believed his position at Layton had many elements of the dream job.

My mother, for her part, was interested in moving back home to the Midwest because of the cold and snow of the Vermont winters and the mud of the Vermont springs and the black flies of the Vermont summers. Not to mention all year round the warp we lived in, somewhere between the hardscrabble life of the real Vermonters and the artiste vacationers, giddy with their views and the mountain air and their leisure. My mother was ready to leave all of it, and it was a fine time, because the band she played in had gone through a difficult period and split up. She was free of them. Not least, I think she believed that if we stayed in Vermont, her tomboy daughter would one day take off into the hills with nothing on but a loincloth, nothing but her bare hands and sharp new canines to get herself some bloody grub.

Many friends expressed sympathy for us both before and after the move. They had the idea that Elvira and I were being wrenched away from Eden, taking that long fall from the fragrant warm garden to the gritty gray world where, it is true, Elvira would have to wear clothes. Fully dressed and in a brownstone, we would be cramped.

Outside we would be in danger from both the careless ways of the rich and the careless ways of the poor. Chicago would be beautiful in a man-made way, but the splendor would hardly be noticeable because of the exhaust and the grime and the noise and the litter. The natives jogged with their dogs and could not break their strides to clean up after them; it was no better, probably, than a medieval city, the chamber pots being emptied out of windows right into the street. And there would be people, people everywhere. That would be the worst of it, I thought, the feeling that you were always in someone's company. But I got tired of what seemed like pity, and I did want to point out to the chorus that Wellington, Vermont, was hardly Shangri-La, that at the church suppers in Wellington you could get a hot dish with beets called red flannel hash. Furthermore, the librarian, Mrs. Hegley, based on her extensive knowledge of her neighbor's moral behavior, either excused her patrons their fines or did not. My father had been a selectman, and I had heard enough of his conversations about the difficulty in getting monies for the school, for the library, for much of anything beyond snow removal within a week of a storm. Both my parents, I knew, worried about my education and my sensibility in a community where I was the only boy in school during deer-hunting season.

All this is not to say that Wellington wasn't a good place and that I don't still miss it. I was taken from Vermont before I could think to want to leave it myself, and so for me Wellington is the ideal, my old backyard there my deepest sense of home. Right away after the move I longed for it, in spite of the fact that I'd been in a conspicuous position, the kid of a proselytizing socialist schoolteacher and a city-slicker piano-playing mother. To make matters worse, we had no television, not that, as my mother used to say, I didn't absorb most everything I needed to understand about our culture by respiring. Inhale, I got *The Simpsons,* exhale *Beavis and Butt-head;* inhale *Letterman,* exhale MTV, every single song, every single leer. When we finally did get a television, when we moved to Chicago, I watched it that first summer, up in my parents' room, without moving from the bed.

Our family from the beginning did have its share of contradictions. For years we had no boob tube, but in one room we had two computers. My mother nursed both Elvira and me until we were embarrassingly old, talking, walking, assembling seventy-five-piece puzzles, yet she had a weakness for nitrates, for bacon, for Fluffernutters, for sponge cake. She played in a band specializing in antique music, but she often borrowed my CDs. She swiped my *Waitresses* disc presumably so she could listen to "I Know What Boys Like." She was capable of a lot, my mother.

In Vermont I used to make off into the woods, off into the hills, doing what boys have been doing for millenniums, damming up creeks, sitting in trees, getting cold and hungry, and coming home. As my mother put it to her friends, I had had time for reverie. She was either proud of me, on account of it, or proud of herself. It was in the spirit of reverie, I'm sure, that I sat down at the desk in the upstairs office in Chicago and logged onto the computer and found myself in Beth Shaw's e-mail file. I was a senior in high school. I believe it was that message in which she said, more or less, "This is an old story. There is nothing new in it. His name is Richard Polloco. I could tell you that I have been waiting for him for a long time, but that is the sort of ridiculous thing that people in my position say. Here I go anyway. I have been waiting for him for a long time."

I should mention at the onset that I copied every message, except for the first one or two, to the best of my ability, during that year of my mother's restlessness, that year, as I sometimes call it, of Northern Aggression. I printed out all of the messages and stored them in a file folder that I kept in the back of a cabinet in my room. I can account for this archive building quirk when I remember that I am my father's son, an historian by blood, a gatherer of primary source material, a compiler, a boiler-downer. It was a difficult job, but someone had to make hard copies, someone had to pull the words from thin air to have, to keep. I know with certainty, therefore, that on October 14 Richard Polloco addressed Liza38 in the following way through cyberspace: "Hello my screech owl, my foghorn on a misty night, my kettle rattling on the stove, my pot of spilled India ink, my mail-order Hatteras hammock, webbed with dew on a damp fall morning." I record that passage to remind myself at the start that he was not usual. To remind myself that it was perhaps not possible to resist a man who would call her something as apt as "my pot of spilled India ink."

That first I-spy day I read her line, "I have been waiting for him for a long time." I got up and went to the window. I knew that I was going to read on, but I was going through the motions of deciding whether or not I should read on. I remember looking out to the street, out to Roslyn Place, to a car trolling along in the search for a parking place. There were never parking places; parking was the major preoccupation of many residents and every visitor. Up on the second floor I could feel the anger of the driver, the leaking rage he was trying to contain on his fifteenth loop around the block. I had a flash of our house in Vermont, the deep worn red of the clapboard, the hill up the back, Larkey's Hill, the place on top where you could see all the way from Killington Peak up through the Northeast Kingdom to Canada.

I was getting ready to apply to colleges in Vermont and New Hampshire and Maine. I was sifting through application material, writing essays that were supposed to show off my organizational skills, my seriousness, my stunning individuality. What did anything matter? I returned to the desk, stood over it, and scrolled down a little farther. She had seen him a year before, the message said. She had seen Richard Polloco at the wedding of one of my older cousins. She had been waiting for him, then, for exactly a year.

I remembered the occasion of Carol and Jim Carodine's wedding, not because it was a lavish affair, five short maids of honor in blindingly green dresses designed for leggy girls; not because the groom stuttered during the I-do's, as if he was unsure; and not because at the reception the piano player got drunk and puked into the potted palms. No, it was the preparation that was memorable, trying to get to the church on time. "You pick your battles," my mother often so wisely said when she discussed child-rearing with her friends. Despite her wisdom she was a lousy picker. She not only chose the wrong fights ideologically, but she also had an unerring sense for those that she could not win. Carol was getting married in a limestone Congregational church in the sight of God, but more important, in the sight of 325 guests, all of whom were going to be appropriately dressed. My mother had had both my father's and my suits cleaned for the occasion, and for herself she had gone out and spent my grandmother's money on a silver-green dress that changed color depending on where you were when you looked at it, and what sort of light, natural or not, was shining on it. Minty was always willing to pay for the goods that would show off her still attractive, nearly forty-year-old daughter to the best advantage. Mrs. Shaw, following the prescriptive, had purchased a dress for Elvira. It was a sailor sort of dress, navy blue with a red sash at the neck, gold buttons, and red trim, something that my mother thought might appeal to the warrior in my sister even though it was in fact a dress.

As it turned out, my mother thought wrong. Elvira was not interested in looking like a seafarer at Carol's wedding. When I told my friend Karen the story of the sailor dress, she pointed out that, what do you know, the word "dress" in the Middle Ages meant to arrange, to direct, to put in order. Mrs. Shaw, as always, was doing what she could to manage her daughter's appearance, with the hope that, at the least, an outfit would make Elvira's husky voice come up to girl pitch. There were other steps, drugs or hypnotism, that were supposed to work wonders, but my mother had not yet taken advantage of the medical profession or New Age techniques to subdue my sister, to rein her in.

Elvira, as my mother might have guessed, had had her wedding wardrobe planned for weeks. She'd been adding details to her uniform and her hat based on the pictures in her Men-at-Arms Series. You could hear her in her bedroom, her foot hard to the pedal of the sewing machine my father had garbage-picked from the Korean laundry right around the corner. In Vermont Elvira had gone through her Native American loincloth phase and went on to a brief Napoleonic soldier spasm—this is what growing up without a television does to a person. She did look good on her white pony, wearing her blue jacket and the tricolored hat—the plume, I believe, was not authentic—and her tall black riding boots. Once she got going on the Civil War, however, her development was arrested. There seemed to be no movement forward, through World War I, World War II, Korea, Vietnam, right on up to the Persian Gulf. There was to be no Desert Storm on her horizon, with camouflage fatigues, a machine gun, and sunglasses. Elvira in her pre- and early teens became more than a Civil War *buff.* For some reason she found that word deeply offensive, as if it relegated her to a class of persons who were merely interested and knowledgeable about that period of history. Because in fact Elvira was living our nation's great conflict. *She was there.*

Sometimes I wondered if it mattered to her that we'd moved from the country to the city; beyond the obligatory complaints it seemed not to have registered. Certainly she had an initial rush when she learned that we'd be living within walking distance of the Historical Society, the building that houses Lincoln's last dispatch to Grant, as well as his deathbed. That thrill aside, when she woke in the morning on the bedroll she had on the floor of her room, I felt sure that, Wellington or Chicago, she heard shots in the misty yonder, took a swig from her canteen, and pulled on her dusty boots. My father had bought the brogans for her in Kentucky, Civil War reenactment brogans they were, true to the period, identical one to another, neither left nor right. The idea was that if the soldier marched long enough in them, he'd mold them to his feet. In the evening, as she got back into her blanket, I've no doubt that a maudlin song, something like "The Faded Coat of Blue"—*no more the bugle calls the weary one*—tinkled in her ear while she gave up a prayer of thanks that she, Elvirnon Shaw, 11th Illinois, had lived through the day. Not a nurse, never, no angel of mercy on the sidelines, but Elvirnon, the drummer boy, the solemn lad who kept the beat.

To the wedding Elvira was planning to wear one of her uniforms that resembled the 1st Maine Heavy Artillery and not her usual 11th Illinois getup. She was not without whimsy back then, and she admired the 1st Maine red braid that went in a riblike pattern across the chest on the coat. She'd fashioned gold epaulets on the shoulders from chunks of sparkly padded upholstery material my father had gotten in the alley behind the sofa shop on Diversey.

That morning of Carol's wedding, at breakfast, my mother brought in the sailor dress in its see-through bag and hung it from the molding over the door. She'd decided to spring it on Elvira at the last minute, the surprise-attack plan. She hung up the dress, and then she busied herself encasing a loaf of bread in an extra layer of plastic wrap. If you are nervous about what's to come, a task such as that makes more noise than you'd expect. The plastic comes ruckling off the roll. Each small sharp tooth of the convenient metal saw on the package rips, molecule by molecule, through the sheer membrane. If you are anticipating a scene or a fight, you can hear the rupture, the crescendo of the filaments as they are cut, one from the next.

My father for the moment was out, power-walking along the lake, he said, although I suspect he spent his exercise allotment having coffee and rolls down the street and reading the paper with no distractions. Elvira was sitting at the table innocently eating her sloosh, the favorite dish of the other team, the Rebels, cornmeal swirled in bacon grease, wrapped around a ramrod, and cooked over a campfire. In a concession to the twentieth century, and in keeping with the fire code of Chicago—a code that precludes building open fires—morning after morning Elvira roasted the precursor of a corn dog over the right front electric burner of our Amana Colony stove.

My mother wanted Elvira to wear that dress. You could feel her will the upcoming drama toward the right ending as she scrupulously rearranged the contents of the freezer compartment to make room for the loaf of bread. She had probably entertained any number of opening statements and prepared herself for the necessary rebuttals, and maybe she had even come up with the perfect psych-out line—but here, now, the time had come. What to say? How to begin in the presence of the real live girl? Plan one was sweet talk, including the figure my grandmother had spent on the dress. Plan two was thunder and threat. Plan three: nothing left but Beth Shaw's own nervous breakdown, shudders and tears, writhing on the floor, tongue hanging out, the last appeal, have mercy, mercy.

My mother closed the freezer door, took a breath, a deep breath, slowly revolved like a fashion model, off the ball of one foot, and said, "Is your suit all set?" She said this to me, Henry, the warm-up act, the routine before the headliner. "You've got your tie, and are your shoes polished?"

Should I make trouble of my own? Go for the middle of the road? Mess with my mother's mind? Quick, whose side, after all, was I on? "Aw, Mom," I said, "do I have to wear a suit? Couldn't I go as a die or a salt shaker or a breast, dig out some of those old Halloween costumes—"

Elvira, no slouch, turned from her ramrod and looked right at the plastic bag hanging in the door. She narrowed her eyes at it. "Nice dress," she said, two words that so dazzled my mother they left her speechless. If she had not been taken by surprise, she would have rushed at her daughter, kissed her, murmuring pretty nothings: Do you think so? Your grandmother spent a fortune on it, you'll look like the rest of the girls at the wedding, this will make me feel so normal, and all without a struggle, you blessed child, you lamb, you sweetheart.

As it was, in my mother's exhilarated pause, Elvira shook her head. "It's not bad," she clarified, "for a dress." My sister, in what might have been a first, seemed not to want a fuss right at the start. She was apparently going to be both resolute and serene, as if puberty were suddenly working backward on her, making her civilized, mature, and reasonable. "In case you're wondering," she said quietly, "I'm not wearing it."

"But—"

Elvira shook her head again. "No" was all she said. She turned herself around and went back to her cornmeal.

There was certain to be escalation. It was unfortunate that Elvira's calm had given Mrs. Shaw hope, that she'd press on for her cause. "So long," I said into the thickening air of the kitchen.

"Elvie. Elvie. Couldn't you wear it for one hour, for the service?

Couldn't you? It would make your grandmother so glad, and really it's not asking much—"

I was getting my jacket on as quickly as possible, out the front door.

"I told you, I'm not wearing it! Do you understand?"

I walked up Clark Street, bought a carton of California rolls from the sushi joint, and ate them in the comic book shop. They would need a good forty-five minutes to work through the stages of the brawl. I'd go to the bookstore, see if Karen was there. Although Chicago and environs have something like 27 million people, it was possible to bump into Karen as if we were living in Wellington. Karen is the most generous-hearted person I've known—outside of my father, that is—but every now and then she'd disappear into her bedroom for a few days to be alone, to write or paint or read. She was the kind of girl you could tell about my mother trying to force Elvira to wear a dress, and she'd say, "Hmmm. Dress, you know, in the Middle Ages, meant to arrange, to direct, to put in order." She wouldn't insult you by saying anything else, by drawing the obvious conclusion. She had black hair that was always, I hate to say it, a little greasy in a no-gloss sort of way. I don't think she could help it. A poet, she wore a cape, a beret, long black skirts, shirts that buttoned up to her neck, and sometimes she smoked cigarettes on a six-inch holder. Although she did cover herself pretty much from head to toe, she seemed to carry her 180 brave pounds, her fifty inches at the hip, her double D cup breasts, with confidence and even élan.

I'm solid enough at 150 pounds and nearly six feet tall, but I'd been told that Karen and I were quite a duo, in a Mutt and Jeff sense. In those days I had dark hair down to my shoulders, and it was usually clean and shiny and in a ponytail. It was cool, I thought, the sign of an individualist, to have long hair at Jesse Layton. There were only a few of us. I had the rimless glasses of a thinker, according to Karen, just the specs Socrates would have worn if he'd been nearsighted. Elvira said they were dweeb glasses. It was my mother who had gone with me to pick them out, and she had assured me most vehemently that they were not sissy-boy frames, that they made me look as if I knew myself. I remember how she said it. "No," she'd insisted, "you really do look as if you know yourself." *Those glasses allow you to fool everyone, Henry!*

The morning of the wedding Karen was not in the bookstore. She was not waiting for me to show up in the literature section. I picked out a few paperbacks and tried to read, but there wasn't much point without the ritual we went through, she telling me to reshelve the true crime, my gasping for breath when she made for Henry James. There was nothing to do but head back to the homestead, if in fact it was still there, if in fact it had not imploded.

When I walked into the kitchen, the observance had not yet concluded, although the location and the players had changed, as was to be expected. It was not difficult to hear the voices from upstairs, my mother shouting at my father behind their closed bedroom door. Through the arch I could see Elvira in the living room, sitting on the floor, sorting her Dixie trading cards. She was wearing her light blue wool pants, the coat with epaulets and red braid, the belt with the circular brass plate, bearing an eagle motif, the black hat with gold braid and a black plume stuck in the red string that went around the brim. This was a combo 1st Maine Heavy Artillery uniform and the more restrained 11th Illinois. She had her white dress gloves on her lap and her saber by her side. Later, by about a year, when she was invited to be part of a hardcore Wisconsin infantry unit, she would never have allowed herself an ornament that was not strictly in keeping with the regiment. As I remember it, the wedding was her last stand as a fanciful reenactor, someone who felt free to tinker with the past.

When my parents finally came downstairs, we all went out to the car parked up the block and without discussion drove to Carol's wedding. I would have liked to ask them a few details about the conflict, just for the record, in particular how long the kitchen phase had lasted and when and how the tussle moved up into the boudoir. In the car my father blew his nose as if he'd been the one storming and crying. My mother turned on the radio to a station that played seventies hits. All the way to Carol's wedding we listened to songs such as "Run Run Run," "We've Got to Get It On Again," and "Nice to Be with You." The bedroom fight had probably begun as usual: my mother accused my father of leading Elvira down the path of one of the goriest phases of our nation's history. He had more than encouraged their daughter to become a fanatic; her life was going to be wrecked because he had led her astray with his own enthusiasm; she had few friends her own age; she never played with girls; she had no interests other than nursing along her hatred for General George B. McClellan and her divided love for Grant and Lee. Where was this going to take her?

My father would probably have shrugged his shoulders and tried to make the point that studying history never really *took* a person anyplace. As much as he liked to think it, studying history didn't alter the course of the present, didn't change very many people's behavior. It was interesting, reading about the past, that was all. It was fun.

"Fun? Fun!" My mother's lines. This so-called fun was ruining Elvira, taking her out of the current—that's where it was taking her. It was turning her into a certifiable weirdo. Pretty soon she'd be unable to be part of the mainstream, even if she wanted to, for God's sake, the die was just about to be cast. Elvira would grow up to be a woman with curly black hairs on her chin and down her neck, someone who wore heavy boots, chains, tattoos, a strident person no one could stand. Beth Shaw didn't have to get any more specific about what type of female she meant. How would he like it, she shouted at her husband, if she dressed their own Henry in drag and took him to transvestite balls? What would Kevin say to that? What then?

Perhaps my father calmly reminded my mother that as for convention, she had breast-fed Elvira until she was four years old. Elvira slept in the family bed until she was eight. It was Mrs. Shaw who had pursued an alternative education for my sister, sending her to an otherworldly place called Mill Farm School. Maybe he told her that if Henry really wanted to be a drag queen, he wouldn't stand in his son's way. I doubt, however, that my father responded directly to any of my mother's charges. Should he become an historical figure, his biographers will dispute whether or not he was fueled by generosity or wisdom, or if, in fact, he was the sort of man who freely plied out enough rope for his adversaries to hang themselves.

We got in the car and drove to Lake Bluff, to the monolithic limestone church where Carol was going to be married. Because of the morning's skirmish, we were nearly late. It wasn't bad enough to walk up the aisle just ahead of the bridesmaids in a community where most of the women were wearing the same Laura Ashley dress. No, we had to walk up the aisle just ahead of the bridesmaids with Elvira in her 1st Maine Artillery uniform and her saber clattering at her side. Naturally the only available pew was near the front. Look, *clank, ca-clank, clank,* at the Shaw family! My grandmother, Minty, stiff and straight as usual, was the only person in the church who was not facing the procession. I'm not sure I've taken a longer walk in my life. My mother, gliding down the aisle, did her level best to distract in her silvery green dress that now and again gave off a velvety glint. She might have been wearing water, the way she moved in that dress. My father had his hand on Elvira's shoulder. What force could blind a man to his mother-in-law's terrifying erectness; what disability beyond deafness inured him to the congregation's collective gasp at the sight of Elvira? He had his hand on Elvira's shoulder because he was proud, always proud of his drummer boy. For my part, I was sixteen and by rights remote from them all, sure that I was ready to leave them. I kept at a distance, a good ten, fifteen paces behind.

It may be safe to say that Richard Polloco noticed Elvira first, before he saw my mother. Even without the uniform she was striking. It was the dark hair, I think, curling around her face that drew attention, and her enormous blue eyes, the simian roundness of them, as well as her stubby freckled nose, a good strong jaw, enough lip to play the trumpet, and the knobbiest legs you ever saw on a little kid. In front of the dais at the reception she hiked up her wool trousers to scratch her calf before the 325 guests in their suits and Laura

Ashley dresses. She never did anything to dissuade a stranger from thinking that she was an I-could-care-less kind of boy. She called herself Elvirnon in public, in twentieth-century venues, shamelessly, as if it were a real boy's name.

Maybe it was that itch at the reception that began the motion, that propelled my mother toward the dais, toward Richard Polloco. First, Elvira, imagining herself alone in the bathroom, pulled up her pant leg on the dance floor and went at a scab, scratching with her ferocious girl claws, making it oozy. Next, Minty took her slow and certain strides over to my mother, pulled her away from cousin Sally, pointed out the behavior going on, up front and left, and commanded Beth Gardener Shaw to take her daughter in hand, to be firm. To change her. Minty had a large bun at the back of her head; she walked in that regal way, all the movement in her legs, the rest of her upright and seemingly immobile. She believed that anything could be bought and did not understand why a private school such as Jesse Layton, with exorbitant tuition, had not provided her with a new and improved granddaughter. My guess is that my mother had never argued very successfully with Her Highness. How can you fight someone who has worn a bun for sixty of her seventy-five years and furthermore foots the bill on a regular basis for fun, style, and edification?

Down in the church basement Beth Shaw may well have been in a rage not only at her imperious, busybody mother but also at her grossly misguided and intractable husband and her impossible and uncivilized daughter. Without the aid of Maybelline my mother's color was high, her eyes shining. It was at the reception that she saw Richard Polloco, and either he noticed Elvira and her legs, and my mother, or perhaps, as I said, it was only Elvira who captured his attention. He was playing the violin in the band that Carol had hired, and at one point after the piano player had had a little bit too much to drink, my mother went up on the dais and took over, because she could play from just about any period you could name. Richard Polloco had on a tuxedo that was the wrong fit for him, top and bottom and girth. The legs were too long, the arms too short, the waist too high, the shoulders too narrow. He looked like a freakish overgrown boy, not least because his shaggy hair was growing into his eyes. He was flushed and sweaty and probably uncomfortable in his suit, but he was at ease with the music, as if the schmaltzy tunes could make a tight tuxedo feel like a bathrobe. It turned out that he, too, was a substitute, filling in for someone who'd had a death in the family. He welcomed an occasional wedding job, to stave off starvation. Surely he noticed—he must have noticed—the music that came from the piano once my mother sat down at the instrument.

Back to the beginning: Elvira was scratching her leg, Minty was telling Beth Shaw to discipline her daughter, and my father, always interested in structures, had his face up to the limestone as if he were making a geological survey of the basement wall. My mother never whined at Minty; she didn't shout. She seemed to grow cold and still. It was her skin, the pinkness all the way up to her glittery eyes, the heat of that color, that betrayed her fury.

"I do the best I can, Mother," she said before she turned away from Minty, to the dais, to him.

There Beth Shaw was, all those months before she formally met him, looking straight at him with the fever in her eyes. There was nothing in his face, in his skull, that would have met Minty's Waspy standards for the father of any of her future grandchildren. Minty probably didn't look at people like Polloco, didn't see them. His was a broad Slavic face, and his long nose, his slightly hooked nose, had the stereotypical aspect of a religious heritage not our own. Inside his fleshy mouth there were gaps between both of his eyeteeth, structurally a detail that suggested Just Off the Boat. There was the other simple fact of his terrible haircut, the indication of general Bad Taste. He might later say that he had stared at my mother when she turned away from Minty, that both of them stopped their motions, that they were stunned for just a minute, stunned in that gaze.

There is almost no way of knowing anything much about the past, my father says. He claims that he decided to study history after reading Byron's *Don Juan*, after reading these lines:

All human history attests
That happiness for man—the hungry
    sinner!—
Since Eve ate apples, much depends on
    dinner.

I think I am not making up this next part. When my mother turned from Minty, the band was playing a semislow dance version of the Josie Cotton hit "He Could Be the One." Not too long after that song the piano player got sick, duty called, and my mother joined the musicians for the rest of the evening. My father sat by while the group went through a list of past Top 40 songs, each one more appropriate than the last. "I'm Shakin'," "Let It Be Me," "Eternal Flame." The lyrics described my mother's sensations and maybe even her hopes. At one point my father went back into the kitchen, well after the buffet table had been cleared, and managed to scrounge two more chicken salad sandwiches on buttery croissants, vegetable salad with peanut sauce, a slab of roast beef, and another slice of cake. Ahead of his time, and rooting for the other side, he had always believed that Eve had had a bum rap, poor girl, she just wanted to eat an apple. He tapped his foot while Richard Polloco moved closer to the piano, to better hear my mother, to better play off her riffs. Two dinners in one night! I am the hungry sinner, my father imagined. Let them play until morning and he'd get yet another meal out of it.

Chapter Two

My mother could never have home-schooled Elvira without losing
her mind or harming her child, but she did recognize that her daughter would not fit the mold of a public school kindergartner. Elvira
was never going to be a girl who is anxious to please, who obediently
colors inside the lines and sits quietly on the rug during story hour. It
was my mother who took the pains to search out an alternative and
finally settled on the Mill Farm School. We were living in Vermont
in that long-ago time. At the start of Elvira's education my mother
claimed that the Mill Farm School was perfect. She actually used that
word, perfect. It's fair to say, I think, that it was Beth Shaw's misfortune to have enthusiasms, bursts of idealism. My father's good
cheer and optimism, however, were sustained qualities, based, as they
were, on the general futility of the human condition. With his knowledge through history of man's depravity and cunning, not to mention
the whim of unpredictable forces, he figured a person might as well
whistle away and live it up. During Elvira's kindergarten year it was
no surprise that my father became Maud Andelar's champion; it
was he who wished Elvira could stay at the Mill Farm School for all
the grades, including high school.

Maud, as the children called her, ran the kindergarten through
sixth grade, out of her house, on the New England farm that had
been famous at the turn of the century for its Morgan horses. My
father admired Maud, revered her, in fact, because she managed
to teach her pupils the usual and expected material in short order,

leaving plenty of time for individual and group projects. One year all fifteen students tromped on piles of wet wool every afternoon, laid out on shower curtains on the porch, until, after months of this, the eighteen fleeces congealed and became felt. On that wool they did every dance in *The Circle Dance Book* while Maud played the piano. When the felt was finished, the group built a yurt out back true to form, a structure that would have been proud to have a real Mongol owner and stand on the plains of Central Asia.

In addition to the gang activities there was the leisure at Maud's for each student to pursue his own interest. You'd go into the house, and at the kitchen table a ten-year-old boy was building a rocket, a first grader mixing up salt dough for her Mayan temple, the autistic kid reciting the phone book under his breath. Elvira was the one by the fireplace making a diorama of that most poignant scene of her war, the surrender of Lee to Grant at Appomattox Court House.

My father was responsible, certainly, for introducing Elvira to the romance of the Civil War, but no one could have made her a fanatic. That, I'm sure, she did on her own. No one forced her to sit in the bathroom for hours reading catalogs called *Servant and Co.* or *The Blockade Runner*, both outfits that carried complete lines of mid-nineteenth-century clothing and accessories. After a while my mother blamed Maud too, for leading Elvira on. She claimed that Elvira became obsessive because she spent so much time in the perfect environment to pursue a single topic, to develop tunnel vision. And if anyone's an expert on obsession, it's Mrs. Shaw. Still, my mother could not bring herself to uproot Elvira, to place her in the third grade, the fourth grade, where she'd have to sit at a desk and read *Mr. Popper's Penguins* and *Beezus and Ramona*, following along with the class. At Maud's Elvira made hardtack when it was her turn to provide the snack, and she wrote an autobiography of Major Sullivan Ballou of the 2nd Rhode Island, a work that focuses primarily on the first battle of Bull Run, where he died. His death, from a saber wound, takes up twelve of the fifteen pages of this version of his life story.

Maud taught Elvira to sew, and for one five-week period at school Elvira didn't do much else but work on her regimental uniform. My mother seemed not to take into consideration that while sewing, her daughter was learning measurement, patience, craftsmanship, design, history, and the importance of reading the fine print. My parents did not argue often, but when they let loose, it seemed to me that the fight was usually over Elvira. We could be having a normal Saturday, say it was winter. What else was there to do but spend the afternoon sledding down Larkey's Hill? My mother was at home, at her station with hot chocolate and marshmallows, my father in the dining room doing his schoolwork. After the sledding and the cocoa I'd play some duets with my mother, she on the piano and I on the cello. I suppose some might say our life looked idyllic. Maybe it was idyllic in that Dylan Thomas sort of way, the sky-blue trades, prince of the apple towns, all that singing, more or less, like the sea. My father sat at the table scrawling on his students' papers while I attempted, not so much to keep up with my mother, but to play my cello as if I were in the same piece. In the yard, past the shed, Elvira was trying to get the goat to haul her around in a wheelbarrow over the snow.

Out of tune with my time and the splintered families around me, I knew when I was small that our worldly home was composed of the sun and the moon, the planets and the Shaws, the four of us holding together with a force that would not fail, would never cease. That knowledge was something so deep within myself it was usually unknown to me, doing its independent and vital work, much like the steady ticking of a heart. It is questionable, I think, whether it's better in the long run for a young person to have that kind of faith. I also understood that if there were meteors and asteroids cracking into heavenly bodies far off, producing a little heat, a little light, there was also my mother, sparking up, at the ready for the quarterly blowout she had with my father. In spite of those disruptions, perhaps even because of them, the Earth continued to whirl its way through the solar system.

It could happen on that same winter afternoon, that idyllic day of sledding and cocoa and music. Somehow my parents could end up in their bedroom, my mother, at least, taking her requisite number of paces, turning to squarely face her opponent.

"We're standing before our own child!" my mother would fire off. "Our own child," she'd rave. "We're standing by watching the immolation!"

"Immolation?" my father would ask in his good old bewildered way. "Torching a person? Making a sacrifice, killing yourself by—"

"Oh, yes, yes, exactly, Kevin. That's exactly what I mean."

"Bethy, 'immolation' is a strong word. That's all I'm saying, and it's probably not one to use—"

"Look! Will you look at her?" My mother was jabbing at the windowpane, pointing at Elvira. Her own little daughter was pelting the goat with firmly packed snowballs from behind her fort. Not only was she stoning the goat, she was gleeful about it. If anyone was near to being immolated, it was Tiggy.

Sometimes I'd walk into the middle of the room when my parents were brawling. It took no small amount of courage to do this. I'd have to talk myself into it, remind myself that there were rewards, of course there were rewards. I'd open the door slowly, check to see where exactly they were in the room. I'd walk to a place between them and say in a normal tone of voice, "Why are you yelling?" I wouldn't ask it of either one of them, but my mother would take the question personally. If she had begun to quiet, all of her flared up again when I spoke, her bright tongue flashing in her open mouth, wide open to the dark red hollow down her throat.

"We're not," she'd bellow, "yelling."

What was there better, in its way, than that scene, my small mother trembling open, the hot sound of her breathing toward me, the swimmy heat and flush of the air?

"You could call it yelling," my father would say.

"And why wouldn't we be yelling! Why wouldn't we?"

I'd have to remember, for a minute, what the argument was about. Elvira. That was it. That and nothing more.

"Why not see it from this angle, Beth? Excuse us, Henry. Be with you in a minute."

My father was talking as if my mother were her normal down-in-the-kitchen self, as if they were conducting a conversation about dinner. Somehow he was able to speak from outside the thrill of the room. He was standing in the corner by the hissing radiator, his arms folded over his chest. "Elvira's developing a passion," he'd explain, "and it seems to me that it's probably immaterial what the passion is. All the while she's learning how to tackle an interest, she's learning how to find information she needs, and she's weaving that knowledge into her life in a way that feels useful to her."

"Passion," my mother repeated.

"It's a skill," he said, "that will hold her in good stead for the rest of her education, forever. So many of the kids I teach don't have the slightest motivation to—"

"A skill?" my mother spit. "A skill." She started picking the stray items off the floor, a sock, a shoe, a book, a pen, a battery, a pocket-knife. "She is beaning a poor defenseless goat with icy snowballs, what a skilled person she is becoming, yes, I'd absolutely have to agree with you there. A skill!" Head down, she was moving over the floor at an impressive speed, snatching at the debris as if she might gobble all of it up.

My father removed the plastic insulation from the window, with great effort opened the frozen casement, and shouted, "Elvie! Cut that out. We'll pour hot lead on you if you don't stop. Tiggy looks like she's about to die." He shut the window and turned to Mrs. Shaw. "If you feel strongly about this, we could move her to the public school."

I'm not sure, but I think it's possible that my mother said, under her breath, "I hate—I hate your guts." My father continued to speak, and often it was curious what happened to my mother when he went full tilt into his lecture mode. Sometimes she began to fold back into herself, the quivering maw of angry Beth Shaw growing smaller and smaller, the trembling going inside, going, going, her mouth snapping shut against the last of it. She could do that, swallow the rage, like a fire-eater, all of that heat apparently snuffed out with a gulp.

"We both know how fierce Elvira is, Bethy. We both know she'd do well in most any situation." He meant, and my mother knew it, that their daughter would stick to her guns no matter what school she attended. You can take the girl out of the Yankee, but you can't take the Yankee out of the girl. My mother must have understood what my father was up to; whatever instincts she did or did not have, she surely realized that he was trying to call her bluff. Beth knew, and he knew it too, that she did not have the strength to remove Elvira from the Mill Farm School.

Kevin talked on then, remarking on the few good teachers I'd had, one in third grade and one in fifth. My mother yawned. I got up from the floor of the linen closet, my place of retreat, and went all the way downstairs. The argument, what served as their subject, had not gone much of anywhere. Beth got busy in the kitchen making soup, chopping the thick woody carrots from the garden with vigorous strokes. My father went to his table to grade a stack of tests. Elvira had come in from the cold and without self-consciousness taken off her clothes. She stood naked, pink and shiny, in front of the wood-stove. As if nothing had happened during the afternoon, at dinner my father told us an amusing story about the custodian at school, and my mother complained about Georgina, the fiddle player in her band. My father laughed at Beth's imitation of Georgina's bowing technique. When Georgina was tired, she played as if she did not have enough muscle in her arm and her face to keep her instrument tucked under her chin. My father listened to Beth's reconstruction of an argument she and Georgina had had about the tempo in a piece called "Waters of Holland." In the end, as he got up to clear the table, he said to my mother what any person likes to hear: "I don't know how you do it." He shook his head. "I don't know how you put up with that woman."

.　　.　　.

I have no idea how long most people can sustain awe, but Elvira had reverence and wonder for at least five minutes when we visited the Museum of the Confederacy in Richmond. The sight of Lee's uniform and the resplendence of his sword nearly brought her to her knees. When we passed by the house where Lee lived for two years following Appomattox, my father was discreetly overcome. His lower lip momentarily went out of control, and he bit it, on the sidewalk before the brick row house, the only one of its kind left on the block, with the green shutters, the tall windows, the yellowed curtains. I guess we can't help thinking, against our better judgment, that the objects that touched an historical person are themselves possessed of a certain grace. Despite my mother's reservations about Elvira's interest, it must have impressed her that her daughter, out of reverence, for a full five minutes, was speechless.

In Vermont, and later also in Chicago, my father took his students and Elvira to Civil War reenactments, both locally and out of state. Those weekend events were equal part flea market, camping trip, and costume party, and in the middle there was usually a battle, what amounted to a cops-and-robbers session. At night, after the dead had risen from the slaughter, the hardcore reenactors made do without tents, just as many soldiers did in the real war, sleeping against one another, turning together at intervals, settling down again, a line of weary infantrymen hugging the next stranger for warmth and comfort.

Ordinary people from ordinary walks of life dressed up and took on personas of privates and officers, drummers and shysters, preachers and cooks, long-suffering wives and patient fiancées. All the campers brought what they could for the spectacle. Some showed up with horses, some with cannons; others brought only their first-person impressions, their gift for Civil War gab. One summer my father purchased a daguerreotype camera with the big black hood, and he hauled it to every site and set up as the regiment's photographer. The families who brought their own cannons rolled them out of their garages, loaded them into their pickups or horse trailers, set them off a couple of times over the weekend—*Boom! Boom!*—and hauled them home again.

Springing to the call can be a cumbersome and expensive proposition, even without a camera the size of a phone booth or a two-ton cannon. You can run up quite a bill buying the uniform, the brogans, the canteen, haversack, cartridge box, shoulder strap, waist belt, belt buckle, cap box, tin cup, tin plate, wool blanket, hand-forged tent stakes, the tent—not to mention the rifle, the saber, and the scabbard. For a few years in Vermont Elvira and my father kept a nag named Betty, "the steed," they called her. I have to admit that it was rousing to watch the cavalry, Kevin Shaw in it with all his heart, charging across the open field, kicking good old Betty and shooting his pistol into the dusty air.

For Christmas the year Elvira was twelve, she got an authentic reproduction 1853 Enfield rifle musket that probably cost around five hundred dollars. After she unwrapped it, put her hand to her mouth, stared at it, said she didn't believe it, she held that gun in her arms, rocking slightly, as if what she'd opened were a baby doll. My parents had surely found a time when we were out of the house to have a bloodbath over that present. I suspect that finally my mother went through a list of alternative gifts and realized that there was nothing, not one thing, that would make her only daughter happy. On that Christmas morning she seemed to be a graceful loser, a good sport. She clicked her tongue, she smiled, she sighed.

As I said, Elvira went to the reenactments, not as a girl on the sidelines, not as a nurse taking a sack of amputated limbs into the woods to bury, and not as an ingenue in hoopskirts waiting for her beau to come home. It was Elvirnon who went to the campground with his drum, his fife, and his 1853 Enfield rifle musket. It was Elvirnon who filled his haversack with a flabby carrot, a potato, a pair of dry hand-knitted socks, and a tinted photograph my father had made of my mother. Elvirnon was not just scornful of reenactors who did not take the trouble to dress with attention to authentic detail: he was disgusted by them, by those who are known in reenactor circles as farbs—short, obviously, for "far-be-it-from-authentic." Farbish behavior included eating packaged food, smoking cigarettes, using a sleeping bag, and wearing a watch or modern-day eyeglasses. Among all of the boy reenactors Elvira hung with, not one of them knew the true identity of Elvirnon Shaw, 11th Illinois. It is a fact that there are more than three hundred documented cases of female soldiers who impersonated men, and Elvira and my father believed that going to the reenactment weekends incognita was not in any way tampering with an event and its players who were striving to be authentic.

My mother made something of a living playing the piano, and she occasionally did research for documentary filmmakers, searching out appropriate tunes for their subject matter and hiring her musician friends to work on the sound tracks. She was a piano player for a big-deal Civil War documentary, one of the ironic details to know and tell about our family. When she got the job, Elvira for a short time was polite to my mother and nearly tongue-tied. Through her music Beth Shaw expressed the typical sentiments of a classical pianist: beauty, the briefness of rapture, and let's not forget sadness, sorrowing, the grandeur of lost passion, lost youth. There was her daughter, head over heels in love but not with life, not with all that was grace-ful, comely, and fair. No, little Elvira was crazy about carnage, the gorier the better; little Elvira lived for scenes of wanton destruction. My mother must have looked at Elvira, and instead of being able to think characteristic mother thoughts—my treasure, my dear one—she thought, Where did you come from? Who are you? Perhaps, folding laundry in the bedroom, holding up Elvira's clothes or underwear, the one pair of flowered panties she owned, she might have felt a rush of tenderness for her daughter, a tenderness that was welcome, that came upon her suddenly, unexpectedly. She'd stop, run down the stairs, hoping to find Elvie, embrace her, appreciate her purely, for herself, for the girl she was at that instant.

It was not Elvira's habit to wait around for such moments. She might be halfway up Larkey's Hill, tearing through the underbrush, trying with all her strength to reproduce that unknowable screech, what historians think sounded something like a banshee squall, the bloodcurdling cry, what's known as the Rebel Yell. When she did show up in the kitchen, late and dirty and ragged, other feelings might have displaced that tenderness my mother had meant so deliberately to keep uppermost in her mind.

In addition to Mrs. Shaw's discomfort with the hobby, and her sense that she'd been robbed of a primary emotion, she probably did have real fear for Elvira, for her future. My mother had been raised by Minty and my Grandfather Dwight in an upper-middle-class suburb of Chicago, and so she might well have wondered what there could be but a future of pain for a woman who cannot be a part of conventional society. Poor Elvira! Think of the anguish, being on the fringe of real life, not having a family, not producing roly-poly grandchildren, going from spiky-haired woman to spiky-haired woman, marching in so many parades, spending vast sums of money on therapy, keeping a houseful of cats. It is possible that my mother was hardly thinking of herself when she railed against Elvira's upbringing.

Liza38 eventually went to a counselor over her beloved, although long before Polloco came on the scene, she might have gotten some use from a professional on the subject of Elvira. I guess she didn't think it necessary, since she had plenty of friends she could talk to about her daughter, if the need arose. It has been said about her that she's an artist, and so it's not surprising that when we moved to Chicago, she managed to acquire several friends who were also supposedly artists, that she surrounded herself with artistic "women friends," she called them, as opposed to beast-of-burden friends, non-denominational friends, or Boytown friends. I used to wonder, and still do, if there is a limit to the benefits of self-expression. At any rate, my mother was quick to identify her own kind, however this is done, by visual cues, from fashion, by verbal tip-offs, or by animal instinct, the electrical crackle up the spine, the quickening of the heart. It was a few months after we came to the city that she became part of a book club, a powwow that once a month almost always met at our house. It is no secret, I don't think, that book clubs are formed so that women can quickly dismiss the novels they have sworn to read, moving on then into their real subjects, inexhaustible topics such as their midlife crises, their incipient menopause, motherhood, their own repressive mothers, and finally, settling down to their favorite agenda item, marriage and men.

Sitting in the kitchen on book club nights, eating the leftover desserts my mother would have gotten at the French Pastry Shop, I overheard many things in the dining room that were an excellent supplement to my education at the Jesse Layton School. I did not know before, for instance, that bad marriages cause women to contract cancer of all varieties, although most commonly unhappiness metastasizes in the breast. The members agreed unanimously on that point, as if they were doctors and scientists rather than painters, poets, musicians, and dabblers in herbs and salves. From this chorus, this unified shrill, there were the standouts: Glamorous Pam, whose beauty was legendary in the neighborhood; Christine, who taught kick boxing before it was fashionable; Lucy, the master gardener; and not least, no, not least, Marcia of the wiry hair, unmarried, scrawny Ms. Butler, head of the English Department of one of Chicago's little-known universities. Although I do not believe in reincarnation, do not hold truck with the business about past lives, I know unequivocally that in Marcia's previous time here on Earth she was a vermin, a rodent, a rat.

Even after Marcia had been artificially inseminated, after she had grown rotund, she seemed to want to be a vision in her silk scarves and long dramatic skirts. If her women comrades had been true friends, they would have prevented her from making her monthly visits to the fertility doctor. Because I knew, even before Richard Polloco came on the scene, that no flesh-and-blood individual, no actual person, can satisfy the kind of lofty desires we can't help harboring. If Professor Butler had contemplated Elvira just half as long as she'd contemplated her own navel, she would have saved the thousands of dollars she'd blown at the clinic and certainly spared herself the disappointment that she had no idea was guaranteed.

Look at Elvira, I would have liked to shout at Marcia. And do study the deep satisfaction Beth Shaw derives from her daughter. What, I wonder, did Mrs. Shaw say to the group, to her friends, about her struggles with Elvira? Did she tell them that she had never gotten over the shock of her own baby girl, that with each stage the shock was compounded? Elvira did have amazing knobby legs, for one thing, legs that were bowed, going in their stringy way from the bony ankles to the bony knees. There was something about those legs that always, when I saw them after not having seen them for a while, made me want to gawk at them, at their strangeness and at their pitifulness, the old-man quality about them.

Did my mother tell the group, say it right out, what was obvious? *Elvira does not want to be a female. The tomboy phase is going to last for the rest of her life.* The book club members could have seen for themselves that Elvira cultivated a husky voice, kept her hair short, and when she grew breasts, slouched so they wouldn't show. Did my mother admit that she hadn't been able to take Elvira to *The Nutcracker,* hadn't read her *The Secret Garden,* no chance of passing on the tea set, the dollhouse, the smocked dresses, all the small things that in Elvira Shaw would have kept little Beth Gardener alive? She might have told them that in lieu of doing those celebrated girl things with Elvira, she'd done many of them with Henry. Six-year-old Henry danced up the aisle with the under-seven crowd in their taffeta dresses after seeing the Boston Ballet. Was my mother too ashamed of her daughter to recount the droll stories, the short anecdotes, to give the club an idea of our family dynamics? The summer trip, for one, to the Plimouth Plantation, the reenactment Pilgrim village in Plymouth, Massachusetts, where Henry was thoughtless enough to point out the fire extinguisher behind the door of the thatched cottage, the single detail in the whole place that was not authentic. Zing, Elvira's knee, that knob, went right into his ass. I suppose it would have taken a certain amount of daring for Mrs. Shaw to be proud of her daughter: a girl who cared enough about her nation's history to give her own brother a shiner on his flat butt.

All those years ago at 432 Roslyn I spent a good portion of my waking hours plugged into my headsets up in my room. While I was downstairs, I managed to exercise my natural brotherly right to sanguinely torture the younger sister. When well mannered, liberally educated parents get divorced, they are usually quick to assure their children that the split had nothing to do with them, that Mom and Dad had insurmountable problems with one another, et cetera. Any child worth his salt knows that this is a load of horseshit. Parents get divorced because they cannot stand to have one more family dinner together. I'd get Elvira going during the meal, trying to trip her up on a Civil War fact that she had not yet absorbed into her marrow. Because she couldn't imagine otherwise, she assumed that I knew what I was talking about, that Civil War trivia was common knowledge.

I'd say whatever came into my head. "What was the cost of a barrel of flour in Richmond, January 1864?"

The thing is, she knew. She *knew*. She'd fire back, "Two hundred and fifty dollars."

My father would nod, yes, that's right.

"How many men served in the Union and Confederate military?"

"Bor-ring," she'd say. "Between 1.5 million and 2.2 enlisted in the Union, during the war, and about 600,000 to 1.4 million in the Confederate service."

Sometimes I dimly remembered a few key facts from all the talk that went on in our household, and I could pull up a fairly impressive question. "What day and year was a Northern city struck by Confederate sabotage?"

Bingo, she'd get it. "November 25, 1864, Confederate conspirators coordinated a bunch of fires in a dozen New York City buildings but did not do serious damage."

On rare occasions I'd make up a question. I'd ask her something that had no answer, as far as I knew, no basis in actual fact. "What American tradition was established by the U.S. government on Monday, September 12, 1862?"

That one stumped her. She put her head down, nearly into her Welsh rarebit. You could just about hear her thinking, American tradition, American tradition. After a while she said, "In April 1864 Congress stamped 'In God we trust' on coins—is that what you mean? That's a motto, though, not a tradition."

I had to think fast, had to think whether to give her victory or lead her down the garden path some more. When she'd figured out that I'd asked her a phony question, food would fly, she'd cry and storm. She once pulled my hair so hard she got a large tuft of it in her white-knuckled fist. This surprised even herself. *"Dad,"* she screamed, *"kill Henry."* It was interesting, I always thought, that she appealed to our mild-mannered father to do the job. She knocked her chair to the floor, tears streaming down her face—"I hate Henry. *I hate him."*

My mother had to occupy herself in some way during the year that she was waiting for Richard Polloco, after she'd laid eyes on him at my cousin Carol's wedding, and before she exchanged words with him twelve months later. Little did she know that his love notes would stream into our household, into her e-mail letter box, mixed-metaphor Richard Polloco on the doorstep of her electronic highway.

"Dear Liza38," he would write after their first tryst in Wisconsin.

When are you coming back? Miss Lucille Van Heusen wonders when you are coming again. The stationmaster has asked after you. The butcher, the baker, the candlestick maker. Not to mention the man in the tub. He especially is waiting, he is waiting, he is waiting.

In that year before she met Richard Polloco the second time, in that interval, she gave piano lessons in our house to a few students. She made two unlikely CDs, one with a Celtic group and another with a klezmer band. She practiced regularly. If I had been listening carefully, I might have noticed that she'd started playing Bach and Handel with a Romantic period abandon. Even before she was sure of Polloco, before she'd seen him again, she was playing as if the Baroque masters had written about restlessness rather than the glory of God. What teenager listens to his mother play the piano? An acquaintance once asked me that question. How could I tell her that it was not a matter of listening. A person didn't have to listen to Liza's music. It was with you. It was in the air and it was in the way she moved across the kitchen and it was in her voice, in the spaces before she spoke and afterward. It was in her hands as she gestured for you to hang up your coat. I don't approve of this kind of holy art crap on general principle, believe in things as they are, rose is a rose is a rose is a rose. And yet it has been said about her improvisations, her artistry, that she is an original. I think that this could be true. Watching my mother play the piano is at once to be let in to observe an intimacy and also to sense the wide world, an expansiveness I would not begin to know how to name. In spite of the movement going through much of her body and the lyricism or tumult coming from the keyboard, when I picture my mother playing the piano, I think of a stillness, a pinprick of a place inside her that is profoundly still. I wonder if a sublime quietness is at the heart of creation. If I have made up that concept, if it is way off the mark, it is only because I learned to imagine it from watching her.

Once a year she gave a recital where she played her own arrangements of works from ancient times up to the present. Once a week, in Chicago, she played with three other musicians in a group called Juice of Barley. They primarily played English country dance tunes, music that most people in this century have never heard outside of a Jane Austen movie. The group traveled and gave concerts, but their main purpose was to provide dance music for extremely nice and well-intentioned middle-aged Wasps, people who had had their heyday in the 1960s. They did their yoga, they ate low-fat meals, they thought their investments were interesting, and every Tuesday they gathered in the La Salle Street church basement to dance English set dances with names such as "Dick's Maggot," "The Maid Peeped out at the Window," and of course the flagship song, "Juice of Barley." The group, Juice of Barley, rehearsed in our living room, first playing the straightforward melodies and then improvising, taking liberties.

All this to say, my mother was busy enough, as far as I could see, with her piano, her friends, and she also had Elvira to contend with, which must have consumed some of her restless energy. She may have worried about me too, although I think my parents were less concerned about my character and abilities than they were about the world into which I was going to be thrust. How many times had I heard my mother telling her women friends that I was a wonderful boy, a model son, someone who rarely gave her trouble—when the next minute the house mole was upstairs logging into her e-mail account to see what had happened in the latest installment of the Richard Polloco story? Because I was self-directed and well behaved, so they thought, my parents, in regard to me, had the luxury of worrying about the future in general, about genetic engineering, crime, pollution, corporate takeovers, the closing of mom-and-pop-grocery, book, and hardware stores: all those problems and failures that were going to fall into my generation's lap.

My mother was often quiet at dinner when I teased Elvira, when Elvira demanded that my father have me drawn and quartered. Kevin would lean back in his chair and, as if he had nothing but time, as if we were not in a crisis, he'd remind us that history is not a contest, that Elvira had done a great job coming up with whatever arcane details she'd summoned to answer my fake question. With me he used that endearingly optimistic parenting tactic, the one where you try to appeal to the youngster's better nature. "Elvie is working pretty hard to master the facts," he'd say, "and your help is indispensable."

Mrs. Shaw would get up from the table and scrape the dishes, place them carefully in the dishwasher, put plastic wrap on the leftovers, open the refrigerator, peer into the shelves, rearrange a few things, close the door, examine the lists hanging there from the magnets, jot down a reminder or two. *Beware the fury of a patient woman.* Every now and again my parents climbed the stairs to the bedroom, to their appointed rumble.

One September evening the year I was seventeen, my mother went to a party at Olivia Ann's, a musician friend, and in a small house on West Cornelia she saw Richard Polloco for the second time. I've been to enough of Liza's parties to imagine the scene. Olivia Ann has dyed-blond hair, an enormous mouth slathered with red lipstick, and breasts—huge breasts, breasts that look like objects of war rather than the means of nourishment or healthy playthings. She was probably at the piano banging out old show tunes, songs from obscure musicals such as *The Vagabond King* and *Flora, the Red Menace.*

It is already clear, I'm sure, that I knew things people my age were not supposed to know.

At this party some of the guests were standing at the piano singing along, some were out in the yard smoking dope, even at their ages and with their infirmities, and some were drinking wine and discussing their children, their cholesterol, their therapies. I'd guess that Richard Polloco was not singing, he was not smoking dope, but he was probably drinking wine, standing before a plate of cheese and crackers, talking to whoever also happened to be hovering around the food. When my mother came into the room and saw him, she may not have wasted much time in being coy and trying to attract his attention. She was almost forty years old, seize the day. She made a beeline for the coffee table. Adding her to the scene has the absurd effect of changing the particulars in the background. The trays of cheese and crackers have become instead platters with long flaky dates wrapped in bacon, and also there are filo triangles stuffed with spinach and chèvre. When I was very young, I assumed that my father did the regular work of keeping the Earth revolving on its axis, but it was my mother alone who transformed ordinary objects or made a marvel appear where before there had been nothing. At first that was how I thought of her music, that she somehow spun it out of the air. She had a cleverness and a quickness, cutting figures from paper or pulling a lump of clay into a fantastic figure, or coming into my room on her hands and knees growling or dancing or singing or doing cartwheels, becoming someone, for a frightening moment, other than herself. At night, if I woke up afraid, how many times had I stared at the wall and the shape of her was there, so much larger by night than by day. I'd close my eyes, knowing she'd stay, knowing she'd be above me so dark, so thick and warm in her nearness, until the sun came back up.

She has short curly black hair, just as Elvira's had been in those years before Polloco. She has blue eyes that are often a little watery, and the smallest, most even teeth I've ever seen. They look like baby teeth, my freak-of-nature mother, and they are all the same length and width, one size fits every space, or so it seems. She's not very tall, but she's slender and is commanding enough so that she appears to rise above some of us who actually do have height. Or perhaps her length is in her torso. When she plays the piano, it seems as if a tall person is going to stand up and bow. And there she is, a shrimp.

Richard Polloco was not wearing his snug tuxedo, so he may have been even more appealing at second glance. My friend Karen told me once that bad dressers are often very attractive to females, that both married and unmarried women want to take the mismatched man and clasp him to their bosoms. If this is true, Polloco must have had to fend them off from all directions. He seems to have had an orphan's sensibility and was only too glad to take donations from anyone who offered. That night, at Olivia Ann's party, he was wearing a pair of jeans that a music industry tycoon, a college friend, had been kind enough to send him. If they were in fact the same pair I saw him in many months later—and I wouldn't doubt that he owned one pair of pants at a time—they were tight in front but drooped in the back. He was also wearing a large brown wool sweater with moth holes at the neck, the detail that probably pushed my mother over the edge.

What little I know about Richard Polloco sometimes seems like a great plenty. So I imagine that already at the beginning of the story he was ticking off the potential conclusions. It would end before it began. It would end the next morning. It would end sometime in the near future, and badly. I think it's possible that as they headed out the door, Beth Shaw thought, Henry! After all, she used to tell me, long ago, that she would always watch over me. And I used to think, when she sat on my bed in the soft shadows of the night-light and stroked my hair and talked, that I would always, always stay where she could see me. I couldn't help recalling—not thoughts—but flickers from a far-off time. And so I imagined, even though of course it was ridiculous, that as she walked away from the party, my name came to her lips.

Oh well, and is there anything more interesting than the story of a man and a woman coming together out of nowhere? A lot of people live for those stories, stories about fate and love, and don't want to know much about what happens in the great beyond, after the initial conflation. To picture my mother a lover, I had at first to break her in my mind's eye, hold her over my knee, like a stick, bust her in two. When that was done, when I had changed her like that, I could see her in a different way. I could put her through the motions like a jointed puppet, all dancy in the limbs, loose, nothing to hold her up but me.

Chapter Three

Most summers when I was growing up, we went to a camp in Massachusetts, a place that seemed to have fallen out of time. As a child I had no idea that the Shaws, the four of us, were removed from our century, and so for many years I did not understand that Silverpines was something outside of contemporary American culture. The camp was for families, for musical families who wanted to spend a week singing folk songs and learning English ritual dancing. I still don't talk about it much. My friend Karen could picture it, but she lived in a fantasy all her own. If she'd had her wish, she would have been Edith Wharton either during the period she was motoring around Italy with Henry James or when she was having the affair with Morton Fullerton.

I once tried to explain family camp to another friend who was usually sympathetic to my lost-in-the-past parents, but she scoffed and wondered when they were going to get a life. I never told anyone else in Chicago about going there. That is to say, Silverpines was the best place I had ever been. I imagine, for example, that it's the place I experienced the purest kind of happiness. The sort you don't question while it's coming over you, that takes you by surprise.

We went to Silverpines because year after year my mother was hired to play the piano for the week of English country dance classes. The camp was in an old-growth pine forest on a spit of land between two very deep and very clear lakes. There were small cabins among the trees, a carpet of last year's needles underfoot, needles that had softened in the rain. All day and much of the night music drifted through the trees, and although I did not admit to listening, I actually thought that, in a way, there was nothing quite like the quaint melodies, the two violins, an oboe, weaving in and out of my mother's rhapsodic interpretations of the old tunes. Now and then it made me wish I'd been born in a quieter era, if there is such a thing. At least born in the 1950s, when I could have grown up with the sweetness of the Paris Sisters, the Everly Brothers, and the Shirelles. But I was born in my own time, and I've logged more than enough hours with the music I was supposed to claim. That is how I know, then, as my birthright, that there are no simple hopes that are not false. That pure happiness, for one, is a fatuous concept. That is also why I continue to believe in simple hopes, why I take it upon myself to resist, when I remember to, the ironic detachment all of us came with who were born or raised during the Reagan era.

At Silverpines my father was the lifeguard, a job he enjoyed, much as he enjoyed everything he did. He was an enthusiastic and sociable dancer, a favorite among the wives. They loved him in part for his grace. He could talk and move at the same time without making too many mistakes, he was gallant, and also he had a silly streak. His dance card was always full.

When I was sixteen, nearly seventeen, the usual thing happened that is supposed to take place at camp when a person is around that age. My mother would say that this is an old story. Her name was Lily. I plan never to meet or know another person with her name. Maybe that's corny. It probably is. My mother might say that a little corn is essential to a good story. We, Lily and I, had been going to camp for years. Our families knew each other because her father played many ancient instruments, including the hurdy-gurdy, and taught ritual dancing for the eight-, nine-, and ten-year-olds. The morris dancing we learned as children requires a set of four couples, eight dancers who skip like hell in various figures, knock sticks together, or flick their white hankies heavenward. The origins of the tradition are lost, but it probably has something to do with the pan-European agrarian fertility rites, and celebrations at sowing and harvest time. By the Industrial Revolution it was a bonding deal for the men in the English Midlands. They'd get up early on May Day, dancing at establishment after establishment, begging for beer with their performances along the way, getting drunk and then drunker as the day wore on. A lot of the older women at camp did morris dancing for a workout, morris dancing, the pagan precursor to the aerobic worship of the body, minus the spandex and the hand weights. The mystery of family camp runs deep: children swallow the instruction whole, as I once did, dancing with bells strapped to their legs as if they were doing a regular twentieth-century activity.

The year that Lily was sixteen and I nearly seventeen, the Shaw family pulled up to the registration table at Silverpines in the Ford station wagon, a vehicle that in its own right made us look like a throwback. We'd been in the car for two days, sleeping and listening to my mother reading her old favorite, *84 Charing Cross Road.* Outside of Worcester Elvira and I had at last submitted to the monotony and stillness of the drive, and we were curled in the back, drooling into our pillows. We got close to Silverpines, wending our way up the gravel path, through the woods, almost there, almost to camp. We could hardly rouse ourselves for the obligatory rush of excitement. I had trouble opening even one eye. Lily, it seemed, was a member of the Greeting Committee, but she was not with the crew handing out maps and job descriptions. I got the second eye going, took a look. She was not explaining to every parent what to do in the event a rabid raccoon was sighted. She was standing beyond the table, set apart, all by herself. She was smiling past the front seat of our car, past my mother. In an instant I was alert, as if her gaze were a search beam, finding me, settling on me. Another cornball moment.

She was waiting for me, I thought. For no good reason I can provide, even now, that's how it struck me. She was possibly waiting for anyone her age to come along, or waiting to see if there was going to be someone who might make the week worthwhile beyond the skipping and singing. Still, I took her gaze personally. I was sleepy, I was not thinking at all, I hardly knew where we were. It crossed my woolly mind that the camp director had stuck her there for the understandable purpose of beautifying the Welcoming Event. And yet it seemed to me, in my state of stunning illogic, that she had allowed herself to be used because she was waiting for the Shaws, for Henry Shaw, to arrive.

Lily was gladly following in her parents' footsteps, in no danger of running off to join a death metal band or trying out for the cheerleading squad. She had long blond hair that for daytime purposes she wore in a bun or in two braids. When she let it down, it was as if Anne of Green Gables had morphed into a sex kitten. She wore skirts, skirts that were frothy, skirts that were almost transparent, that went to her ankles. Her tops that summer always had thin straps. One of those straps, the day we drove into camp, was twisted at the small knob of her shoulder. The way she stood in the scrap of a shirt made you both want to look and think that you shouldn't. It seemed in that naked clavicle as if she were showing off something that was ordinarily private. You were required to look at those beautiful bones, required to study the shape of her breasts, to see that yes, in fact, they were perfect. Her expression—hey, it's just me—seemed innocent enough, as if she had no idea that her breasts and those bones and the shirt straps were making an impression, were giving a person a cause.

She played the fiddle, danced with a morris team in her New Hampshire town, wore clogs, sang rounds with her friends, and did not eat meat. I sometimes thought during the week that I should find someone else to be attracted to, someone who was rebelling against English ritual dancing, a dark-haired girl with a pout, a sneer, a punk who was stealing off into the woods to drink the parents' stock of gin. There were occasionally teenagers who did not want to get with the program, but they'd usually end up down with the kitchen crew, college students who reputedly spent their time in the staff ghetto having group sex until the early hour came to cook bacon and oatmeal, pancakes and scones.

Lily and I circled each other for a couple of days, pretending that we didn't always know where the other was across the room, sitting at a meal, dancing down the line, swimming out to the raft, heading to our cabins to bed. We had one formal conversation, and then another that was slightly less stiff. And one more exchange when we were playing in a string quartet. I said something about one of my favorite disaffected and melancholy goth-pop singers, Robert Smith—or maybe I quoted a line from the song "The Perfect Girl." I might have expected an expression of disapproval, a scowl, or the furrowed brow of disappointment, or even gape-mouthed shock. She lowered her eyes, stopped looking at me altogether. My musical taste seemed to have erased me from the scene. She blinked, I was gone. She really was an amazing person. What could I say that would color me back into the picture? As we played, I could feel the noise of my cello stretching beyond the notes on the page, sprawling past their pitches, past the length of the quarter notes and half notes. In the pause at the end of the movement I said, "I think I need a conductor."

Evan, the violist, said, "We're hanging together. We sound okay."

"Not for you," I said. "No, all of you sound great, very good. You people must practice. Did you, by the way, know that Lully conducted his own music? He'd conduct using a staff and he'd bang it on the floor. At court, in front of Louis XIV, he was pounding away and he hit his foot, he hit it hard. One, two, three, one, two—Ouch! Damn it! And the wound festered and became gangrenous and he died."

Death was always seductive, wasn't it? Especially when the goner was a seventeenth-century French composer, somebody she could admire? I had been staring at Evan while I dispensed that valuable historical information.

"I swear, Henry, you've always known the weirdest things." It was Lily, speaking, and to me. I couldn't tell if she was complimenting me or not. At first I thought yes, but when I glanced at her, she had her nose in her case, rooting around for her rosin. I thought no, she thinks I'm a geek, she thinks I'm a loser. All through the rest of the rehearsal she looked at me only one more time, as if she didn't want to, as if she couldn't stand to lift her eyes and see that I was still across from her.

At night, in the large outdoor pavilion, we danced to our parents' music. We danced those English country dances the gentry used to do in their manor houses in the seventeenth and eighteenth centuries. There is a lot of walking around in a skimmy sort of way, but you have to keep track of where you are, what you're doing, backward and forward, moving in figures of eight, making kaleidoscope patterns, the whole room flowing in and out of the long lines. Lily and the other girls always wore glitter on their eyelids in the evening, another touch that made it impossible not to stare at them, to make sure you were seeing straight, to make sure you weren't having floaters.

In most of the dances you momentarily hold hands, you may skip for three or four measures, but the main event, aerobic or otherwise, is eye contact with your partner. If you are half crazy in love with her, that opportunity to gaze is as terrific as it is intolerable. I'd been dancing since I was two years old, and if I was a model son, as my mother claimed, it was in part because I could handle myself on the dance floor. I knew that Lily was an obvious choice, that she had a prettiness many guys my age would probably like. She laughed easily. She was just coy enough to make you wonder if she was being coy. She didn't wear a bra, and you could see her perked-out nipples through those tops with the thin straps. She had the same shirt in just about every pastel shade on the color wheel.

At home, after I'd talked to Karen and shown her the pictures—the one with the other girls and Lily, her arms up, the silky blond hairs in her pits in full view—Karen said, in her usual incisive way, "Oh, I get it. Do I have this right? If I'm earth, salt, maybe a little water, then this Lily is light, dew, and a gust of wind." She had put her hand on my shoulder and said, "Poor Henry," in a way that confused me and then made me angry, and for a few minutes confused me again. She was not someone capable of much guile, but that expression of sympathy was one of her rare, manipulative moments.

Back at camp, through the long nights in my cabin, I tried to figure out how I could kiss Lily and also possibly take off her shirt. By and large that is what I imagined, more than the rest of it. When I went further in my dreams, usually she became someone different, someone I could not always see, someone who didn't matter. In my waking dreams I wanted to slide those holy straps off her long arms and touch her small breasts, the both of them, and I placed her kneeling as I did this. I'd kiss down her neck, kiss back and forth over those breasts, put my mouth to her nipples, first one, and slowly find my way to the other. I pictured her throwing her head back and pulling my hair as I moved across her chest with my tongue. I wondered if out of her pretty mouth she might make a noise, something unexpected that wouldn't necessarily jibe with her two-braid, sweet-girl looks.

After all this time I still find it remarkable that people do come together, that they carry out their imaginings, sometimes exactly as they have hoped. It surprised my mother, that year of Richard Polloco, that she wished, and months passed, and she wished some more, and what do you know—he appeared before her, eating crackers and cheese. The surprising part, I guess, is not that the wish comes true, but that the wish, what was unreal and illogical, something of the hazy future, is in the present, is suddenly a piece of the story of the here and now, the day-after-day.

I'd not yet had any kind of serious girlfriend. I don't count the short experiences, nervous kissing in winter after a school function, the gropings, vague in feeling and actually in purpose, that went on down at the beach in summer. The direct feelings I had for Lily were new to me, dangerous, I thought, and important and crucial. Every move I made or didn't make I believed had bearing on the rest of my life. It was because of the importance of each gesture that I didn't have the courage to take her by the hand. Why should she want me to touch her? I was not handsome; I was quiet, witty only sometimes, and usually under my breath. I knew useless things. Taking her hand seemed a test so terrible I knew it was better not to try, better to keep thinking that the next time I might just reach for it, hold it, hold on, no matter if she wanted to wrestle away. I sometimes thought she was disgusted by my meekness, my inability to show myself to her, not to mention converse with her intelligibly. I couldn't be sure, couldn't know if she thought of me, or if there was an impossible accord between us, so that in fact she was waiting for me to do my part, to take charge, to lead her somewhere, into the bramble, to kiss her, to lift away her shirt.

Near the end of the week she and I were leaning on the railing of the pavilion watching Elvira's group perfecting their Northwest morris routine, a dance with swizzly sticks, all wound around in different-colored ribbons. Elvira was wearing her Yankee private uniform: light blue pants, darker blue overcoat, brass buttons, no trim, nothing fancy. The night before, I had advanced up through despair and on into depression, where I expected to stay for some time. In a way I didn't care anymore what Lily thought, or what I did to offend her. The week was almost over. Suppose I had had a chance, I had repeatedly blown my cover and she had come to know without a doubt that I was an idiot. It probably didn't matter what I said or did or didn't do. So I started telling her about Elvira, about her loathing of General McClellan, her secret infatuation for General Lee, her effort to love Grant in spite of his drinking. I explained how she went to the reenactments in search of what's called "the magic moment," when time collapses and suddenly you're marching to war, to your probable death; it's 1862, and the country is spread before you in its bucolic glory. Elvira refused to remove her sword from her belt during the dance, and every now and then the ribbons of her stick, which she was supposed to twirl, got stuck on the sword as she brought her arms into position.

We got to laughing, Lily and I did, laughing so hard that after just a minute, to avoid getting in trouble, she pulled me by the elbow, away from the class, away from the pavilion. We found ourselves running down a path, in and out of streams of sunlight that were coming through the pine trees. We were holding hands, running and running down the soft path until we were beyond the perimeters of camp, on someone else's property. Right before we came to a clearing, she let me go and went ahead, down a slope toward the water. I came after her. It was this moment, this place, that we had been waiting for. In many respects what I had been dreaming about unfolded, only I had neglected to imagine that she would return the attention, that she might have also imagined what my body would feel like to her hands and her mouth. We had torn away from camp; the pavilions, the cabins, the dining hall, and all the people were gone, floating off from us. No one did disturb us, not for the rest of the night, the thinnest crescent moon on the horizon. She was at once Lily, light and dew, a gust of wind, and also, when she wanted to offer herself in that dark-girl style of my wayward dreams, she could, and she did. Sometimes, even now, it's hard for me to say the name of that common flower.

It was in the fall, after camp, when my mother again met Richard Polloco, at Olivia Ann's party. Not so long after that evening she took the train up to his cabin, just over the border in Wisconsin. It was in October that I became an observer to my mother's secret life. The journey to Tribbey did in fact feel to her like a crossing to another country, another dimension. I had a friend once who adjured me most solemnly to confront my mother with this past of ours, to have it out, to see it from her point of view. What Grace didn't know is that I possess the files, and so she could not understand that most of the knowing is in the letters. There is probably very little either of my parents can add to the story except their own brand of confusion. They would ruin it with their perspective, their middle-aged wisdom.

I started out trying to study history in college, but within a couple of months I switched to literature. I often felt shame, looking at the pictures of the dead in battle, or portraits of effeminate princes, or the death masks of kings. I could hardly stand to read the bloody histories of the ancient rulers, and I hated to know that so-and-so had become distracted by women, poisoned by a brother, killed out of carelessness in his tent, or died without glory of a bad cold. I hated, too, thinking about whole populations in terms of economics or ideologies. I disliked the sweep of history, but I also couldn't stand the intrusion on real past human beings, what seemed like spying. I had had enough of that already. I knew Richard Nixon's story before I could sing the alphabet song; it had been drummed into me that espionage for all parties was an indignity and immoral. There are many places that have had the good fortune of eluding history, villages and farming communities and busy populations that have had the luck to live and die, the evidence crumbling into the earth, gone. With Elvira's fixation on the war, and my father's running political and historical commentary, and my mother, and why not count Polloco too, I have had enough history to last my seventy-year life expectancy.

There was another person at a different time whom I told about my mother's affair with Rpoll, and I mentioned my tracking—to a certain extent—that relationship. The woman was amazed that I had had the strength to do so, that I hadn't shut down—done, she said, the denial thing. Or else, she wondered, why hadn't I acted out, taken drugs, sold drugs, vandalized property, brought home girls and screwed them on the dining room table? She kept referring to my strength. But that was not what I had, not strength. During the year of Richard Polloco I often worked through the fractured logic proving to myself that very little mattered and also that I was not helpless. I was, after all, virtually an adult, although I had no job prospects, no placement as of yet at the college of my choice, no assertiveness training for my résumé. I was, nonetheless, only months away from legal adulthood. I could acknowledge the existence of Richard Polloco and decide that he was no concern of mine, to the whole life I had before me. I could hold the Shaws up and then hold myself up, examine them and me, keep us apart. Sometimes I'd decide to hate my mother. That was something I could reasonably do. I'd watch her sitting at the piano looking very much as if she were in her life, knowing full well that she was not. I'd figure to leave home earlier than planned, not to run away exactly, but to strike out on my own. Pack my bags, say good-bye to the folks, and not turn back.

Little did I know that years later the refuge I'd find was in this story itself. It is a sorry thing to admit. I cannot, at this late date, believe in what was once the fresh drama of silence, exile, cunning, the smithy of the soul, unfettered freedom, all of that business. I can't stand, either, the idea of any kind of art as therapy or personal catharsis. In the end the story seemed to be the only home I could make, or the home I'd been looking for all along, a poor shopworn story, gussied up as best as I could make it. Strange, maybe, that an invention is the one place to belong. When I entered the story in the night, in my apartment, alone, in yet another city, the emptiness that is so near the shore of the world did not seem quite as close. And I knew of that stillness where music and also surely language begin.

I could gaze all those years back and consider why I had stayed in Chicago, why I hadn't taken serious drugs or wrecked the Ming dynasty pottery in our neighbor's brownstone for attention. Of course there were many reasons to finish high school. Running away, for instance, would require a certain amount of cash, and I didn't feel that I could ask Minty to subsidize my travels. I could argue against leaving, against staying, and in the final round understand why it was better to remain in Chicago until my scheduled departure in the fall. The true reason, however, one I would not have acknowledged, was with me like new muscle, flexing, growing, becoming. By the force of my self, because I had to eat in the kitchen and sleep in my bed, because I moved through the house, my mother, I believed, had to stay in place. This wasn't something that I thought; it was purely an action on my part. I never did tell anyone that there were some moments when I could feel so chillingly what my mother, longing for Polloco, must feel. That sensation, hers, was somewhere between the sentiments of "I Love How You Love Me," by the Paris Sisters, and the words of The Skeans: "Every time you kiss me your tongue cuts through to my heart."

The first time she went to Richard Polloco it was September, a cool morning, blue sky, the leaves just beginning to turn. She took a cab to Union Station, and when the Hiawatha was announced, she put her bag over her shoulder and walked along the platform. The train was giving off steam and the platform was wet, glazy. In his dark uniform the conductor was down the way motioning the passengers to enter at his door. My mother may have said to herself, "God, dear God, here I am boarding this train to Wisconsin to commit adultery." I know from so many of her messages that she did not take her transgressions lightly. She may have been seeing her own body from the outside, watching a woman by her name going through the motions that other women, both living and fictional, have gone through, and there she was, taking the same steps. I imagine her wearing a blue dress she wore a lot in those days, a soft dress that had buttons up the side, and on her feet her brown leather pioneer-woman boots. She probably had on her velvet hat that pressed the curls down around her face, so that all in all she looked like a bohemian from another era, like one of those unconventional and ultimately tortured Bloomsbury characters or a heroine from a deadly D. H. Lawrence novel. She was Mrs. Shaw in costume, a woman who was perhaps in love with the romance of herself.

My mother probably didn't notice the crowded streets with bungalows, didn't notice that as the train went northward the lots became bigger, the trees more dignified, the houses more expensive. She looked out the window but did not see the houses thin out altogether until there was nothing but cornfields, the stalks and ears in golden tatters in the sunlight.

The station just over the border in Wisconsin looks like a Russian outpost, a Chekhovian white clapboard structure in the middle of the plains, a place where you'd willingly sit and wait for hours if there was a chance a train would come and take you anywhere else. My mother's friend Jane was quick to point out that although many women their age were committing adultery, right and left, none of them was doing so with a violin maker who lived in a log cabin that had gingham curtains. Most of them were doing *it* in cheap hotels, so cheap the management had the TV remotes bolted to the night tables. My mother, according to Jane, had chosen well.

In addition to my mother's contribution to the Civil War documentary, there is another ironic detail about Rpoll that I hesitate to mention. It is not only that my generation was born with an ironic sensibility, it is also that ironic details are a feature of the natural world, incongruence there for the taking. Maybe, too, the War Between the States is still present in our lives, more than we know until we start paying attention. It is a fact that Richard Polloco lived in a cabin that was built as a model of the Indiana cabin Abraham Lincoln was born in, a structure that was displayed at the World's Columbian Exposition in 1893 and later purchased by the Van Heusen family and transported from Chicago to Tribbey. Imagine Elvira's astonishment when she heard that piece. Polloco rented the place for one hundred and fifty dollars a month from an aged family friend, Miss Lucille Van Heusen. It was part of his rental agreement that he run errands for her and help her with household chores. The country, he told Liza, did not exactly suit him, but neither did the city. At a small workbench in his entranceway, he made the violins that he sold to a shop in Boston.

The cabin was held together by wooden pegs and mortar between the logs. I know this because my mother did take Elvira and me to visit at a time when my father was at a teachers' convention. Outside there was a sweep of land that even in November had its charm, the long lanes bowerlike, a prairie with bleached and hollowed stalks waving in the wind, and the wide sky above. Inside the cabin there were two lanterns hanging from the rafters, hooks by the door with a series of straw hats, the kind the peasants probably wore in Russia when they were going off to make hay. There was a tool chest by the hearth, a bird's nest and stones on the mantel, a swing outside, a tree house. A leather latch on the door. *Just lift the latch and come in.* A slant roof. Mist rising off the field out the back window. A patchwork quilt, a window seat with white-and-green-checked pillows, and wide pine floors. At odds with the time period there was a computer in the corner, but it was tastefully covered with an Indian print cloth. The other inauthentic detail, the brand-new woodstove, had a kettle clattering away on it for a ready cup of tea. In other words, if my mother hadn't already thought she loved Richard Polloco, the sight of the cabin convinced her that yes, he was the one, the love of her life—no wonder she'd been waiting for a year. She would gladly have waited another five if it was certain she could have him in the end.

I owed my own romantic encounter to Elvira. If I hadn't brought up my sister in conversation with Lily, if we hadn't started laughing, if we hadn't run down the path, we would never have gotten to the grassy clearing by the water, the place we stayed until we woke and it was almost morning. When my mother and Richard Polloco were in bed all that long day, that first time she visited, they probably talked about who had led them to each other, to whom they owed their debt of gratitude. The obvious first choice was my cousin Carol, for getting married, for hiring a band for the reception. Second choice went to a man named Sam Horton, who played the violin in the wedding band but had had a death in the family. He had called Richard to see if he'd be a substitute. So thanks were definitely in order to Sam Horton's Uncle Stan, who had dropped dead in Minneapolis. Olivia Ann deserved a nod too, for inviting the future lovers to the same party. And why not offer up gratitude to a force, an unseen power, a celestial body that was choreographing everyone's movement? It is so much easier to justify a thing when apparently it was meant to be.

In bed, too, they would have discussed how my mother had jumped off the dais before the last song at the reception, how Elvira had been so tired the family had had to go home, how there hadn't been time for an introduction. Still, in their glances they had quickly recognized that they were kindred spirits, and of course in their playing there was the proof. It was unfortunate, they had both thought, that they were so close, as it were, and yet so far. They would have gone over every word, they believed, of the conversation they had had at Olivia Ann's. Halfway through the party it was Richard Polloco who suggested they take a walk around the block. However, it was my mother who stopped at the alley crossing, who said to him,

"The trouble is, there is a trouble." Her mouth was dry, her legs shaking.

"Trouble?"

"And it is," she said, "it is that I'd like very much to kiss you." She strung it out like that, with more than enough words.

Richard Polloco, in his ingenuous way, said, "*You* would like to kiss *me?*"

"Yes, yes, you see, I would."

They did that routine many times in the months to come. One of them would say, "The trouble is, there is a trouble."

"Trouble?"

"And it is that I'd very much like to kiss you."

And the other would say, with mock surprise, "*You'd* like to kiss *me?*"

"Yes, yes, you see, I would."

Thus began their private history, the gathering of sayings and jokes that belonged to them, that had no currency anywhere else. After the kiss Richard Polloco asked her to move closer to the light of the garage, so he could see her better, so he could watch while he kissed her. Hand in hand they moved solemnly and stood under the fixture of a brown one-car garage. She lifted her face to him. She may have been flattered enough so that it didn't occur to her to avoid the light, in case someone else from Olivia Ann's party was also taking a stroll. They went from light to light, kissing, and after some time he said to her, "If we keep this up, you might never again play the piano." I suspect he made that remark because of her ardor. The joke was not original but she laughed. She said wouldn't that be just too bad?

She would remember their walk so often in the months to come. Because sometimes Richard Polloco, the fact of him in her life, the reality of him, was—she hated to think it—a millstone. She didn't know if she could carry the burden, she couldn't imagine being without it, she knew very well what she wanted in the moment, the moment! But getting there, to the moment, and waiting for it, and longing for it, and being without it—all of it was terrible, wonderful, awful, she didn't know. And sometimes she couldn't tell where she was, in what life. Was she in Tribbey, was she in Chicago, was she between the two? The bloom of romance! The bloom of romance! If she could conjure up that encounter in the alley, if she could close her eyes and see him leaning over her, and catch his voice, then—then there came the relief of feeling, pure feeling, and she'd remember that aside from the struggle, she loved him.

"*You'd* like to kiss *me?*"

As they went from garage light to garage light, Richard Polloco began the story that in the absence of daily life would become their ballast, would hold them together through the year to come. He had been born in 1947, he told her, in a small city called Kovel, in the Ukraine. There was a past, he said to my mother, a long story of chaos and terror for the Pollocos, through the Bolshevik Revolution, the Red Terror, famine, the war, his father's imprisonment in Siberia, in one of the harshest labor camps in Kolyma. His mother had died or killed herself, after his birth. He would like to know why she had given up hope, had drowned in the bath. So many relatives—aunts, uncles, grandparents—gone. There had been many cousins, and for the most part they had disappeared. His father's younger brother had gotten lost and was one of thousands of children who had roamed in packs across Russia like wild dogs, stealing, begging, killing. Richard Polloco, in Tribbey, Wisconsin, was trying to piece together the horror stories of his relations, was trying to see across two continents and an ocean. The fragments were with him, my mother explained to her friend Jane, were like bits of glass that he kept under his skin, to make him mindful.

Beth Shaw brought his hand to her lips as he spoke and kissed his short fingers. What was the worst thing that had happened to her, or to her family? Minty's brother Clarence had studied art history and become a homosexual, though no one talked about his proclivity. One of the great-aunts had been committed to a mental institution. Somewhere along the line there'd been a couple of alcoholics, a ne'er-do-well, a divorce. No, my mother's sadnesses and the family's failures were common, the simple ones that are bred in the bone. She kissed his fingers and thought, atrocities. It was as if she had been surrounded by history for so much of her adult life, general history, history that did not belong to her or anyone she had actually known, and here, all of a sudden, in the form of the orphan man, was a specific history, a person with something real that had happened to him, that had wounded him. He was a person she might be able to comfort, a man she could lead out of the dark past, going from light to light to light.

Chapter Four

It used to irritate me when Elvira got on her high horse about General Lee, as if, little abolitionist that she was, her heart belonged to old Marse Robert. I'd read some things about the general, including the plaques at various battlefields, and knew that Lee invariably credited himself with honor. He could decide to fight for the Union, weasel his way out and stand for Virginia, send the boys to be butchered North and South, and along the way, no matter what, he'd speak in terms of honor, of acting honorably. He was his own brilliant spin doctor. Elvira was all wrapped up in the Lee tradition, in the myth that Lee was a man who could not hate, who loved his enemies, who always, like Christ himself, turned the other cheek.

At dinner, to goad her, now and again I'd say things that she didn't completely understand. I'd recite a line I'd read somewhere as if it were mine. I'd say, "I think Lee had a very high tolerance for ambiguous loyalty." She knew just enough, though, to guess what I was driving at, to feel her nerves twitch. There are some people you want to give yourself over to, can't help it, and no amount of talk or good sense can make you change your mind, put an end to the affliction. Elvira loved his silver hair, his distinguished beard, his penetrating gaze, his sad eyes. Tender Lee, ingenious Lee, Lee who could have outfoxed anyone if he'd had an army even half the size of our team's. The general, the slave owner, hated the war more than anything, hated that the Union was broken. The good general loved Virginia best of all and would do anything for his state, even lead hundreds of thousands of men honorably to their deaths.

It drove her wild when I said things such as, "I think Lee had a very high tolerance for ambiguous loyalty." My remarks often made her leave the table, leave her dinner to bang the doors through the house until she got to the third floor, to her room, to the heavy walnut door that made the loudest noise, that had the most satisfying reverberations.

When we moved to Chicago, my father grew a beard, and it was said in reenactment circles that he looked like Grant, that there was a striking resemblance. As far as I could see, the beard was where the similarity began and ended. My father had curly reddish hair and horn-rimmed glasses, a round face, a full bottom lip, nothing like the thin line of Grant's mouth, and neither did he have the high forehead, the smooth straight hair, the somber affect. "Go easy on her," he'd say to me in his good-natured way as Elvira slammed her door once, twice, again, again. The brick brownstone that had been built to endure after the Chicago fire quaked; the dishes in the cupboard rattled. The architects who believed in permanence had not anticipated a force like Elvira.

That Sunday when my mother first went to visit Richard Polloco, she had probably gone through her list and was able to account for all of us. She might have been reasonably satisfied. I was doing plenty, playing in a doubles Ping-Pong tournament a group of forty-year-old Jesse Layton alumni had going in the basement of a nearby synagogue. The Emanue-El B'ne Jeshurun basement was the place where Henry Shaw lived his secret life, the suave ace Ping-Pong player, with a new blade and a rubber that cost seventy-five big ones. Also that day I was finishing up homework, walking the streets, and on my headset enjoying the dark and angry and sorrowful strains of yet another rock star who would kill himself. The morning before, Elvira and my father had driven to Enos, Indiana, for a skirmish with the 15th Indiana. My father no longer had his steed, Betty, but even without the horse trailer it was a production, packing up the musical instruments, the weapons, the food, moldering to authentic perfection, every bit of clothing and personal effects, as well as the bedrolls, the tent, the coffeepot, the skillet, the hand-carved wooden spoons, the tin plates, and the iron cauldron.

Elvira had been unofficially invited to join a hardcore group, the 28th Wisconsin, a group that carefully picked its men from regiments around the Midwest, men who were rigorous about authenticity, who took the call seriously. The 28th Wisconsin was going to participate at the reenactment of the battle of Shiloh, in Tennessee, the following April, and already Elvira was more diligently than ever, day after day, working on her first-person impression, on Elvirnon, in the hopes that she'd be asked to go south with the regiment. Among other worries, my mother fretted that the faux deep voice Elvira used might permanently damage her vocal cords. Over the weekend in Indiana Elvirnon would get to strut his stuff before the officers in the 28th Wisconsin, for final approval. The Shiloh bash wasn't going to be what's known as a mega event, but it promised to be a classy affair, with select groups from both Canada and the United States. Elvira's fondest wish had long been to be singled out and asked to join an exclusive unit; she dreamed of marching with the real men. And although of course it was difficult to choose, it is possible that Shiloh was her favorite battle, the slaughter that was the turning point of the conflict, the massacre that informed both sides about the nature of the war they were fighting.

When my mother came home that Sunday, after she'd been visiting Richard Polloco for the first time, the reenactors had been back from their trip for several hours. Their gear was still all over the entryway, and because it had rained in the morning, the wool blankets and jackets and trousers were wet. There was that nice animal smell, barn odor, in our downstairs, undoubtedly a favorite house fragrance of Mrs. Shaw's. Elvira had stayed up all night with the guys and was in her room sleeping off the excitement. At the kitchen table I was beating my father at chess. He didn't believe in playing dumb to let younger people win, but when I was small, he'd turn the board around the minute it became clear that he had me cornered. He'd let me finish out on his side. When I was seventeen, I was often able to outsmart him, but I always offered to turn the board before I took his king. It had become a ritual, this staged generosity, the fake offer to be the loser. He'd consider my suggestion earnestly, but then decline, saying his piece about how it was good for a person's character to get trounced, that losing to me was excellent preparation for old age and geezerhood. He always said so with esprit de corps.

I was in the middle of my part of the rite, telling him he should turn the board before I whipped the pants off him, when my mother came in the front door. She had told my father that she was going up to Wisconsin for the day, to Tribbey, to rehearse with a violin player she'd met, that they were going to do a gig in Milwaukee for a dance. I guess all of that was true.

She came into the kitchen, said hello, went to the sink, turned on the water, and reached into the cabinet for a glass. She let the water run for a long time, waiting for it to get cold. There was no mention of the mess in the hall or the warm smell of sheep, a sign for the astute person that at the least she was preoccupied. Or guilty. *Who was she now? Now that she had made her crossing.* She might have asked herself that question. She stood with her back to us, with her hands on either side of the sink, as if she were bracing herself for the drink or whatever it was that came next.

"It looks like I'm finished," my father said to me, squinting at the board, trying to retrace his steps, to recall the disastrous move.

Without turning around my mother said, "How was the reenactment?"

"Terrific!" my father said. He carefully set the pawns into their velvet places in the chess box. "Elvie got her wish."

"Her wish?"

"The 28th Wisconsin finally did invite her to go to Shiloh in April. They're a great bunch, and they've given her a lot of encouragement. We should all go down there, make a vacation of it."

"Uhh," I think was the noise my mother made.

"There was a court-marshal yesterday afternoon, the two skirmishes, and the hanging of a deserter this morning."

"Elvira was thrilled," I said. "The guy gagged for a full five minutes."

Liza38 faced us then. By rights she should probably have looked flushed or dewy, a vision of loveliness. She was not, however, at her radiant best. She looked tired. She looked as if the sight of my father engaging me in a game that resembled war, coupled with the news of Elvira at the hanging, was more than she could abide.

It was the next day, Monday, when I read my mother's first e-mail on the subject of Richard Polloco. "This is an old story," she wrote to her friend Jane. "There is nothing new in it." I remember I went to my room after I'd read the entire message, including the description of the cabin. I sat on my bed, like a stranger might, on the edge. A gentleman caller. I should sit at my desk, I thought, get busy, sharpen my pencils, start my calculus homework. Alternatively I should go downstairs and inform my father that our life was about to change. Good idea! I had more than once overheard my mother tell her book club intimates that I had been born middle-aged. I should talk to Bethy, that's what I should do; take her aside like an uncle, a grand-father, point out the error of her ways. Sure, why not, Henry? Ask Mother to come up to the bedroom, tell her firmly that you need to speak to her.

What was going to happen? Wouldn't this teach me to look at other people's mail, I thought, and then I stood up and said no. Out loud I said, "No!" What the fuck was my mother doing? That question was more to the point—what the fuck did she think she was doing?

Were we going to break up, like other families, so we could be the picture of American normalcy? Would my mother move away to Wisconsin, take the piano, the battered gray recipe box, the framed photographs that went along the stairs? Nothing but the bare wall where once there'd been the pictures of Elvira on her steed, Henry at the summit of Mount Washington, the old dog Beastie barking up a tree at a bear cub in our backyard in Vermont. And then, oh Christ, no! And then, in my mother's absence, would my father go on dates with women twenty years younger than himself, my age practically—would he marry someone like *Lily?* Lily Shaw, Ms. Lily Graham Shaw, the new, updated Mrs. Kevin Shaw! My mother and Richard Polloco, this thing they had, would lead to Lily becoming my stepmother. Lily, kissing my father as he went off to work in the morning; Lily, stern and humorless, in the matron mode, pouring me orange juice, fortified with calcium; Lily's black string underwear hanging in the bathroom to dry before another night in my father's bed.

I went outside. I walked very quickly down the street. It was funny—oh, yes, it was funny—that finally we had a family drama that didn't directly involve Elvira. It was a melodrama, a Keystone Kops deal, my mother tied to the tracks, my father—or me!—racing the train to rescue her. It was a mistake, of course it was. They, my mother and what's-his-name, had probably only had coffee together, played some music. My mother had a busy enough schedule—she didn't have time to go out of state. I had read the screen wrong, it was someone else's message, our e-mail provider had screwed up, everything was fine. Everything was fine.

I made the error then of imagining my mother at the piano. She played her instrument as if not only her fingers were hitting the keys. All of her body was conspiring to make that music. Even if her hands were cut off, she would raise her head and howl, and out of her mouth would come a melody, a haunting line, a fragment you'd spend half the day and night straining to remember. Everything was fine, my mother was a passionate person, and it therefore followed that my father—the twinkly historian, the hearty reenactor, the gung-ho dad, the even-tempered fellow—could not pin her down or contain her or hold her. He might not even know to want to do any of those things.

I remember looking up, finding myself at the North Avenue Beach. It was a syllogism: My mother is x, my father is y. Therefore x and y do not fit together, x and y are mutually exclusive. What she was made of, it seemed to me, was unknown to him, and what he was, of little interest to her. Wait, I thought, could that be true? How was it that I had lived with my parents for seventeen years and never understood those key facts about them? I knew the legend of their meeting, that fateful day in Montpelier, the mistake that led her to the wrong room on campus where my father was working way ahead with fellow ideologues on what would turn into Senator Eugene McCarthy's second bid for the presidency in 1976. Neither one of my parents was enrolled in the college, which made the chance encounter more chancy and the story about destiny. Beth Gardener came into the room looking for her band members and saw my father, pencil stuck behind his ear, explaining his strategy to the three others at the table. He was quoting from *The Peloponnesian War*, something about how brave hearts must always be brave, and inexperience must never be used as an excuse for misconduct. It may be that I have Thucydides to thank for my very existence. Bethy stood listening to Kevin Shaw; she looked at the pencil lodged behind his pink ear, the auburn curls scattered down his neck, his crooked glasses that were held together with tape. He paused to ask her if she needed help, but it was one of the other men who got up to show her the way, who tried to chat with her in the hall, make a date. I guess there was nothing more that she wanted in the moment than the thrill of what seemed like virtue and gentleness in the man with a stubby, chewed-up pencil, the man who was speaking so poetically. It is not an inconsequential detail that my father fell in love with her without first hearing her play the piano. What, then, or with whom, I wonder, did he fall in love?

Using an addition, or perhaps subtraction that did not follow the usual properties, I could figure that the four of us added up to the Shaws, but my mother and father were a one plus one that equaled zero. They were wrong as a pair, I could see that; they'd begun for misguided reasons—they had no real foundation, nothing solid to stand on for all these years, nothing beneath their feet but quaggy muck. Was it right for a young woman in that time, with her interests, to be captivated by gentleness? What the fuck had she been thinking?

"Get a grip," I said to myself. I was too old to feel smothered by anything my mother did or did not do, too old to be frustrated by the inadequacies of my parents all the way back to their ridiculous courtship. I could walk up and down the beach, walk off what was bothering me. I could spit into the wind. I could stand very near the water where no one would pass by, and I could cry, I could yell. Talk was supposed to be good, a washing-clean of a person's troubles, even before you'd identified the real problem. I could return to the house and go up to the second floor, close the office door, lock it, and call Lily in faraway New Hampshire.

I went so far as to go home, climb the stairs to the second floor, close the office door, and sit in front of the phone. We'd only spoken a few times since camp. We had been writing letters to each other, but because I had no hope of seeing her for a long time and because she was beautiful and knowledgeable in a certain way, the letters, the phone calls, seemed pointless. Lily was the kind of girl any geek should be lucky enough to have for a first experience. More than lucky: her attention was on the order of divine visitation. She had made it seem so easy. *Put your arm there, your hand here, that's right, oh, you're so good, know just what to do, a natural.* It had been she who controlled each of our movements, but she'd made me think that I was the one, that I was a dude, the big moment Henry she had always wished for. Without very many words and in less than eight hours at Silverpines she had given me a fantastical version of my own self.

She was in New Hampshire and I in Chicago, unalterable details. I had probably already lost her to someone else. I wanted to call her up and tell her not exactly about my mother, but that something had happened. I wanted to convey the information without having to say anything. This method of communication had worked for us before.

And when she'd gotten the gist, what then? What did I expect gorgeous, capable, coolheaded Lily to do? Did I think her pity for me would propel her to Illinois? I kept picking up the phone and setting it back on the receiver. Lily lived in Hanover, New Hampshire, with two devoted parents in a colonial house. She sang in a Balkan choir; she practiced the violin; she did her homework; she was planning on going to Sarah Lawrence; she'd probably never had a day of sadness, beyond the usual childish squalls that don't amount to anything once a person is in adulthood. I'd pick up the phone and dial her number, and my silence would be a sign to her. She'd know immediately that she should come to me. Lily, taking the Greyhound to Chicago, a drunk hitting on her all the way from Toledo. She'd arrive in a long frothy skirt with her silky hair in a bun. The wind would blow her this way and that. She'd find it funny at first, but then the trash on Halsted would disgust her. The homeless people, the blacks and Hispanics, not the select ethnic types who went to Dartmouth, the real city poor, would frighten her. The smell on the subway would upset her stomach. She would be no good in a big city.

After dialing eight or nine times and hanging up, I found that I had committed her phone number to memory. When I got through to her, she might tell me to come to her. We could both crack open our savings accounts, leave our parents, and meet in some place—how about a haven? A haven that would reveal itself, a shelter in the forest, a warm forest, a green autumnal forest, with a path to a bed of dry leaves and why not a little moss, a pillow of moss.

"Jesus Christ," I said into the receiver. I should call Karen and ask her, beg her to come and read to me from one of her favorite impenetrable Henry James novels, a reassuring five-hundred-page book in which life gets the better of the sensitive character who has no courage. I sat with the receiver in my ear and my index finger on the Off button. From downstairs I could hear the scraping of the chairs in the kitchen and the clattering of the silverware in Elvira's hands as she prepared to set the table. Where other families microwaved or carried out, Mrs. Shaw insisted on the serious old-fashioned thing known as dinner, five out of seven nights of the week. We were apparently going to do it, have dinner, as usual. Elvira was unstacking the glasses, pulling apart the sticky tumblers, filmy from the dishwasher, and at the same time asking my father if he thought she was getting too pudgy to look like a starving drummer boy. The rations, what were typical issue of both North and South, were often riddled with weevils and maggots. Many hardcores struggled with their weight for the sake of authenticity. I could smell the winter squash, the tang of the burned butter in the pan my mother would be using to cook the chicken breasts.

Maybe they had called me. Maybe she, the woman of the house, had yoo-hooed and I hadn't heard. I could stay in the office, wait for her to come and rout me out. I'd say I was busy playing with myself while I read her e-mail; I'd be down when I was finished. "Oh baby, oh glory, fucking glory." I'd moan that kind of thing as I sat in front of the screen. Or, instead, I could go to dinner and look at her. Maybe I'd know better; I'd know what the business was about. I'd get a sense of it. I'd show up, see, eat enough to keep me going, and then I'd—do something. Something, that's what I'd do.

It took a good deal of my strength to make my way downstairs, along the hall, and into the kitchen, where she was serving the food into four unequal portions, depending on our appetites, which she knew so well. It seemed there was a resisting force, a substance denser than water, that I was walking against. I could feel my heart beating, walking through my own house. My heart was thumping in my chest when I was only going to dinner.

I came into the room. She didn't look up at me, didn't say, Why are you walking so slowly? Are you all right? There was no Hello, no How was your day? She let a chicken breast slide off the spatula onto my plate, and the hot squash half she passed to me in her hands as if it were cool porcelain.

"You really think it didn't hurt that Bernard guy when they hung him?" Elvira was saying. "There were rope burns on his neck afterward. That part was for real, Dad. That was not phony." This may well have been the sixth or seventh time Elvira had asked Private Shaw the question about the hanging. How was it that I was sitting at dinner with my mother and father and Elvira, as if the e-mail message had never been written by my mother, and sent to Jane, and read by me? As if I didn't know that my mother had gone to Wisconsin the day before to visit a man named Richard Polloco, the violin maker, in his log cabin with the straw hats in a row on their pegs and a boiling kettle on the woodstove.

I felt as if I were at a great distance from my mother, as if I were looking down at her, as if I could see into her, as if she were no relation to me, not even an acquaintance. She was eating her squash, taking a dab, an orange dab on the end of the spoon, and putting it on the tip of her tongue. She did the same with a shred of meat. She was clearly not very hungry, poor love-sick Liza38. My father was cutting his chicken up, cutting the whole piece before eating any of it, putting the butter on his squash, a little salt, getting everything arranged. "There were the curtains on the scaffold I told you about," he said to Elvira, "in those few strategic places. I agree, the hanging looked real, and the noises he made were—"

"Please," my mother said, "would you mind? We're trying to eat." To Elvira she said, "I have a friend, this man I went to see yesterday, named . . . Richard. Richard Polloco."

What? Had I read the message correctly? She wouldn't bring him up if she was deceiving my father, if she was deceiving us. Would she? Not in front of all of us. Not at *dinner*. And yet she could hardly say his name. She wanted to both hold his name in her mouth and say it, say it again and again in our presence. Richard Polloco. Polloco, Polloco. Richard. "He lives in a log cabin."

Elvira said, "What's so good about a log cabin?"

"It's sort of a curiosity," my mother said, ignoring Elvira's tone. "It was built for the Chicago world's fair in 1893, as a replica of Lincoln's birthplace."

"How come it's in Wisconsin?" My mother had snagged Elvira. If Lee, in my sister's mind, was our Lord, Lincoln, in spite of the fact that he kept McClellan on the job too long, was God Almighty.

My mother explained the short history of the cabin, how it had come to be owned by Miss Lucille Van Heusen and rented out to Richard Polloco. She described in great detail the construction and the furnishings, the dollhouse up in the loft, the children's book titles, the arrangement of the dishes, the swing in the yard, the tree house.

"Sounds like you didn't have much time to practice, to get ready for your gig." I'd meant to say it. I'd said it. I kept my head down, looking at my food, but I heard her, the laugh, the nervousness in it, the snort of indignation that came first. I had an idea then how she felt about Richard Polloco. I knew that I had read the message correctly. She got up to find a tissue. She blew her nose, went to the wastebasket, threw the Kleenex out, walked over to the counter, and got another, repeated the maneuver. When she'd recovered herself, she said, "We'll have to visit there sometime. I'll have to take you."

"I'll go," Elvira volunteered.

I have often wondered why I didn't learn to pick out chords and crummy leads on a trashy guitar. The music I admired was fierce and raw, and it wouldn't have taken much to try to imitate it up in my bedroom. Why was it that I couldn't muster the genuine article, couldn't do more than whimper or slash my bow across the cello strings? I like to think that I knew even less than I do now. I couldn't know, for one, that a love affair can live almost entirely in the imagination. First, you dream of the lover without meaning to, and next with intent you fantasize about her. Once you are in her bed and her company, for the longest time, and sometimes for too long, you cannot conceive of yourself without her, without the tonic of her body, her laugh, her gaze. At some point the thing turns. It's as if a spear of light comes into a dark room. With that first glimmer you sense what it will feel like to break loose, to get outside, to breathe normally, that old in-and-out, and to see for yourself the sunshine, the trees, the shrubs, the street, people going to work, the day up and under way.

I was seventeen and did not know very much, although I had the weight of the world on my shoulders. I thought that if I'd been a pet, I would have barked and barked at my mistress's heels, trying to keep her from drinking the poisoned water, keeping her from danger. In those days my heart, I guess it was, sank more or less every day. I was no longer a boy, not yet a man, nowhere near as industrious as a dog. I had nothing in me then but useless sorrow.

Chapter Five

When my mother's book club discussed their selected novels, they seemed only to have regard for the female characters. It was as if the men were put in the fictions only to damage the women. Professor Marcia Butler, star member of the book club, single and artificially inseminated Professor Butler, was often talking about "the inviolate self," a term she'd gotten ahold of from Willa Cather. It was a thing women were supposed to find for themselves, some kernel that no man or animal could penetrate or wreck or remove. She bandied the phrase around so much my father couldn't help but take up the cause. He'd say, "Henry, you and your inviolate self want to play a game of chess?"

Although Ms. Butler professed to want to talk primarily about the assigned book, she couldn't help trumpeting her own theories, ideas that highlighted her superior intelligence. The others in the club unabashedly used the novels as springboards into contemporary life and in particular their own problems. I remember once being in the kitchen when Glamorous Pam got all hot and bothered out in the living room. "Where," she said, banging on the coffee table, "in mainstream American fiction do we read about sexuality from a woman's point of view? If women write about sex, they are considered threatening and brutish. When my mother first told me about intercourse, she explained that it was something I would want to do and that in most circumstances it was unforgivable. Can you believe it?"

They all started talking at once, about the times their mothers said this and then that, and how whacked out it had made them, how much money they'd spent in therapy as a result. Lucy, at one end of the room, was telling Charlotte how her mother put her on the pill, at age thirteen, ostensibly to make her skin clear up. Professor Butler had risen to go to the sideboard, to get a cup of hot cider, and there, to the visual artist named Janice, she gave a mini-lecture about how language is culturally determined to show an antifemale bias. She was asking Janice to think for a moment about the gender content and context in the language that is used to describe human fertilization. "Consider this," Marcia said. "Consider how egg is used to connote passivity, and sperm activity."

Janice, the good citizen, nodded. Yes, she was thinking. What else could a person do in the presence of such a mind? Beth Shaw was trying to stick to the club's purpose. "Yoo-hoo," she called, sounding very much like her own mother. "Can we get back to the book? It bothers me that the author doesn't forgive her character, what's-her-name, Catherine, until she gets into trouble for her adultery. She's likable only after she's been punished. Did anyone else see it that way?"

Interesting question, Liza38.

"Sex and punishment have always gone together for women!" one of them said. "If we cheated on our husbands, wouldn't we all expect to get killed accidentally, or our children would die, or we'd lose our homes, our money, we'd be cast out?"

"Yes," Beth said, her head in her hands, "yes."

Professor Butler was still holding Janice hostage at the urn, delivering her sermon on the sperm and egg. "When the scientific understanding of the process later changed," she was saying, "the description of the egg was modified in terms of aggression, the femme fatale, the lock and key. There is, you see, a new male bias."

Back to the discussion, a woman named Barbara made her suggestion, based perhaps on a personal wish. "The fact is we live far too long. To ask a couple to stay married to each other for their whole extended lifetimes is just too much in this day and age. Marriages should be renewable every fifteen years, no pain, no penalty, if at the fifteen-year marker you want to shake hands and part company."

I sometimes thought of the nine of them sitting on the floor, Indian style, around the coffee table, as a coven, although technically a coven has thirteen members. All the candles in the house were on the table, lighting their faces, casting shadows. There was often a murmur, a building of their voices, until out of the babble came a fact, a truth, an imperative. Yes, they all agreed that holy matrimony went on far too long. Women tended to get married before they knew themselves, before they'd made contact with their inviolate selves. Another fact: it takes ages, years and years, to train a man to be even moderately sensitive and to equip him with the expertise to carry out ordinary household tasks. By the time all the information has been dispensed and processed, the trainer is worn out.

Women, take charge! Women! Do not put up with those of the species who are not in touch with their spirituality and cannot sort the laundry by color and fabric.

I'm sure they came to their conclusions with the look of pleasure on their faces, just as individuals who enjoy casting spells might appear around the boiling cauldron, the light of the fire beneath catching the glint of their beady eyes.

One night during book club I got to the point where I could no longer remain a prisoner in the kitchen. I had to walk through the living room to get upstairs to the office. They had right away strayed from the assigned book and were again talking about goodness and sexuality, about how, when a woman marries, she suddenly thinks she has to be Mrs. June Cleaver; she has to leave behind her former lusty, bestial self. That was the gist, as best I could gather. They were probably more than a little drunk when I came through the arched doorway. It was Pam who hollered across the room, "Henry! Henry! Have you been eavesdropping on us all this time from the kitchen?"

"Of course," I said.

"Listen to him," she cackled. " 'Of course.' I want you to know that everything we said about mankind does not apply to you. We're old and jaded. But you, you're smart, and your mother tells us that—what did you call him, Beth?—perfectly amiable, that you are perfectly amiable. That sounds so Jane Austen. I love it! I love it."

"Don't let it go to your head," Marcia said to me. "You're not God's gift to women. Not yet, anyway."

"Yes, yes, he is!" Pam shouted. "We want you for an honorary member, Hen. You can set us all straight and—"

"*You* are free to go." It was my mother speaking, so kindly coming to my rescue.

The day after I read my mother's first message, on Tuesday, I managed to get out of bed, in five minutes thoroughly study for my Latin test, check Liza38's mail, and walk to school. I had spent a good part of the night writing a few things down and listening to music. You can waste entire seasons watching jerk-off and gross-out movies, and you can imagine that you're both wise and cynical, but in the end you can be as much of a sap as the next person. You can listen to the song "Rape Me" and maybe enter the darkness and ugliness to get a thrill, and turn around next and listen to some sad Sinéad O'Connor ballad; you can decide that love is a deadly business or that some woman somewhere has the power to save you.

I tried again to think of an equation that would explain our lives: Love plus my parents. What did that equal? Two children, a brownstone paid for by my grandmother, two adults with satisfying careers. What else? I thought, briefly, of my father's body, the thick swirl of light brown hair on his chest, his white back with the small red moles. I asked myself how much time I wanted to devote to thinking about my parents in the first place. This preoccupation of mine was my mother's fault, or I was sick, or I needed a distraction, a small, short war, marching orders from the sergeant. For some reason it was easier, in a way, to picture Richard Polloco with my mother than to consider my parents together. No, wait, I said to myself, that isn't right. I was tired enough to have to think it through again. Wasn't Richard Polloco—wasn't he a fantasy? Had I read that e-mail? Why, just why would Liza pack off to another state for something she could get at home? I thought of my parents' bedroom, or rather I recalled how it smelled, how stuffy it was. It was the stench that came to me. Kevin, like a bad boy, left his dirty underwear on the floor, at the spot where his feet had come through them. The smelly socks, inside out, were twisted, flattened, one of them a bookmark in the dusty stack of books on the dresser. There was a staleness particular to their room, the trademark marriage odor, perhaps. But I had never interrupted a scene between them; never, even as a child, as far as I knew, stumbled upon them *in medias res*. From my vantage point it was hard not to think that if you had the chance, you'd fuck day after day, year after year. I couldn't fathom what really could keep a person from doing it morning, noon, and again at bedtime.

All through the night I couldn't shake irrelevant thoughts, dangerous in their simplicity. At the school playground my mother used to sincerely and enthusiastically say, "Wheeeee," down the slide with me. Out back she'd wade in the creek and ride on the toboggan and skate on the river. I was nostalgic for everything, for the five minutes that had just passed, for the sky-blue trades of my childhood, and certainly I was nostalgic for the time before I'd read the e-mail. When I was little, my mother, in her early twenties, was still practically a kid herself. This was a strange but true fact. She might have felt that she was hardly more than a girl playing house. She used to make bread and cupcakes, she knit sweaters for me to wear, she played goofy songs on the piano. I couldn't help wondering what had changed. Elvira had been born; Mrs. Shaw had made a career for herself; she traveled a lot; she got older; we left the sharp, clear air of Vermont to move to Chicago. I had grown up, hidden the parts of myself she would disapprove of, careful not to alarm her. Sometimes it seemed that nothing was the same down to the very air, and then I looked at Elvira, kooky Elvira, and my father and mother, and there I was too, even-keeled Henry, benevolent Henry—so my mother said—and as far as I could tell we were in our same corners, where we'd always been, at our places.

I had fallen asleep trying to name the thing that was different about us. When I woke up, I had twenty-five minutes to get to school. Time enough to check the mail. She would think I was finishing up some last-minute schoolwork. In the office I turned on the main switch, waited for the machine to boot up, felt the little bit of stubble on my chin that took a week to break through, opened the file, waited for the modem to connect, bit my thumbnail, strained toward the voice, "Welcome." There was a message, yes, and it was from him, Rpoll. I could read the communication and save it as if it were new mail. Our Internet provider had thought of everything, had thought of prying sons and lecherous mothers. Mrs. Shaw could log on and read her love letter, innocent as a lamb.

Dear Liza38,
We lived at Augusta and Hoyne, did I tell you that? It's still Chicagoland's Ukrainian neighborhood—living where you do, so uppercrusted, you may not know this. We will go to my old haunts and buy chocolates from Mrs. Lozovan, chocolates that have pictures of cows on the wrappers. Moo cows, Lizadiza, with long lashes. We will stroll past St. Vladimir's and the sun might then very well shine. Sometimes when I am visiting those streets, a terrible strangeness comes over me, borne from time passing, from my father, my cousin Rudy, the barber Rocko, being gone from that place, gone from all places. Rudy, remember, was my Aunt Galina's juvenile delinquent boy. We used to run through the streets, two immigrant urchins, dirty and foulmouthed. We stole candy from Mrs. Lozovan and shot at the mangy cats with our slingshots, and later, in high school, we did our share for the drug traffic. We ditched school and rode the El into the worst neighborhoods, and any number of times almost got ourselves killed. But I had what Rudy did not, my violin and my violin teacher, Mr. Albert Perrin, to steer me on my wavering path

toward third chair, second chair, and finally concertmaster of the Youth Symphony! Also, I had Mr. Toti, the Italian woodcarver, who taught me the rudiments of woodworking and the auxiliary joys of sniffing glue. Liza, what will happen to us? I think that that terrible strangeness would go away if you could be with me. Come to Tribbey, listen to my stories, take them off my back, make me right as rain, and do, above all, tear the buttons from my shirt again. I have sewn them on with heavy-duty thread and when you arrive will add duct tape, for extra protection. Get them off me if you can. Kiss me, kiss me, I'm waiting. RP

Kiss me, kiss me, Jesus Christ, tear the buttons from my shirt. *Again?* I should click on the Delete icon, I thought, get rid of the message. He used to kill cats with a slingshot and wait on dark corners in the night to hand over drug money. In his bedroom, in a tenement on a wide street, with no trees, nothing green, he played his violin against the noise of the traffic and the El train. I could delete the message if I wanted to. Kevin Shaw was the boy who'd been in love with steam engines and rockets, who'd been the editor of the school newspaper and an average second baseman. He was in bed every night at nine-thirty in Cleveland Heights, Ohio, dreaming about hitting a homer with the Indians. Delete, I told myself. Easy— click, click. Two motions of the index finger.

If I got rid of the message, what, I asked myself, would then change? Richard Polloco would still be in Tribbey and Kevin Shaw in Chicago. My mother would write to Rpoll without knowing that she'd missed a message. Right away he'd shoot back a clever response. Vaporizing a single communication was not going to alter much of anything. Clicking on Delete was not suddenly going to make Polloco dull or give Kevin more dimension. It occurred to me that I could save the message. I could save it and print it out and have it. I didn't think that it might be useful at a later date or that I'd end up printing all the correspondence, that I'd end up with a file. I didn't really think, beyond the idea of having the one, just to keep, much as you take a shell from the beach or a leaf from the woods.

I couldn't help wondering what—what if I wrote Lily letters like this? *Lily, Lily, come back to me, tear the buttons from my shirt, kiss me, kiss me.* Surely she would jump on a train, a bus, a plane; she would pound at the door, trample my mother and Elvira and my father, take the steps by threes to get to my room. If there was a God and if he was merciful and also slightly insane, maybe he had brought Richard Polloco to me, for me! To instruct me in the fine art of epistolary courtship.

It only took me another beat to rethink the purpose of the letter, to realize that, asshole, the message had nothing to do with me, that my mother and Richard Polloco were trading life stories. There was possibly nothing worse. He was telling her about the things that mattered to him, and if she was going to do the same, then there was no stopping them. There was no stopping them even though my mother was not this Liza38 character. She was Beth Shaw of Roslyn Place, a Midwestern woman of Puritan stock, someone who had no business running off with an immigrant from the Ukraine.

The clock in the hall chimed once. Seven-thirty. I had ten minutes to get to school. First, I routed the message to my own disk. The beginning of the Polloco archive. Next, I dutifully clicked on the Keep as New Icon, for my mother's satisfaction. Up the stairs, I found clean clothes, put them on, stuffed my homework into my pack, looked around wildly, as if I had to be sure the smoking gun was covered, the bloody cloths hidden. She—Lizadiza, Beth Shaw, Mother—so many inviolate selves she had to keep track of; she was in the kitchen. I didn't go in there to eat breakfast or look at her or say good-bye.

I went out the front door. The leaves on the maple trees had turned yellow and were beginning to drift to the street. The sky was blue and the breeze was cool, so that I wished I'd grabbed my sweatshirt on the way out of the house. There were enough trees on our block to have produced leaves that covered the sidewalk in some depth, but they were damp and limp. When I tried to shuffle through them, they stuck to my shoes. They should have been crisp, should have made a crackling noise. "Fuck you," I said to the leaves. I was breathing hard, too old to cry. "Go to fucking hell."

The leaves had no spines, and something else was missing, so that I had to stop for a minute, look up, turn around. What was it? What else was gone besides the family I thought I'd had, and Lily, the person I believed I needed? It was something large, something else, I said to myself, that was essential, in the way air is necessary. The citizens of Chicago are not allowed, by order of the law, to burn their leaves. I had to take another breath, and another, before I realized that I was missing the smell of fall, the thick haze of smoke down the road, the old men, the husbands, the mothers, the widows wearing bandannas, with their rakes, standing in the yard at the burning piles, feeding the fires. All through my town in Vermont on autumn days the smoke seeped through the chinks in the windows. Out of the cool sweet air it settled on the laundry hanging to dry; it lined your nostrils. The chill of September and October was always warmed by the smell of burning leaves, the fragrance that went along with apple picking, early darkness, stacking wood.

I turned onto Clark Street. The drunk, no matter the season, was as usual weaving in and out of traffic, yelling at the cars about the Good Samaritan. I could see, up ahead, the line of Volvos outside of Jesse Layton, and the rich children climbing out of the backseats to go to school. I choked on the air that was polluted city air and not the superior polluted air of the country. I wanted to be back in Vermont, where I wouldn't have to see homeless Pete or the mothers in their sweat suits on their way to the Health Club. There wasn't anyplace in the city I could go where someone else wouldn't be, nursing along his or her own misfortune. I wanted to be one narrow state away from New Hampshire Lily. Lily. *You.* Down by the water, that night at Silverpines, when, with her light fingers, with both her soft hands, she had touched me, she had also whispered, "Tell me, Henry. Tell me what this feels like. Tell me now."

I couldn't think of her saying that without seeing Richard Polloco. It was Richard Polloco lying next to my mother, Liza38 on her side, he bent over her, whispering in her ear, his hand moving slowly down her back and her behind, teasing the tangle of hair between her legs. "Tell me," he was whispering, "tell me, Liza, what it feels like. Tell me now."

I had to hold still by the iron fence at Jesse Layton. All by myself I had ruined that image of Lily, the sound of her voice, the words she had said to me. Why had I let Richard Polloco, a man I had seen once, overtake the only privacy I had, the privacy of my memory? How could I let that happen? Somehow, what Lily had said to me just then was his doing.

I hung there, by the fence. I wanted to stay, I wanted to go some-place else. Eat or not eat. I could move, it wasn't worth going any-where. This was how schizophrenia probably began, this very way, mixing up your girlfriend with your mother's lover and subsequently hanging on a fence. A student named Cathy Greber came along and said, "What's the matter, you all right?" Even though she'd asked af-ter me, I felt as if no one had seen me; no one would ever come up to find out if I was sick. Cathy had several medical problems, one of which gave her a pop-eyed look, another a tic, the corner of her mouth every few seconds spazzing into her cheek. At my father's sug-gestion and pressure from Layton itself, I took Cathy Greber to the homecoming dance when I was a sophomore—a fact my mother con-tinued to broadcast year after year when she talked about my sterling qualities. I had hated that dance and seriously considered climbing out of the bathroom window, anything to get out of there.

When Cathy asked me a second time if I was okay, I said that I was fine, I might have the flu, I might go home in a minute. I was still slumped against the fence when Karen came, walking quickly, in a hurry to get to school on time yet not in any way panicked. She al-ways tilted her head when she walked, and moved her lips, reciting poetry to herself, in her own verbal trance. But she noticed me. She stopped, straightened out, and said, "Tell me."

Tell me. Tell me what it feels like. Tell me now.

"Henry," Karen said, "have you impaled yourself on that fence?"

In the moment it annoyed me that she didn't ask me any further questions, any further specific questions. "I don't think so," I said.

When she realized I wasn't going to elaborate, she took me by the arm and led me up the stairs and into the building. What good is this going to do? I thought. The bell rang. We were late to calculus. Mr. Kuhn ignored us stumbling to our seats. I paid attention as best as I could, lagging behind Mr. Kuhn, catching up, slipping, getting close again. At the start of the next class, Asian history, we were sent to the library to work on our research papers, and in my carrel I was able to wonder what Lily would have done if she'd come upon me draped over the fence outside of Layton. Lily might have mothered me, might have coaxed me to admit my troubles. *You can tell me, Henry.* Who was to say that Karen's tack wasn't as good as or even better than fantasy Lily's strategy? Karen had so wisely taken me by the arm, wound me up, set me on my course.

Most people my age, I figured, sat in their rooms at night listening to CDs, because our music, we thought, pierced through the teenage armor we imagined we'd built up, and showed us, we believed, ourselves. We all listened in the dark, dreaming about the musicians, about knowing them the way the 12 million other people who had bought their recordings did not. I sometimes wished it were only I who had ever heard Nirvana, and at other moments I felt that even in my room I was in an amphitheater, the open sky above, in the soothing crush of strangers, listening to the fury of one small-town punk. That fury was something I would have liked to appropriate, for a short time, on the condition that I could leave it behind, make for home when I needed to. I think I did understand that fury can take a person into itself, that there is sometimes no knowing how the rage will use you.

I was perfectly amiable, so Mrs. Shaw said, as if I were an eighteenth-century lapdog. She who knew nothing. Sure, I had plenty of acquaintances at Layton. I was in the chess club, I took photographs for the yearbook, I assisted in the computer lab, I made it to about half of the cross-country meets, I hardly ever practiced the cello and therefore I was tenth chair in the Youth Symphony. With the group of Layton alumni, men my parents' age, I played Ping-Pong. I usually finished my homework. I shut up and did as I was told. On occasion I went to parties and down to the beach and to the jazz clubs, the punk clubs, the blues clubs. I wasn't a loner, I wasn't a jock, I wasn't straight-edged, I wasn't technically a geek because of my long hair. I was nothing or I was everything. Perfectly amiable.

Whatever it was, it didn't matter, maybe because I hadn't caught up with myself. I hadn't really arrived in the city, in the neighborhood, in the school. Maybe I hadn't even adjusted to the Chicagoness of my transplanted family. There should have been plenty of things to like about the city. I could walk out the door, down the block, and buy a CD, a book, play games at the arcade, eat a knish, a piece of sushi, get a good cup of coffee, stroll by the lake thinking grave thoughts, consider myself mature, go to foreign films, and hear bands on the cutting edge. We had left Wellington nearly four years before, and yet I felt as if I hadn't arrived in Chicago. I'd wake up in the morning trying to figure out where I was, looking out my window from my bed, at the patch of sky. I often had the sense that I was suspended, neither here nor there, hovering somewhere over the Ohio River Valley. "He's so well grounded," my mother would say, "and kind! He took the handicapped girl, Cathy Greber, to a dance."

On that Tuesday in late September I came home from school, mashing the leaves into the sidewalk and breathing the air that had come up from Gary. When I walked into the house, my mother was at the piano, playing Gershwin, playing—of course—playing what else but "The Man I Love." I stood staring at her, at the way she shook her head and moved backward and forward, emoting, I guess. Was it an act, or did she feel so moved she had to throw herself around like a drunk?

Why are you playing that song? What is it, Mother? Anything special about "The Man I Love"? I was standing in the hall, trying to tell myself that she often played Gershwin, nothing unusual about her choice. Elvira and I used to beg her to play certain pieces when we were small. We used to like Gershwin quite a bit. It struck me then that considering her generation, she was old enough to play "The Man I Love" with no sense of irony. She loved Richard Polloco. She was an artist in love, and so naturally there was a pitch to her feeling that the rest of us could not appreciate. For her, perhaps, there was nothing complicated or absurd about expressing her emotion in the middle of our living room. She loved him, she loved him—that feeling was all she knew. She would only ever play "The Man I Love" for Richard Polloco, for Rpoll, for Richard "come rip the buttons off my shirt, kiss me, kiss me" Polloco.

Elvira at that time had a new friend named Hilare, a girl her own age, a pre-woman, a baby woman, an individual who not only seemed to enjoy her femininity but was also fearsomely in touch with her inviolate self. She was bossy. She had a gigantic singing voice and had been in several musicals at the Victory Garden Theater and a drama at Steppenwolf. In addition to her prima donna references she had padded puffed-up lips, movie star, duckish lips. My father called her "the infant phenomenon." Elvira, from what I could see, had a crush on her. Hilare would say Elvira do this, Elvira do that, and stubborn, door-banging Elvira would mutely fetch and tote and haul, trying to please every one of Hilare's whims. My mother did not like Hilare, and also she had no sense of humor about a girl it was probably best, in terms of self-preservation, to mock. She seemed to think that Hilare was destined to be a loose and unlawful teenager, that the slack hair that hung in her face, and her purple lipstick, her pasty skin, were the signs of a wanton future, a future that was upon her.

I was stuck in the hall, listening to Gershwin. My mother did not look up from her own muscly hands. There was no flash from her fourth left finger, because at some point in the preceding weeks she had removed her engagement diamond and her wedding band. She was a free woman!

The girls in the kitchen were eating something that made Hilare say, in a voice that came screeching down the scale, "*E-e-uuuuuuuu.*" My mother should have been pleased that Elvira was playing a nonviolent game that did not involve historical reenactment, with a person of her own gender, and better yet, with a girl who seemed to be headed for heterosexuality. But Liza did not like Hilare of the prospective nipple ring. Mrs. Shaw, who had wanted at one stage of her life to be the Earth mother to end all Earth mothers, overflowing with generosity and blueberry muffins and craft projects, had discovered within herself the bitter vein of disapproval. She seemed not to like Elvira much either, although certainly she would have hotly disputed that charge. The fourth time the screech, the *E-uuu,* came from the kitchen my mother abruptly quit playing "The Man I Love." She said, "Goddamn it," from between her clenched teeth, and put her head to the top of her beloved Steinway piano, the instrument my grandmother had bought for her when she was twenty-three. She groaned. She did not rise from the piano; she ripped away from it. Like an unexpected summer blow, all hot air, she swept into the kitchen.

She was wearing a new getup, or at least an outfit that I had never seen before. Clothes that were not Kevin Shaw clothes. Apparel that might appeal to the violinist, Mr. Fashion. A thin black sweater that had a V neck, a white lacy thing underneath, and a pair of red pants. Red pants.

"Would you girls consider," she hissed, she flashed, "eating something else if that cheese spread revolts you so much."

As she often said, you pick your battles. Hilare was a thoroughly modern child who did not think twice about the propriety of mouthing off to a friend's mother. She had not gone to Jesse Layton for nothing. In the Layton brochure, on the front page, the president of the board proudly describes and supports the school's tradition of promoting Self-Expression.

Hilare said, "Well, sor-rie," in a tone of phony contrition.

Elvira had lived with my mother for a long time, longer than she had gone to Layton, and she wisely changed the subject. "We're going rollerblading in the park," she said.

Regrettably it was not the right subject. "Oh, no, you're not," my mother said.

"Why?" Elvira was wrinkling her nose, the one expression that made her pixie face look piggishly unattractive.

"Because, it's going to get dark soon," my mother said. She was probably envisioning Hilare at the Fullerton Beach with all the stoned high school boys and the miscellaneous heroin addicts, Hilare polishing her moves. That was why not. Would Mrs. Shaw rather her daughter be a lesbian or a hooker? It was such a tough choice: Lesbian? Hooker? Lesbian? Hooker?

"It's not going to be dark for an hour and a half," Elvira said.

I held the coatrack in my curled index finger and considered letting it fall. In the kitchen my mother began the list, the dread litany. "You've made a mess with this cheese stuff, what's the caramel doing on the table, you got a C on your spelling test last week." You could hear the anger building as she was tabulating all of the omissions and errors, the evidence of laziness, willfulness, carelessness. "You left the paints out upstairs and didn't wash the brushes, how many times have I told you to clean the brushes? Those new jeans I got for you that Minty paid for—I don't want to think how much they cost— were on the floor in your room in a wad. No consideration—"

"Wait a minute. Wait just a minute."

We looked, the three Shaws in the room, at Hilare. Hilare, the Jesse Layton student who had been misled in the school's best tradition since kindergarten. She had demanded that my mother wait, not once, but twice. And then again. "Hold the phone," she said.

My mother cocked her head, as if she couldn't hear in Hilare's frequency, as if she couldn't make out the words coming from the biggest trap in Chicago's musical theater. "If you were in court," Hilare was saying, "these arguments, you know, to keep us from going skating, would not hold up. The judge would, like, blast you out of the water."

Although I was on the girls' side, to be sure, I had a moment of pause. What was the world coming to? Without a doubt, teenybopper Hilare needed someone to beat the shit clean out of her. I was in the hall, but there was a vibration through the house in the silence that followed. It was perhaps all of our hearts beating, a collective fear pounding from each of us while we waited to see what was going to happen, while we wondered how Mrs. Shaw would strike.

In that quiet we looked to her. We looked until we could see the hint of her private happiness, the slightest smile on her lips, the shine in her eyes. "Fine." She said the word softly, almost gleefully. "Go. Go out in the park. Let it get dark. Maybe, maybe someone will come along and ki–" She thought better of that sentiment and reduced the perpetrator's offense from manslaughter to felony. "Maybe," she said, "someone will come and beat you up."

She was down the hall, past me, without seeing. She took the stairs by twos, went into the office, and turned on the computer. I could hear the hard drive boot up and the wheels of the chair as she scooted herself into place at the desk, making ready to leave us, to go to him. And I could see why, for just a minute, a man who made violins in the stillness of the woods, who lived in a log cabin all by himself, who had a swing in the yard, a tree fort where no boys and girls ever played, a collection of children's books that had ink drawings of mothers and fathers of the 1950s and adorable daughters with bows in their hair and dresses with petticoats underneath–I could see that what Richard Polloco had might be something my mother wanted, that the tableau in Tribbey was perfect, complete, because it did not include us.

There were many days early on when I thought I might impersonate my mother, that it would be sport, at the least, to compose messages in the style of herself and send them to Richard Polloco. It was tempting to tell him that she'd changed her mind, she no longer wanted to speak to him, that he was inconsiderate, slovenly, self-absorbed, and—what else? As far as I knew, those were not adjectives that described the woodworking violinist. Theoretically he had conducted himself dishonorably, although it's possible, I suppose, that my mother may have made it difficult for him to act otherwise. I didn't yet know that they would try to break up time and time again, that one more Dear John letter would be just another blip on the screen. I understood very little about him beyond one crucial fact: he could write. It was no mystery why my mother was smitten by him, and if he spoke in a way that was anywhere near his writer's voice, there was no hope for the continuation of the Shaw family.

Many of his messages, even the trivial ones, the quick notes dashed off in a hurry, had the coziness of a morning in bed, the barbs of intimacy and a well-turned phrase keeping the reader near.

"Dear Liza38," he wrote on October 26:
I know I'm supposed to love Horowitz. How can I tell you he does nothing for me? Liza, I confess he does nothing for me. You are undoubtedly saying Gadzooks in just that way you do. You will possibly not be able to love me with this new

knowledge. But stay, oh stay oh stay. I'm putting my money on the Russian lad who's still in diapers—he plays as if he could get to hell and back, his face is fresh, his lunacy not yet hardened by alcohol or disappointments in love or the smell just around the corner of death. If you would come up here and play for me, play "When Johnny Comes Marching Home," a Goldberg Variation or two, and "Tenting on the Old Camp Ground," I could make more violins faster, and in no time, no time I tell you, become independently wealthy. We could run off to a South Sea Island where I'd sit beside you in the sand and make you a pookah bead necklace. My future is in your hands, those lily-white ones. I remain, RP

I had never heard Mrs. Shaw say Gadzooks in my life. She proba- bly would like being on a South Sea Island for a while—who knows how long? She'd walk for miles on the beaches listening to the tropi- cal birds and the beat of the natives' drums, and pretty soon she'd be playing her same old music with a brand-new twang. It would be music that predictably enough would come into you through your heart. She'd send us postcards of the blue skies, the blue waters. *Miss you! Love you!*

My father was funny in one-sentence segments, but Richard Pol- loco, it seemed, was charming in his lethal way by the paragraph. That was about the best I could do in my efforts to size him up. Al- though in the first several weeks I read scores of my mother's mes- sages, I could not quite get a handle on her tone. I could not always tell if her earnestness was straight up or if she was mocking herself in the unlikely and hilarious role of femme fatale. Did she really think, for example, that she had been waiting for him for a long time, as she had written to her friend Jane? She couldn't seriously believe that out in the wide world there was a single preordained person and a woman had only to wait for the magic activation moment in order for *poof!* Strolling out from the fog, himself, The Guy. Young persons my age and until we reached the age of twenty-one were allowed with impunity to indulge ourselves in that absurd and seductive notion, but she, at her stage of life, was not.

In those first weeks of the Richard Polloco experience, for some reason quite often our computer screen froze or the provider wouldn't respond; it was one thing or another. I like to think that the heat of Liza38's guilty conscience interfered with the circuitry of the mother-board. I was doing nothing but blithely coming home from school the first time she had technical problems. I set foot in the front hall. She was down the stairs so quickly she rammed into me, grabbed my arms, all breath she was, her watery eyes gone dry.

"Henry," she gasped, "you've got to help me."

"What! What's the matter?" Was the FBI upstairs? Was she bleeding internally? There'd been gunfire! We were going to scream down the street in an ambulance while she told me her dying wish, while she expired in my arms. "What!"

She was doing the difficult job of holding still, so that the skin on her hands, those lily-white ones, were stretched to the thinnest translucence around my big wrists. "I—can't," she said, "get—on-line."

I looked hard and I looked long into those beseeching blue eyes of hers. Right then there was nothing—not jewels or a cruise ship or money, not even Polloco himself—that she wanted more than the machinery to be up and running. I could see this in her fierce little pupils. "Oh, no!" I finally whispered. "Oh God."

"What? What do you think it is?"

It hadn't taken me much time, more than a second really, to understand the possibilities in the situation. At her tender age my friend Karen had given me plenty of lectures, and so I had been made to understand that there is a variety of ways in which different cultures throughout the world torture bad women, women who have strayed. Some stone them in public. Some kill them quietly. In America we tend to reduce them to poverty. "Let me think." I said it slowly, as if there were a veritable banquet of software and hardware problems from which to choose.

"I've—I've got to get on," she said. "I've just—just got to get on."

"Okay," I said. "Sure."

I set my backpack on the floor, squatted, took out a pencil, in case I needed to do some complicated algorithms to get the dolly in working order. Computations that might take, oh, a week or two. I ambled up the stairs after her, sat in the office chair, adjusted the setting for height and back support. Stood and fixed my belt. Sat down. Made a fine tuning with the smaller black knob under the chair. Tweaked the larger one. You may recall that Liza38 was rather stumpy, staturewise. I blew my nose. Balled up the tissue and tried for a three-pointer all the way over to the wastebasket. I squinted into the screen that had most likely been immobilized because there were a few conflicting extensions in the system. Usually, shutting the thing off and starting it again unscrambled the works for a while. First, though, I tried clicking on every icon. No response! It's always a good idea to check the connections, the plugs, the ports, the phone line, the printer cables, and why not clean out the mouse while we're at it, get some cotton swabs and a little alcohol.

She would have liked to scream at me, I could tell, to shriek for all she was worth. *Get me on, Henry.* I could feel the urgency, the desperation, in the way she clutched the back of my chair and breathed as if she were running and running and not simply standing still.

"I wonder," I said when I'd finished with the mouse and set it sparkling upon its pad. "We might have to call the technical support number."

"Will they tell us?"

"They do the best they can," I said. "To tell us. After, you know, you've been on hold."

In an effort not to cry she closed her eyes, sucked in some air, held it. Good girl, Liza. Perhaps he had written her a message telling her he couldn't go on; he should never have gotten involved with a married woman. As she was reading along, wouldn't you know it, the computer had had a seizure! Or maybe she had written him to say she couldn't manage it anymore. She had come to her senses. It seemed to me that both of those messages were just waiting to happen. Possibly she'd written the letter of no return, clicked on Send—whoops! Wait! Wait, wait, wait, she'd changed her mind.

It did seem natural that my mother would have second thoughts once in a while. A person didn't in every moment wholeheartedly love the object of her affection. Even I knew that. Maybe she was feeling burdened by his future being in her lily-white hands. She probably sometimes believed that she was willing to risk everything for Richard Polloco. She could leave Roslyn Place without a second thought, throw us away, go off without a pang. But there must have been other times when she considered what a strange thing love was. Why had she let it take her from the people she cared for most? She must have had occasions to wonder. For no reason she might, for an instant now and again, have been freed from the tyranny of her feeling and therefore been able to see him clearly. It might have crossed her mind in those troubling flashes that she didn't even admire people like him. He could have made a real living, produced more violins, made a name for himself, and he certainly could have practiced more, been disciplined and ambitious. He wasted an awful lot of time rereading Rex Stout mysteries and sitting down at the one bar in Tribbey watching football and talking to any of the old drunks who were planted on the stools. Maybe it wasn't charming after all, the way he bit into an apple, as if he were rabid, as if he were attacking it, going to get the better of it. Would she, for the long haul, be able to lovingly wash his stack of crusted dishes, and scrape the burned oatmeal, the burned noodles, the burned Spaghettiing-Os off the bottom of his three pots? When she considered his failures and a few of his slovenly habits, she'd have to shake herself. She'd have to remember that it was his boyishness, his wide-ranging curiosity, and his hungry-dog appetite that had been appealing in the first place.

Up in the office, when she could no longer control herself over the computer's malfunction, when she started to tremble, and when her breathing down my neck became irregular, I said, "Wait a minute. Let's try something." I made elaborate motions, pressing the various keys and finally hitting the one under the desk that shut the machine down. "Hold the phone," I said, starting it up again. "Here we go."

My mother sank into a hard wooden chair, put her hands into her face, and said, "Oh Jesus. Thank you."

I had several opportunities that fall to come to her rescue, and each time I made the fix I always wished right away that I could take it back, that I could make the whole system irreparably bomb before her eyes. It goes down again, I said to myself more than once, I won't get it working. I could make as many promises as I wanted in my spare time without exactly remembering how grateful she was when I waved my wand during the crisis and all was well again. I would not have admitted that her trust in my ability to make it right for her was actually worth something to me. Her way of thanking me was usually simple and, naturally, from the heart. She might fold her hands on the top of my head while I sat at the desk finishing up, and she'd put her chin to her knuckles and rest there, breathing normally into my hair. She might stand before me and smile sweetly, shaking her head a little, as if to ask, What would I do without you? Once, she did go so far as to say, with hideous solemnity, "Henry, I really hope I can repay you for this someday."

I'd get out of there while she checked her messages, or sent her own, restored to happiness. When she'd done her writing, after she'd left the room, I'd tiptoe down from my lair to see what it was that had nearly driven her over the edge. Here's the thing that bewildered me in the beginning: in those first few months it was usually unaccountably nothing, nothing that I could find in old or new messages, that would have given a person cause for such psychotic behavior. I'd read along over the tender insults, the sly references to favored body parts, the passages about longing, about the strength of their love, the yearning toward the next assignation, the recapitulation of the last meeting. What was the problem? Why the insanity over a frozen screen when she only needed to say yet another Coochie-coo and receive his adoration?

After about the fifth freeze-up and my coming to her aid, a ritual it was by that point, I realized, as she was sweating and choking, going cold turkey, that she was frantic to communicate with him. Period. She had to have him. She had to have him ten times daily, had at the least to have that writerly voice of his, or she had withdrawals, couldn't cope, couldn't function, couldn't breathe.

There must have been a part of her, then, that wished to be free of the great and ungovernable need inside her; and so sometimes I thought I could write to Polloco, in anticipation of her future feelings. I could let him know that the whole of it had come clean for her. With one short communication I could speed up the story, bring on its inevitable conclusion.

I once went so far as to try to type out a message.

"Dear Richard." She would use his Christian name for a message that had as its serious business the end of their love.

Dear Richard,
Last night, very late, my son, Henry, came downstairs to talk to me.

She would tell him, succinctly, how I had changed her life with my deliberate words. Because I would say just the right thing, and she would see the error of her ways. I would spare her any embarrassment, of course, as she wept. I'd tell her that we wouldn't speak of it again, that it was over now. Afterward, I'd run for the office of senator for the state of Illinois, get elected, wear a suit and tie at all times, and give long speeches about school prayer and keeping the National Rifle Association vital.

I thought about Rpoll in his cabin, at the desk where he kept his eyesore, his Macintosh SE. He might read the message I'd composed in my mother's name and wonder about the sentence structure, the general tone, my fairly regular use of correct punctuation. If I got carried away, he might think, Is my Liza on uppers, on downers? Has she had electric shock therapy? I pictured his writing back, to ask her what had become of her phraseology. Her messages were often filled with private jokes, so that it was impossible to understand what she was saying, although the basic intent was usually not obscure.

On October 21 she wrote, "Dear Kreplach."

What the heck was a kreplach? I had to look it up in my un-abridged *American Heritage Dictionary*. My mother was calling her lover the name of a small pocket of noodle dough filled with ground meat or cheese, usually boiled and served in soup. A German won-ton. I guess she had had enough of her Wasp culture, enough sing around the campfire, recite Shakespeare sonnets, go to Grandma's lake house on the weekend. What she wanted was kreplach, a little terror to go with it, a portrait of Stalin, and Lenin too, a sad Ellis Is-land story, the fractured hope of the immigrant.

"Dear Kreplach," she wrote:

> I have been trying to play the Schumann, the Kreisleriana as you suggested, whatareya trying to do, kill me? Do you think I'm not tortured enough, I have to have another madman in my life? It is a long journey to your house, not to mention the even longer path past the rose garden. I sit at the piano playing that storm, how'my supposed to hold it together from here to there, again not to mention the fact that I'm not going to see you until Saturday, I need you, are you going to wear Checked Pants, what has become of your finger?

Liza38 had dispensed with standard English punctuation and seemed to be writing her messages to Rpoll in the voice of a Jewish mother. Maybe the most dangerous aspect of her affair was the fact that writing to Richard Polloco had altered her voice, had made her unrecognizable. He had confused her about her own self. She'd be-come the Helene Hanff of Chicago. In her afternoons at home she was probably smoking cigarettes and dribbling gin over her treasured used bookstore copy of the Latinate Bible. I wasn't sure I was up to imitating the character she had created for Mrs. Shaw, even if I could pin it down. That character, it seemed to me, was attempting, in vain, to be as delightful and fluent as Rpoll. She was embarrassing herself pretty badly, and I wondered if he knew it. My friend Karen once pointed out to me that the trait I have, always taking the long view, is at once a negative and a positive feature of my personality. It stood to reason that if I wrote Polloco under my mother's name, and if I lambasted him or tried to change the course of events, and he read the message and wrote her back, there most certainly would be trouble. My mother would log on, read his message, and ask herself what he was talking about. *Whatdaya mean I said you were an insensitive asshole?*

I doubt that it would take her very long to trace the misunderstanding to me. She'd find me out, and then what? Would she haul me off to family therapy? Would she expect me to be complicit, to honor her secret? Would she pay some kind of price to keep me quiet, offer me a vacation, a bigger allowance, a noisy and loving foster family in the suburbs?

I wanted to send a message to Richard Polloco, to see what would happen. I made believe, however, that my mother, if she caught me, had it within her power to make me feel responsible for her having taken up with a lover in the first place. I didn't know I felt this way at the time, but I have since studied literature, read more Henry James than I care to admit, and been to film school. All of that education was supposed to give me tools to think about the world, but I'm sorry to say it taught me to think about myself. In the year of Polloco, without knowing, without examining much of anything, I feared that my quietness, my failure to take hold in Chicago, had led my mother to another kind of reassurance. I'm fairly sure it is true that somewhere within my amiable psyche I believed Polloco was my fault. Rpoll had nothing, nothing, to do with the fact that my mother was grateful for all of the wrong things in her life, that she had no idea what to appreciate, and that she was greedy. It was my own flimsy character that had made her tumble into bed with the golden-tongued musician. I did consider that her transgressions were perhaps partially my father's fault too. He was so wrapped up in the Civil War, so committed to his students, that he seemed not to be present. He spent one fall corresponding, in the persona of Mary Todd Lincoln, with about a dozen people on the subject of some lost photographs of her late husband. Who wouldn't want to run away to Wisconsin? And let's not forget Elvira. We can also hold her responsible for being the wrong daughter, a girl who had come to my mother in someone else's place. Still, I had to shoulder the blame, because living with a son's unhappiness, an unhappiness you cannot treat, might be like having a wound that cannot be bound up, that will not heal.

I dared myself to write in the style of Liza38, the mercurial style of herself, but the truth is I didn't have the nerve. This story might have begun with the scene in my office, my writing to Rpoll and clicking on the Send icon. That is where I would come into focus, effecting the drama's swift conclusion. As it was, I sat at the computer and I'd think of a dozen reasons why writing wasn't a good idea, and when I'd gone through every one of them, I'd feel something sink, the fantasy Henry fading, a little more of his brazen strength ebbing away. There I was, the helpless spectator. It wouldn't be too much longer until even in my own mind there was nothing but the real person, stark in his weakness.

During those first weeks, when I had a wayward thought that I didn't want to entertain, I'd make myself turn to Karen, to the idea of Karen. I'd bypass Lily and go to a reliable source. What, I'd ask myself, would Karen say? Karen, with the black hair that was so dull my mother wondered if she dyed it, to get it such a flat color. Sometimes Karen did look as if she were a fifty-year-old masquerading as a teenager, a being who had come down to us from another sphere, to show us the way. If I told her about Richard Polloco, she'd take me for a walk, and in a short paragraph she'd explain the whole matter. She might say, "Henry, first of all, this affair of your mother's does not have anything to do with you. Think of it as one must a Greek tragedy. The players don't really have personalities. They hardly have character. They are set in place by the gods to fulfill their roles. Therefore, Clytemnestra has no choice but to kill Agamemnon. Your mother is getting older, so she's going to dry up one of these days. You've heard of menopause, right? My mother is going through her change—hot flash, cold flash, smiles one minute, throws a fit the next. Your mother, sweetheart, just wants to fuck someone's brains out. I'm sorry to put it bluntly, but that's how it is. It's purely biological. She's playing her role as the Menopausal Woman. Think of the last egg hobbling down the fallopian tube, shrieking for one last sperm."

In fact, a few years later, when I did tell Karen the story, that is more or less the monologue she delivered. Lily would not have been able to lay it out for me in such a fashion. She'd ask me what I thought, and I'd try to put it into words, to explain that I felt responsible. She'd say, "Oh, no, Henry! Do you really think it's you?" Lily had infinite sympathy, a brand of sympathy that is probably one of the deadlier sins. Or maybe nothing I thought about Lily was true. I probably had to define her in a certain way so that I wouldn't drive myself crazy, missing her. In any case, what Karen would say, what Lily would say, was academic because there was a very small chance that I was going to tell either one of them about Polloco in the near future.

That fall, to have someone to talk to, besides the boyfriend and my father, Mrs. Shaw occasionally went to a psychic, a practice that was out of her range of experience. She also went to a beautician on Lincoln Avenue and had gold foil papers wrapped into her hair, to change the color. It was a time-consuming and expensive procedure that covered up the three or four gray hairs at her temples. I know about the salon because I happened to be walking past the storefront and saw her at the mercy of a man in a tight black shirt, tight black pants, tight permed blond curls. Her judgment was obviously failing her. I found out about the psychic the way I discovered most things— that is, my mother wrote Jane all about it.

There was a place on Clark Street where my mother went, the

apartment of a woman named Shirana Gilden. The client rang the bell and climbed up the rickety flight of steps, and at the landing the husband, who was wearing nothing but boxer shorts, led her into the hall. In some kind of Indian dialect he shouted the equivalent of "Stella" into the dark interior. The priestess sat in the living room, smoking thin ladies' cigars and watching television. That fall there was lumber by the sofa, sheets of drywall in stacks against the windows, and sawdust deep into the pile of the blue shag carpet. The husband was remodeling the apartment, presumably buying nails and spackling compound as the tarot money came into the coffers. He must have loved my mother. The children were usually in the kitchen, crying or arguing, banging their bowls of rice on the table. Shirana always quickly moved the scraps of wood that obstructed the path to the sofa and turned off the television. I know these details because once, actually twice, I went there too. Having a tarot reading seems like a useful thing to do when you cannot or don't want to depend on instinct or self-knowledge.

I don't know if my mother got a cut rate because she went often, or if every time she paid a visit she had to pop twenty-five bucks for the privilege of Shirana's insights. She kept going back, partly because she couldn't stop herself from lying, as Shirana laid out the tarot cards and asked her personal questions. When Jane asked her what purpose it served to deceive the psychic, Mrs. Shaw had a pretty lame and self-pitying reply. She told Jane that she felt a great deal of shame, the shame of not having what she needed in her marriage. "It's awful to admit," she wrote in a message, "that your needs aren't being met." She had two kids with high IQs, a certain amount of fame, a brownstone in a classy neighborhood, a husband who did his share of housework. Poor Beth Shaw. She believed, apparently, that not having whatever she absolutely had to have was more shameful than breaking her husband's trust. She wanted very much—provided the tarot cards told her she could do as she pleased—to give herself up to their wisdom.

Shirana told my mother the usual: be careful tomorrow but take a risk on Tuesday, save your money, your career will take off, drink a lot of water, you will find true love, you are an unusual and talented person, and most important, your children will not be juvenile delinquents. They will turn out all right after the requisite rough spots. She also told my mother ancient secrets garnered from the spirits flying around the room, in particular an amusing nugget that should have made me laugh. It should have done nothing more than make me snigger.

I learned about this tidbit after school one afternoon in November. I had gone up to the office, logged on in a perfunctory way, going through the motions out of habit. *Yes, I always come home, creep upstairs, raid my mother's e-mail file so I can keep up with her every move.* I wasn't paying strict attention as the system connected to the provider and the file popped open and I began to read. As usual, my mother had written to her friend, couldn't take a step without telling long-suffering Jane about it.

Dear J.,

I went to the psychic this morning to ask her about Henry. It's mixed up, I know, but I have as much guilt, or shame, I should say, about going to Shirana as I do about the rest of it. If Kevin knew! Even he would have difficulty finding tolerance for this lapse. Richard wishes I would get the scoop about pork bellies and what the next invention like Velcro will be. I pay the money because I just want to know that nothing bad is going to happen, that I won't be punished.

About Henry. I'm sure he's preoccupied. There's his future and all. He doesn't know where he's going to college, what he's going to study, what will become of him. He's been very quiet. When I ask him if he's okay he smiles at me as if I'm a demented old woman. He's always been the sanest of the Shaws, but lately he has me spooked. Is he going to erupt at some point, rob the Quik Mart, kill the cashier? I talked to Shirana about his broodiness. She said, "Ah, Mrs. Shaw, you and Henry were married in former life. Husband and wife. Very close, very strong bond. Very close, but also sometimes enemies. It was love match, very deep."

This information explains everything, do you not think so?

Love, Beth

If I had felt strange when I read my mother's first message to Jane about Richard Polloco, it was nothing compared to the oddness I felt then, reading about my life with Mrs. Kevin Shaw. I was married to my mother, without having had to murder my father or pluck out my eyeballs. How lucky! On the dark side, if I had been my mother's spouse, I was now cheating on my father, or else he was cheating on me. Not to mention herself, betraying both of us with Polloco. What did she mean: "This information explains everything, do you not think so?" Was the question a joke? And incidentally, did she think she could use Rpoll's phraseology—*do you not think so?*— without my noticing? She had no voice of her own, that much was clear. *There's his future and all.* What a stupid thing to say about the life before me. *There's his past and all.* What were our names five hundred years ago? What did I call her? Did we have preposterous endearments? Hold it! Stop! Mrs. Shaw had been making a joke; she wasn't serious about the past-life situation. I was supposed to laugh and call each one of my friends. I was supposed to say, Listen to this! Instead, I was wondering, in spite of myself, in spite of my expensive education, if there was some kind of wacky truth to Shirana's hindsight, if that's why I was both drawn to and repelled by my mother's infidelity. It was impossible not to consider the details. Had we been Sumerians, or French Revolutionaries in the 1800s, or Native Americans, pre-Columbus, living our short grateful lives in the brutal wilderness? Wherever we'd lived, had I been patriarchal and stern, or sensitive and wimpy? Did we sit around in the evening drinking coffee and telling each other stories about the neighbors? Did she revere me and follow all of my directions? Did I beat her?

I remember distinctly when she left me to go to the hospital to have Elvira. She came into my room and she sat on my bed in the steady little blaze of the night-light. I know this sounds improbable, when I was all of four, but something unspoken passed between us. Why else would I remember her face that had grown so round, the beauty of the fullness, and the way she made me feel? We more than looked at each other. We gazed. Let's say we gazed with a kind of rapture.

"It's just been us, up until now, Henry," she said after a while. "When I come home from the hospital, we'll have to open our circle a bit. We'll have to make it bigger. That's not always easy, but we'll help each other do that."

I had no idea what she was talking about, but it didn't matter. It was the two of us, always on the same side—we had nothing to do with a circle. It had always been the two of us, and my father across the way, the admirer, the breadwinner, the dishwasher. I didn't see why that would change because she was going away for the night to have a baby. Although when she left the house, while I listened to Minty stir on the cot in the living room, I turned in my bed, and no matter how I tried to draw the covers up to my neck and huddle into them, I still felt cold.

That fall in Chicago my mother used to go and see Richard Polloco at least once a week. She could leave early in the morning and be back in time for tea. Sometimes I doubt if my father knew she'd taken the trip to Wisconsin, although quite often she'd sit at dinner and tell him tales from the Polloco family history. I'd eat the balanced meal in front of me, listening to my parents discussing the plight of the Russian Jews in the Ukraine. How interesting it was. Again, I'd wonder if my mother was out of her mind, gabbling about Polloco to my father, or if it was I who was delusional. She'd munch her carrot stick, talking about the violin maker as if he were an eccentric find, someone she'd dug up so she'd have stimulating dinner conversation. A story for her husband. My self-appointed task was to stay on, long after

Elvira had stormed up to the attic in her nightly upset. I ate my pie while my father went off on a tangent about the genetic testing of the Tsarina's German relatives and the impostor, Anastasia. I ate my peach pie, trying to determine how quiet I'd have to get before my mother got genuinely spooked. Holding my own counsel between Mr. and Mrs. Shaw, I imagined that we were all shouting at each other. We were angry enough, all of us, to hurl things, to slap, to get hurt. I'd look up and realize that my mother was saying something about the Ukrainian famine of 1932, that they were still exchanging facts about Polloco's ancestors, and that I was still pushing the slurry of peach filling around on my plate.

Supposing I said to my father, Pop, why are you asking such inane questions about Richard Polloco's grandfather? Don't you see what Mom is really trying to tell you when she talks about the Bolshevik Revolution?

Or I could wink at the Momster and say to Dad, Kev, I've got a special deal going with your wife, always have, always will, so listen up for a minute. There's something you should know about her—heh-heh—friend, the Rpoll.

It seemed remotely possible that at a specific point I might say a word or two to my father, that the moment would come and I'd know right beforehand that it was the time, and also I'd know exactly and sensitively how to explain what was happening to us. Meanwhile, she arose in the morning, Liza38 did, and made breakfast, elaborate meals, muffins from scratch with buttermilk and fresh blueberries, or she'd do a lengthy waffle production, sifting the flour not once but twice. She poached eggs and gently situated them in the green egg cups, alongside the sectioned grapefruits and the morning buns, the softest flakes of buttered pastry with cinnamon, all of it melting in one sweet river down your throat. Her breakfasts were legendary in the year of Richard Polloco. They were her penance, her hard labor for her past vices and upcoming sins. She'd pack a lunch for Elvira with organic figs, Brie and crackers—this for a kid, as if Elvira were the one who was going off to have a picnic with a lover. She'd make my father's favorite lunch, an apple, a ham sandwich, a couple of Oreos, as if he were the child. She'd ask me if I had enough money for my daily fare of roast beef and coffee. We'd go out the door—"good-bye, good-bye, have a nice day," she'd call, so merrily—and then, without our noise, in the sudden quiet, it was as if she'd never had us, as if we were strangers who had come begging for food and clothing, who were gone from her life.

She'd take a taxi to the train station, and by eight forty-five, if all went according to plan, she'd find herself outside of Tribbey, Wisconsin, climbing down the metal fold-out stairs of Amtrak's Hiawatha service destined for Milwaukee. Once again she was back in the country. If there was a delay, and often the trains ran late, she'd have to wait in the lounge at Union Station. It was a mixed blessing, the holdup. She was wound tight, what with all the excitement in her life, and she'd been having trouble sleeping. The waiting gave her time to rest. She had never been so tired. "I'm so tired," she said out loud, walking down the street and sitting at the piano and standing in line at the grocery store. In the afternoons at Roslyn Place often the fatigue would overcome her and she'd lie on the sofa, and just when she thought she could let everything go, just when her legs began to get heavy, he'd come to her. She'd see him clearly, and she'd lift her head a little, to meet his lips. If only she could sleep folded up against him; if only she could comb through his hair with her fingers before that sleep, and watch his lovely closed eyes as he moved to kiss her breasts. All of a sudden she was alert with longing. How could she sleep on the sofa or anywhere else when she wanted him, when she had to have him, when she could hardly breathe? There was no hope—she might never again go down into that rich dreamy state where life got scrambled up, might never again experience the REM cycle, never wake feeling revitalized. But on occasion, waiting for her train, she was able to fall asleep in the station. She was that tired. She'd curl up on a bench, on a hard place, like a sailor she was, or she'd drop off sitting, head down, like a bum, like someone with no address. And it probably felt right too, that she had no place, no home, no self.

When she got to Wisconsin, he'd come to pick her up in his VW

Rabbit, a car you could no longer buy parts for, a vehicle that was held together with bailing twine. That car, I'm sure, was part of Polloco's appeal. Because they fondled each other on the way to his house, he had to shift and drive with one hand, with his left hand. There was a certain danger and an absurdity, crossing his arm to get to the gearbox, the car steering itself—look, Ma, no hands!

To get to the cabin, you had to walk past Miss Van Heusen's house, and if she was out in her garden, you had to say hello and have a formal conversation. Everyone knew what everyone else was thinking: Miss Van Heusen could see that Richard had got himself a woman; Richard knew that Miss Van Heusen understood that he was going to get some satisfaction. Mrs. Shaw knew that Miss Van Heusen felt how much Lizadiza couldn't wait to get to the cabin, and so the old lady took extra time explaining to them how long she had spent raking the leaves in her yard and why she had bagged some of them up and why she had burned the others.

What my mother and Richard were able to do, once they were at last inside, in the alcove, once they'd pulled back the counterpane, once they were safely in bed—what they were able to do, beyond exhaust themselves in the usual way, was make a story out of nothing. That is easier said than done. There was, without the ballast of daily life, very little to hold them in their private world. And so they set about conjuring, doing the impossible work of building what they thought might be a solid structure, out of what proved to be flimsy materials in the end, out of words and touch and some musical notes.

During the short day they lived in their culture—the culture of bed, I suppose you could call it. There was the first frenzy, the popping off of shirt buttons and so on, and after some time they'd settle in, on their backs, Richard Polloco absently moving his fingers up and down my mother's arm, she doing the same at his collarbone. Most of life does not take place in bed, unfortunately, but at certain points along the way it almost seems as if all of life could or should take place there, preferably on a firm mattress and beside you the person who thrills you. Eventually Richard Polloco would roll out of the sheets, go to the wilds of the room, wrestle down some victuals from the shelf, bring her back something to eat. An enormous orange. A cookie broken in half, the sandwiches in her bag that she bought at the station. Relaxed and with a full stomach, he told her horrific stories, what had gone on in Russia, in his parents' time, in his grandparents' time. I will not use this history to tell his story; I will not. He'd go on about Lenin and the Red Terror. He included devastatingly personal details, the way any good narrator must. He explained that when his grandfather was about to be executed in a dark wood far from home, he put his hand up, to stay the gun. He asked for a chance to say farewell. Because there was no one standing by, no one he knew, he embraced and kissed his executioner.

My mother surely gasped, put her hands to her mouth. How terrible to be alone! She cried at the thought of it and Richard Polloco cried too. They held each other and wept for those who had had to love, at the last minute, the soldiers who killed them. How terrible, my mother kept saying, between her sobs, to be alone.

The first time I went to Shirana I made the mistake of taking Karen with me. This idea that I'd been married to my mother—although I didn't believe it—had stuck in my craw, and I thought that if I went and had my cards read, I could test the psychic. I could see for myself if there was anything to her method, and then I might ask her other, more probing questions. For entertainment I could find out what civilization I had passed through with good old Liza. I could get Shirana to hypnotize me, and at the least I could use my extraordinary grasp of historical detail in the writing of my personal essay on my college application.

Karen and I were sitting in the bookstore on a Saturday afternoon, she with a fresh copy of Anaïs Nin on her lap, and I, next to her on the window ledge, with the paperback *Rand McNally Road Atlas*.

"Where do you want to go, Hank?" she said, leaning over to see what state I was browsing through. I was on page 98, in the Vermont map, looking at the veiny roads and rivers, the dotted green patches that meant mountains, so many of the places I had walked and swum and canoed. I found a physical comfort in the bold blue lines, the principal highways, and the thinner red lines around Barre, the blank spots in Orange County, and the dot of Wellington. I could look at the map and forget the bookstore altogether.

I glanced down at Karen's Mary Jane shoes on her short wide

feet, her white socks with black spades, the hairy crossed leg, the long black skirt that she had hiked up to her knee. That much of her outfit was enough to remind me that she consulted her horoscope now and then. I closed the atlas. "How about going to a psychic with me?" I said. "That place a few blocks up. For a tarot reading. A tarot reading from a witch-type woman." I spoke as if we took that kind of trip every few days, as if we were going for pastry and coffee. Once I said the words out loud, I realized that if I were actually going to go, I had no desire to walk alone into the apartment of an impoverished woman who might have supernatural powers. I needed Karen to come with me. "I think it would be, um, a kick," I said.

"A kick? A kick, Hank?"

It's a dismaying thing, to be known long enough so that you cannot even try out a new expression. To avoid that particular type of humiliation, my mother traveled to Wisconsin, where she could experiment with alternative gestures and phrases, becoming someone other than the usual and approved Beth Shaw. For a brief honeymoon period nothing she would say to her stranger man could smack of phoniness.

"I don't think a tarot reading is going to help you much," Karen said.

Ah, but she was assuming that I wanted to go to Shirana only to find out if Lily would make a magical appearance on my doorstep at a specific moment in the months ahead. I had in fact received a letter from Lily the day before in which she casually mentioned that she might be visiting Northwestern University in nearby Evanston sometime in January. She was a junior in high school, starting to think seriously about her future. Although she wanted to go to Sarah Lawrence, she was no doubt being wooed by colleges around the country and felt obliged to visit the prestigious institutions that wanted her. Or could it be true that the college tour was only a pretext to come to Chicago so that we could meet? I had stopped talking about Lily to Karen, in large part because there was nothing to tell. It was probably middle-aged of me, to understand that sometimes there is nothing of any use to say. If I did have a few instincts at work, it was my better nature that told me to shut up on the topic of Lily in front of my good friend.

Possibly Lily was going to visit in January, and if she did, we would see each other. Either something would happen during our meeting or it would be a bust. That's about as far as my own psychic powers had informed me. I would have liked to take off across the country, running; better yet, running like an Athenian youth, flying with a torch in hand, all the way to New Hampshire, to Lily's doorstep. A little dramatic something, for show. I'd learned that in matters of love the ball usually gets rolling because one person wants to see what, if anything, will take place, if, say, she marches up to an acquaintance in an alley or a clearing by a lake or anywhere else and then—why not?—kisses him. That defining moment may or may not guide the players on a path together, whether for an evening or a week or a lifetime. My mother had been on the phone with Lily's father, the hurdy-gurdy player, and had invited Lily to stay with us if she did come to Chicago. Her invitation made me realize that my mother had no idea that I was sort of, somewhat, involved with Lily. Too bad for Mrs. Shaw, that there wasn't a long paper trail for her to nose through, to get the information she needed. Lily and I hadn't been writing as often as we had at the beginning. I'd had trouble finding much to report, and she seemed to be busy with her music, her friends, her theater group, her dancing.

"At best the tarot reading will give you confidence." Karen was still talking in her knowledgeable way. She leaned over and pushed the novel she'd been reading, *A Spy in the House of Love*, back into its place on the bookstore shelf. A spy in the house of love! Karen had been reading *A Spy in the House of Love*, as if I needed another bizarre detail in ordinary life to complete my day.

"Jesus," I said.

"That's not necessarily bad," she was saying, "but at the worst the cards will make you think that something terrific is going to transpire, and when it doesn't—"

"I'm just curious," I said. "A friend of mine recently did it, and she found it pretty interesting."

"What friend? Who?"

"Liza. Her name is Liza. I don't talk to her much. We don't live in the same, ah, state, but we go back a long way. I mean, a long way."

Karen, both in real life and in my imagined conversations with her, was almost always saying what seemed in the moment to be the politic remark, the wise comment. Or, if there was nothing to say, she, too, kept quiet and got on with her business. That kind of marksmanship was as irritating as it was astonishing. "It's for a joke," I said. "For something to do. Instead of getting stoned. Instead of wishing ourselves backward in time."

Karen zipped up her black sweatshirt, pulled tight on both strings of the hood and tied them underneath her chin. She, who wished to be Willa Cather or Edith Wharton; she'd take Virginia Woolf, suicide and all, if that part were offered. Her hair stuck out of the wimpleish circle around her face. For someone who was not beautiful or cute or pretty, who often had an ashen pallor, she did on occasion, and probably without even knowing it, shine. Her face was framed by the sweatshirt, and in the hot bookstore her skin had turned pink. She looked radiantly plain. "Sure, Hank," she said softly, without the slightest edge of recrimination or hostility. "Whatever you want."

Her calm was never studied or forced. She had been raised a Jew and a Methodist, but she was the closest thing to a bodhisattva that I knew west of the Ganges River. She had forgone Nirvana out of compassion for others, in order to save what she could of humanity. Centuries ago, in her all-important past life, she had a shaved head, she was a man, she wore yellow robes over her bony frame, she renounced material comfort and possessions. She knew everything. I would have liked to say to her, to shout, My mother goes to Wisconsin to fuck. To fuck! What am I supposed to do about it? Am I even supposed to try to do anything about it? What does it matter? Does it matter?

But you can't yell at a bodhisattva and feel good about yourself afterward. Instead of shouting at her, or saying anything relevant beyond testing my private theory about her former incarnation, I said, "Hey, what are the points of Buddha's Noble eightfold path, anyway?" I was probably more of a geek than I gave myself credit for. Still, that was the thing about Karen: you could behave like a moron, you could ask her a ridiculous question out of context, and even if you'd never spoken about the subject, she'd run with it.

"I don't know what this has to do with anything," she said, "but, let's see. Wait—no. I don't think I can really say them the way I used to." She meant it! She used to know them. She was just as wigged out as Elvira, but on a different channel. "I more or less know the eight verses on training the mind, though. My favorite ones are six and seven."

"Refresh my memory," I said.

"Verse six. 'When others out of jealousy treat me badly with abuse, slander, and so on, I will learn to take all loss and offer the victory to them.' These verses are fantastic if you want to seriously be a martyr. Number seven goes, 'When the one who I had benefited with great hope unreasonably hurts me very badly, I will learn to view that person as an excellent spiritual guide.'"

"Whoa," I said.

"You're supposed to cherish the most ill natured beings, to consider them precious jewels."

"You're sure the rules aren't tongue-in-cheek? Maybe they're supposed to be funny."

"You've got a point, Hank. I've always thought those Buddhists were a laugh a minute, now that you mention it."

I wondered if being a Buddhist was dull, wondered what you were left with if you rid yourself of every one of your emotions. Imagine, for example, Liza cleansing herself for spiritual purposes, having, for starters, to peel away her various selves. "My mother would make a lousy Buddhist," I muttered.

"Let's face it," Karen said, "most of us would make lousy Buddhists. Is this why you want to go to a psychic, to find out if your mother is going to change her religion?"

Mrs. Shaw had some kind of religion, although I wasn't sure it had a name. She had always been devoted to music, and now, in addition, she had taken up Polloco and Passion and the Phallus. The three Ps. She was a hedonist, she was a narcissist, she was a slut. Without answering Karen's question I slung my backpack over my shoulder and walked out of the store. She had not finished adjusting her wimple or gathering her bag or her umbrella. I didn't wait. Because she was an unusual girl, she did not hang back; she did not fold her arms over her chest and become sullen. She did not make quick work of it and tell me to fuck myself, and neither did she whine or preach. Perhaps she considered me the ill-natured being in her life, the wretch she was supposed to worship. She caught up with me, she took my arm, and together we went along Clark Street, until we got to the blue door that was between the shoe repair and the used record store. The handwritten sign was held up by two thumbtacks. "Tarot readings by Shirana. Twenty-five dollars."

"This is where I mean," I said. Karen herself turned the knob, and when the door didn't budge, she leaned into it with all the force of her broad shoulder. Up the stairs she went. Not seconds after she knocked on the inner door, the husband appeared, baring his chest. He had a hammer in his hand, and he looked at us, the menacing teenagers, as if he would gladly pound us to pulp. We could see down the hall into the living room, to the Mastermind, watching her soap opera, her instruction, the place from which she probably gained her extensive knowledge of human relations. She had the dark skin of an Eastern Indian, but American designer frames that might have come from the discount eyewear store on Irving Park Road. They were large pink frames, the inventory that hadn't sold in the eighties.

"What have you come for?" She called it out, staying put, although she did mute the television. I liked that: What have you come for? Not, What do you want, or What can I do for you, or Scram. What have you come for?

I want to know if my parents will hold our life together, Shirana, O Holy Bespectacled One. I want to know if we'll burst apart and scatter to the corners of the earth, or if what happens next will be slow, inexorable, if gradually there will be nothing between the four of us but distance. Will I go to college, lost; my mother move to Wisconsin, lost; my father stay in Chicago, lost; Elvira shuttling between, lost? And about Lily. Is there any hope? This, all of this, I have come to ask and to know.

"I–," I began. "I–"

"He wants his cards read," Karen said, moving past the husband. "How much did the sign say out front—twenty-five dollars?" She reached down into one of her Mary Janes and removed a five-dollar bill that had been rolled into a tight cylinder. "Here," she said to me. "I've got this much."

"Okay," I said. "Oh! Right." Payment was required up front, but of course. I followed Karen into the living room, opened my wallet, and along with the five put two tens on the table, cash my grandmother had recently pushed upon me. The sight of the greenbacks seemed to work wonders on Shirana's limbs and also, presumably, her chakras. She bounced to her feet, unrolled Karen's bill, pocketed all of the money, cleared the coffee table, dusted it with a grimy cloth, turned off the television, shooed her children away, the three of them who had come creeping out of the corners. She felt around in a drawer in the television cart, clearly a junk drawer, and finally extracted a deck of cards. She kneeled—kneeled down before us. I liked that touch. We had money and therefore we were worthy of her reverence. She had insight and we would do our turn bowing before her, provided her long view wasn't too gloomy. The whole thing was beautifully syncretistic. She looked up at me, longer than is considered polite, taking stock, I guess. "Say your name, sweet," she said.

Sweet? Was part of the payment for her affection, for something you couldn't get at home? I didn't want to say my whole name. I didn't want her to know that I was any relation to my mother. "My whole name?"

"Yes," she said, nodding, as if the visual cue would help me understand her verbal instructions. "Whole name."

"My whole name," I said, "is David Andrew Westly."

Karen turned her head sharply and stared at me. She still had her sweatshirt hood tied under her chin in that nunly way. If Shirana hadn't already figured out that I was going to lie, she knew then, by Sister Mary Karen's look, by her censure.

"Put your hand on the deck. That's right. Hold it there for a moment." I did as Shirana said. I think I even closed my eyes, to make a show of effort. It shouldn't matter, I thought, that I'm lying, because if the cards are good, if they are accurate, they will tell my future regardless of my name. No doubt my mother had used the same logic when she'd lied to Shirana. Two peas in a pod, we were. A chip off each other's block. How was it, I wondered, that average citizens, change in our pockets, a family tree that included individuals on the *Mayflower*—how was it that Mrs. Shaw and I, in search of solace, had come to this squalid apartment, to Shirana, with her noisy children and frightening husband? Shirana, I thought, could have used a toss or two of the cards on her own behalf, some way to get herself out of her own situation.

She was setting out the cards, telling me about myself, by way of asking questions. "You are involved with someone right now?" she said, studying a card with a man hanging upside down by his foot. "She is far away, yes?"

I nodded.

"She has caused you some pain, but you are experiencing life, learning something you've wanted to understand for a long time."

"Uh."

"Yes?" She examined me again. I stared past the pink tint of her glasses into her knowing eyes.

"Here," she said, pointing to a card that had what looked like a sperm swimming up the middle, a few ugly wolves, a hand reaching down. "You are alone, see? This is period when you feel cast out, when things aren't going so good in the family."

I looked again into her face, and this time I could see my reflection in her glasses. I was a teenage boy with dark hair, dark broody eyes, the wire-rimmed glasses of a pseudo-intellectual, not some brawny beer-drinking guy who played rugby and screwed any girl he could. How much effort did it take to figure out that I was just beginning to experience life, that I did indeed feel cast out, that I was having problems with my family? I had paid my money and she was getting away with cheap calls. "No," I said. "It's going fine. That part actually, with my parents, is easy. No problem."

"I'm seeing tension here, trouble between you, between your father, between your mother."

"No, no, they're great. Sometimes I feel as if I've known them before, in a way—that's how well we get along."

"You will have work ahead of you," she said, ignoring me. "Work to separate from them, difficult work, but positive, as you become a man." She was flipping the cards down so quickly it was hard to see them. "You and your chum here have a strong friendship. It will last you, stay, even when you are grown. You will be close by."

"Oh," I said. *Chum*. I wasn't really listening anymore, I suppose because we'd both lost what little faith we'd had in each other at the start. She went through the rest of the deck casually, it seemed to me, and I nodded when it was required. I even murmured, "Wow," a couple of times, when she said that my sister had unusual interests, when she said that my father was the type of man who was keen on his work. I couldn't figure out her accent. She had sounded Chinese when my mother described her, in the message to Jane. "You and Henry were married in former life. Husband and wife. Very close, very strong bond." In person, although Shirana dropped her articles now and then, she used the expressions of a British subject—*keen on his work*. My mother, perhaps, was trying to develop her skills as a storyteller, and for Jane she'd made Shirana into a simple character, streamlining the scene but maintaining the essential quirkiness. "It was love match, very deep." My mother seemed to feel an obligation to amuse her audience. She could first write to Jane, polish the images, the accents, the details, and when she was good and ready, she could present the masterpiece to Rpoll. Or finally, she could tell Kevin, when the story had been honed, all the punctuation in place, not an extra word.

As Shirana was getting to the end of the deck she said, "I see, David, that you worry, you worry about convention, yes?" I must have squinted or frowned. "A little bit, you care what others think, you care about the rules?"

"My father's a socialist," I said.

She nodded this time, as if my father's political affiliation clearly had something important to do with my own attitudes. Moving on to the last card, she said, "There's a big event coming up soon, after Christmas. Big event." Lily, visiting Northwestern! Who cared about rules or convention? The blond folk-dancing beauty was in the plan after all.

"Thank you!" I said. "Thanks very much."

There had been no mention of my past marriage with Mrs. Shaw, but maybe you had to pay yet again to receive information about former lives. I backed out the door, mumbling good-byes while Karen lingered, asking Shirana about the type of cards she used, about the paintings on them that had been done by an English noblewoman. I waited at the bottom of the stairs for my chum to come slap-slapping along in her retro shoes, the patent-leather jobs of the sort she'd been wearing since she was three years old. She called them her Protestant shoes.

We walked back down Clark Street for a while without saying anything. I wished that we could see ahead, that the misty path before me would come clear. Perhaps Shirana had seen forward to the apartment Karen and I would share in Madison, Wisconsin, and later another flat in New Haven. We often found it easy or convenient to slip into each other's company. When I finally told her about my mother, when I was twenty, she put the story into a perspective that diluted its power. She thought she was doing me a favor. She talked about menopause and how that transition affects a female's sex drive. She made me read a feminist essay on the institution of motherhood, a tract that described how mothering leaches away a woman's identity and her self. For a few days I was thankful to her for, in effect, taking the story from me, for putting it on a shelf in a dusty library along with thousands of other stories that were alike. But after that short time had passed, I wanted all of what was mine back. I did in fact feel childish about it. I wanted again to try to understand that year in terms that may or may not have been as profound as biology or convention or the institutions holding us in place. I didn't tell Karen that I wanted to take the story as far into the idea of my family as I could. I didn't attempt, either, to explain what I meant, because I hardly knew myself.

Strolling down Clark Street, Karen may also have been thinking about our individual and mutual fates. I tried to concentrate on the immediate future, to figure out if I should start the inevitable conversation about what we'd just experienced with the psychic, or if, instead, I should wait and spend my energy building my defense. Undoubtedly she'd say something. It was unlikely she'd keep still, that she'd hold back her opinion of Shirana. Certainly she'd want to make a statement about my behavior. I should probably take the lead, apologize for dragging her along, and offer to pay back the five dollars, to return to my house and dredge around in the change pots. It had been nice of her to jump-start the session by offering the cold cash.

"Henry," she said before I could make the move. "Henry—David Andrew—whatever your name is. Now and then I think I know what's wrong with you, and then other times I don't have the slightest idea. The last month or so, something's different. You've become skittery. In case you didn't know, in case you really are a mannequin in disguise, you're important to me. It's usually possible to have a conversation with you, for one, which is more than you can say about most people at Layton. So, I'm happy to hold your hand if I think that will do any good, but I feel sort of dumb holding your hand if it's your foot that's bleeding—you know what I mean?"

I kept my eye on the pavement, intent on taking purposeful strides.

"I guess," she said, "I need to know if you're going to tell me what's eating you. It would be good if I could at least think that someday I'd figure out what's going on, without having to try to piece it together from all of these clues that may or may not add up to the whole story. I don't get, for instance, why you wanted to go to Shirana in the first place. You, Henry Shaw. That's so freaky. And also, why did you lie?"

I pictured telling Karen, but even then I believe I had an idea that her explanation might rob me of something vital. I couldn't hear the sentences she'd say, the paragraphs, but I could see her calmly laying it out for me, using her hands, waiting for me to understand, clarifying when necessary. It would make sense, the way she told it, and I would eventually understand the deeper motivations of the main players. It was tempting to tell her, to be done with it. "My mother—," I said. "My mother—"

"Your mom?"

"She's been sort of strange lately." No, that was wrong. "Strange" wasn't the operative word. *My mother is leaving us. She's already gone.*

"Strange?"

"My mother's psychic told her that in a past life we, she and I, were married! I was married to my own mother."

Karen stopped on the sidewalk. "Wait," she said. She dragged me to the meter so that the other pedestrians wouldn't have to skirt around me. I had to think what I had said, to figure out what had prompted her reaction. Whatever I'd said I hadn't planned on; I'd said something to fill the space, to make a noise.

"Henry. Henry." She put her hand to her brow, as if my presence were giving her a headache. "What some psychic says about your mother and you does not automatically turn you into Oedipus, all right? I do occasionally cast my horoscope, I know, even though astrology isn't exactly scientific, even though it was developed in Babylon, way back, when astrologers knew of five planets, when people didn't know their asses from their elbows. Why should I take my chart seriously? I ask myself that, and yet the system is so old, so ancient, and whoever developed it along the way had real knowledge of human nature. It's a system and it's put together logically, although, as I said, it's certainly not scientific. So yes, every now and then I indulge myself. It helps me understand the people in my life. Gives me perspective." She looked at the meter, to see that it, too, was paying attention.

"Tarot cards can be used the same way, to understand potential and character, but when so-called psychics use them to predict the future—I don't know. That's toying with magic. Voodoo. You've got to consider the fact that the psychics are people in the here and now who have to feed their hungry children. One person, based on her own screwy vision, told your mother that you guys were married, and then she probably went to the grocery store and bought several pounds of salmon steaks. I guess the real question is why your mother went to the psychic. Now, that's an interesting question. That's not something she normally does, is it?"

She rarely missed a beat, Karen didn't. A few more minutes of her clear thinking, and, like Shirana, she'd see forward. She'd see that my mother and Richard Polloco, in another two weeks, would be walking across the Michigan Avenue Bridge, across the Chicago River. The city would be lit up around them, the water sparkling in the floodlights, the night air chill, their faces cold, their noses pink. Polloco would stop, open his arms to the city, to the splendor of the architecture and the glittery water. "It's beautiful," he would say, "so beautiful we have to kiss." My mother would protest, afraid that her neighbors or her mother or her husband or her children might for some reason be passing by and see her in that compromising position. Mrs. Shaw would say that they couldn't kiss, they shouldn't, they mustn't. The refusal would make him all the more ardent, and in the end they'd have their kiss on the Michigan Avenue Bridge: cool lips, chill air, warm mouths, dark bridge, lights in all the windows, up and up, on either side of the river.

"You'd think with her music," Karen was saying, "she wouldn't need too much else out of life. I don't have a musical bone in my body, so maybe I don't understand how it works, but it seems to me that if you had that in you, if you were constantly making music, it would be a way of seeing. Doesn't it? From my vantage point it looks like a magical way to live. Your mother, she's a Scorpio, right?"

"November 8," I said.

"So she's secretive and intense and passionate. Big deal if she was your wife in a past incarnation. Maybe you had a good marriage. Maybe you even had fun. Maybe you, the Libra that you are, kept her on an even keel. Now you get to be her son. This has nothing, nothing, to do with sex, okay? You are her son in this life, this one you are living in at the moment. Having a passionate, intense mother is probably a little easier than having a passionate, intense wife, but I'd say that all around you're pretty lucky. Suppose it's true, that you knew each other before. You must have wanted to return, to be with her. You must have wanted to come back for a reason. Maybe it was for simple old uncomplicated love. That's what I think, Henry. I think you came back out of love."

The next weekend, during the teachers' convention in Chicago, I went with my mother and Elvira up to Tribbey, to meet Richard Polloco. It was a good day, a fine day, to be sure, for that particular visit, because in the morning my father was busy attending lectures and arguing with his colleagues about the virtues and drawbacks of block scheduling at the high school level. In the afternoon there was a meeting with the Layton administration and staff to discuss the implementation of site-based management. Nothing made my father happier than the concept of worker control. It was too bad, my mother said, that Kevin couldn't join us, too bad that the one weekend Richard Polloco was free, Kevin had a commitment.

Early Saturday morning my mother and Elvira and I took a taxi to the train station, and just as she always did as part of her Richard Polloco routine, she stood in line, purchased the tickets, bought a cup of coffee and flooded it with cream. Walking carefully with the hot liquid, she led us to the lounge, where we waited for the boarding announcement of the Hiawatha train, heading for Milwaukee. I was reading a contemporary novel by a woman whose name I don't remember, a book that was already supposed to be a classic, a book I read from beginning to end that weekend without registering much action or dialogue.

My mother was sitting up straight on the edge of the pale green plastic molded chair that did not conform to any variety of human posture in that room. Elvira, next to her, her two front teeth clamped on her lower lip, oh so cool, was drumming on her canteen and nodding her head to the beat. Mrs. Shaw put her hand out to still Elvira and then must have thought better of it. Instead of trying to reform the girl, she took a breath, closed her eyes. Maybe she had a new habit of prayer. Anything, she'd recite incantations, try sorcery or hocus-pocus, if it meant she'd hold together. She was probably nervous, since what she was doing—taking her children to visit her lover—was slightly unconventional. As I got to thinking about Liza and this visit of ours, it seemed likely that she was a wreck.

After all, she was putting herself into a potentially revealing and dangerous situation. In the presence of Polloco, Elvira and I might notice our mother's makeover, her presto chango personality. We might ask ourselves, or each other, why she was suddenly so sparky, so interesting, so delightful, so attentive. Liza38 was going to want to behave as she always did with her man, to show him that she was her Richard Polloco self, but at the same time she'd have to find a way to shield that self from us, to maintain her matron act. Break a leg, Mrs. Shaw. Say an abracadabra, six Hail Marys, whatever it takes. Get up there on the tightrope, skip and jump, stand on your head and boil an egg. And don't forget to relax!

My sister's drumming was not loud, but it was steady. Make no mistake that Elvira Louise Shaw was with us, the wild card. It must have crossed my mother's mind that Elvira might pull something in front of Richard Polloco. An Elvira episode that would embarrass everyone, that would shed light on the real Beth Shaw, the frowsy married woman with the noisy troubled daughter and the quiet troubled son. I could see through to any number of blurry scenes, the only clarity this fact: in the company of strangers no one but us, Elvira and me, had the power to disappoint my mother, to humiliate her, to expose her. Funny, that a mother puts a fair amount of energy into educating her children, providing dental care, nutritious food, and cultural experiences, and what the boy and girl know best is how to disgrace her.

What was going to happen? This question, as I've said, seems to be at the root of most romantic encounters, and at the root of disobedience too. Sometimes I'm very sure that that question was what propelled my mother, more than anything, more than her unhappiness with my father, more than her passion for Richard Polloco. What would happen if she kissed the ragtag man in the alley? What would happen if she went to visit him in Wisconsin? Would anyone at home see that she'd been transformed? Wouldn't it be interesting if she took her children to visit him in his log cabin that was a replica of Honest Abe's birthplace?

On the way to Tribbey, I was reading whatever book I was reading and not looking at my mother and not listening to Elvira talking to Mrs. Shaw. For one thing, Beth had been on the phone with Lily's father that morning. They were old friends from Silverpines days, when they themselves had been teenagers. My mother, over the telephone, again urged Lily to stay with us if she did come to Chicago to look at Northwestern University in January. She chattered at Paul as if she had no idea that Lily and I had spent the night together at camp, that I had been writing to Lily, that I stopped thinking about Lily only when I was reading Liza38's e-mails. It still seemed inconceivable that my mother was unaware of my past with Lily. But if she had known, if she had been even half conscious, she might have realized that she should have consulted me first, before she offered up my free time to Lily, as well as Elvira's bedroom, directly across the hall from mine.

On the train my mother was saying to Elvira, "Do you remember that day I took you to Mill Farm School, to check it out, to meet Maud? When you were five? We came up the driveway and you turned to me and said, 'Mom, I know my name, and I know my address and telephone number, but I'm not exactly sure how the earth was formed.'"

Elvira snorted. My mother pressed on. "Remember when that horse of Maud's, Champ, got sick, and you had Maud bandage up your ankle to match his foot? And the time you hid Peter Lindman's harmonica, and when you found it, magically, in the drawer with the cookie cutters, Maud gave you a peafowl feather as a reward?"

Elvira put her head down and laughed at her badness. "I hated that Peter Lindman," she said. "He was always playing that stupid harmonica."

"How long did it take? Three days, I think, before your conscience overcame you. You woke me up in the middle of the night to confess."

"I had to give that feather back to Maud," Elvira murmured. "You made me."

"Yes," my mother said, "but you didn't have to apologize to Peter. Maud decided that was unnecessary. She was probably grateful to you, to have had an extra three days free from 'Yankee Doodle Dandy.'"

Beth seemed to be chock full of memories, short clips featuring Elvira the genius, the cutie pie, the imp. I got to thinking that maybe treachery is the only interesting story, that there's not much to a narrative unless somewhere along the way the main character, the lover or the beloved, becomes a turncoat. You could say that the Civil War was nothing more than a marriage spat, the thing in the middle of the long years together, the midlife crisis followed by forgiveness, habitual bickering, old age, and amnesia. Maybe it was impossible to be a strong country or couple or family unless you'd fought a little war, either against a common enemy or amongst yourselves. I was pretty sure that there was no such thing as simple, uncomplicated love, as Karen claimed. If I had come back from my peaceful grave to be with my mother in yet another incarnation, maybe it was to prove something, to settle a score. I wasn't used to thinking in terms of shaming anyone or exacting retribution, but perhaps it was time to consider the hard line. King Henry II locked up his wife, Eleanor of Aquitaine, for fifteen years. Maybe that's who I'd been, King Henry, and history, repeating itself, had called for me to come again and put the old girl away.

Before the train had cleared the city, Elvira appeared to know that this was her day. She had taken off her boots, and she was sitting sideways in her seat, cross-legged, facing my mother. Beth Shaw had asked her to remember a few small scenes from the past, and once Elvira got going, she seemed bent on recalling as much of her life as she could retrieve. "You should have seen Dad that afternoon he was riding Betty in Vermont, up Larkey's Hill. Dad was posting even though Betty wasn't trotting. She was walking! He didn't even know Betty was walking—it was hilarious. He thought she was going at her full speed."

My mother was leaning away from Elvira, but with her face turned toward her, so that it looked as if she were listening to her daughter. "What are you reading?" she asked me in an instant when Elvira was taking a breath.

I held up the book that was in my lap.

"Is it good? Tell me about it."

Tell me. Tell me what it feels like. Tell me now.

I glanced across at her, at her blue eyes that always seemed about to tear, those eyes that made her seem tender. I said, "We're reading contemporary novels in school. Things like this." I pointed to my mass-market paperback. "We should be reading *Hamlet* and the *Oresteia*." Works, I wanted to say, about mothers driving their sons crazy.

"You read those last year," she said.

"You can't read them enough." Liza38, I said to myself, you just cannot read them too many times.

When we got to the station Richard Polloco was there, waiting for us. My mother was solicitous of Elvira, helping her climb down the metal fold-out stairs, as if the amazon were a demure girl child who couldn't handle the great big steps of the great big locomotive. Mrs. Shaw made a gesture to assist me, but I acted as if I hadn't noticed her motherliness, the sudden bloom of it. Richard Polloco was standing on the brick pavement in an enormous white coat with a fur-trimmed hood. His shoulders were at his ears, his arms straight and stiff, his hands in his pockets.

He stood, waiting for her. I couldn't think why I had allowed my

mother to drag me to Wisconsin for this moment. When she'd wondered if I'd come along, I had had to concentrate, to understand what
she was asking me. I'd laughed, figuring she was making some kind
of joke.

She'd repeated the question: "Do you want to come with Elvira
and me to Tribbey, to visit my friend? The violin maker?"

"Your friend."

"You might be interested in the woodworking shop."

"The woodworking shop." I tried to remember if I'd ever expressed an interest in woodworking. Her recklessness was stunning. Maybe she was planning on taking us into the Tribbey forest
and leaving us. It dawned on me that Hansel and Gretel's father and
stepmother hadn't been starving, not at all. They'd wanted to ditch
the kids so they could bang the shithouse door out of each other.
Mrs. Shaw probably wanted me to visit the man so I'd figure out how
to find her when she ran away, so we could have a weepy reunion at
some later date, when I was in my thirties, when she'd figured I'd let
bygones be bygones. Or else she wanted me to come along so I'd see
how far superior he was to her other friends and relations.

"You could bring your cello," she'd said. "For a threesome."

"A threesome."

"Henry, why are you echoing everything I say?" She'd asked me
this in an irritated tone, as if I were the peculiar one, the offending one.

I was standing on the pavement at Tribbey, wavering still, wondering how I had come to be in Wisconsin staring at the stranger
who was known to me. My mother kissed him on both ruddy cheeks,
put her arm around Elvira, and made the introduction. She beckoned
me to come nearer. Richard Polloco removed his cold hand from his
pocket and extended it to me. I stared at the thing. A beat too late I
bent to tie my shoe. It was as if all our movements were taking place
in slow motion, the hand pulling itself out of the deep pocket, that
hand with the short fingers, the squat palm, unfolding at me, my step
back, the long beat, my intention revealed—*I'm not touching you.*

My mother made some bright comments. Well! What a beautiful

day! Elvira can't wait to see the cabin! Everything with exclamation points. The three of them moved together toward Richard Polloco's VW Rabbit, Elvira skipping, asking questions about the cabin as if she were seven years old, my mother throwing her head back, laughing at Ricky's clever answers. At one point he stooped to talk to Elvira, she, of all people, shedding her years and her disposition. She nodded, wide-eyed, solemn, at an offer he seemed to be making, the promise of a sucker perhaps, or a mint patty, a pinwheel. Had I come for this, I wondered, to see an unraveling? Was my hateful job always to bear witness? It was plain to me as I followed along behind that if there was to be a new family configuration—Elvira, Henry, my mother, and Richard Polloco—our previous roles were breaking down, were nearly gone, in spite of our own characters.

The cabin had all the features my mother had promised. The pegs in the floor, the pegs holding the walls together, the loft with Miss Van Heusen's dollhouse, the old toolbox, the gingham curtains, the swing and the tree house, the slant—the fetching slant of the shingled roof—the straw hats hanging in a row, the lanterns overhead, the kettle rattling on the woodstove. There was a closet in the bathroom full of bent cardboard boxes in a jumble, what I took to be Polloco's junk from whatever past life he'd inhabited. I went back out on the porch while the others were inside taking off their shoes, and I felt that terrible homesickness again, for Vermont. I missed the shape in the near and far distance, of mountains, what was so grotesquely absent in the Midwest. I could never shake the idea that there must have been some kind of mutilation, an amputation, to reduce a countryside to such awful flatness. The clouds over the lake could only do so much for so long in a day to masquerade as landforms.

When my mother appeared at the door of the cabin looking for me, when she asked me what the matter was, I almost cried out, like a child, "I miss Vermont." What, actually, had my parents been thinking when they decided to move from Wellington? She came toward me, and I believe she might have had some understanding just then. Her face had in it the old sympathy, and for the briefest of moments I let myself meet that expression. "Henry?" she said. I wanted to tell her what I'd finally put into words, that being more or less on the Central Plains I felt exposed. I felt it in Tribbey, I felt it on Roslyn Place. It was driving me out of my mind, feeling naked. I wanted to know if, after all the years away, she felt the same, if she missed the comfort, the safety, of the mountains. I was about to ask her when Polloco loomed up behind her. "Hello?" he said, as if he hadn't yet met me, as if I were a stranger on the porch.

We went inside, and my mother unpacked the lunch she'd brought in her knapsack. There were large Granny Smith apples, a vegetable salad with barley, and the homemade chicken soup she'd made in our own kitchen. Elvira, oblivious to the tensions in the room, did most of the talking. Mrs. Shaw had not anticipated the pleasure of her daughter's coquettish company, and she was paying, ostensibly, strict attention to Elvira's Abe Lincoln narratives. She appeared to be fascinated. Perhaps it was my mother's single-minded devotion through the day that brought out in Elvira her latent girlishness. It was hard to say if it was Liza's sham or Polloco's magic touch that transmogrified Elvira, that made her seem not only feminine but innocent. Maybe it was Rpoll's sheer animal magnetism that made her want to please him, the same force that had appealed to my mother. Or possibly the fact that he was so charmingly depressed prompted any female, regardless of her inclinations, to want to cheer him up, entertain him, drive away his rainy day.

Whatever the cause, Elvirnon was fading, and in his place stood the precious flower, her dark curls around her rosy face, the sweet light in her blue eyes. I could see that Elvira, in our new family, was going to be the good child, the one who could do no wrong. Liza must have felt as if the world itself had shifted, the plates underneath us wobbled, and the heavens above rotated; there was, for the first time in years, a visible chance, albeit a small one, that Elvira would not grow up to be an NRA card-carrying bull dyke. What a load off Mrs. Shaw's mind!

Although the girl guest was fluttering those pretty little eyes, she was at the same time telling Richard Polloco the critical facts about her favorite battle. It was the dispassionate observer who made no mistake, who understood that the babe moves were merely superimposed upon her real self. "Can you believe," she said to her host, "that Shiloh means 'place of peace'?" Flutter, flutter went her eyes. "It's a Hebrew word. Place of peace, give me a break. It was one of the bloodiest two days of the war. More men were killed at Shiloh than in all the wars put together in America."

"Is that so?" Richard Polloco said.

"No, that's not right." I was speaking to my sister. "I don't think you've stated it correctly." She could flirt herself into femininity, but she had better get the details straight. "More men were killed at Shiloh than in all the wars in America up until that point," I explained. "Later there were other dramatic losses. Seven thousand fell in twenty minutes at Cold Harbor." Those five sentences were about the extent of my contribution to the conversation during the afternoon. I didn't actually know what I was talking about, but I was fairly sure the Cold Harbor statistic was accurate.

Elvira turned her enchanting baby face to me. She narrowed her eyes, clicked her tongue. "Big whoop, Henry."

Yes! Attagirl, turn ugly on us! Smash the teacup, hurl a goober at your brother! Even a small show would send Richard Polloco running for cover, and for a moment I felt a surge of optimism.

"My dad," she said, turning back to her host, "my dad and I are going to Shiloh, to the reenactment there this spring. Well, technically it's a living history. We're not going to re-create the entire battle. The hardcore reenactors, by the way, don't like to be called reenactors. We refer to ourselves as living historians."

"That's good to know," Polloco said.

"I've joined the 28th Wisconsin. In case you aren't familiar with them, they are really, really super hardcore guys. No farbs allowed."

"Farbs?"

" 'Far-be-it-from-authentic.' You do not want to associate with any farb or anything farbie, it is so totally gross, what they do. You know, bring ham sandwiches in Baggies, and bananas, and smoke cigarettes. It's unbelievable."

"Unforgivable," Richard Polloco said, shaking his head.

"The hardcores, they go on twenty-mile hikes all the time, for the fun of it."

He stole a look at my mother, as if to say, That's exactly what we do around here for fun.

"Plus they don't use tents. They sleep on the bare hard ground. So if they invite you into the regiment, it's kind of an honor."

"I should say," Polloco said. "And at your age."

Elvira giggled, all shoulders and grin, as ingratiatingly cute as she'd been in her life. "Everyone thinks I'm a boy. There's this twerp who always shows up at the Midwest events, and her big thing is to chase me and try to kiss me." She did the cuddlesome laugh again. "My friend Al, he hasn't even figured out I'm not a boy. It's awesome, the things I hear around the campfire."

"We don't want to know," Mrs. Shaw said.

"We don't?" Polloco leaned forward, waiting for more.

"Elvira can use thirty-five different expressions for breast," I couldn't help adding, a figure she had boasted about to Hilare.

"Not that many!"

Polloco raised his eyebrows.

"Okay, a couple of the guys can get pretty—descriptive. They do get slightly barfed out. I've seen them try, well, some outrageous things, total guy displays, where they, oh God, they—"

"Elvie, could you pass the bread—"

"Don't get me wrong—they aren't disgusting all the time. They've been nice to me, and, not to brag or anything, but they're complimentary about my first-person impression and my uniform. It's just about completely hand-stitched now, and my boots, my brogans, are from Kentucky—"

She went on and on, through the soup and the salad, the apples and the brownies. Either Richard Polloco was entranced by her or he was pretending to be entranced by her. Every now and then he'd glance at my mother, or rather, periodically the two of them exchanged a glance: Isn't Elvira sweetly eccentric? Aren't I, Richard, being charming myself, in my conversation with her? And haven't I, Beth Shaw, done a perfect job raising my child?

My mother had produced a model daughter after all, a girl who was pleasing her lover, and Polloco, if not exactly fatherly, was proving that at least he was capable of being engaged by a young person. And scoring additional points, he knew enough not to try to draw me out. I could like him for that one thing alone, for the fact that he ignored me.

Still, I thought of making a scene. I could start an argument over Lee, get Elvira boiling about her hero, riled enough to break her plate, throw a little crockery around. Bringing up Lee's dishonorable traits would be the simplest and most covert way to incite a riot. There were probably any number of things I could do. *You,* I could say to Polloco. *You across the table, yeah, you. I used to be married to this broad. She's my dame.* Or I could wax poetical about Kevin Shaw. I tried to think how to do that. Living with a high school teacher is probably not that different from living with a coal miner. They are down the shaft, they are cleaning up from being down the shaft, or they are preparing to return to the shaft. And it's hard to get poetical about someone who is always cheerful, unless you want to go the limerick route.

I could come right out with it, and stud to stud ask Polloco; I could say, *Is she a good fuck this time around?* Alternatively, I could finish my lunch, get up, and examine the books and the few things on the wall. I ate my barley salad, took my plate to the sink, and went over to look at the deer skulls and a bird's nest on the mantel, the usual collections from a country life gathering dust. Underneath a hunk of granite I noticed a photograph, and I moved the rock so I could take a look. It was a black-and-white photograph of two boys, but even without the full spectrum you could tell that the blond kid was pale, pale all through himself. There wasn't the life in him that the other boy, the main boy, had, the star of the photo. The primo boy's hair was slicked to the side, and he was looking right at the camera as if he wanted to know what lay before him, as if he could almost see the shape of his lonely future. It occurred to me that the boy who had more color was Polloco, at the age of eight or nine. And I remembered then some of the messages Rpoll had written about his cousin Rudy, how the two of them had stolen candy and sold drugs and prowled the streets when they were growing up together in the Ukrainian neighborhood in Chicago. So that was Rudy probably, the thin boy, the one who looked resigned.

When the lunch food was cleared away, by Mrs. Shaw, we took our places. Richard Polloco, the grown man, had his violin out of the case and was tuning it. I had not brought my cello. After my mother's initial suggestion at home that we play trios, we had not discussed the matter, which was just as well because there was nothing I wanted to do less than stumble through a Baroque sonata with the two of them. Liza sat at the upright piano, her hands in her lap, watching him, trying to look as if he were nothing to her. Her face was flooded with happiness. Elvira, like the good girl she had suddenly discovered within her range, curled up in the window seat, waiting to listen to their music. Waiting raptly. *This is going to be the most beautiful experience of my life!* She was doing a magnificent job of proving to my mother that it was my father who had created the monstrous Elvirnon out of someone who was perfectly and normally feminine. Kevin Shaw, incidentally, was also in his place, in Chicago at his conference, earning a living and thinking about improving the world.

While I stood at the mantel studying the photograph of young Rich, I got a glimpse of another thing about Polloco that held my mother; what it was, outside of the romantic cabin and the seductive fact of his bachelorhood and his writing talent, that appealed to her. The boy in the photograph—the boy who looked as if he knew enough to grow up, but of course didn't know anything—that boy, frail and bold at the same time, was there inside of the man who was playing the violin across the room from me. He was playing a Gypsy tune, what sounded like a lullaby or a lament, and it occurred to me that my mother, watching him and taking up the melody, was playing the song to the boy, the boy I was staring at in the picture. It seemed to me that my impression was right, and that in spite of myself I was letting my mother give me an understanding of her attachment to the man. It was through the music that I felt it, and knew it.

I had been old enough for several years to apprehend that astonishing idea that all adults truly have once been children. It almost made me laugh, standing in front of the photograph, to think that my mother had fallen in love with a long-ago boy, a specter, when she had a living and breathing son of her own.

Without putting on a jacket I opened the door and went into the cold November day. Screw them all. I wanted to keep looking at the picture and not look at it any more. Maybe my mother's love for the violin player was based on a past she couldn't have, couldn't enter, couldn't in any way be part of. A few weeks before, I had wondered what it was about our family that had changed, and I saw, standing in Polloco's yard, that perhaps the thing that was different about us was me. I was going to leave home. It's possible that my mother was looking ahead to a future that seemed so blank she could only think to fill it with the largest and most forlorn figure that had crossed her path. Not too many years away she'd find herself alone with Kevin Shaw. That was quite a concept. They might play chess in the evenings, fighting without any bluster about who was going to turn the board for whom, who was going to win. I wasn't sure how they were going to stand being alone in that house together. What would he do with his unusual combination of gusto and plain sense? How would she single-handedly absorb his energetic reasonableness? Would she schedule bridge parties and bus tours and backpacking expeditions so they could enjoy, really enjoy, each other's company? Maybe she'd give up and settle for several big dogs or toucans, a whole family of ferrets.

I went into the yard and I climbed into the tree house. Their music was coming through the thick log walls held in place with pegs and mortar. They were playing a lugubrious English country dance tune called "Fair and Softly." I could see Elvira in the window seat, listening as if she were a charmed seal who had come out of the sea, who had opted for land. This, then, could be part of my adult life. Elvira and I would change to fit the setting and the personalities of our parents' new mates. My father's general enthusiasm was almost always with him, so I thought, like a cloud circling him, like bees buzzing around a large petally flower. That joy of his was insistent. The ignorance or happiness or denial, whatever you wanted to call it, was impenetrable. I considered how he was sealed up in his own complete self. Sure, the Big Emptiness was out in the world; sure it was and he knew it, and so what? In whatever matter was at hand, he didn't particularly need anyone to make him glad, and also it seemed that there wasn't much you could do to alter the condition of his own good cheer. It was beyond the scope of my imagination to picture him with anyone else besides my mother, but that was probably my own failing.

Richard Polloco, standing in the cold, at the station, hunched inside his jacket, had had a sadness, just as the boy in the photograph knew sadness. Richard was someone a person might affect. In the Polloco drama my mother was the angel woman, come to make him laugh, feed him a good lunch, play the piano part to the Gypsy tune he'd written, the song that he'd dedicated to his Aunt Galina, one of the strong who'd survived Stalin's purges, one of the few Pollocos who'd escaped. Beth came to Polloco with so much eagerness you could have mistaken her for Kevin Shaw. How amusing that thought was. My mother, in order to fully minister to her lover, had had to take on some of the traits she most resented in her husband.

I stayed outside while the three of them in the cabin moved the chairs around to the table and found some cards and played several hands of what looked to be triple solitaire. I had never thought of my mother as a game player, although she'd put in her time with Elvira and me at war, crazy eights, and rummy. I had never known her to use a game as a way to pass the time with an adult. Eventually she came outside and found me, up the tree with my confused thoughts and no hat or coat or gloves in sight. She scolded me without meaning a word, knowing, as she did, that I was well beyond chiding. It was a correction only for show. I came down and got my jacket from the porch, and then with Polloco we all went for a walk.

Wisconsin is very much like a Vermont that has been stretched flat. Much of Polloco's state, I believe, is in the same planting zone as my old home. On the property near his cabin there were pine trees, and in another stretch oaks and maples, and periodically there were clearings with a few gnarled apple trees and the picturesque stalks of dried weeds. I was not unhappy to walk ahead and imagine that I was alone. It was blustery and overcast. The palette of the landscape— a series of reddish browns and faded greens and a gold that has been slowly bleached away into the finest absence of color—was suitably mournful. Polloco had put on worn hiking boots and pointed his nose upward, as if he were a dog trying to pick up a scent. He seemed to be a fan of the great outdoors. Elvira loped beside the Mr. and Mrs., chattering at Rpoll about the hanging she'd witnessed in Indiana. It was a pleasant tour of the Van Heusen acreage, or whoever owned it, and I could see that Liza's days, when she visited, were full of so many good things, including exercise in a bucolic setting.

Right after the walk we climbed into the car and drove to the station. Elvira, in an uncharacteristic maneuver, threw her arms around Richard Polloco on the platform. Your future stepfather, I said to myself. My mother, I suppose, also embraced him. I boarded the train, turned at the last minute, and said, "Good-bye." I was saying good-bye to the photograph, not to anything else; not to the man, not to the place, not to the stationmaster standing on the steps.

On the way back I imagined that my mother sat scrutinizing me as I read my book. Not for the first time I wondered if something serious was wrong with me. What I needed, I thought, was a pill, surely a drug that was on the market; a small, ordinary white tablet that would dissolve my self, the troublesome *I*.

When we got to Chicago, I told Liza that I needed to move, that I was going to walk the four or so miles home, and without waiting for her to answer I took off. I made my way through the Loop and up Clark Street until I got to Shirana's blue entrance. I took the stairs by twos and tapped on the inner door. A small girl appeared and pointed into the living room, to Herself, in front of her shrine, she who was watching an old western and eating a chapati.

"David," she called.

"Henry," I said, moving toward her. "My name is actually Henry."

"Ah," she said.

"I'd like to hear my cards again, see them, whatever it is you call it. If you don't mind. If you have time."

"Sure, sure, dear," she said, clearing the table of the tools and magazines. "Take off your coat." She clapped her hands and the children disappeared, the cat ran away. She looked at me quickly, long enough to understand that I was in trouble. "You came without your friend," she observed as she set the cards in a stack. She reached out and took my hand, put it on top of the deck, held it there, and closed her eyes. "Sometimes it's good to be on your own?"

I shut my eyes too and nodded. After my vibrations had been absorbed into the cardboard, she patted me, took the cards from under my palm, and began laying them out. I stayed as I was, dreaming myself into her words.

"There is a woman in your life, a magnetic woman. She is someone you want to love, but you're having trouble loving her. You must wait for another woman. There is always another woman for you, Henry." She laughed, a quick ha-ha. "Lucky Henry, I call you," she said. "But for now, Lucky Henry, you wait."

I could hear the cards moving through her hands and onto the table, her breathing as she leaned over to translate their meaning. "You don't like to wait, but you are good, a good wait-er. Not the worst thing, yes, knowing to sit still? In spring, do you see here?" I opened my eyes to look, not unreasonably, at a picture of a flowering tree. "In spring there will be change. Great change. In spring you will reap, excellent time for you. Very fine time for you."

I slapped down my money, said that was all I needed, she could stop right there. I didn't care if nothing she said was true. That thinnest stream of lies was enough to live on, enough to get me through the long winter.

At dinner that night after our trip to Wisconsin, my father was talk-ing about the concept of moving from forty-minute class periods to block scheduling at Jesse Layton. He was intrigued by the idea and seemed to be thinking out loud how he'd manage a ninety-minute history class for freshmen, how he'd keep them active, keep them thinking, keep them awake. He did not believe in using movies dur-ing class time, because, as I've said, he was a throwback. My mother wasn't listening to his ruminations, but as usual she had the look on her face of attentiveness. When her piano career goes to hell, she can play hags and queens, she can do Shakespeare in the Park. Elvira may have been pondering the afternoon, including the novel experience of having been a good girl. She was understandably quiet through supper, eating slowly, staring at her plate, chewing, reflecting.

Again we were in our places of the moment, what seemed to me our rightful places, the four of us in our house at 432 Roslyn, and in the outer world, Richard Polloco was sitting at his table eating din-ner by himself or possibly with Miss Lucille Van Heusen. My mother should not be counted fully present in our circle. Still, we had her in a certain way. If she meant her body for Polloco, she had it wrong. Her physical self in the kitchen was ours, and it was a small thing, I thought, that if her mind was tending toward Tribbey, let it go, let it be gone.

Our narrow brownstone had four stories. The basement was

nicely finished, but it was filled with junk and the Civil War equipment. The kitchen and living and dining rooms were on the first floor, the office, bath and my parents' room were on the second, and Elvira and I had our rooms in the attic. The patch of ground in the back was nothing but a tangle of ivy. What the house lacked in width was made up for in high ceilings, so although the building had an old-fashioned grace, it was drafty and uncomfortable in winter. We hardly ever ate our meals in the dining room because it was cold and, with the exception of holidays and book club nights, the table was never clear. That was the space where my father's schoolwork was laid out, in addition to his books and miscellaneous papers that were all over the office, the room we shared. The living room was taken up by my mother's grand piano and her shelves of music, one sofa, and a coffee table. Our neighborhood was filled with rich couples who were knocking the daylights out of their walls, putting in big blond kitchens with granite surfaces, ranges built into the islands. Even though Minty had paid for our brownstone, my parents didn't have the money or time to strip the dark trim and cover the worn stairs with carpeting and paint over the olive green in the kitchen. In Vermont we had had a whole house, a saltbox house, reddish brown clapboard, on twelve acres, a house with passages that opened into many small bright rooms.

I sat at dinner remembering Richard Polloco's cabin, the view of the field, the low ceilings, the warmth of the woodstove. My mother might be thinking of the same details, caught, she must have been, between this world and that. I watched my father talking, his fisted hands opening and clenching, again and again, as he described the frenetic movement of forty-minute class periods, nine of them in a day. My mother, across from him, was still doing her impression of an interested helpmate. "Uh-huh," she was saying. "Uh-huh. Oh! It sounds like block scheduling would be worth trying."

If my father had once looked across at her, he might have seen how bogus her act was. He might have noticed that she was absent. Since recently I had been observing, with discrimination, both of my parents, doing this for the first time in my life, it had occurred to me that my father might be self-absorbed. I had gone through a stage when I was about thirteen, a stage that lasted a few years, when I thought he was an imbecile. Everything he did struck me as clownish and asinine, and I avoided being seen with him in public, and at home I kept my distance. During that time I had never considered that he might be selfish. At seventeen, although he no longer irritated me in that old way, I had trouble determining what moved him. He was always volunteering to be on school committees, attacking problems, but not, it seemed, to be the man who saves the day—no, not to be heroic. Sometimes there was very little *I* attached to his deeds and his opinions, and yet he did manage to do whatever he wanted. He could justify every place he went and every nutty part of his hobby because it was in the service of history, in the service of teaching and his vocation. When I was young, he was often out at meetings, which might have been difficult for my mother. She would have been stuck in the town of Wellington, with two small children and her overriding need to practice. All the same, my father's job was often thankless. He was a teacher because he believed his profession to be worthwhile, whatever the pitfalls. He loved his children because we were lovable. He loved his wife because—because why? I could not trace an answer through to a satisfying conclusion, couldn't say the precise reason. She was his wife. Therefore he loved her.

Even when my father started listing his colleagues' sentiments about block scheduling—Harvey for, Celeste against, young Brad undecided—Kevin had no need to parade his own preference around, demonstrating his long experience teaching in many different classrooms. You could tell that he was not afraid to try something new. He'd never been afraid, even though he had once gotten fired. It didn't matter to him, really, if he taught in ten-minute segments or had all day to play at history. He more than understood his subject and could break it down into convenient components, and by and large he knew how to involve his students. Where my mother lived inside her music, so that you couldn't have one without the other—or at least, that's how it seemed to me—my father stood aside from the stories that were history, as they rolled on by of their own accord, and while that happened he pointed out to you all the interesting things that of course you wanted to know, that you could see were fascinating once you noticed them.

That night at dinner, while he was getting excited about some of the more extensive projects he could do with a ninety-minute class, I thought that he was the best person I knew. I was ready to throw my allegiance to his side. I didn't think that he could be distracted from the purpose of his useful life, a life that required no declarations, no titles, no applause. It was possibly because he had no ego that he was more fully himself than anyone else I could name. "Some of the Layton kids," my father was saying, "are already, even as freshmen, writing at such a high level. What they could do if they dedicated themselves to a research project for a concentrated period, instead of running around trying to catch a whiff of nine subjects every single day."

"That sounds great, Kev," my mother said. She had her hands on her chin, leaning on her elbows, watching him from across the table. *She's not listening to a word you're saying! Dad! Look, look at her.*

"Yep," he said, "it's definitely worth trying." He was slathering butter on his corn bread, apparently unconcerned about his future. He wasn't the least bit fleshy or even thick around the middle, but when he'd turned forty, he'd stood and asked us, over dessert, to admire the beginning of his paunch, the first sign of the declining years, he said, and a life well spent. His own father and an uncle had died of a coronary, family history that seemed not to hold sway over his eating habits.

"How about dousing your bread in a bowl of whipped cream?" I said. "You've got a quarter pound of butter right there on that two-inch square. Go ahead, live it up." It was fine to talk about animal fat, but nothing else. More than anything I had to manage the conversation. In my own company I had been trying to stop thinking, because the few times I'd let myself go blank, from some small place, on one thin thread, there came to me a kind of sense. Maybe it was a Buddhist- or Zen-type payoff. Into the clear empty head comes wisdom, or at least field tactics. The perfect sense required that at dinner I speak only about saturated versus unsaturated fat. It demanded that I protect my father from the knowledge that my mother was gone. I wanted him never to find out. I saw, too, that I must somehow shield her from his knowing, if it came to that. Sit, I wanted to say to my parents, as if they were pets who would heed my command. Stay. Stay right where you are.

My father said to me, "Have you forgotten that I've taken up power-walking? I can eat anything as long as I have the right shoes and those nifty black pants from the sports shop." He was about to put the greased-up square in his mouth when he stopped himself. He remembered that we'd been away. "Hey! How was Wisconsin? How was your trip?"

Whoops, Bud, the buzzer is sounding, wrong question, guess again. You, madam, don't answer him.

One false move and she might reveal her true feelings for Richard Polloco; she might say, "Oh God, Kevin, it was awful. Dick and I couldn't fuck because the children were there."

It would be best if Elvira nattered on, but she seemed lost in her own reverie. I could not let my mother say anything that might incriminate herself. It was up to me; I needed to fill the immediate space with my own version. "It was okay," I said. "The trip. It was good. The violin player rents a cabin, the pseudo Lincoln birthplace—but it has the feel of an authentic pioneer cabin, if you block out the computer in the corner. He showed us the shop where he makes the instruments. I guess he's got an exclusive contract with a store in Boston. He never practices, he says, but he sounds very consistent, the few times I've heard him play. You probably remember him from Carol's wedding, how his playing stuck out in that tacky band. He's a better musician, actually, than any of Mom's other friends."

I could imagine that it would bother her, that he never practiced, considering his talent and his aspirations. He had told her once, through an e-mail, that he would like to have been a classical violinist.

He's an undisciplined slob, Dad.

"It's kind of a weird town, Tribbey is." I was still talking. "There doesn't seem to be anything going on there. Zip. Zero. The old neighbor woman, Miss Van Heusen, I guess she plays the piano with—him, and he gets a quartet together once in a while, people from Chicago. It's not like Wellington, where at least there was a library and the women on the hill with their instruments, and Mom playing a dance once a month. There is seriously nothing happening in Tribbey. Everything looks closed up, shut down for the season."

My mother was staring at me as if I'd been dead for days and had suddenly and unaccountably sprung back to life. I thought of the photograph of young Richard and the other boy, probably his cousin Rudy. I couldn't remember it very well, couldn't think if his, Polloco's, expression had been one of knowledge or bravado or resignation or pure innocence. Maybe it was all those things, a set of impossible contradictions, within one boy. I would have liked to inspect it again. I wondered what age Polloco was when he learned that his father had been in the gulag, in Kolyma, starving and doing hard labor. My mother must have pored over that photograph, must have picked it up from under the rock on the mantel and stared at it, trying to somehow extract the child from the paper, pull out a human being from ink and light.

"They think there's an Indian mound," I went on, "an Indian relic on the property."

"Gee," my father said.

My mother was still looking at me with an expression of alarming happiness. "I didn't know you had such a good time today, Henry," she said. "I didn't know you were listening to the conversation."

The place mats Liza had set out had a texture to them that ran through the weave irregularly. I followed the pattern with my finger, wondering what it was like to read Braille. I did not want to be breathing the same air that she was breathing. To avoid exchanging molecules with her, I moved from the table, went to the stove, and I stood there, looking down into the burners. Elvira took my departure as her cue to begin pestering my father. She would not go to Old

World Wisconsin for the living history weekend if her friend Al was having his adenoids removed. What if that girl, Samantha, showed up, the chit who always chased her. Where could they go next weekend? Where could they find a wide-open field, so she could shoot her muzzle loader?

"I don't think I told you," my mother said in the middle of Elvira's demands, "that Paul and Julia Graham's daughter—you remember Lily—is coming to visit Northwestern and the University of Chicago in January." She was speaking to my father, getting down to the business of family life. "She's going to come on the ninth and stay for a night or two at Northwestern, and then one of us—maybe you could do it, Henry—will need to drive her down to Hyde Park."

"That's easy," my father said.

"But, Dad, do I have to have a hunting license just to shoot off a round of blanks?" Elvira had her hands on the table, hoisting herself over her plate, waiting for an answer.

"I thought she had her heart set on Sarah Lawrence," Mrs. Shaw said. "I can't picture Lily at the U of C. Too formidable, too many intellectuals. I know she has plenty of time to decide, but last summer wasn't she excited about Sarah Lawrence?"

"I don't think you need a license for target practice, Elv," my father said, "but we should definitely get a hunting and fishing regulations booklet."

"Henry, wasn't she?"

Into the stainless hood of the Amana Colony stove I said, in a return to my regular old laconic self, "Your muzzle loader, Elvira, is a single-shot loader. You, of all people, know that it does not have rounds."

In five short weeks I was going to drive to Evanston and meet Lily in front of a designated dormitory. I pictured her wearing a thin wool coat, standing in front of the building, shivering, looking down the street, waiting for me. I'd park illegally by the hydrant, and even as I was jumping from the car, she'd be running to me, calling out her hellos and also my name. We'd drive back to the city, put her bags in Elvira's room, eat dinner with the family in what, realistically, might prove to be the most awkward meal of my life, taking the prize from the Richard Polloco luncheon. It would probably be the one night that Elvira kept quiet, refusing to blabber on when I needed her most. She was talking again, and I wanted to go to the table, put my hand on her mouth, tell her to save it, to keep all the words inside, to be let out later, at my direction.

When my mother began to do the dishes and my father went into the dining room to work on his lesson plans, I allowed myself to go upstairs. They were secure, for the moment. I was ready to leave home, more than ready, to leave the four of us, but only if we could be summoned, the whole group, when I said so. Shirana had remarked that I was conventional, that I paid attention to the rules. I was sure that I was permitted, as their son, to exercise moral judgment over the Shaws, even if I did so with no one else, including myself. They had chosen, after all, to play a certain game, and it seemed to me that if you entered into it willingly, then you had to observe the regulations. If you stepped out of bounds, it followed that you could lose everything. You might very well end up with nothing.

One of the women I began to tell this story to much later, insisted that I was exactly like Hayley Mills in *The Parent Trap*, the movie about prepubescent twins who try to reunite their parents after years of separation. She found it adorable, this effort of mine, reducing me to two blond-haired ten-year-old girls, both up to their eyeballs in mischief and love and goodness. I took her comment as a sign that I had to break up with her immediately.

During that family dinner, after the trip to Tribbey, I'd decided that my parents could not come together in our house until they were past their troubles. It was fortunate that my father went to bed much earlier than my mother. Elvira and I had to fill up what space and quiet we could so that Mr. and Mrs. Shaw would not ever take stock. Karen had already told me that one of my dominant moons or houses or planets, something astrologically important, was in Cancer, and if a person is born in any way under the crab, he will be a homebody. Perhaps nothing more needs to be said about the importance to me of the Shaw family. Home. I had a moon in Cancer and therefore my parents had to stay together; therefore my parents had to stay clear of each other to remain inseparable.

And anyway, how did it work, practically speaking, that a couple split up when they had known each other for so many years? It took place all the time, to plenty of people we knew. I could see that it might be easy to divide a household, arrange for the children to be here and there at certain hours, take a lease on an apartment. But if this happened to us, wouldn't my mother always be thinking of my father, even when she didn't want to? Didn't any revolution carry with it the risk of nostalgia, a longing for the old regime? Richard Polloco would periodically say a line and Liza would react, and it would remind her of the way she'd been with my father, or she'd hear herself saying the exact words to her new husband that Kevin had often said to her. Wouldn't she even, on occasion, want to call Kevin, to tell him a funny, very short story, something only he would understand because they'd once shared a house and children, shared the common language of daily life?

I wondered if Shirana could answer questions about details in the here and now, if she was perceptive about actual living. It did seem unlikely that a person could see far ahead and back too, and in addition understand what lay right before her. I should probably visit her again, when I got ahold of some money, and ask her about my father, ask her what he could look forward to in the spring. I could call Minty, tell her that her own little Beth was getting laid regularly by a man not her husband, and if she could pop for the psychic, I could find out some more dirt on the subject. I had all of the winter to get through, including Lily's visit, before April, before Shirana's promise of deliverance. *In spring you will reap, excellent time for you. Very fine time for you.*

The day after our lunch in Tribbey, on Sunday, my mother was downstairs practicing with the Juice of Barley. My father was doing the grocery shopping—a willingness, incidentally, the book club women included in their prescription for the ideal husband. The husband from heaven. Elvira was out on the streets with her loud-mouthed friend Hilare. I had a moment on the second floor by myself, and I logged onto Liza38's account to see if she had documented our afternoon in Tribbey. I remembered the last message I'd read from Liza to Jane, the one that chronicled a short trip the fornicatress had taken with The Man, to Minneapolis, to play for a dance. In the middle of the night in some motel he'd woken her by saying her name. He had hovered above her, saying it once. Other men might have whispered *Beth* to her before, but there was a devotion in the way he'd said it, or the way she'd heard it. In her message to Jane she'd intimated what had happened in those private moments. He'd found himself awake; it was as if he'd had to say it, the beloved word. She'd opened her eyes, coming up from a dreamless place, coming up into the warmth of his large body. Without much fumbling they found each other, the sound of her name ringing down through her as they held still for a time, clasped, in the dark. Slowly, then, they began to move.

Downstairs Juice of Barley played a tune called "The Famous Ratcatcher" while I retrieved my mother's most recent message to Jane. It is with a sense of embarrassment for her that I copy her messages. If I were the Hayley Mills good-girl heroine of the movies, I would destroy all the documents in my Richard Polloco archive. It is cruel, I know it is, to have your own words, your own poor self, trapped as it was years before. Nonetheless, she wrote these words. They are hers. They cannot be taken back.

> Dear Jane,
> This one thing I call my own, is it so big and so terrible? Will I have to pay for this joy? We were sitting at lunch in Tribbey today, Elvira talking to Richard as if she'd known him all her life, as if we were all old friends. Henry was on guard. I can't say what he knows. If only I could tell him this whole story and along with it give him understanding. Kevin is my family. He and the children are my home, the place where every night there is food on the table and in the morning the rhythms of work—in other words, he goes with the life I know and need and love.

Richard. Richard is my home in quite another way, in a disembodied, airy, floating space that doesn't seem to require physical boundaries or regular time. We go together, he and I, in a way that is separate from the workaday world. In a way that feels primitive, basic, irrefutable. To see Henry and Elvira in our disembodied, airy, floating space both confused me and gave me hope, and here I am in Chicago, split and split. Love, Beth

Disembodied, airy, floating space? Clearly she was out of her mind, although her writing skills were improving; she looked to be coming into her own even if she was having a psychotic break. A lot of people would have been grateful for Beth Shaw's routine, her house, the food on the table, waking up in the morning, having a life that she understood. Some days she didn't change out of her pajamas, her nightgown with the blue stars all over it. She played the piano in the morning, she ate lunch, she argued with her booking agent over the telephone, she did musical research for various documentary filmmakers who consulted her. All of that she did in her white flannel nightgown speckled with blue stars and gold stars. She had gotten herself into a situation where she was split and that was just too bad. It was no one's fault but her own.

After I read her e-mail to Jane, after the other members of the Juice of Barley had gone, I went downstairs. My father had appeared with the groceries, and my mother was in the kitchen helping him put the food away. "Do you remember," she was saying to him, "when we took the kids camping in Maine—when was that? When Henry was five or six? Elvira was barely walking. Do you remember the storm?"

"You made us sing," my father said. "You were screaming through the wind for all of us to sing."

"You thought we should recite the Gettysburg Address, in unison."

The two of them, my father and my mother, were working in the kitchen together, laughing. Laughing. It struck me that my mother lately had been asking all of us to remember certain scenes from our family life. Was she planning to bolt, planning, in effect, to take the files, the family history, the memories with her?

Later, at dinner, she did it again. She said, this time to me, "Do you remember at Silverpines when Suzy Dyerman threw up during the mummers' play? She was supposed to be the doctor, and she opened her mouth to speak and began vomiting. Dad threw the doctor's case to you, and you started doing the part as if nothing were wrong."

It had been one of my favorite valiant moments, and I wasn't sorry she recalled it. My father had tossed me the satchel, and almost without knowing it I'd stepped into the role. I was there saying the lines I'd heard a hundred times, while Suzy Dyerman was whisked off the platform. I'd even ad-libbed during the cleanup operation. A few lines that had brought down the house.

"It was so disgusting—God, it was gross. We'd had split pea soup for lunch, and the barf was like a river of green slime." Elvira loved that puking incident. "Do you remember, Dad," she said, "the time Claire and I went skinny-dipping and Brian came down with his flashlight and was shining it on us? What a creep!"

"He was reminding you that you needed a lifeguard," Kevin said.

"He was not!"

"Remember?" my father said, turning to me, caught up in the exercise. "Do you remember at the Plimouth Plantation when the boy got bit by the pig—"

"That special Pilgrim breed," Elvira said, "and the Pilgrim lady wouldn't help him? She told him he should pray, and his finger was like a fountain, spurting blood."

"It was a trickle," I said, "a trickle of blood. It was not a head wound."

My mother was smiling, staring and smiling, transfixed like the madwoman she was. Without blinking, without moving, she said, "Elvira, you got so angry at Henry that day because he showed you the fire extinguisher in the plantation cottage."

"He was such a jerk, trying to rub my nose in the fact that the place wasn't authentic. I clobbered him."

"Poor Henry," Mrs. Shaw murmured. "Poor Henry."

I was wondering, as my mother held still, in her trance of remembering, if she was weighing her future with Richard Polloco, a future that would be without a past. She was testing the weight of the family history, the stories—that's what she was doing—to see what they were worth.

One afternoon in December, on the way home from Jesse Layton, Elvira was seized by the urge to have her head shaved. In the summer she had herself shaved patches above her ears, but that winter day she stopped in at the barber, and for good money Mic Conelli sharpened his blade and sheared off my sister's short black curls. As I picture it, she had been walking home, she'd looked first at her reflection in the used record store window, she'd stopped and stared. Could it be? She looked hard at her own prettiness, at the curls around her face, her dark lashes, her sculpted features, cheekbones to chin. "Shit" was all she said. Beyond the reflection, inside, she saw a poster of a bald rock star, and she thought, That's what I need. That's exactly what I have to have. It was terrible timing, her beauty coming on when she had at last gotten her wish, to be a private in the 28th Wisconsin.

After the haircut she went to Walgreens to buy a stocking hat for the occasion. She put it on for the cold walk home, and she felt that underneath the green knit cap was the secret and the genuine Elvirnon. At Roslyn Place she went straight to her room. Across the hall I was at my desk working on my calculus homework. Not long after her arrival I was aware of the shape of her in my door. She was standing, her new hat in hand, waiting for me to pay attention.

"Henry," she finally had to say.

"Uh-huh," I said, keeping my eye on the paper, on my figures.

"What do you think?"

So I did look up, a loop of my head, another look, the classic double take. She was as bald, as naked, as a whole wet, blind, newborn animal. You don't realize what a positive thing hair is until it's gone. In the first place, hair makes a dinky head appear larger than its actual size. It is to a person what frosting is to a cake, a frame to a painting, a halo to an angel. Although it is now the fashion, for me baldness still has no attraction unless the individual is gravely ill and I talk myself into admiration. Elvira's hair had already been short, but taken to the next level she looked stripped of an essential part of herself.

Either Mom's going to die or she's going to kill you. That was my first thought, beyond how god-awful she looked. Moreover, Richard Polloco wouldn't think she was cute anymore. I had hair past my shoulders, which I usually wore in a ponytail. I pulled the rubber band off and let my straight dark mane fall down my back. "You, me—what's wrong with this picture?"

"I know, I know, we're backward!" She put her cupped hands to her mouth and giggled into them, the return of the Rpoll-inspired girl creature.

"Why, honey," I said, "you can't do a thing with that skull of yours."

She laughed out loud. It was strange to hear her regular throaty laugh coming from the face that was smaller than it had been that morning. I wasn't going to bring up the subject of her mother directly, not while she was giddy and triumphant, but I did say, as she left the room, that I would start my prayer wheels, why not, wouldn't hurt. I said, "Are you going to make a splash, or sit at dinner hoping that no one will notice?"

She ran her hands over her follicles. "It's just hair," she said, beginning to rehearse her defense. "It's not like it doesn't grow back."

If she had been a few years older and had more range, she would have put on an evening gown and a tiara and come sweeping down the steps, puffing on a cigarette and calling everyone darling. She was, however, limited by being Elvira at the age of thirteen. Right when the rest of us, all friendlylike, were sitting down to dinner, she marched into the kitchen dressed in her 28th Wisconsin uniform. She stood at her place and made the noise of a drumroll on the table with her fists. She looked my mother in the eye. With her thumb and index finger she plucked the hat from her crown.

"Just think how much we'll save on shampoo in the next six months," I said.

"Wow!" my father said.

My mother covered her mouth with her hands, what a person does instinctively when looking upon a scene of horror. It was not the girlish gesture Elvira had used up in my room. "No, Elvie," she whispered. "No."

Elvira pulled out her heavy artillery, a little prematurely, I thought. "It's just hair, Mom," she snarled. "It's not like it doesn't grow back."

Beth bowed her head, going into her prayer mode. My father, who could not keep his curiosity at bay, asked, "Does it itch?"

"Nah," Elvira said.

"Not until it starts sprouting," I said. "Then every single hair is like an egg hatching."

"Shut up," Elvira spit. "What do you know about it, you dipshit hippie?"

I raised my arms, surrendering.

Mrs. Shaw continued to look at her plate of linguine. She muttered, "Your dinner is getting cold." That is the fallback line mothers through the millenniums have used to keep from blowing their stacks at mealtime. "You'd better eat while it's still warm."

There was nothing more that night, nothing, that is, if you don't count Mrs. Shaw's silence. Of course in that quiet was the beginning of the boil—but I wasn't thinking of the weeks ahead. I was foolish enough to be amazed that the short scene was over, that there'd been no blowout. My father had the good sense to talk to me, to leave the females to their own thoughts of fashion. He had a strict code that forbade either of us from asking the other about teachers or students at Layton, but we were allowed to discuss the basketball team and to talk about specific plays and the strengths of individual athletes. Elvira, slouching in her chair, seemed to be disappointed in everyone's reaction. She may have realized that she would have gotten a dramatic rise from my mother if she'd grown her hair long undercover and one day done it up in a fancy braid. After dinner she banged herself up to her bedroom, my mother went to a rehearsal, my father did his schoolwork, and I performed my archival duties in the office.

That night I documented the first of the breakup messages, what would serve as a prototype for the many adieux to come. I had not logged on for four or five days; what a lot of catching up to do! I thought, after I'd read the messages, how admirably my mother had kept her cool at dinner, considering the stress in her life. It was he who had initiated the split, he who'd dumped her.

Dear Beth,
I have long made it a rule not to get involved with a married woman. This time I broke my rule. The situation becomes more difficult. It is better to end this now. RP

Such a somber message, and terse, from the man who was usually so lively with his pen. She replied within forty-five minutes.

Richard, Richard. You are my beloved, the companion of my body, the guest of my heart. I do not want to cause you pain. I will miss you more than you will know. I cannot bear this.

What followed was approximately thirty-six hours of inactivity in her account. During that time Beth Shaw, as far as I could remember, had not taken to her bed, and she had not been working up pieces written by mentally unbalanced geniuses of the Romantic period, no Schumann cascading through the rooms of our house. But then maybe I'd missed the crisis while I'd been away at school, at my Youth Symphony rehearsal, and a party at Karen's house, where her exotic parents discreetly supplied us with some excellent hash. At about the thirty-fifth hour it was Rpoll who broke down and in effect came riding, riding, riding. His message said, "I miss you. Write me." At the ready she shot back, "I love you. Write me." And so on. The following day there were flowers delivered to our door, roses as I recall, yellow, a vase of them which my mother put on her piano.

Meanwhile, we all had our theories about why Elvira went to such lengths, as it were, with her hair. Karen, going a little overboard perhaps, came up with a home-remedy-type castration theory, something about how Elvira had primal anger against the universe because she'd been born a girl, and one of the ways to express rage within a conventional middle-class family, a family that encouraged sweetness and niceness, was to commit acts of aggression and mutilation against herself. What Elvira really wanted to do, deep down, Karen surmised, was go on a castration spree.

I'm sure my father thought Elvira had a lot of starch. If there was anyone who had an inviolate self, it was his daughter. The fact that she felt no pressure from her Jesse Layton peers to conform, that she had her eye on her own goals, made him proud rather than anxious. He may have believed that she was onto something, that she was a model for us all, true to her principles.

My idea was the simple one. Elvira's breasts were getting larger by the day. She shaved her head to take attention from her shape and also to prove to herself that she was as much a guy as the next fellow. There was the regiment to think of, her commitment to the hard-cores. My mother did not speak about Elvira's sleek, bold style, and if, in the immediate aftermath, she had a theory about her hair, she kept it to herself. She was in any case awfully busy, patching it up with Polloco and tending her flowers, the posies that probably cost him a month of rent. She did tell Minty about the new hairdo in the family, over the telephone, trying, to the best of her ability, to be both the good daughter and the good mother. "I'm not sure if it's lack of respect," Beth was saying into the receiver. "I think of it as a very strong will." She was huddling into the wall, as if she were at a public phone on a noisy street. "I know," she said, "I've tried." Bethy listened and then this, my favorite part, the argument a person hopes will work every time. "It's just hair, Mother. It's not like it doesn't grow back. It's just hair."

In the days that followed, Mrs. Shaw was brisk in her quietness. My parents had taken up the habit of playing a few rounds of double solitaire every night, a practice Liza38 had apparently learned from the companion of her body, the guest of her heart. I'd come downstairs thinking everyone was asleep, and they'd be in the kitchen slapping down the cards as fast as they could. I'd think that I was supposed to start talking at them, to distract them from each other, but they were so absorbed in the game they'd shush me, both of them, as soon as I'd opened my mouth. I'd stand over them and every now and then offer some advice. "You can put your three on that four, Dad."

"Where?" my father would say. "Where?"

My mother, and presumably Polloco, held to the rules with an iron fist. They did not believe in fudging a card here and there to keep the game moving, but my father was all in favor of cheating if necessary—being flexible, he called it. Taking creative liberties. "You're a cheater," my mother would say. "This game does not count." It certainly was a comfort to know that Mrs. Shaw held herself and her husband to such a strict accounting.

Christmas was coming, and as she always had, she was bracing herself for the family gatherings, the cooking and the shopping. She played the harpsichord in three concerts of Baroque music at the Shubert Theater, performances that she claimed would have been fun if she'd been twenty years younger. Coincidentally Polloco had also been hired to be part of the ensemble. Liza mentioned that fact to Jane, as well as the detail that he would be in Chicago to spend the holiday with his aunt. Whether or not Mrs. Shaw could find a reason to slip out of the house to meet him on Christmas Eve or Day was something that probably plagued her.

I was occasionally on her mind too. When she asked me what I wanted for Christmas, I shrugged and said I didn't know. Traditionally I had been the hardest person to buy for, the son who didn't demand much. Usually I asked her for CDs, some software, or a modest piece of hardware. When I told her I couldn't think of anything to want, she scowled. She said, "You're going away next year, and there's nothing you need?"

"What could I possibly need?" I said amiably.

"Surely, there's—" She stopped when she saw the look on my face. Perhaps there was a mocking aspect to my bearing and demeanor. She started coughing, the very image of the romantic consumptive. I did not ask her if she was unwell, or offer to thump her on the back. Before she left she managed to say, "If you come up with something, let me know."

My father bought a tree at a lot nearby, and it was he and Elvira who decorated the Scotch pine in time for Mrs. Shaw's holiday book club meeting. She, as I've already intimated, was so terribly busy. The night of the club I got home well after dinner from a Ping-Pong practice. I came into the kitchen, only to hear the uproarious laughter of the women who as always were supposed to be discussing serious literature. I had been avoiding them ever since the Shirana episode. I figured that my mother might have mentioned to them the joke about our having been married before, and I had no interest in meeting Glamorous Pam's eyes or having an exchange with any of the others about my past associations. Who knows, perhaps the book club had been with Mrs. Shaw and me all along, in our previous lives: the ladies-in-waiting, the backup band, a whole slew of daughters.

In the middle of the hilarity, I tried to sneak from the kitchen through the dining room. I heard the toilet in the downstairs bathroom flush, but I wasn't quick enough to get past the powder room and up the stairs, out of sight. Just as I stepped in front of the door, it opened.

"Well, hello there, guy." It was The Marcia, standing before me in a patch of light.

"Ah—hi," I said. *Crone.*

She was getting to be more pregnant as a result of her insemination, and the softness of her face was startling in a person who had formerly been so angular. According to my mother, she'd been talkative about her weight gain, and that, too, was surprising in a cerebral individual who scoffed at the concerns of the average American woman. "Have you been working on those college applications?" she said.

"Those ones," I said. "Yes, I have."

"Where do you fancy going?"

I was even-tempered—that much should already be clear—but in spite of my own disposition I could have happily knocked her down and kicked at her with the hard toe of my hiking boot. I fancied like hell doing such a thing.

"Anywhere in the Northeast," I replied.

"Back to your roots! How interesting. And what are you planning on majoring in?"

"Um. I—"

"Have anything in mind?"

"I—I was thinking about women's studies, actually." I said it with all the earnestness I could muster.

Out of the corner of my eye I could see the jolt pass through Mrs. Shaw. *What? Women's studies?* She looked so lovely when she was alarmed. She sat up very straight and the color came high into her face. Most men who major in women's studies are probably cake-boys, every mother's worst nightmare. Beth already had a pre-lesbian daughter, and so she was counting on me to be the family breeder. I was the one she would be able to hold up: Here, meet my son, Henry Shaw—you see, I did something right.

"It's been sort of a dream of mine," I said, going up the stairs, leaving the obvious unsaid, that Marcia had for all the years of book club been my inspiration.

Imagine the many, many things Beth Shaw had to think about that December. There was Elvira's baldness, the announcement of my future course of study, Christmas coming, not to mention the daily work of keeping up her correspondence, and in addition her full travel schedule. To top it off, midmonth, she confessed to Jane that even though she knew it was insane, she couldn't help thinking about having a baby with Polloco. A little half brother or sister for Elvira and me! I believe I did not save that letter, that the contents distracted me from my purpose. I rarely printed out Jane's replies, although she often had sound advice about eating well and getting enough rest and holding on to real life a little longer, just a little longer. Since my mother had added a baby to her fantasy, including, no doubt, the precious tiny clothing and the search for a name, both first and last, she probably never got to sleep.

I don't think I slept much either. I was waiting for January ninth, for Lily—light, dew, and a gust of wind. For Christmas, Mom, I want time to pass. I want to get to Lily. *Lily, the companion of my body, the guest of my heart.* That message Liza38 had written to Rpoll wasn't half bad, I thought: companion of my body, guest of my heart. It had a certain ring to it. It was practically poetry.

I couldn't concentrate, couldn't get anything done. I came down with a bad cold and ended up taking my mother's sleeping pills. She doled them out to me as if they were gold and silver, the last of her precious supply. The small silky tablets knocked me out, stilled all brain activity, and when I woke, I felt as if I'd been outside of my body doing a prescribed deed for it, taking it for a long walk in a dark tunnel. Living with sleeplessness and then going dreamy half the day is, as my mother would say, part of the old story.

I attributed her silence to weariness, a simple mistake. I felt a glimmer of hope when she sat at the piano with her shoulders sagging, her hands motionless on the keys. She'd gaze out the window and heave a sigh, poor Liza. Surely she looked at Polloco every now and then with a coldness in her eye, and also in her heart. On occasion she must have seen him as he was, just another person, another body with its awful needs. Not someone to break your neck to love. Logistically it was all so cumbersome. How was she going to keep Richard dangling at the end of her rope, and be dangled herself by him, with work and Christmas looming, Minty coming over to discuss holiday plans? There was also her husband to consider, making sure he got his crumb in the morning and evening, and she had her friend in Vermont to keep up with, so many letters to write, phone calls to make! And if those duties weren't enough, she had a depressed son, and a daughter who was likely to come home any day having had a sex change operation: Surprise! I felt as if somewhere out in the weeks ahead there was the possibility that exhaustion would catch up with Liza, that she'd step off the Hiawatha in Chicago, thank the conductor, and bring all of herself home.

I imagined her in the fall driving me to Vermont, to any college in Vermont, and her crying, crying at my going. Her display would make me uncomfortable, and I'd whisk her down to the end of the hall, out of sight of my roommates. I'd wish she'd drive away. But I'd also have to resist the urge to laugh, to toss my hat in the air, celebrating the sorrow, celebrating the bond that was so strong on her side, so much stronger than the frayed line that held me to her.

During Christmas dinner at Minty's we sat around the table, the Shaws and my three uncles, the two aunts, six cousins, including Carol and her banker husband, Jim Carodine, the happy couple who were responsible for bringing Rpoll and Liza38 together. It was an overcast day, the light in Minty's dining room was dim, and for many hours the afternoon seemed to be hovering at dusk. At six o'clock in the evening we felt as if we'd stayed up until three in the morning. I remember my mother that day, her hands in her lap, her silence, that awful quietness posing as graciousness. She wanted so much not to be with any of us. She was perhaps imagining that we'd take our annual Christmas Day walk around Minty's neighborhood in Lake Bluff, and while we were gone, while she stayed in the kitchen and did the dishes, a hooded man would jump from the bushes and gun down Elvira and me and Kevin. With one round of ammo we'd be gone. Bravely she would forge ahead without us. Richard Polloco would comfort her, she having joined his league of sorrow. All that long afternoon at Minty's she watched the front door, as if at any minute, when we happened to turn our backs in concert, she'd get up, leave her folded napkin at her place, and skulk along the hall. She'd carefully close the front door. She'd be down the stairs and away, away to her rapture.

I sat at dinner watching my grandmother at the work of hostessing, instructing her son about the carving, reminding her smallest granddaughter to keep the butter moving. It was a big job, being Minty. I did wonder about her briefly, how she'd grown up as a minister's daughter and married Dwight Gardener when she was twenty-three. Outside of her stiffness, those are about the only facts I know about her. She seemed to be overlooking Elvira's fashion error, and as usual she gave her grandchildren one hundred dollars in crisp new bills, two fifties for each of us.

After the table was cleared, Mrs. Shaw managed to get a group together, eight or so, to play a game of mass solitaire. Young and old alike were throwing cards into the center of the dining room table, as much riot as had ever taken place in Minty's house. That bacchanalian joy, of course, was thanks to Richard Polloco, he who had introduced the cards, no cheating, into my mother's regime.

Minty had warned the relatives about Elvira's hair, and some of them had good-humored comments to make about the brightness of her head. There was the natural "Won't you lead my sleigh tonight?" Elvira plastered her pate with stick-on bows and stood at attention while my father announced the rather old news, Elvira's invitation to reenact with the 28th Wisconsin. He explained that this was like being asked to be on the Olympic team. Elvira, he said, had already done a few events with the group and would have the privilege of touring with them in the spring, to the battle of Shiloh and on into the summer at various Midwestern camps and also possibly Gettysburg.

There was a murmur through the living room, the sound of tepid enthusiasm, feigned approval. Later, I figured out that my father had brought up the 28th Wisconsin to put Elvira's bald head into perspective for the relatives, to inform them there was indeed a reason for the coiffure.

In the pause between the opening of the gifts and charades, my mother gouged a few of the chocolate candies out of the frosting on the cobbled walk that led to Minty's annual gingerbread house, made by the wife of the Hungarian gardener. Jim Carodine was standing next to Mrs. Shaw in the living room as she shamelessly dismantled the pavement and from the shutters popped one M&M after the next into her mouth. "Does your husband know this about you?" Carodine asked her.

She gasped. "You won't tell him, will you? You wouldn't tell him!" She pulled out the red gumdrops from the dormers and mashed them in her hand before she turned her back on him.

In spite of the weeks that I had lived waiting for Lily to arrive, I still wondered, when the hour came, what there was that had led up to my being in our Ford Escort, parked in front of the dormitory on the Northwestern campus. It was my habit, my need, to have to retrace my steps, and that time was no exception. There had been the path at Silverpines, we had run and run and come to the clearing, or maybe I had dreamed the chase, made it up. Maybe, after all, it was nothing. I didn't know if I had ever seen her in winter, if we'd been children together, packed in our snowsuits on a mountain slope. Maybe we had a history that went back further than we realized. Since camp we had written letters and talked on the phone a few times, without having much to say. I asked myself after the calls if it was our desire to see each other, the inadequacy of the phone connection, that rendered us mute, or if she no longer had any interest in me. When we spoke to make the arrangements for the visit, she seemed fixated on the details of her trip, all the times and places she had to keep in mind. It was a five-minute conversation, and when I hung up, I wondered if she was someone I even knew.

I was sitting in the Ford, thirty minutes before the appointed time, in front of the Noyes Cultural Center, when there came a knocking at the steamy window. I wiped a circle in the glass. There she was. The girl herself. Lily. Early—she had come early and it was Lily and actually there she was. Instead of a college-woman-of-the-Northeast wool coat, she was wearing an ugly gray parka that looked as if it belonged to her father. In keeping with her interest in folk art she had arranged a scarf of blue and silver threads at her neck. What I did next baffled me. I didn't open the door and jump out. I didn't throw my arms around her, as I'd imagined doing, all of a sudden a hearty, demonstrative, ebullient personality pulling the country girl in her thin wool coat into my embrace. I didn't speak or shout or whisper or croon or stutter. That whole sequence, not doing anything, seemed to take forever. And then, what I did, as if I were reacting in a deep sleep, what I did, crank by crank, was unroll the window.

"I'm here," she said, and she must have been shrugging her shoulders because her parka heaved a little, up and down.

"Hi," I said, looking through the window at the coat that seemed to have swallowed her. I could hardly see her face because of her scarf, the glittery threads, and the snow drifting to the ground too. *It's Lily, L-I-L-Y, you mental giant, you dumbfuck.*

After I'd unlocked the door—and it was no easy job with my mitten, trying to grasp the puny knob—I opened the door, tried to get out, and realized that what was restraining me was my seat belt. *Jerk, moron, asshole.* I unbuckled and did at last jump up, somewhat in the style of the hearty, demonstrative, ebullient personality I meant to be, and I took that parka in my arms and pressed hard against it, trying to feel down to the girl inside. No such luck. But she did pull my face to her mouth, and I thought then that everything was going to be fine, that we, she and I, were all right, that we'd come through six months without anything being lost. That's how new I was to the business of love.

She had more of Elvira's gift than I remembered, on the way home, talking, telling me, remarking, making note of the details, being able to recount in a stream, going on tangents and returning to the main point even after following a tangent of a tangent. If I had been a blind person, I might very well have been able to find my way around the Northwestern campus after her thorough description of it. She was facing me as I drove, as I kept my eye on the road, all that snow and ice and glare. It was probably, I considered, the yearning, the absence of a physical presence, that had made it impossible for us to speak to each other over the telephone. She told me a great deal about the two girls who were supposed to host her, both biology majors, both of them from Kansas. They had so much studying to do they'd passed her off on a music major down the hall, a good thing, because Lily had been able to go to a choir rehearsal and sing along through the first section of the B Minor Mass, a mass she'd sung in Brattleboro the year before. She sang the second soprano part of the Kyrie for me. She described the conductor, the people in her section, the choir room, the accompanist, the old Baldwin piano, and the battered score they had to read from. It had been thirty-five relatively long minutes since we'd kissed outside of the Cultural Center. When exactly had Lily become a talker?

For an instant—no more than that—I had a wayward thought that men put up with a lot of noise in order to get what we want. It was no wonder that early on, the males of the species figured out that we should spend our day in the workplace, where there might be quiet. I'd have to tell Marcia I'd changed my mind, I didn't really want to major in women's studies; I'd decided that I didn't care about the female brain. I only, I'd say to her, want to bang this one girl.

I was wondering how I should break it to Lily, that I was capable of discourse, when she said, "Hell-o! Henry, I've been jabbering a mile a minute. I must be nervous." I had parked in the alley and turned off the motor. She leaned over and kissed me. It was surprising, the way a girl who looked that delicate could kiss, no clue that her small mouth could be expressive, that there could be so much heat and light when my eyes were closed and the car was cold. I thought, too, about how all of her had opened to me last summer, how her pleasure was seamless, how her body had rippled out from the tip of my finger, at the place she showed me. All of her turning from the point where I held her.

When we went in the house there was a flurry at the door: my mother coming to greet her, to greet the Grahams' lovely daughter, so grown-up; my father also hovering, taking her coat and hanging it in the closet; Elvira saying, "Hey," in her voice that seemed to be growing deeper.

"Your hair is so great, Elvie," Lily said, as if she meant it. She tittered when she asked if she could touch it, but she was appreciative when Elvira bent her head, when she stroked the soft bristles.

I kept my hands on the luggage, didn't watch all that stroking. Lily came up behind me, asking my sister about the buttons on her uniform, were they replicas, Elvira going into her song and dance about how some people piss on their buttons to give them that essential Civil War patina, but then you have to put up with the stink. Lily tried to exchange a glance with me over that one, just the way Polloco and my mother had done. I went up and up, dragging her duffel bag which turned out to contain a chemistry tome, the history of the Western world, her English literature anthology, and a hardbound copy of *David Copperfield.*

My mother didn't usually kick Elvira out of her room for a guest, but my father was in the middle of doing grades, and clearly the office was no place for an optimistic visitor who lived with two organized parents. It was going to be ideal, being alone in the attic together. We would not have to make do out in the freezing temperatures, in the cramped backseat of the Ford Escort. Even if we hadn't liked each other, how could my parents think that we could pass up this opportunity? It was remarkable, I thought, how dense my mother was.

At dinner Mrs. Shaw gave us each a glass of wine, as if we were European teenagers—and what was this for? I wondered. Was Bethy trying to impress Lily, to show her what a groovy mother I had? Lily made her eyes go big, gave me a smirky little smile, and took a sip. "Thanks," she said. "Thanks very much." There is nothing more ridiculous than drinking with your parents, and although I could imagine developing a taste for fine wine, I found it nearly impossible to swallow the warm and mellow cabernet my mother had probably paid too much for at the organic superstore. What got us through dinner was not only the chemical-free wine but Silverpines gossip. My mother actually did rise to the occasion, doing imitations of the cast at camp, the techy violinist who always spent more time adjusting his microphone than he did tuning, the ninety-eight-pound piano player, Elise Gunn, who played contra dance chords as if the music were Rachmaninoff, the clarinetist who wasn't very good about handing the tune back to the other musicians when his riff was supposed to be over. It turned into a charade-type game, the rest of us guessing whom she was impersonating. Lily, in a bold move, did her impression of the Silverpines grande dame, Fiona Porter, who used to poke around in the bushes with an umbrella to make sure no one was humping on the property. Liza laughed into her chest. The idea! Sex at Silverpines!

My father, in the most challenging act, both for performer and for audience, mimed the warped canoe that was impossible to steer. After we gave up, not having known that inanimate objects were in the rules, Elvira went over to the refrigerator and lay down on the floor with her tongue hanging out. "The camp dog after he's been shaved for fleas?" Kevin said.

She barked at him, nipped at his heels.

It seemed that my turn was next. I took an easy shot at Grisha, a man who always appeared at Family Camp, the foremost clog-dancing expert in the country. English clog dancing is like tap dancing, but you do it in shoes that weigh three pounds apiece. In his black clogs with gold rivets Grisha danced up and down steps, climbed on chairs and tapped, jumped off them, tapped some more, often using a broom and a hat as props. His real name was Kim. He'd learned to dance from an old woman who had clog-danced regularly on the radio for a weekly talent show in the 1930s. Imagine how hard up people must have been, to listen to tap dancing on the radio.

At camp, when I was eleven, I had taken a workshop with Grisha, so I could fake some of the moves, and once I got going, even after everyone had stopped laughing, after Lily made the winning guess in two seconds, I kept dancing, into the living room—blame it on the wine—and they all followed me, my father doing something like the twist, my mother floating like Isadora Duncan, Elvira snapping her fingers to her own boogie beat, Lily waving her hands over her head. Mrs. Shaw sat at the piano, and for a while we did a sort of free-form square dance to Liza's interpretation of the Madness hit "It Must Be Love." There we were, for ten minutes or so, the Shaws at our best.

When Elvira flopped down into a chair and my father went off to clear the table, my mother suggested I take Lily for a walk around the neighborhood, that we go to the Cafe de Bon Bon up the street for some dessert. I had considered introducing her to the Fireside Bowl, a venue for punk in a working-class Latino neighborhood on the North Side. Bands from all over the country came through hoping for the mostly white crowd to pay attention for at least a song, to spit on them to show their approval, to howl along. But the idea, I reminded myself, was to get Lily to like me some more. I suppose I half wanted to see what it took to rattle her, how deep the veneer of the good girl went. I'm not sure how deep I hoped it went, if I wanted her to be as idealistic as she seemed, if I hoped that there was nothing more complicated in her than a thin dark streak, a shallow streak. It was imbecilic, I knew, to believe in pure goodness.

My mother's proposal that we go to the Cafe de Bon Bon was genteel. Perhaps she envisioned Lily and me sharing a chocolate soda, two straws in the one tall glass. Lily, being either generous or politic, asked Elvira if she wanted to join us. That way, she might have figured, my parents wouldn't suspect that later we were going to go up to the third floor, that pure Lily in her faded jeans and boxy blue sweater was going to first remove her pants and then pull that unisex sweater over her head, that underneath she'd have neither brassiere nor underwear.

Elvira, as it turned out, was going to sleep over at Hilare's house. It was below zero on the plains, and add to the temperature Chicago's famous windchill factor. It was too bitter for a long walk, and as for the Fireside Bowl, that venue was probably best left for another visit. Lily explained to my mother that all of a sudden she was feeling awfully tired, seeing as she'd stayed up most of the previous night in the dorm. She seemed fairly convincing. "Thanks so much for everything," she said for about the eighth time. "Thanks very, very much."

"Make sure Lily has a good towel," my mother called up after us. "Get her a blue set, the ones Minty gave me for Christmas." My grandmother had presented my mother with huge Egyptian cotton towels that were called bath sheets, towels that could be used in times of hardship for winter coats.

When we got to the third floor, I said to Lily, "You can come in my room, but with a condition or two."

"And what might those be?" she said with mock haughtiness.

I told her that I was going to bare my soul to her. "I'm going to bare my soul to you," I said. It was a good sign, I thought, that she laughed, saying, "Your soul?" I explained that I was going to let her peruse my CD collection if she promised not to hold my taste against me. Before I would let her past the door, I said, I wanted her to understand that I did not have any Balkan women singing songs about making hay, there were no Palestrina double choirs, and I did not have *The Fireside Book of Folk Songs* on my shelf, and if that was okay, if it was really okay, she could come in a few steps.

"I don't know," she said. "Do you think I can handle it? Do you think it might be too much for me?" She was whining a little, slinky even in the slight movements of her head and hands. She pressed right against me, pushing me across the threshold. She kissed me and I drew her in, I closed the door. I had thought we might have a preamble, at least until we were sure that my parents were asleep downstairs, but six months is a long time to wait even another forty-five minutes. There was more than a good chance that my father, at nine o'clock, was already in bed, engrossed in his bible, Howard

Zinn's thick history of oppressed peoples. My mother was probably in her on-line home, sending her kisses and hugs through cyberspace, kisses that had to be translated into telephone signals, put into data packets by the TCP, passed by the routers, some of those Xs and Os taking different paths, in order to be reassembled at their destination. A long journey for a couple of scratches, but those were what she trusted the lover man waited for, in front of his screen.

It was deep in the night, after we'd finally fallen asleep for a while, when I woke up, when I leaned over her and said, "Lily." I said it once. I said it as if I'd needed to. It was only after I'd spoken that I realized the history of that smallest of scenes: I was doing something prized that Richard Polloco had done to my mother. Lily had been asleep, but my speaking her name made her lift her head and instantly arch her back. In my memory at least, she is the most responsive person I have ever been with. It was as if my mother had taught me what a woman would like, taught me without my asking, taught me without my permission. I felt dishonest, as if I were pretending to be someone who was not in any way like myself. I was thinking about that a little later, as we lay, our legs twined together, her damp body against mine.

"You're so quiet," she said. "Is something the matter?"

"I was, ah, thinking," I said, truthfully enough.

"What about?"

"Lily," I said, trying out the trick again, whispering in her ear.

"Yeah?"

So much for the name thing being some kind of charm to bypass ordinary communication.

"I want to play you some music." I got up and rummaged around on my desk for a CD, for one song that would explain everything. I cannot recall exactly what it was I put on for her, but it was probably one of Nirvana's sweeter tunes, "Pennyroyal Tea" or "All Apologies." I tried to tell her how I understood the music, that when I listened, I felt a part of the great blackness in the world. I'd never said that out loud to anyone, but when I spoke in my room, in her presence, it seemed true and not at all pretentious. I found something like comfort, I said, even though the band's sensibility might have been suspect. They'd become famous and rich and mainstream, and yet in their own angry way they were still singing about the terrors of alienation and hatred. They were singing about sadness too, and beyond all that, a darkness. I said to Lily that a person could get spooked by the music, down to the bone, and feel alone with the group and feel thrilled by that togetherness. They'd always had an easy entry into the darkness, and sometimes I wasn't sure which was more frightening: the thing itself or the door that was hanging open for them, for all of us, that led to the void.

A woman I went out with once, a hostile type, told me that what she really hated about me was the way I sometimes made her feel when I whispered a secret to her, a tidbit she believed was for her, and only for her. She'd just about give up on me, she'd said, when in my quiet, sincere voice I'd share something private with her. She went so far as to say that I was poison to women. I hadn't been able to think what I'd told her that qualified as a secret, but I did remember back to the feeling I'd had with Lily that night, when I told her about my favorite bands and, later, about my mother. She sat hugging her knees to her chest as I justified my feelings about Kurt Cobain, and I could tell then that it didn't matter so much what I was saying. There was a quality to the moment: the small yellow flickers of the candle by the bed, my voice, her attention, and outside somewhere beyond our light, a void we thought we could imagine.

When I'd finished talking about the music, Lily eased herself back into the bank of pillows. She said that the rage of the groups I listened to did frighten her. She was right to register the fear, I said, even though a lot of the players were junkies who could hardly get out of bed to get to their next gig. Maybe because of their obsessions, they were reliable messengers, fighting their demons, both personal and those that are bred in the society. She nodded, as if she were a student, finally grasping a concept. I loved how she looked, her hair over one shoulder, her easy nakedness, the earnest expression on her beautiful face. She was thinking about what I'd said, and when she'd thought enough, she pulled me to her. She knew what she wanted and I understood what she wanted and I let her lay me down.

After some time had passed, I said that I'd missed her. I strained to say more; I was almost going to say more.

She answered me between her kisses. "Do you think," she said, "I haven't missed you every day?"

"I'm not sure," I said. "I don't know."

"Henry." She drew out my name, Henreeeee. It was as if she, too, were holding her secret near.

It may be because we wanted to whisper about love to each other, but could not yet say the words, that I began, instead, to tell her. There was nothing in the dead of night that seemed wrong about trying to explain. It had been a strange fall, I said, an unusual fall. "My mother," I said, "my mother, these past months, has been having an affair, a real affair, and I found out about it. I'm the only one who knows." Not counting Jane. I did not count beleaguered Jane. It seemed important, in the telling, that I was the single person who knew.

Lily popped up. "What—what did you say? A love affair?"

"It was wrong of me to read her e-mail, but it happened more or less by accident. Even if I hadn't done that, I've seen them together."

There had been a sighting, not a week before. I was certain it was the two of them, at about Lincoln and Fullerton. I was a block behind, but I'd spied them, walking along as if it were their neighborhood. My mother was swinging her bag as she never did in real life, and although they weren't touching, they were walking in sync. If they'd been in a three-legged race, they would have won. Mrs. Shaw, in an e-mail, had told Jane that her body felt different when she was in the presence of Rpoll. Her concept of herself changed the minute his eyes were on her; she had a new shape; she was transformed. And I could see, watching them, that she was right, that her joints were springy. Down the street he and she were talking to each other. He was making small gestures, she larger ones. They stopped to laugh— they couldn't walk and laugh at the same time. She poked him in the ribs, he tweaked her nose, and they moved on. While no one was at home they might have been upstairs in the marriage bed. I could have come upon them in the middle of the day if I'd left school sick. The enraged husband from the past life coming upon the adultery scene.

"Are you sure, Henry?" Lily said. "How do you know?"

"I've read about him, in my mother's messages, but you can tell, you can tell just by looking at them." I wondered if that was true, if anyone seeing them would know.

"Oh!" She was kind enough not to say, "Oh, Henry," which sometimes made the speaker think of the candy bar, so that the subject at hand was temporarily blurred.

"And so I sort of have the file on my mother, and I haven't told anyone, and I haven't been sure what to do with the—information, if you're supposed to do something with that kind of data, anyhow. What does it matter? I keep asking myself if it matters. I'm out of here in a few months, my mother can do whatever she wants. Why should I care?"

"Of course you care."

"When I wrote to you, I wanted to tell you, but—"

"Oh," she said again as she exhaled, as if she were nearly as pained as I had been the first time I'd read the message to Jane. As if the wind were being knocked out of her, and she had just enough air to say, "Oh."

I suppose we choose to tell certain people certain stories based on what we know of them, based on how we figure they'll react, based on the amount of compassion they'll have for our predicament. Lily, I guessed, would have nothing but sympathy for me. She would hold me, hold my head to her small but high and rounded breasts with the pink nipples that were never anything but alert. I told her, as she rocked me, everything that had happened. I told her that my mother took the train up to see Richard Polloco. I told her that he lived in the log cabin, that he made violins, that we'd been to visit him, that Mrs. Shaw regaled us with the Polloco sagas at the dinner table, that there was often a tight-lipped quality about her, as well as a private happiness or amusement or madness that she seemed to think no one else noticed. I said that sometimes her comments were off the wall, and I wondered if she was becoming deranged, if she was having symptoms of early Alzheimer's or just plain dementia.

Lily and I had grown up around musicians who you'd think were more prone to dumping husbands and wives than the average non-musical population, but most of the Silverpines families were intact. We had both been led to believe in a kind of permanence.

"Your father doesn't suspect?" she asked.

"No," I said. "I don't think so."

I remembered a morning a few weeks before when I'd come downstairs to Elvira and my father in the kitchen. He was talking to her in a way that was familiar. "It's the two of us against the world, Elvie," he was saying. "The two of us."

"Yep," she said. She was leafing through one of her catalogs, captivated by everything else she needed to buy in order to complete Elvirnon.

I assumed they were discussing the reenactment life, Elvira and my father with their secret, set against the men. He started when I came full into the room, as if he'd forgotten I lived in the neighborhood. He hadn't slept well, I thought. It annoyed me that he looked terrible, that there was a hole in his right sock, that he put his hand to his hip when he walked from the table to the sink.

"You're battling the world today?" I said.

"Considering it."

"How long you figure it'll take?"

He stood still for a moment, calculating. His eyelids were red and his shoulders were sloping in a manner that did perhaps evoke General Grant after a drinking binge. He'd gone to bed early the night before, as I recalled. My mother was out, and he had fallen asleep in front of an old person's nature program on public television. "It is probably more than a twelve-hour job," he said, "even if we skip lunch."

Elvira demanded to know what we were talking about.

My father left it to me to answer her, to tell her that there was no content to our bantering. Years later I determined that that morning

Kevin had not been discussing reenactment with Elvira, that he was not lending her his support. He was speaking for himself, speaking of his struggle in his own house. How to keep Beth Shaw? While she was off at a concert or a party he must have asked that question into the dark room again and again. The mysterious vibrations I'd sometimes felt may have been pacing down below. Maybe he'd been walking back and forth in his bedroom wondering if he should wait or shout, move to a motel, shake her, give her ultimatums. Should he ignore her, get himself another woman, or should he try, as best he could, for however long it took, to love her, to keep some sort of love shining upon her? In his backward way I'm sure now that he was talking to Elvira that morning because he was trying to think of himself for just a minute as a man who had a team, who had a little help in the job of tackling his particular world.

Up in my attic room that January night Lily asked me if my father suspected, and first I said I didn't think so, and then I said, "No, of course not." I believed it was not in his nature to know. I couldn't imagine the scene in which my mother confessed or my father dragged it out of her or they simply acknowledged what each other knew. I couldn't fathom how they'd go on, how they'd get into bed and wake up the next morning and make coffee and eat their cereal. It wasn't possible for him to know. Skipping ahead, past the idea that he would never find out, I did tell Lily again that if my parents finally split up, I could handle it, especially since I was fleeing the coop. I would be all right, I said, but I didn't understand how my mother could do it to Elvira.

To myself I wondered if Liza imagined how it would be at holidays, when I came home, with just one of them there, my father's things gone, or a space in the living room where the piano had been. Did she think it would be nothing for Elvira and me to make the trek up to Tribbey, to sit around Polloco's cabin drinking tea for the weekend? To sleep in the tree house so the two of them could get it on inside, making pigs of themselves, making their racket? If my parents got divorced, I wouldn't come home anymore; I wouldn't go near where they were. I said so to Lily and the thought of that made her cry.

I held her against my chest and kissed her hair, comforting her this time, for my mother's disobedience. I was grateful to her for feeling it the way she did. In the candlelight, in the middle of the night, I didn't wonder why she wasn't giving me advice or saying much beyond "Oh" and clicking her tongue. As I've said, I've since learned that confiding in women, telling them a choice piece of information, allowing them to be privy to your hurt, is like administering a sure-fire aphrodisiac. I have not always felt the same, and have certainly not always wanted to receive and hold the priceless story of a failed relationship, a gross injustice, the awful childhood, that a woman has been glad enough to foist on me. I'd like to think there are stronger bonds than unhappiness; I'd still like to think that. I said to Lily that there was nothing for me to do but pass the time until I could go to college, get away from whatever future my mother was forging for herself. She cried some more. One of the things I remember about her is how she looked when I stopped kissing her, when she was most ready for me, when she had her head back, her mouth open, her tongue, searching, like some wild hand in the dark. She'd have her eyes closed, waiting for me, waiting for me to come into her. After all this time I can still think of her that way and wonder where she is, and wonder why, why she isn't in the entry ringing the bell to my apartment, why I am not standing below her window, calling up to her.

Before she was awake in the morning, I went downstairs to the bathroom. I wasn't to the second floor when I heard enough noise to understand what was taking place in the kitchen. I went down half a flight farther and stood on the landing.

"Someone else would not have let that happen!" My mother was shouting at my father.

"I'm not responsible for Elvira shaving her head," my father said. "Blame it on Sinéad O'Connor or Michael Jordan. I never encouraged her to stop at the barber."

Finally, two months later, they were going at it over Elvira's hair.

"If you thought about it," my mother cried, "if you actually thought about who Elvira is, you would know that she shaved her head to punish me. She's taking it upon herself to do to me what you have never had the strength to do. She is acting out your wishes. Subconsciously she thinks what she is doing to me is for you."

"I don't know what you're talking about."

"Well, *that's* a surprise! It's time to wake up, wake up! You've never taken a minute to—"

"Beth, Bethy. Elvira is a child. She is not—"

"Elvira isn't a child! She's a savvy adolescent who clearly knows how to drive a wedge between her parents. I'm all in favor of letting children find themselves, but I'm not convinced that Elvira is who you think she is, the tomboy of all time. I think there is a completely different aspect of her personality that you've squelched, just as you've encouraged the other. She has been led astray."

"Led astray?"

"Someone else," my mother said, "would not have let this happen."

Now, if Polloco had been her daddy, Elvira would go to school in strapless evening gowns. She'd undoubtedly be planning her life around the Miss America Pageant.

"We'll never know that," Kevin said slowly. "She is who she is. We'll never know who she would have been if she'd had different parents, a different sibling, if she'd lived in a different place. I don't understand why you keep making that point."

"I make the point," my mother said, pounding on the counter, "because you have the capability still to affect what direction she takes. When she shaved her head, all you said was 'Wow!' That's all you said. When she comes home with tattoos up and down her arms, what then? Will you say, 'Great, Elvie'? You support everything she does. You wait for me to show the disapproval." When he didn't return the volley, she said, in a relatively quiet tone, world-weary as she was, "I'm sick of it. I'm sick of being the heavy hitter. I'm tired of your thinking that everything is always fine."

My parents had perhaps chosen this moment for their blowout because Elvira was gone. Or maybe I was mistaken and there was no choice involved. It happened when it happened. In any case, Elvira had been away for the night and they had a few more free hours to wrangle. It wasn't perfect, fighting when a visitor was upstairs, but Mrs. Shaw had tried so hard to be on her best behavior at home, cooking breakfasts and playing cards with her husband, and she could no longer hold back, no matter who was on hand to listen. It was the same argument they'd had for years, with the addition of the Richard Polloco line: *Someone else would not have let this happen.* She had proof from the man himself, that Elvira would have been a delectable little girl in a flowered dress if she'd been under the proper male influence.

I was sitting on the landing, listening, when Lily came padding downstairs in her bare feet, and otherwise dressed. "What are you doing?" she said, sitting next to me. Before I could answer, she began kissing me. In my life to date I don't think I have been so crazy about kissing anyone as I was on the stairs, kissing Lily, while my parents quarreled in the kitchen.

My mother had revved back up and was yelling. "You've allowed Elvira to perpetuate a lie. You're the one who encouraged her to do the reenacting. It's nothing but a lie!" In the middle of her own tirade she lowered her voice and said, "Oh God, I wonder if the lovebirds can hear us." Although she spoke softly, the sentence was distinct. *I wonder if the lovebirds can hear us.*

Good old Kevin Shaw said, "Who?"

"Jesus," my mother muttered, "you are so thick."

I was engaged in the make-out session and was not paying strict attention. I heard the word "lovebirds," but the sound of the various letters did not have meaning to me at that moment. For one thing, I was at the ready again—where, I was thinking, did all that gung-ho up-and-at-'em come from? A big thank-you, I wanted to say, to who-ever was responsible—Mom, Dad, the city water commissioner, the great ape.

Kiss, kiss, irrepressible moan, stroke, stroke, all the while my mother holding forth. "I'm serious, I am dead serious about this, Kevin. How do you think those boys are going to feel when they find out that all these years they have been confiding, talking smart, talking big, all these years, to a girl? A girl! Have you ever considered their feelings? I don't even want to think about what the men in those groups would do, those burly hard-drinking men. But I know that the boys have trusted Elvira, and they're going to feel hurt and ashamed and silly and embarrassed and betrayed."

In his regular way my father said, "A good training for what future women will do to them."

At that one I pulled away from Lily. What had he said?

"A good training for what future women will do to them?" Liza38 repeated it about twenty decibels louder, reversing the principle of the echo. And again, louder still, "A good training for what future women will do to them?" She threw down a saucepan. "Oh for God's sake, you're impossible." She whacked another pan on the counter and came flying from the kitchen. Lily and I sprang up, grabbed our undone clothing to ourselves, and ran as fast as we could back to my bedroom, where we stood against the closed door, breathing hard and laughing. "A good training for what future women will do to them," I said, and we roared and we howled and we fell on the floor shaking with the drollness of that sentence.

Later, when we went down to breakfast, the Shaws were back in the kitchen, moving around each other as if nothing had happened. My father greeted us cheerfully. It was my mother who asked if Lily had slept well. "Were you comfortable in the attic, Lily? Not too hot, not too cold?"

It came to me then, her musing earlier to her husband. *I wonder if the lovebirds can hear us.* She was offering up her very own prize-winning pancakes. She'd won a blue ribbon for them at the county fair in Vermont, and she was flipping them onto Lily's plate as if it were a universal truth that the way to a girl's heart is through her stomach via the boyfriend's mother. In general I am not a believer in epiphanies, I guess because I rarely have them, or if I do, they are usually not reliable. But just then I had a ping. Ping! A measure of clarity, an epiphanette. The details all added up. My mother had given Elvira's room to Lily. She had served wine and also arranged for Elvira to be out of the house. There was the remark about the lovebirds, and that smile of hers and the comment about hot and cold. My mother may or may not have known about our summer romance, but one thing was certain: she had meant for us to come together in the night.

"Pancakes, honey?" Mrs. Shaw said to me.

She had planned it, that Lily and I get together. She had gone so far as to play "It Must Be Love" on the piano for the Shaw family hoedown. I tried to look at her, to glare, to glare evilly, so she'd understand that if she called me honey again, I might have to kill her. It had been her plan. What was worse, I wondered, that it was her plan or that without knowing I had followed her plan?

"I have to go all the way to Montpelier for the Balkan choir," Lily was saying.

"Who's directing this year? Two or three, Henry?"

"Gillian Ryan. She took it over from Mary Brant. Her voice is incredible and she's very tough. Some of the girls have complained about her, but no one has dropped out."

Although I had not responded, my mother had put a stack of pancakes on my plate. She might have had any number of reasons for thinking she should assist me. Number one: Henry's so uptight, he needs to get laid. Number two: Henry sticks his nose into my business so much, what he needs is a squeeze of his own. Number three: better sic a sex bomb on Henry before he becomes a women's studies pansy boy.

"That's a testimonial to Gillian," my mother said.

They were talking as if they were old friends, Lily and Liza38. There, at breakfast, Lily was telling my mother about the music in her life, the Bach she'd sung in Brattleboro, the Balkan music in Montpelier, the quartet in Hanover. Not an hour before, Lily and I had been kissing on the landing, complete, I thought, in our understanding. I left the pancakes on my plate and went to the cupboard to get the box of Frosted Flakes. The two of them were utterly absorbed, talking about singing in half-step harmonies. Kevin was reading the editorial page of the newspaper and periodically snorting. What I'd done in the night is offer up to Lily classified information. I had given the files directly into the hands not only of a stranger but of someone who might be my mother's spy. While Lily and I were hiding in my room, everything had turned upside down: Kevin and Beth Shaw had reunited in the kitchen, and Lily, somehow, had gone over to the other side. It was I who had been forced out. *Pancakes, honey?*, my ass. It was difficult to say, between the three of them, whom I disliked the most. First, Kevin, for nothing in particular if you don't count his passivity. Second, Beth Shaw, for so many reasons I could not enumerate them. And last, Lily. What had my mother said to my father about Elvira's eventual coming out to her reenactment friends? "I know the boys have trusted Elvira, and they're going to feel hurt and ashamed and silly and embarrassed and betrayed." To which my father had so wisely remarked, "A good training for what future women will do to them."

After breakfast Lily and I walked up the few blocks to Walgreens for some toiletries she needed, something unspecified and no doubt feminine. Out of all the people in the neighborhood, there was my chum walking along Clark Street, wearing her black cape, black beret, and her good old Mary Janes. On one arm she had a tiger fur muff, a ratty thing she'd found at a vintage clothing store. "Hank," she called in a register that was higher than usual. Karen was the only person who called me Hank, a privilege she had granted herself. When she got close, she stuck her hand out to light, dew, and a gust of wind. "Hi," she said. "You must be Lily."

Lily giggled, an idiotic, empty-headed girl giggle.

"You're just how I pictured you," Karen said. She was not without malice, my chum wasn't. I hated her too. I hated her for being the only girl I could fall back on. I hated that she understood Lily's essential nature. In addition, I hated her theatrical getup. She looked big and manly and impressed with herself. She looked like Gertrude Stein. Most of all, I hated her for calling me Hank, for claiming me in that simple and powerful way. "Where are you off to?" she said.

I looked past her, to the drugstore. "The University of Chicago."

"Really?" Shouldn't Lily, she meant, be focusing on the junior college in the state of her birth?

"Really," I said, moving on.

"Nice to meet you," Lily called over her shoulder. To me, a few steps farther along, she said, "Does your friend always dress like that?"

"Like what?" I said.

In the day we spent together, walking around Hyde Park, we could have been strangers who happened to be on the same pavement, going to the same places. How was it that we had been joined in the night and could not carry on a conversation in the daylight? We kept bumping into each other, or I'd stop and look and she was five paces ahead.

"Are you okay?" she asked once.

She didn't mention my mother or the situation, although she did tell me the tales of two friends of hers whose parents had split up. It turned out I knew one of the girls, Heather Wood. Her mother was certifiably insane. Mrs. Wood had been institutionalized for three years before the husband finally gave up and sued for divorce. I didn't think that the Heather Wood story was exactly comparable.

At the U of C Lily had a meeting with a man in admissions and we had a tour of the campus. It would have been good of her to apologize for schmoozing with my mother, any excuse would have done, for her going into the enemy camp. Some few lines I could believe. In the night she'd said very little, her thin "Oh!" I had told her what I shouldn't, and she had pretty much disregarded the story or used it in the wrong way—I wasn't sure which. The telling had ruined what small right thing there was between us. By candlelight, in bed, our great strength, it had seemed, had been my trouble and her sympathy. But it was after all nothing.

The end came quickly. There was traffic, we had to rush, and so there wasn't time, at Midway Airport, to go in with her, to wait at the gate. She kissed me on the cheek, climbed out of the car, got her bag, and was gone, running, inside the terminal. I was rid of her, and rid, too, of all the feeling I had garnered for so many months. Funny, that there was a great peace in the emptiness, surely something Polloco felt after a visit from my mother.

It took me about four days to recover from Lily's stay, to recover, that is, from being blank, from feeling nothing for her. For two days or so I was free of her, but on the third day I began to miss her. Not her, exactly, no, not the girl, but the old feelings I had for her, the desire for her, the desire that belonged to me. I started to remember how she'd pitch herself into me, how she could kiss me in about the same place on my mouth and each time it would be different, a slightly different kind of kiss. Sometimes I had what amounted to tender feelings for her because she looked like such a fragile girl and at the same time she seemed to like a little roughness, what experience had probably taught her. I didn't let myself imagine that experience, didn't want to know about any of it. She had asked me to drive into her up in my room, and when I did, she cried to herself, as if she were hurt. I'd asked her if she was sure, and the asking made her grab hold of my arms and thrust herself at me. She would do the work, I gathered, if I wasn't going to try to please her. Her lust and the hurt, all mixed up, kept coming back to me. I'd get to thinking about her need, the mystery of it, and there I was back to my pre-visit state of hope and expectation and impatience.

I got so I could easily fantasize about her without remembering how much I'd disliked her. Even after the rumor mill had swung into gear, I still had trouble listing the reasons I should no longer dream about her. It was in the week after she left that I got a message from a friend of hers, Gretchen, a girl I hadn't seen in a few years. She had been a Silverpines camper too, of the long-braid variety, homespun parents, flossy skirts, hand-knitted socks, and a repertoire of Victorian parlor games. "How *are* you?" she wrote, as if we were pals who had been separated for a couple of interminable days.

Lily. It was Lily's gossip, I thought so right away. Possibly I was paranoid, maybe I was psychotic, or maybe every single fear was justified. So what if Gretchen had occasionally e-mailed me out of the blue? This time was different; this time she *knew* because Lily had told her about my mother and Richard Polloco. The news was streaming out and out, as far away as Hanover, New Hampshire, and farther east, in Salisbury. How long before Lily's mother knew about Richard Polloco and then how quickly the musicians on the eastern seaboard would hear about the affair, and after that, how many days before my father got wind of it? Everyone would know, and all of us, except bald Elvira, would suffer shame. I could already imagine the shape of that feeling, the weaselly thing I'd have to beat back just to walk down the street in the morning.

As I sat in the office sentencing myself to future humiliation, I thought that I could hardly blame Lily for my mother's fuckup. In the end it wasn't her fault that the world knew about Polloco. There was no point in blaming the messenger. The best I could do, I thought, was quit Roslyn Place, never to return, when I went to college. My parents, if they were together, could leave messages on my answering machine. They could stay in a motel and arrange, if they could get ahold of me, to have dinner at a restaurant. I might in the summer, for a week here and there, go with my father on camping trips, but I'd make him understand that we weren't to talk about any event that happened after 1865.

I was planning to write Gretchen, but before I did I went down to the kitchen to get something to eat. My mother was sitting at the table with Marcia and another book club member, Barbara, and also Glamorous Pam. They were socializing outside of the strictures of the book club, something that was probably illegal under the by-laws. Since Marcia had gotten pregnant, she'd become more chummy with people like my mother, experts in the child-farming line of work. Hilare, talking in her stage voice about brands of English muffins, one of which she had in her hand, and Elvira, listening to her every word, were just going into the pantry, where the toaster was kept.

Marcia was even larger than she'd been at the December meeting. I don't know if she'd ever been married, but I liked to think that years before she'd been a wife, that the bedeviled Mr. Butler had woken one morning, come to his senses, and walked out, for good. The four women must have been on their usual topic because as I came into the room I heard my mother say, "Why am I leaving my husband? I'm leaving him because I beat him!"

Around the table they screamed with laughter.

"I mean, the shit out of him," she added, as if clarification were necessary. She said that line quietly, so the young things in the pantry wouldn't hear.

I stepped back and started to walk the other way, toward the stairs. That's what I meant to do, what I thought I was doing. I found myself, instead, in the kitchen, standing in the doorway, the sweep of the room before me, the women drinking their tea, the girls behind the pantry wall. Marcia's stomach was keeping her an arm's length from the table, and therefore she had blueberry muffin crumbs down her gigantic sweater, the kind of mess that on her future child would drive her over the bend. All of it, present and future, were not images the artificially inseminated head of the English Department would have liked us to entertain.

What nonsense was coming out of my mouth? I was staring at Marcia's fat middle, and I was quoting a study, something I must have fabricated, because I certainly didn't read the *New England Journal of Medicine*. As for newspapers, I read the movie reviews in the *Reader* and nothing more. "When you gain over forty pounds in your pregnancy," I was saying, "there is an 85 percent chance that your child will have a cleft palate."

I already knew Marcia had gained forty-five pounds: what person in Chicago didn't know that statistic?

I swear I might have done something cinematic and Italian, might have, with my bare forearms, cleared off the counter, knocked everything, Cuisinart, cutting board, knives in the wooden block, dishes— all of it to the floor. Right when I was about to do that, who should come around the corner from the pantry but Hilare. She was passing her hot English muffin from hand to hand. She started talking as if all along she'd been in the conversation. "I know someone who had a baby," she said, "with that turkey baster thing? It got screwed up, though, because she got the wrong glop out of the bank, you know, where you choose the dad, and instead of this genius scientist she thought was the father, it turned out to be this really creepy guy who'd killed a couple of people. So she was stuck with a criminal baby, a psychopath baby."

We were all gaping at Hilare—everyone, that is, except Elvira, who continued on buttering her muffin at the counter as if nothing untoward were happening. "Cool," she said. "That's way cool."

"They didn't figure it out until the kid was in preschool. He took a knife from the kitchen and starting chopping off a girl's fing—"

"That's enough, young lady," my mother cried.

I loved that, young lady, how antique it sounded. My mother had risen up from the table. "You have been rude so many times." She was shouting at Hilare, shouting through her gritted teeth, so that her voice had a guttural roar. "So many times. I don't know if anyone, anywhere, has ever informed you that you are not the center of the univer—"

"Waidaminute. Waidaminute." Ah, Hilare, *ma chérie*. The infant phenomenon had her hands on her hips, her feet far apart, and she was projecting, projecting just fine. "You guys are in here talking about beating your husbands, like we can't hear what you're saying. That's so nice, talking about beating the—*beep*—out of your husbands, and I'm just reporting a fact about a baby, something I thought you'd find interesting, considering, you know, that your friend here is storked."

"Storked," I believe I repeated out loud.

My mother was quivering, trying to get beyond the chair so she could do whatever violent thing she would naturally do without first thinking. She had not ever spanked us, but she had been known once or twice to grip Elvira by the shoulders and shake vigorously. There have got to be times for chivalry, occasionally, in our age, and it seemed to me in the moment that if I had any gallantry at all within myself, I should try to use a little of it. Hilare, after all, had done a noble thing, even if it was unwitting. She had burst into the fray and she had done so with perfect timing.

I stepped between my mother and the future debate team captain, and looking at old Liza38, I said, "You ought to be ashamed of yourself." Wheeeee! I'm only about a foot taller than my mother, tall enough certainly to be her elder. I can't tell you how exhilarated I felt, saying that to her. *You ought to be ashamed of yourself.* I wanted to say it again, out loud, but I knew that repeating a good line spoils the punch. I was nodding my head, though, pursing my lips—I couldn't help it—I was gassed! I was hum, hummy!

She was caught. Caught by her perfectly amiable son, the family breeder, the one she was someday going to be proud of. If she had been innocent, she would never have hit me. As she was not innocent, she reached up and with her strong pianist's hand she slapped me. One firm stroke across my cheek. Whop. It had the dull thud of a bird striking a window. It surprised me and also it hurt. One motion of her hand across my cheek—you are guilty, so guilty, Elizabeth Gardener Shaw.

I have sometimes wondered what kind of hero a person can be in our time. As a boy, in Vermont, I used to imagine that I was running courageously down the slope, flag in hand, dodging the bullets, making it safely through the ranks, to our side, the right side. It seems almost impossible to take moral action these days except, for what it's worth, in small and private ways. Even recycling, however, no longer has the thrill it used to when it was a new imperative. At any rate, that afternoon in our kitchen, my mother, I think, saw in me a dignity she had hoped I possessed, although she'd never dreamed she'd be battling against it. She had slapped me. In front of Marcia, the perfect mother-to-be, she had whacked her son. In the stillness right afterward, her hand in the air, she did not look horrified. She did not look contrite. She was defiant, I could see, itching for more of a fight.

The left side of my face stung, but I did not touch it. I didn't change my expression, didn't reprove her or let her know right off that something between us was damaged. I understood that instantly, before she did. I looked down at her from my paternal height without blinking. Let the sense of what had happened come to her slowly. *You have hurt yourself more than you have hurt me. Young lady.* It was really a very prissy moment, I admit it. There is a fine line between dignity and prissiness, and it's true that I probably crossed over it for just a minute. Before I ruined the scene, I turned to Elvira and Hilare and said, "Come on, girls."

They followed me as if I were the Pied Piper, into the hall, where in record time we put on our coats, slammed the door, got away. They were right behind me, looking up at me, not watching where they were going, tripping over the cracks on the sidewalks. They were in awe of me, the victim, the hero, the scolder, the everything all wrapped up in one older brother. It's doubtful I'll ever be in a position of such valor again. I owe that moment to Hilare. She was a great and terrible punk of a kid, and I hoped I'd never see her on any other occasion. But for that afternoon I could treat her like a princess, give her the thanks she deserved. We went into the snowy park, and I chased the two of them, as if they were three-year-olds and I the favorite uncle. I gave them a long time to run, and when I caught them, I pushed them into the bank and mashed just a little bit of snow into their faces. They screamed and ganged up on me, gave me the business. We would have gotten cold if we had not been fueled by so much righteous indignation. I considered finding some pot and teaching them to smoke, coming back to Liza laughing our frozen heads off. Of course, it was entirely possible that Hilare knew more about where to get the good stuff than I did, that she was already on to meth and heroin.

They were too old for ice cream, too old to acknowledge it as a treat, and in any case it was the wrong season. And so we acted as if going for coffee were something we did every day. Elvira didn't say much, but when she did speak, she referred to me in the third person. My brother does this, my brother does that. It is a sad thing, no doubt, that that afternoon is so far one of the high points, if not the highest point, of my life.

What was going to happen next? That enormous age-old question. My mother would rap on the door in the night and ask to have a talk with me. She'd demand that I apologize to Marcia. Or she'd be so overcome with guilt, because of both her transgression and the slap, that she'd prostrate herself before me. I was mildly curious about her next step, but not so eager that I headed straight for the kitchen when I got home, to find her. I went upstairs, trashed the message from Lily's friend Gretchen, the one in which she said, "How *are* you?" What she really meant was, I know about your problems—tell me about them—and your mom! I disposed of the communication. I checked my mother's file but there was nothing new. She had not yet confided in her loved ones about her freshest sin. I went downstairs, found the note on the kitchen table from Mrs. Shaw reminding us that she had a rehearsal and would be gone and that my father had a meeting. There was meat loaf, she said, in the refrigerator. Before I swiped a bottle of wine from the pantry and took it up to my room, I practiced the cello for ten minutes. I would read my history assignment, and while I waited for the next big scene, I'd drink myself into a stupor. I was sure that something would happen, that before the night was over I would hear from Mrs. Shaw. Perhaps I'd get a memo from her. Perhaps from this time forward we would speak to one another only through e-mails, inhabiting that disembodied, airy, floating space she so loved.

At one point, while I was trying to read an essay about Chairman Mao, Elvira came into my room. She stood around, she went to my shelf, she pulled out a CD; she sat on my bed, yanked the shade up, and looked down at the street. She did not notice the wine bottle, that it was nearly empty. "Hey," she said at last.

"Hey."

"So, why did Mom, like, slap you?"

I continued to read as I said, "Because she's having sex with Richard Polloco."

"Ick! God, Henry—gag me! You are so disgusting." Without asking for more information or verification she pounded off to her room making retching noises.

I noted that I seemed to have lost control over myself, that I was the last person to know what was going to come out of my mouth. "Oh well," I said. Elvira had plenty of armor to shield herself from what she considered unpleasant. She didn't like something, she shaved it off, she spat it out, she marched on ahead. She'd probably wallop all of us in the end.

The next day I went to school without stopping for breakfast. I wondered how long I could go without seeing Mrs. Shaw. If I planned carefully, I could live in the house for weeks and never bump into her. Maybe my father kept himself busy for a reason, so he never had to spend much time around her. Maybe she wasn't kidding and she actually did beat the shit out of him when they were alone. Smack across the cheek, smack, and a sock in the gut. Anything, all of it, was possible.

When I got home in the evening, my mother was again away, that time teaching a workshop on improvisation at the Old Town School of Music. So she said in her note. The awful thing about this life, of course, is that often when you expect something to happen, nothing does. In her absence Elvira and I had dinner with my father. It was a quiet meal, and after Elvie disappeared, Kevin and I stayed on, talking in a desultory fashion. I admit that I probably didn't pay as much attention to him as I might have, under the circumstances. The few occasions I had checked I'd found nothing of interest in his e-mail correspondence with his fellow historians and reenactors. He was not really the one I wanted to see over dinner; the substitute he was, the stand-in. But after all, he may have been thinking the same of me. Liza38 had said in a very short message to Jane that deep down, beyond his fun-loving aspect, my father was stoic, that his Norwegian mother had given him more than enough of her stolid Scandinavian genes. The two pen pals must have had a phone conversation right before that message, because Liza had said only a sentence about my father's temperament, an afterthought to the conversation it must have been, a footnote. Perhaps she'd been explaining away her husband, telling her friend that he was a natural when it came to endurance. If I'd thought more about him then, I might have sensed that Kevin Shaw's enthusiasm was at a low ebb.

"So, Henry," he said, "what are your plans?"

"You mean for tonight or for the rest of my life?"

"Either one," he said. "Both."

"Let's see," I said. "Um. Have a fulfilling career that pays me the fantastic sum I'm worth, meet the girl of my dreams who coincidentally thinks I'm the man of her dreams, and eradicate terrorist groups by teaching them about sing-alongs—is that what you mean, what you had in mind?"

He frowned, nodding. "That sounds pretty good. Just make sure the dream girl doesn't think you're going to solve her problems. There's a lot of pressure on us, to save the day, to be something more than we are. I'm afraid the idea of courtly love is still alive and well after eight centuries. It's best if both parties understand at the start that you're going to be two flawed people stumbling along through the years, making it up as you go."

What did he know about Lily? Why was he telling me this? "I haven't met her yet," I lied, "so I'm not too concerned about it."

"It'll be interesting," he said, closing his eyes and slumping a bit so he could rest his head on the back of the chair.

"I've learned a lot about women from the book club," I tried to say jauntily. "Especially from the brain of the organization, the man-hater."

He did smile at the smear, without opening his eyes. "It's tempting to make fun of just about everything, but you want to remember that occasionally life can get fairly serious."

I couldn't believe that he was telling me about the graveness of life, me, the heavyweight champion of depressed teenagehood. And did he actually think that Mrs. Shaw's book club meetings were important summits on the female seat of thought? I knew I should have asked him if he was all right, if he needed some booze or a piece of chocolate. There was Alfredo sauce in his beard, that hairy trap that was sometimes nauseating to look at. Later, by a few years, I regretted that I'd missed an opportunity to hear what he'd learned from two decades of marriage. In the moment I wanted to get out of there, to leave him to lecture himself in his sleep. It used to be that he would play chess to amuse me, to keep me from loneliness after the move from Vermont. We hadn't played in a while, and I did realize, as I asked him if he'd like a game, that I was taking on the possibly long-term job of keeping him busy while we waited. To my relief he said that he had exams to grade, he was hoping for an early night, he'd take a rain check.

As for the other one, it wasn't until the following afternoon that I passed her on the stairs.

"Henry," Mrs. Shaw said, "how are you? I haven't seen you in days."

Forty-eight hours, I could have told her.

"How are you?" she inquired once again.

"Fine."

She began to prattle on about her rehearsals and the workshop she'd conducted and had I gotten enough to eat, had I taken the check for my cello lesson? It was as if, for her, that *thing*—the troubling episode—had occurred long ago. It was one of those bad little moments, probably larger, she thought, in her mind than in anyone else's. Didn't she often make such mountains out of molehills, wasn't she so hard on herself, didn't every parent lose it now and again? I backed away from her, and probably gave her a cold look, so as to refresh her memory.

Chapter Twelve

As the air slowly warmed and the snow grew dirtier, my father and Elvira did their brushing up inside, making their preparations to go to Shiloh, to the National Military Park in Tennessee. They set out the troops on the Ping-Pong table, moving them around, step by step, standing on stools to get an overview or crouching to look the soldiers in their plastic eyes. I had long since given up playing Ping-Pong at home because the table was covered with miniature Styrofoam and twig forests, clay bluffs and Reynolds Wrap ponds. The Tennessee River and Lick Creek went snaking under the net.

The winter was passing, and that April weekend of slaughter and mutilation was going to be upon our family before we knew it. Father and daughter were dedicating themselves to the part of the battlefield called the Hornets' Nest. From photographs, from correspondence with the park historian, from primary source materials and maps, my father was coming to the conclusion that what took place at the Hornets' Nest was not the turning point of the battle after all. At Jesse Layton he had molded several of his students into physical anthropologists. He'd brought them to the basement display at our house to discuss the topography of Shiloh, where the burial trenches were, what the place had looked like without foliage, as it was a late spring in 1862, and what effect the livestock would have had on the undergrowth. That kind of information, crucial information, determined the sort of weapons the soldiers used in what spot and how many died in which place.

My father seemed to be distracted by the scene in a thicket that had occurred over a hundred years earlier in Tennessee, so distracted he couldn't worry about the maneuvers of his wife. To the onlooker his inattention was spectacular. Even without giving up my day job I believe I had noticed that she no longer practiced the way she used to all the years before the advent of Polloco. She'd sit down at the piano, she'd flip through the music, work on a phrase for a while, and wander off into the kitchen. If I hadn't known better, I'd have said that the music didn't matter to her anymore. Perhaps she'd found an activity that was more fulfilling. All her life she'd been putting in her time playing the piano, waiting, I guess, waiting for the real thing, the truest thing, maybe it was, that had been obscure until Polloco came along. Still, there was a long day to fill up, and what was a person to do except sit at the piano going through the motions? It was also probably difficult, if not impossible, to concentrate when she was so often breaking up with the boyfriend.

A few years ago, when I was in film school, I did an assignment that incorporated all of the Dear John messages from the file, so many of them cliff-hangers. Around my apartment I hung up the four or five or six messages that came as a package with every rupture. Usually it went something like this: there was the initiation of the idea by one party, the please don't in response, the insistence that it had to be, the grudging and tearful agreement by the other, followed by the initiator taking it all back. There were nine major crises, a total of forty-six messages in the breakup category. For my project I hung the first two series in the bedroom. I had four of the ardent letters over my bed, the two big weeper letters tacked upside down over the mirror, the comeback-kid letters by the heat register. There was a different set in the kitchen and in the bathroom, the next three in the living room, and the last on the porch. I'd gone to great lengths to procure an Exit sign, under which I'd taped the last message, for the final shot. We were supposed to do a personal-type narrative for the assignment. Karen was visiting, and it was she who held the camera. I'm going around the house reading the messages out loud, shuffling from display to display in my ratty slippers. The camera slides in and out of focus, that kind of thing. It's hard to say exactly what group is my favorite, but if I had to choose, if I *had* to, I'd probably take the number five breakup, the briefest exchange of the lot.

"Dear Richard," she writes, getting the ball rolling:

> I can't leave my family. I can't expect you to wait around until the children are grown, and even though I know you must, I can't, CAN NOT, stand the thought of your taking up with someone else. I am wretched. Do not write me again.

Whenever she ordered him away, he always came back to her, his vigor redoubled.

> Dear Liza,
> Who, then, am I supposed to write? I'm supposed to invite the girls in the neighborhood in, those with the good-size chompers and the long legs? Is that what I'm supposed to do? None of them will be able to bang out a tune like you, none of them will turn "Row Row Row Your Boat" into a forty-minute fugue. I'll try out my jokes, the bread box line, and get nothing but vacant stares. Is that what you ask of me? Miss Van Heusen wonders where you are, this of course is the sign that you must stay with me even with all the afflictions I bring you. If I do not write to you I will write to no one, and if I write to no one then you see I write to no one. It is a very sorry state of affairs when there is no one on the other end. If a man pens a letter in the forest and no one reads it, has he written it?

What else could a woman do but respond as Liza did?

> Dear R.,
> Yes, in the forest, yes, he has written it, I love you, write me, write me.

Karen thought that the final product for my class was a little myopic, as did my professor. "What's wrong with this kid?" he asked me, as if I were not the star of the film, as if I were a character who had no relation to myself. "Why is he so stuck?"

That winter of Polloco, in Chicago, I sometimes thought back to the day when my mother slapped me, and if I felt an incipient sense of shame, I quickly did my best to quell it. I'd remind myself that it was her shame and that I did not ever have to absolve her of it. At dinner, in the weeks after the slap, my mother was watching me. Maybe she was thinking, as was I, that with her slap she was settling an old score, something from long before, from the time of our fabled marriage. With so much stealthy observation going on, our present-day meals were strange affairs. We sat, my mother and I, with the family, and the slap was there too, as if it occupied a place at the table. It was there whenever we asked each other to pass the salt and the butter. It was there between us, so that we could not look each other in the eye. I sometimes tried to consider what it was that I had done in my past life, what could have provoked her to hit me. There were the standard offenses: I might have cheated on her, or belittled her in front of the relatives, or come home late, drunk, and without the groceries.

One night, eating the enchiladas my mother had made, I thought to wonder if she'd been the man and I the woman in our marriage alliance. Shirana had not mentioned who was what. Maybe Beth Shaw had beat me, beat the crap out of me, as a matter of course, just because. Maybe she was a puny, hairy-chested guy and I was a tall, slim woman, and every night she'd come home and wallop me. In our kitchen in Chicago she'd probably slapped me for the old reasons. For my insatiable curiosity. To keep me in place. To stop me from getting uppity.

After we finished the enchiladas, Elvira disappeared, my father got to work in the office, and as I was scraping the last of the ice cream from the carton, I could tell she was about to start in; she was about to mention the slap to me. She was standing at the sink, taking a breath and another. She was building up to it, gathering her nerve. "Henry," she said.

"Mrs. Shaw."

"What's been going on with you lately? You seem distant."

"Distant."

"You never look up anymore. You slink in here, you eat, you slink away. You don't exactly seem like your old self."

I was going to ask her if any of us seemed like our old selves, with the exception of Kevin. He was pretty much always his old self. Instead I said, "I am waiting for spring." And then, "Oh wow, I'm having a déjà vu, you, me, in a kitchen, having this conversation, only it feels so—so ancient. I'm wearing armor, you're working at a tapestry, it's like I've just come back from the Crusades or something." I shook my head, flapped my arms, said, "Brrrrrrrrrr."

"What?" she said. "What?"

"Whoa, that was spooky, really spooky." I left the room, left her standing at the sink, alone with herself, in the company of her own hard hand and whatever past she wanted to conjure.

During the course of the meal that winter it was not unusual for Elvira to haul down one of the volumes of *The Official Records of the Union and Confederate Armies*. It was Minty who had given my father the *O.R.*, all 128 leather-bound books. If love can be bought, then it is safe to say that those books secured my father's affection for his mother-in-law. Elvira, who did not want to part with the sanctioned version of what took place in the Hornets' Nest at Shiloh, was often citing a reference to prove that the butchering she believed in had most certainly taken place in that sacred spot. My father's intention to revise that history had become more intense as the visit to Shiloh drew near, and the two of them seemed able to speak of nothing else.

"But, Elvira," my father might say, "the park ranger, the guy who gave me the idea originally, the man who's there every single day, studying the grounds, made a great point in his last letter. Think about it again. The veterans who fought at the Hornets' Nest were isolated from the rest of the battle, and after the war wouldn't it have made them feel good and proud to imagine that it was in fact they who made a difference, they who not only experienced glory but were the glory?"

"Dad, Dad," Elvira said, "listen up. You've got the 8th, 7th, and 58th Illinois under Sweeny, right? North of the Corinth Road—okay, okay, wait, I want to get back to the detail of the bayonets. The thickets were impenetrable, like you say, and there were what, eleven to fourteen near-suicide charges—"

As was customary at our dinner table, there were often at least two conversations going, one of them swirling around the other. I had mentioned to my mother that at Youth Symphony we had had to audition for our chairs in front of a crowd of people. "I think you should talk to the conductor," Mrs. Shaw was saying to me. "It's not right, that you have to do those challenges in public. How many people were watching the rehearsal? Richard, you know, Polloco, has terrible stories about challenges when he played in the Youth Symphony. I wonder why they can't get a conductor in there with a little compassion."

"He played in the Youth Symphony?" my father said.

"Dad! I'm trying to explain why I think your bayonet theory is incorrect!"

"Concertmaster," my mother said.

My father raised his eyebrows and frowned in an exaggerated way, a la-di-da, bully-for-him kind of look. To Elvira he said, "Tell me again your estimate of the casualties. Let's start from there."

"Thanks for dinner," I said, slinking out of the room. Shirana, when is spring going to come? Lily, where are you? God, help me to escape this never-ending epic recital of events long past and of no consequence.

I had written to Lily, as witty a letter as I could write, about the scene in our kitchen with Hilare and Marcia, minus the slap. She had written me back, and all of a sudden we were off and running, writing old-fashioned letters nearly every day. Her parents had no computer at home, and so we couldn't write obsessively, minute by minute. I did, however, put what I'd learned about epistolary court-ship to good use. "Hello," I wrote, "my Himalayan goat, my hand-painted egg, my winter thaw, my catalog of all natural products, my organic fig juice in recyclable bottles." I did the best I could, al-though of course I was nowhere close to the brilliance of the master. Still, my letters served their purpose. Lily and I, both of us, were soon reduced to that old longing. We never talked about my mother in our correspondence. There was no need to bring up her worn story of desire when we had our own.

When my parents fought, that morning Lily visited, my mother had insisted to Kevin that Elvira tell the boys in her reenactment unit that she was a girl. Liza, in her screwily sanctimonious speech, had made the point to my father that Elvira was as good as lying, she was be-traying the boys, and it wasn't fair to them. This issue did not go away after my parents had made up, or whatever it was they had done. At another dinner, when Elvira was at volleyball practice, my mother again brought up the subject. Kevin listened, nodded, strok-ing his beard in a meditative way. As my mother finished her pitch, he pushed back his chair and went into the dining room. We heard him rooting around in there, at the grandfather's rolltop desk. When he returned, he had his quill and his bottle of ink and a sheet of paper.

"All right," he said, arranging the supplies. He sat down, twisted off the cap of the bottle, and dipped his quill in the ink slowly, tap-ping it on the rim in his fussy way. He spoke to himself as he wrote, and although we were watching him, he acted as if he were alone. He began with "Dear Mrs. Shaw." I'm not sure what we thought we were witnessing, but my mother and I sat there anyway, helplessly. "Dear Mrs. Shaw," he repeated. His writing was both elaborate and tight, the studied cursive of an educated Union soldier, a doctor, in fact.

A matter has come to my attention that has given me much cause for vexation. At present, I have under my care, in the hospital in Savannah, Tennessee, a young soldier, a one Elvirnon Shaw, a lad who fought most bravely near a church named Shiloh. Elvirnon received a bullet wound in the shoulder after a valiant assault, and only after he assisted an officer to safety did he heed the pain of his own wound, only then, madam, did his strength fail him.

Let me make haste to the conclusion of my epistle—

"Can't you just say letter?" my mother said.

Let me make haste to the conclusion of this letter. It has come to my attention that courageous Elvirnon is, dear Mrs. Shaw, none other, I believe, than your own daughter! It is my heartfelt wish to obscure her true identity, to keep her from harm's way, and to afford safe passage back to your loving care, where she may heal her body and her spirit, where she may take comfort in her heroic part in our nation's great and terrible conflict, where she may take her proper place in the bosom of her family as she prepares for the adventure of her adult life.

I await your reply.

I am, your faithful servant,

Doctor K. Shawlin

"There," he said, blowing on it. "I should scorch it around the edges—"

"Shawlin?" I said.

"And just what is the point?" My mother asked this, not unkindly.

"Well, the point. We could send it to you right after Shiloh, and at the next reenactment, the one in Decatur, we'll show it to Al. That would be good, for Al to know first. We'll stagger it, choose a few more to tell, let it spread through the regiments. They'll come to understand legitimately, in a mode that goes along with the game of it."

"Elvira is going to love this plan," I said.

"It will take her some getting used to," my father agreed. "Ultimately she'll have to come up with a different way to participate. I suppose 'coming out,' as it were, will take a good part of the thrill away."

"The thrill of deception," I ventured.

"It has to end sometime," my mother said, firmly, knowledgeably.

I wonder if it's better to know when a thing starts to disintegrate or if it's wise to keep that news from yourself as long as possible. In February my mother met Richard Polloco's Aunt Galina, the mother of his cousin and playfellow Rudy. She was the only family he had left in America. Perhaps any passionate relationship begins its decline when the lovers take a seat in the relative's living room. I have wondered recently how much that visit to Aunt Galina had to do with my mother's feeling of hopelessness. Mrs. Shaw after all did have her own relations; it was not as if she needed any more, and certainly not one as unyielding as Galina seemed to be. Although my mother was often going to Tribbey, two, three, four times a month, and possibly more often, for quite some time I didn't understand some of the more important and subtle facts about Rpoll, about her feelings for him. Sometimes I'd lay off reading her mail. I'd decide that I'd had enough, I didn't want to know, and so I wouldn't log on. Weeks might pass, or at least a week. But then I'd wonder, wonder if it was over, if it had intensified once again, if they'd had a fight, if everyone in the city knew. I'd check. For the purpose of the archive I'd go into the old message file and print out everything, with my mind on the future, on historical preservation. There were often messages that had a Liza38 logic, that made me think the dementia was progressing, messages such as this one, written on February 18:

Dear Jane,

This is how it is, I've figured it out, laid it to a kind of rest.
Richard gives me exactly what I need, conversation and whimsy
and passion and attention, and well fortified I can go home
and be a good wife to Kevin. Kevin provides the foundation,
the stability that allows me to be the fanciful lover to Richard.
It goes something like that. If everyone stays in their places
it works perfectly, subject, I realize, to blowup at any
moment.

That was a dandy. *I have a lover so I can be a caring housewife.* The
paragraph had blue-ribbon prospects. *Let's dress passion up in the clothing of a solid citizen, parade him around for family values.* Our whole
world might go up in flames, but Liza will have been happy, zipping
to Wisconsin for her basket lunch and home again, home again: Stay,
stay, good boy, Rpoll. Sit, lie down, attaboy, Kev, Kevy.

In that same message she'd gone on to write a short paragraph
that revealed to the thoughtful reader a chink of another sort:

Sometimes, when I play music with Richard, I feel as if I'm not
playing, it's very strange. We are not competitors, really, and
we've shared so much and learned a great deal from each other.
This is something that I'm not sure I can explain. He has a way
of overwhelming the piece, but it has nothing to do with volume
or tempo or hogging the melody. It is a peculiar thing.
Sometimes I cannot hear myself.

I think I paused when I read that part. She went on to talk about
the fine time they'd had making a chocolate cake for Miss Van Heusen's birthday luncheon. I hope that after I'd read on, I went back to
the section about the strangeness, not being able to hear herself. She
meant, perhaps, that when they practiced, even then, his past was
large. Those dead Russian relations were always with him, and they
were probably especially with him when he played his instrument
and his own soulful tunes. She might have also meant that Polloco

took something from her. Maybe that's how it was with them, that he absorbed her gifts and held them in himself. That, anyway, has become my theory. Although I did not understand much at the time and didn't sense the sadness in that part of the message, I knew certainly that she was listless when she played the piano. Anyone with an ear must have noticed her lack of spirit. I couldn't help thinking that it would serve her right if she lost her talent. She'd have to get a real job, have to go work at Walgreens, have to stand for eight hours at a time behind a register, have to be courteous and helpful throughout the long day.

After I read that message, I decided that I should really dry out, so to speak, stop going into the files altogether. I asked myself what good they were doing me. Polloco and Mrs. Shaw were going to be breaking up and reuniting again and again, to hell with Kevin Shaw; they were going to be making music in whatever state they were in, until kingdom come. I would be gone, out of touch, and they'd be stuck in their loops: I can't go on, I love you, I'm confused, I'm so happy, I love you, don't write me, write me.

I did stay away for about two weeks that particular time, but as always there came to me a wondering, a let's-just-take-a-look. The curiosity was with me like an itch. What was the harm in one quick in-and-out? Because of my idleness, it was therefore March before I learned about the visit to Polloco's Aunt Galina.

"Dear Jane," Liza wrote on February 26:

Aunt Galina is well fortified against age with plenty of beige face powder, a red wig, lipstick, black eyebrows. She lives on the far North Side. Her son Rudy threw himself onto the train tracks at the Halsted station when he was eighteen. Sometimes I think it is the single fact that Richard will never recover from. Galina treats him as if he's five and he abuses her, gently most of the time. They have an awful bond. She hated me, was contemptuous, shameless hussy that I am. I didn't belong there, in that dining room. I don't belong in Tribbey, I don't belong in this house, nowhere feels right. Beth

Poor homeless, son-beating Liza38, alone in this world if you don't count her two offspring and perfectly good husband. That message was a cry for some advice, at the least. What was her problem? I asked myself the basic questions. Why didn't she just get rid of him? Come back to her place. Didn't she see we were waiting for her? I often had to force myself to remember what was so great about Polloco, and I'd find myself rifling through the file, pulling out a message at random.

> Dear Liza,
> I have gone for a walk this morning, to our spot, and stood in the rain. You do not mind my not having enough sense to come out of the rain. It was very cold rain. At home, still wet, I wrote yet another piece entitled, yet again, "Liza38." Yours, rp

I'd read his messages and I'd recollect how scratches of ink on paper or strings of lethally charming words could make the correspondent's heart go all warm and oozy against his will. I'd recall, too, how you could dislike a person or feel neutral about her in her presence, and then, when she went away, you'd find yourself thinking about the manner in which she ran her fingers down your chest or glanced along the inside of your ear with her tongue, and all of a sudden you felt as if you'd rather not live without her.

It wasn't as if Richard Polloco and my mother hadn't put in some time together, so that they already had a bank of remembrances to draw from. "Those barrel-shaped old-lady twins in the matching pink sweaters are coming to get you," Rpoll wrote. Or "The waiter at the Posthouse mentioned the gravy again. This is of the utmost importance, as you well know." Or "Bread box."

Private jokes, no place for me there, no way to understand their intricate beginnings. But the jokes, more than anything else—the incomprehensible jokes that would have seemed brainless to anyone but themselves—those stupid one-liners betrayed the fact that Rpoll and Liza's bond was still vigorous, that they could break it off and break it off, and in the hearty reunion, safe once again, they could laugh and laugh about a bread box.

In mid-March my Grandmother Minty had a massive stroke in our dining room. I felt that I hardly knew her well enough for her to do such a personal thing in our downstairs. She had come over to discuss with my mother the plans for a baby shower they were going to give for our cousin Carol, who at that point had been married to Jim Carodine for a year and a half. Rumor had it that the pregnancy was not planned, and Minty, for one, could not temper her disgust. "Frankly," she said to my mother, "their carelessness revolts me. It's given me a headache."

I wonder if on occasion it took all of my mother's restraint not to tell Minty about her own recklessness, if she wouldn't have liked to shock the Royal Highness, knock her off her pins. *Hey, Mommy, I've been thinking about having a baby with an indigent musician from the Ukraine.* Mrs. Shaw said, "Jim and Carol are married, Mother, and have been for quite a while. They did do it in the right order—courtship, marriage, child."

They were talking about propriety, and in the middle of a sentence Minty raised her hand to her forehead, felt her brow, and toppled over.

"Oh! Oh!" Beth cried, and then, "Henry! Henry!"

I came running from the kitchen, saw the upset, went back for the telephone, pawing toward it. Beth was talking to Minty, hand to her wrist, trying to figure out just where you find the pulse. Although Minty was out cold, Beth was speaking to her as if she were continuing the conversation about the baby shower. She seemed so quickly to have gotten over the shock of the collapse, or else she hadn't quite realized what had happened. "It's going to be fine," she said in the chilly tone she often used with my grandmother. "You've taken a fall, but Henry is phoning the hospital. They'll come, we'll take care of you. It's all right, Mom, it's going to be all right."

In the kitchen I spoke to the person at the other end of the 911 connection and relayed the information as he said it to my mother.

"Is she breathing?" the man asked.

"Is she breathing?" I called to my mother.

With the fingers, not the thumb, Beth was to pull down from the patient's thumb to the crook of the wrist, roll over the top of the bone, and settle there, to find the beat.

Yes, Minty had a pulse.

Next, taking great care not to move the neck, she was supposed to find out if the airway was obstructed. Minty's dentures had slipped, Beth could see that, and with her hand she reached into my grandmother's mouth and retrieved the uppers. I couldn't recall having ever noticed more than three or four of Minty's teeth, and there all of them were, set out in a grin on the rug. We lived not far from St. Joseph's Hospital, and yet it seemed like a long time before the ambulance came blasting, as best it could, down the narrow street. It was so odd, my grandmother in her suit, only slightly rumpled as she lay on the floor. Later, I learned that the paramedics arrived within five minutes of the call. I would have said that my mother had been at Minty's side, talking in her calm voice, for at least twenty minutes.

When the professionals came in and moved Beth out of the way, she turned to me, to give me my marching orders. I was just then, I think, afraid of her. She had knelt on the floor over her mother, talked to her in the correct manner, felt around in her mouth. Right before the men appeared, she had stopped her chatter. She must have heard the siren and known her private time, the last of it, was about up. She had looked at Minty, and she'd leaned down and put her cheek against my grandmother's. She had held herself like that, as if all she really wanted to do was be near the stern old face.

I was to stay at home, my mother said to me. I should call my father, tell him the news, and keep an eye on Elvira when she returned.

"Should I tell anyone else?" I asked her, without really considering Polloco.

Still, when she stopped, in her tracks, I knew what she was think-ing. *Richard.* Should she call him or send him a very short message, a line or two? Could she? She wanted him to know; she wanted him to know first.

"That's all for now," she said. She was out the front door, gone, I assumed. I went back into the kitchen, was reaching for the phone to call my father, and there she was, in the house again, coming at me. "I'll let you know," she was saying. "They'll be able to tell us how she is." She came close, closer. She kissed me. Right on my cheek, on the spot where she'd hit me. She kissed that place. It was as if Minty, falling over, possibly dead, and my mother doing everything right, and last of all the pause for the kiss, the kiss in the crisis—it was as if all of those large movements should have the power to wash away one little slap. I could give it to her, give up that small hold I had over her. In that moment I was sure I let myself absolve her.

Chapter Thirteen

At one point in my life, after film school, not so long ago, I wrote a column for an alternative newspaper in Boston called "Ask Mr. Sensitive." It may be that I touched bottom then, that there is no farther depth beyond which a person can sink. I was supposed to take questions that were personal or intimate and answer them factually but also, and most important, with an attitude. Sometimes the queries were embedded in a story, a life history, a two- or three- or four-page letter, single-spaced, that included the family tree as well as details of emotional pain suffered and bodily functions gone awry. Very occasionally a few questions came through, a straightforward inquiry.

Question: Why has there been an explosion in the sanitary pad market over the last decade? Sanitary pads take up one entire wall at the supermarket. Is all that variety necessary?

"There is clearly a need for a Ph.D. thesis on this subject," I advised, "a full-length book. What does it indicate about the psyche of the modern woman when she chooses between the Classic, the Sure Curve, the Secure Center, Maxi or Super Maxi, with or without wings? What do these choices tell us about *her*?"

Question: My girlfriend thinks I want to sleep with my mother. She says we get along too well! What should I do?

"Past-life regression is definitely in order." I warned the seeker that he may have been married to his mother in a previous incarnation, and it was essential to consider what the relationship was like. Was he killed prematurely, before he'd had a chance to rob Pharaoh's tomb, get the necklace for his old lady? Had his mother ever slapped him? Was there a score to settle? Perhaps that, more than sexual attraction, was the thing bothering the girlfriend. "Let's face it," I wrote, "who, besides someone out of antiquity or a bloke who is extremely hard up, would really want to screw his own mother?"

I brought what I could to my responses. Many of the letters I received were written by people who didn't realize that I was supposed to be hip and blow them off. All those small stories dying to be bigger ones. The letters were always clipped down to one short paragraph at the most, by the editor, while my informative and insulting answers were two columns in length. All those writers looking for a platform and an audience. Richard Polloco had found his listener in my mother, and my mother had siphoned off some of his history and her feelings to Jane, but it seems to me that even Jane, that big vibrating tympanic drum in faraway Vermont, was not enough for Liza, bad Liza, no-good, guilty Liza38. Being bad had made her want to talk, to tell, to narrate.

Imagine her walking with my father across the bridge, over the Chicago River on Michigan Avenue. She'd remember how Richard had stopped her one night in the fall, when he'd come into the city for a concert, when they were walking in the exact spot, how he'd insisted they should kiss because the city was lit up around them and it was a cold and clear winter night. It was as if they were in a scene with a fantastic backdrop, the two lovers at center stage, and so naturally they should rise to the occasion. My mother, because she was nervous about my father or Minty driving by and seeing her with her paramour, kissing on the bridge, told him they shouldn't, not right there. But in the end they were on the bridge, and it was night, and the city was lit all around them, and the water was lapping and glittering. How could they not kiss? Those moments were what she thought of when she walked in that same place with my father six months later, and in a way, *in a way,* wouldn't it make a good story for him; how much he'd enjoy the story, for the sheer storyness of it, her walking there with a man, over the bridge that is on the site where Fort Dearborn was erected, the major military garrison at the threshold of the Northwest Territory. How fitting that Richard Polloco should have chosen that site for a conquest, the kiss on someone else's territory, a seizure of goods and chattel on the bridge, the light around them and below them too, wavering on the water. Bethy might have been able to put it to Kevin in the historical context, and it's not impossible that my father, always one to enjoy a yarn, especially when the details are right, would have appreciated her rendition. He might well have thrown his head back for a short ringing laugh.

Perhaps as important to survival as shelter and food and clothing is the one person, the right person in your midst, who will listen to your stories and laugh in the appropriate places. I had always taken for granted that Kevin did his telling for my mother. She, as we know, had many outlets, but I couldn't think whom Kevin shaped his narratives for besides Beth. He didn't seem to have a Karen equivalent in his life, his only brother was thirteen years older and lived in London, and I doubt that he burdened his colleagues with anything even remotely personal. I wondered if he told Liza what he knew from his years of study, if in a general conversation he observed that there is very little anyone can do to save a friend or relation from her obsessive passion, that forbidding it or removing it will hardly clear the lover's mind, that there is simply nothing to be done in the waiting but meditate upon battle scenes from ancient wars and play chess.

In the matter of Minty's deathbed scene, Beth made an adequate story from it, for Jane and Rpoll and for Kevin too. A C− for content, B+ for effort. Minty, it turned out, lay in a coma for a week after her stroke while her daughter and her sons sat and waited. Elvira and I went to see her once, near the beginning of her stay. We were relieved to be in the company of Minty's cleaning woman, Cora, because Cora talked to her, smoothed her brow, sang her songs, all the things you'd like to think you could do when a loved one is in a coma, all things Elvira and I were incapable of doing at our ages. We couldn't wait to get away from that place. While Cora fussed over Minty, we stood silently on the other side of the bed.

When we'd arrived, Beth and the uncles had gone out into the hall to talk about their mother's prospects. Although it seemed unlikely that Minty could understand the conversation, her children were respectful in her presence. As always they did not want to speak about unpleasantness in her company. Minty's eyes were half closed, and her mouth was hanging open as she labored to breathe. She seemed to want to grasp something on Cora's hand, and Cora let her fumble around, untangling the bedsheets when necessary. "Yes, ma'am," Cora finally said. "I know what it is you're missing. You're lonesome for that wedding ring of yours, what you lost. I'll find it for you, your Cora will find it. We'll get that ring back on your finger so that either way you choose, whether you decide to come or go, you'll have it with you, yes, ma'am."

She looked over at me and she said, "Your grandmother lost her wedding ring a month or so ago. We turned the house upside down looking for it. My land, how she's worrying my ring finger. I know she's trying to tell me that she needs it. She needs her Cora to get it back for her."

To Minty she said, "Here, Miz Margaret." She was pulling a gold band off her finger and putting it on Minty's knobby hand. "You wear mine, you wear Cora's ring until I find yours."

Elvira and I went down to the vending machines for a while, anything to escape the room, and when we came back, Cora was gone. Beth and my Uncle Chuck had assumed their positions, one on either side of Minty. I couldn't imagine that Minty had ever been helpless before, and I wondered if she knew, if she had any idea of her condition. She was clawing at Uncle Chuck's wrist, in just the way she had gone after Cora's fingers. "Mother," he whispered, "what is it? What do you want?" Elvira and I stood by the end of the bed, again not knowing what to do. Mrs. Shaw had said that this was the time we were supposed to say good-bye to our grandmother. Both of us would have liked to wave at her, a few quick words as we exited. *"So long, Minty. Thanks a lot."* It seemed problematic, saying farewell to someone who was spending the remaining portion of her energy pawing at her son's forearm.

"Maybe she's wondering where your watch is," my mother said to

Chuck. "Don't you have Dad's watch, the Bulgari he got from the company for his however many years of service?"

My uncle leaned close again to Minty and said, "I used to wear it all the time but I got a digital one. It's so much easier to read, Mom, but I still have Dad's watch. It's in my dresser drawer. I'd never get rid of it, you know that. When I come back tonight, I'll bring it. You can touch it. I'll bring it for you."

Elvira and I glanced at each other, remembering Cora and the ring. "Just think what she'd do to your head, looking for your hair," I muttered to her. She cracked up, good old Elvira. Uncle Chuck was having a heartfelt moment with his nearly dead mother, and Elvira was shaking so hard the bed's railing, the tubes and cords, were clattering.

"I think it's time for us to go," I said to Mrs. Shaw. I looked at my ancient, breathless grandmother, someone I had never really liked or known. It was expected of me, I knew, to kiss her. I advanced to the head of the bed, bent over, and gave her a quick peck. The skin of her forehead was dry, and no part of her, not her eyes or her mouth or her hands, nothing registered her grandson's fleeting kiss. "Bye," I said, trying, for an instant, to feel it, trying to know that I would never see her again. "Good-bye, Minty."

Elvira, backing away, said, "Yep."

That was it, the last time I saw Margaret Ellison Gardener. On the way home Elvira took off her hat and swung it on her little finger. She was skipping and turning around and running back to me, going forward, returning to my side. I knew how she felt; I could imagine being that happy, out of Minty's room, away from the hospital.

Later, that night, I sat in the office writing a letter to Lily, telling her about the most recent drama in our family. My mother had come home to get something to eat and take a shower. Presumably she'd called Polloco from St. Joseph's, giving him updates on the hour, claiming her right to be tragic. She was going to spend the night at the hospital so that Minty would have someone beside her in the unlikely event she came to, or when she died. Beth, all wrapped in her large white fluffy bathrobe, her wet hair done up in a turban, was in her room on Roslyn Place. The door was open and I could see her, sitting on the edge of the bed, talking to my father. Kevin had set his book aside, to listen to her. I wonder now if he was hopeful in Minty's emergency. Death often jolts a person into a new awareness, a heightened sense of gratitude. Kevin might have wished that Minty's last gasp would make Liza take a vow to reform. She'd have an epiphany of the sort women have on made-for-TV movies, standing over the bed of the comatose child, almost too late, the eleventh hour for cherishing after all what was truly precious. Maybe through the year Kevin had assumed that the stuff of life would float the Shaws out the other end of the story. It was his mother-in-law, in a final act of generosity, who was going to give Bethy one last push to get her on course.

It must not have occurred to Beth that I was in the office, in the dark, typing in the gray glow of the computer screen. "It's awful, Kev," I heard her say. "This morning, when I was with her, she almost broke my arm. Every bit of her strength seems to be in her left hand, or else it's the only circuit that's still open. She was wrestling with me, and then she started to feel my fingers, one by one." I thought of my mother's firm grip, her long fingers, the elegance of them and the plainness too—and I remembered that she had taken off her engagement and wedding rings, that she didn't wear the symbols of her union anymore. I thought of her hand around a cup of coffee, her hands chasing up and down the scales. It had been quite some time that she had been without the rings. Maybe Minty was looking for a last-minute answer to a question that had been nagging at her for months: Why wasn't Mrs. Shaw wearing her wedding band?

"She was feeling my fingers," Beth was saying. "She was breathing very hard through her mouth and frowning. I started to talk to her. For the first time, the first time in my life, I was really able to talk to her."

"What'd you tell her?"

"I don't know—everything. I talked to her as if she were my priest, my shaman, my therapist. I told her I was doing the best I could, that even if she disapproved of me, this was my path, my journey."

What? What was she going to say to my father next? I started up, thinking to distract them, when Kevin said, "That kind of psychobabble didn't bring her back?"

They both began to laugh. "She probably didn't register any of it," my mother said. "Who knows. But she did get quiet and I did need to say what I said, and I did feel absolved."

"Go, Minty!" my father said. "She could have a whole new career if this phase of her life continues."

"You're terrible," Beth said. She swatted him with a towel. "You really are." I'd say she swatted him with the towel fondly.

He took her in his pale freckled arms and he said, "I love Minty and I'm going to miss her. The world won't be the same." They had a moment of reverence for the dying woman, and I think, when they moved out of my sight lines, that my mother began to cry. She was sniffling and he was mumbling and the floorboards were creaking under the strain of two people standing still in the same place. I sat in my chair trying to imagine what she had said to Minty in the confession, what Mrs. Shaw might have said to a priest, a shaman, a therapist. "You won't approve of this, O Mother, but I have had to go outside of my marriage to have a fulfilling relationship. When I've had sex with Richard Polloco, creative, joyful intercourse, then I can come back home to Kevin and bake up a storm. Give me a sign that you forgive me my trespasses, so I can go right on fucking and cooking when you get to heaven and are looking down upon me."

Question for Ask Mr. Sensitive: Do you think it's possible to be sexually and/or emotionally committed to two people simultaneously?

"Absolutely," I wrote. "However, you have to have plenty of time and money to do so. To successfully manage two equally satisfying relationships, it's best if you belong to the English aristocracy, have a large manor house with different wings, many heavy doors, and a household staff as well. You will not have the energy to adequately care for the children, to keep up your correspondence, and don't even consider trying to hold down a 9–5 job. It's great if you can play a game, cards, for example, in the event one of the parties needs soothing. Also, it's advisable to maintain a psychic on the premises in order to tell you which lover is going to blow his stack when, so that you can avert a crisis, so you can save yourself."

I wrote some of what I had seen and heard at the hospital to Lily. I told her how useful a person can be who isn't even actually quite in this world. Minty's muscular spasm in her left hand was probably a last release of energy in the one part of her that still worked. It was unlikely that she cared about her body or had an interest in her children's jewelry or timepieces, all the trappings of life inconsequential in comparison to her, as they say, journey. It was pretty funny, I said to Lily—wondering if she'd find it funny—that each person who came to my grandmother's bedside and held her hand felt that brain-dead Minty was still proffering her censure. Because Cora had been with Miz Margaret the day the wedding ring fell off her hand, and because Cora was a loyal employee, a saint, in fact, she felt responsible for the loss. Uncle Chuck was guilty because he no longer wore my grandfather's watch. He liked the convenience of a digital watch, but in truth he'd never gotten along with his father and he didn't want to have to think about him every time he looked at his wrist. Elizabeth Gardener Shaw, the good daughter, had a crookedness in her heart. It was a long story, an old story.

After I'd written it down for Lily, the hospital scene seemed like a fairly good anecdote. An A— anecdote. In my telling there were three incidents, the repetition of Minty clawing at the hands or wrists of three persons, triplicity always a sign of a strong tale. There was as well a shaman who reveals the characters' strengths or weaknesses. Liza's story to Jane and Richard Polloco primarily involved herself. She wrote to them about her mother being in a coma and the weirdly blessed state that condition conferred upon Minty and her audience. It was the first time, Beth explained, that she'd been able to talk to her mother. Without having to elaborate she told her correspondents that she'd confessed everything to Minty. The dying woman had been agitated when Beth began to speak, but she'd quieted, as if she were listening, as if she were understanding.

The night my parents sat in their room talking about Minty I thought to ask myself if there wasn't a piece of the story that hadn't yet come clear, something I had failed to consider. Sitting on their bed, Beth was telling my father that she'd confessed to her mother, and Kevin had said, "That kind of psychobabble didn't bring her back?" They had both laughed. I wasn't sure if I was more shocked by his question or their amusement. Liza had clearly been available enough to me through the year: Yes, she had guilt, yes, sexual passion had made her weak. If I was ever in doubt about her frame of mind, I had only to log on upstairs, and her brain, her beating heart, was laid out before me in typescript. What, however, was my father's part? The comments he had made about Minty could not be called sympathetic or even kind, and I began to wonder if he had a supernatural ability to absorb pain, or if he had a complete lack of sensation. He couldn't possibly be so stupid as to be ignorant of my mother's feeling for Polloco, not the way she rattled on about him. What did Kevin imagine my mother had confessed to Minty at her deathbed? Certainly he understood that her unburdening was more than an apology for habitually burning the toast when she was a teenager, or for having lost Minty's monogrammed handkerchief at Sunday school.

I know my mother had sorrow over Richard Polloco, sorrow over the life not lived with him. You could feel the desolation in her, especially when she played the piano. I could hear even in the scrappy way she had been practicing that the music was about him, about missing him, not only in the future but in the past. Assuming my father had sorrow, where did he keep it? Sometimes, when my mother arrived in our kitchen in the evening, after a day in Tribbey, she'd sit down to the simple dinner my father would have cooked, and he'd say, "How are you?"

"I'm getting there," she'd say quietly.

He'd nod, looking at her eating, watching her as she kept her head bowed.

What, I'd wonder, were they talking about? How was a person supposed to penetrate their code? The private jokes of Rpoll and Liza38 were no mystery compared to the plain English my parents used. There was no meaning I could glean from their short sentences.

Jane Hamilton

If I went downstairs in the middle of the night, to get a snack or go to the bathroom, often my parents' light would come through the crack under their door, and I'd hear the murmur of their voices, or their laughter. They talked with the light on; how strange they were. Perhaps only lovers and children speak softly, lying together in the dark. If you are not lovers, you sit up talking. You keep the light on.

Minty conveniently died well enough before the long-awaited trip to Shiloh, time enough to have the memorial service, to write thank-you notes for the sympathy cards, and to begin to move on. It was a sad event for my mother, so sad that way in the back of the congregation during the service I was quite sure I saw Richard Polloco. He had come to honor her distress and to hear her eulogy, a short piece of writing she had labored over for several days. My uncles spoke too, and in addition to my mother's five-minute tribute, she played a French suite on the piano, one of Bach's more affecting suites, when a clipped fugue might have been more fitting, to evoke the essence of Minty.

During the service I did follow along, and I did remember my grandmother, and I did think about her life. Somewhere, though, in all that thinking, the idea of "ambiguous loyalty," a phrase I had read somewhere about General Lee, popped into my head. Lee, who had loyalty in one form to Virginia, and loyalty in another to the Union. Surely my mother, that year of Polloco, was also suffering from ambiguous loyalty. Suffering enough to invite him to her own mother's memorial service. There must have been moments when she was with him, and she'd think, I don't want to–I *cannot*–be without this, this that he gives me. She loved him so much the sight of his shoes made her go soft–the imitation leather boots he'd been able to afford at Kmart. It's a terrible thing when a person's shoes do it to you, make you think you can pay any price to follow him. And yet, after her day in Tribbey, she always had to come home to us. She must have considered how if she left us, if she broke the family, she would long for us, for the life we'd had on Roslyn Place. She might have wondered, too, if Polloco, alone with her finally, could bear the burden of her new sadness.

At the memorial service the man in question was behind a pillar, underneath the balcony, and in the flash that I saw him, I cannot say absolutely that it was he. But who else, I asked myself, was as large and looming? Who else would have had a haircut that looked so painfully fresh?

If Polloco was standing by my mother in her time of crisis, it was my father who saw Minty through to the end. No blood relative, not the uncles, not my mother, no nieces or grandchildren, went with Kevin Shaw and the body to the crematorium. My father, always game for a learning experience, had a tour of the facility before the oven was turned on. He had an informative conversation with the proprietor, who did not usually have anyone standing by during the procedure, he called it. Mr. Jennison not only explained the process but told a few trade stories about the occasional spooky corpse that refused to burn at the normal rate. My father sat in the front room while the gas burners were turned on in the back chamber. Halfway through the roast he went out into the air and breathed. Breathed in Mintified air; breathed in what she'd become. Although he and my grandmother had never had a close bond, he had always respected her, and he was thankful for the life she had afforded him. Maybe respect and gratitude boil down to love of some kind. I think he was genuinely moved at the crematorium, at being a part of what seemed to him an ancient ritual. A few days later, when the urn arrived, he put it in the downstairs hall closet, waiting for a time in the summer when we would scatter the remains up in Michigan, along the lake, by Minty's beloved cottage. Our lives, in the meantime, were supposed to go forward.

After we got back from Shiloh, I went into my mother's file to see what she had to say about the family vacation. Certainly there was much she could have reported about our four days away, but she told next to nothing. "Home from Tennessee," she wrote to Richard Polloco. "Exhausted." To Jane she said, "The reenactment did not live up to Elvira's expectation. Ultimately, probably a good thing."

I have never fully understood why my mother did not try to cash in on Shiloh, the one place she might have believed she was heroic. She did not tell anyone the story, as far as I know, besides her therapist. It did not become something the book club women bandied about, a sock for the ladies to hold in their mouths, to *grrr* over. I have gone back and forth, wondering if the event was shattering for my mother, or if instead, she was so pleased with herself she kept it private so as not to blow her own horn. She had after all been reared not to be boastful. I've wondered if I misjudged her, if by any chance she soon came to appreciate Elvira's deepest feelings and therefore was necessarily ashamed of her own display. I have only ever discussed the incident with my sister. There has never been a coming together for the four of us late at night during a holiday, or a time in the car, when the conversation turned to family highlights. *Remember that night at Shiloh, when Elvira . . .* Of course, when my mother dies, the event might become eulogy material for either Elvira or me; we cannot rule out the possibility that in the limestone Congregational Church in Lake Bluff, Illinois, one of us will tell, and so thrillingly, as we pay our final respects to Beth Gardener Shaw.

That first week in April my father and Elvira loaded a rental van on Wednesday, and early Thursday morning we swung past Karen's house to pick her up. My father had put in his time persuading me to join the Shaws on the trip. It was going to be Elvira's big moment, he said. I was supposed to think of it as a play, Elvira's debut onstage. I protested, saying that she was going to be in the woods the whole time, huffy in her super hardcore way whenever a tourist asked her a question, inquired about her shoes, her haversack, her hand-stitched jacket. My father nodded slowly. Yes, he said, it was true, she would be involved. Still, it was important to her, and in a way it was some-thing of a last gesture I could make, while I was part of the house-hold. He used the word "last" more than I could stand. He pointed out that this trip to Tennessee was our last family vacation before I went off for summer work and to college. It was my last spring break in high school, the last opportunity to travel together.

To maintain my dignity, I told him I'd go if Karen came along. It wasn't so much that I wanted to spend several days with her, but she was never dull and she'd keep me busy, keep me distracted. On the way she and I would sit in the backseat of the van listening to music on our Walkmans and reading science fiction, and the rest of them up front could talk about the high points of Shiloh: Sherman coming upon Grant in the middle of the night under a tree, the hogs feasting on the corpses, the pond turning red with blood, the death of General Albert Sidney Johnston.

How would my mother have given shape to the story if it were she who was telling it? I sometimes think of that weekend, trying, in vain I'm afraid, to see it through her eyes. It is naturally impossible to faithfully report on someone's state of mind at a specific scene when there is no writing left behind. My father and Elvira camped at the Shiloh National Military Park, Karen and Mrs. Shaw stayed in one room at the motel, and I had my own room down the hall. This ar-rangement had come somewhat hard-won to me. My mother had said, "You and Karen can stay together, right?" You're not having sex, she meant, and so it's fine if you share a room, twin beds, after all, at the Pickwick Landing State Park Inn. I'm certain she wanted to be alone, so that in her own way she could be with him, so she could dream of Rpoll, running her own hands over her body in her quiet bed as she drifted off to sleep.

"I don't think that would be—suitable," I said.

"What?" she said. "Did you say *suitable?*"

Karen and I were good friends, but without knowing exactly, I must have had the sense that there was a gate, pretty ragged, a flood-gate that she managed to keep locked against the tide of her feeling. Although I was no Don Juan, Karen is herself a passionate girl, and at the time she had not yet found an outlet—besides her poetry and various religions—for her considerable emotion. It is always easy to say that at a certain point in one's life one knew nothing, but actually it seems to me that what a person knows at each stage, no matter how little, is important to that stage. We probably lose the knowledge that is no longer useful as we move on to another kind of knowing that matters for the next era, very like shedding skin after skin. If I understood before Shiloh that it would not be wise to be alone in a motel room with Karen, then that was one small piece that held me in good stead. A few years later, after she found someone else to love, I was sorry to lose her searing and clear-eyed adoration. Of course, as Shirana predicted, we have remained friends, chums through thick and thin.

About the motel situation down in Tennessee I said to Mrs. Shaw, "I don't think Karen's mother would approve of us sharing a room. She wouldn't like it."

Liza looked at me in amazement. She seemed to be pondering how she could have spawned someone so acutely middle-aged. "It's thoughtful of you," she said, "to anticipate Mrs. Bruckman's feelings."

I was surprised that my mother hadn't found a way to wriggle out of the weekend, that her sense of duty impelled her to spend fourteen hours one way in the car so that she could walk around a battlefield and bunk with Karen, who snored. When Karen couldn't sleep, she sat on the ledge of the tub writing poems in her black-and-white-speckled composition notebook. She, too, was observing the Shaws, filtering us through her Jewish-Methodist-Buddhist-feminist-New Age-leftist lens.

My father had probably pitched the trip to my mother just as he had done to me: Shiloh was the pinnacle of Elvira's life thus far, and something not to be missed. I suppose that fact alone made it impossible for Liza38 to be a shirker. In the old days, back in Vermont, Beth used to dress up in hoopskirts and walk around the reenactments with a basket on her arm, fanning herself with a reproduction fan, but at Shiloh she was a spectator, hiking in shorts and a T-shirt, her purse over her shoulder, a tourist among tourists.

On the way down to Tennessee, driving toward spring, the vegetable world gradually turned green, and as we went south, began to bloom. There was something ominous once we were past the Mason-Dixon Line, ominous in a Flannery O'Connor sort of way, in the dripping boughs of so many willows, and already the signs of what would become extreme in summer, the moss carpet underfoot and the ropy vines hanging overhead, set to strangle the trees that harbored them. I knew the wisteria was supposed to be beautiful, but to me the flowers drooping from their stems looked overblown, unchecked, like mutant flowers, lilacs in drag. The sweetness of the spring seemed false, a harbinger of no good to come. Still, if you worked hard enough to blot out the catfish restaurants, the barbecue pits, the centerpiece churches in town after town, you could almost imagine the Rebs walking through all that greenery and getting both a heartache from it and solace. For us northerners there is not much familiar in that landscape. Yes, there is springtime, the smell of newly turned earth, the wood thrush hidden away, singing, the meadowlark in the wide open, singing. It's the isolation of each town, each small sinking town, that is startling. Driving past the occasional cluster of houses, past the clotheslines full of flapping shirts and sheets, I had the sense that the inhabitants were blissfully unconnected to the larger world. Presidents would come and go, disgracing themselves in their own styles, wars would be waged, but those townspeople in places like Crump and Ramer and Guys would continue to hang out their wash and eat catfish and go to church. And it sort of scared me, the thought of all of them doing that, made me feel as if I'd stepped out of time into a new emptiness, one I hadn't thought of before.

It's hard to say whether Liza38 contemplated the notion of emptiness or not. Maybe my laying claim to the subject was teenage arrogance, and Liza, at nearly forty, did her share for the cause of the big vacuum, the holy void. Perhaps she spent that Friday and Saturday at the Shiloh National Military Park stumbling around howling, cursing the night, and so forth. It's doubtful, I think, that she watched her daughter in drill after drill or that she followed the map and examined every one of the monuments and the burial trenches. At one point Karen and I, in our wanderings, stubbed out our joint and went into the church, not the original chapel that gave the battle its name, but a Methodist church that was finally completed on the site in 1949. It's not the picturesque clapboard replica it might have been, but an ungainly stone building, constructed to weather the storm.

It was hot and Karen and I were looking for a drinking fountain. There, in the sanctuary, my mother was sitting at the piano, playing "Johnny Has Gone for a Soldier," somewhat in the style she used to play it, before she knew Polloco. That day, in that hour, she was perhaps thinking only about the specific tragedy of the Civil War, something you can let yourself hook into at certain national parks, especially Gettysburg and especially Shiloh. She was playing, as I recall, with her arms and her elbows at the old pre-Polloco angle, engaged with the music and the instrument in a way that she hadn't been in months. She looked up, smiling wistfully. Karen and I got out of there as fast as we could. The whole thing struck me as pretty funny, the two of us high, Elvira doing a maneuver in Sarah Bell's Old Cotton Field, my father, on all fours, sniffing the ground in the Hornets' Nest, and my mother, by herself, playing a dirge on the piano. That about summed up the configuration of our family, right there, in the living history moment.

There were at least a thousand reenactors prowling the park, and many thousands of tourists to watch them drill, boil coffee, take naps, charge with the cavalry, heal the wounded, write lonesome letters home, gaze at the pictures of their loved ones, heed the preacher, scare up the cowardly, drink their gut rot, and other self-appointed duties.

What happened to Elvira was simple, the result of a common predicament any cross-dressing girl could find herself in, even in a state other than Tennessee. It was toward dusk on Saturday. Mrs. Shaw and Karen and I had stood by during the day—in other words, for long enough. We were going to drive into the town of Savannah to get a pile of ribs, and surely my liberal mother would allow us a beer to wash down the meal. We were maybe then going to catch a movie. My father was nowhere to be seen, off, we later learned, on the bluffs looking over the Tennessee River, watching the steamboats and testing his theory about the slaughter in the Hornets' Nest on one of the park rangers. Although most of the reenactors were set up near Cloud Field, Elvira's group had chosen to make camp behind the William Manse George Cabin, to the west of the Peach Orchard. My sister was keeping company with the real men, hard-drinking men, some of whom had brewed their own ale and were slugging the muddy liquid out of wicker jugs. There were twelve or so of them, around the fire, watching the spit that had on it a side of venison, the hindquarters of a deer that one of the infantrymen had hit with his car in the last winter, which had thawed on the trip down and was dripping its juices into the flames.

It had been hot enough during the day so that the petals of the blossoms in the orchard had fallen, and in the coming evening there was already an insect hum that was no longer young, that was a full-blown sound of summer. Elvira was sitting beside her friend Al, one of the three boys who had been chosen from other regiments to join the 28th Wisconsin. Her haversack lay on her other side, next to Bernard Hecht, a lieutenant in the volunteer infantry. Hecht had played the part of a deserter at Enos, Indiana, the previous fall, had been the courageous man who had allowed himself to be hung in a way that had captivated Elvira. She was probably in ecstasies, not only belonging to the same unit as Hecht but sitting next to him at the campfire, nearly touching him. Because of the hanging, she admired him more than the average super hardcore who did the usual drill, walking twenty miles in ill-fitting boots, maintaining the soldier figure by starvation, sleeping without a tent. Hecht had a gaunt face, a black beard, and small oval spectacles. Every piece of his uniform was hand-stitched. The ground had been damp the night before, and in his thin blanket he had lain awake shivering until morning. Throughout the day he had suffered from diarrhea. In fact, the Union camp near Pittsburg Landing in 1862 had suffered from dysentery, what they called the Tennessee Two-Step. Bernard, not a reenactor to stoop to using a Porta Potti, had been digging holes all over the scraggly woods of the park. Needless to say, everyone was in awe. There was some speculation about whether he'd taken laxatives in order to make the event true to life. Around five he figured he'd better keep up his strength, get the fluids going, and he'd been drinking from the quartermaster's stash. He had gone through the equivalent of a six-pack when he reached for Elvira's haversack, thinking it his own, looking for his pipe and tobacco.

It was starting to get dark. My mother was hanging over the split rail fence, about twenty-five yards from the campfire, waiting for my father to return. They had long before agreed that Elvira would never be left alone in the company of the reenactors, and certainly not as night fell. Karen and I were more than ready to make our exit, go to town, grab us some hominy, and retire to a he-man adventure movie. Mrs. Shaw was clearly impatient, looking behind her, looking left and right. Where the hell was he? She may have been thinking about how he was always late, how he so often got carried away at the wrong moments. He never had any idea of time, he'd been that way forever, when was he going to get his act together? It's true that there has always been a space cadet component to Kevin Shaw's personality. I'd seen him look up when the bell rang at Jesse Layton, as if the buzz were a novel and unexpected sound, as if he'd never dreamed there could be a passing period, that his class would leave him when they were having such an interesting discussion.

My mother was standing at the fence, Karen was lying in the grass singing to herself, and I was sitting cross-legged trying to read a book in the fading light. I had given up wondering why we were there, given up cursing my fate for being along. I had meant to feel nostalgic about the trip as it was happening, because it was the last time, I swore, I would ever come with the family to a reenactment, or any kind of vacation, for that matter. I sort of wished Lily were with me, although in some departments Karen was more entertaining. Breaking a variety of rules, we'd smoked dope and taken pictures of each other around the Harvey Lamb Mortal Wounding Monument. We'd charged each other at Ruggles Battery, we'd mugged at the Indian Mounds National Historic Landmark, and innocently enough we'd sung through a lot of our repertory: "Don't Wanna Fall in Love," "Make You Sweat," "Blue Savannah," "I'm Your Baby," and "Good Beat."

In my last year of college I did my senior thesis on Henry James, what Karen considered a moral victory for herself. I had through the years come to admire the restraint of James and his characters, even if they were miserable and stuffy and repressed, even if they were loathsome. For example, it is never disclosed to us what article Lambert Strether spent his life manufacturing; that perhaps offending, indelicate object is left entirely to the reader's imagination. Since my turning to James, I have had a prudish reaction to characters in novels sitting on toilets or perspiring in such a way that they stain their clothing. I have no interest in having their pimples pointed out to me, or smelling any of their emanations. It is not for nothing that I was called Mr. Sensitive. For Henry James it would have been unthinkable, the crisis moment of his tale turning on the item I must necessarily describe because I live in my own unfortunate time.

Bernard Hecht took up Elvira's haversack, thinking it his, an understandable mistake since both bags had come from the same mail-order company. He unbuckled the single strap at the center and began rummaging through the contents, a few pieces of bacon, damp sugar tied in a rag, a potato, a flabby carrot, an old shirt—and, what was this? And this? He removed one of the two articles, unrecognizable to the Federal soldier in him, an object that was not animal, mineral, or plant from the time of April 1862. He first undid the packaging, and next he held it, the white rectangle, with a pink underside, up to the fire. He blinked. He had never taken the trouble to get married or keep any one woman around for more than a few months, which might explain why he was neither a stunned nor an appreciative student of the feminine hygiene wall at his local grocery store. He scowled at the thing.

The first sergeant, David Merks, noticed him, broke away from the conversation, what happened to be the retelling of the deer story: the icy roads the previous winter, the swerve, the hit, the instant death of the buck, the quick rescue of the carcass into the back of the pickup, before anyone drove by, as it is illegal to harvest roadkill in the state of Wisconsin.

"What—?" David Merks said, squinting at Hecht. "Where'd you get that?"

Elvira looked then, and she saw it, saw her own Pantiliner, the type she herself had chosen at Walgreens, what happened to be a Sure Curves Thin Maxi sanitary pad, without wings. She was a girl who knew her own mind, provided my mother would take the goods up to the counter and go through the humiliation of paying for them. The particular item, on display for the 28th Wisconsin, was intended for moderately heavy days. Elvira's initial impulse must have been to jump up and grab the pad from Bernard's callused hand, throw it in the fire. It would sizzle away, the plastic liner melt down into a gummy pink drip, nothing but that left. The men might chalk it up to having had a few too many and stagger off to bed. But if she made a show and tried to get it, there was a chance, a reasonable chance, that they'd come to, they'd see through to her panic, they'd know she was in their midst. She hugged her knees, hunching over, trying to get smaller, less visible. She kept her eyes open and at the same time she prayed. She prayed, I suspect, to her best general, her dearest man, to Robert E. Lee. "Get me out of this one," she begged him, staring hard at the hot coals. She had learned enough from my father to know that it is often a seemingly insignificant detail or event that forces the hand of history, that changes the course of the world. She did not beseech the general for protection. "I don't care what happens," she said, thinking to bargain with him, "as long as the secret is safe."

Bernard glanced back to her bag, and he saw, to the right of where he'd been sitting, his own haversack, his eyeglass case poking out of the side. He stood up, holding the pernicious object for all his mates to see. "Gentlemen." My mother, straining still to find my father out somewhere in the dusky woods, turned toward Hecht's deep voice. There was a seriousness in his tone that made the others, the rest of the soldiers around the fire, abruptly stop their talk. They gaped at the—what was it? No, wasn't it a handkerchief, a bandage, a rag, a sock? "Gentlemen," Hecht boomed again. "And scholars. Methinks we have a traitor in our ranks."

I had not known that Yankees of yore spoke as if they were reciting Shakespeare, as if they'd just seen Hamlet's ghost.

"We have a traitor, it seems, in our circle. This—article—is a sign of infection. Filth. And betrayal. Betrayal. I know not how I know this, and yet it is the truth. Someone is among us who does not belong. Someone who has misled us concerning her—her identity."

There was a moment in which the men were stupefied, looking across the fire at each other.

"Someone who knows us when we don't know her, brothers," Bernard said.

The understanding was dawning on them slowly. Huh? A woman, here, right now? "When we don't know her," Bernard reiterated.

Without having to think further, the past came through them, lit through their bodies as much as their minds, all the stories they had told and that a woman had heard, their tough talk, their frank talk, their boasting, their show-off contests. A gash at their fire, a piece of ass? The shock, too, that she might think they were queers, spooning, sleeping against one another, wrapped in their blankets. From the pervert herself!

"Where is she?" David Merks said. "Who?"

I liked Bernard's line a lot: *I know not how I know this, and yet it is the truth.* You had to admire someone who was that far gone, to convincingly pretend that he didn't recognize a sanitary pad when it was right in front of him. To speak so eloquently when the moment was so raw.

Al, Elvira's friend, who was slight and had large brown eyes, sprang to his feet and said, "Not me!" He was pulling open his shirt, to show them, see, he belonged, he was legitimate. My mother, sensing danger, began walking to the fire. The men were rising, leaning toward the spit, trying to size up each other, some of them putting their own hands to their own chests, their privates, as if to assess and certify that they were not the culprit. Elvira, along with them, also stood. Although they no doubt would have caught her sooner or later, she made the mistake, the fatal misstep, backing away just a little, trying to move into the shadows.

"Shut up," Merks said to Al. "Where are you, lipsticks? We'll find you, we'll get you."

"Elvirnon," Hecht said simply.

"Shaw!" Merks cried.

"Shaw?" Al said.

Merks got ahold of her before she could run, before my mother, before I, could reach her. I wondered later if they had rehearsed, planned for that moment, Hecht and Merks, moving the way they did, directly and without consulting each other. Hecht went for Elvira's neck, held her by the scruff, as if she were a cat, and with the other hand he gripped her wrists behind her back. That way Merks could get at her, yank past her coat, at her vest, in three movements tearing it down the front, the buttons popping off and falling into the grass. He was shorter than Hecht, and those squat hands, the backs of them, did not have much, if any, hair. He was feeling her with his bald hands, the damp-looking hands, trying to feel under her shirt, feel through the binding fabric she used to flatten her chest. A third man maneuvered with Hecht, struggling to remove her jacket off her shoulders, past her cuffed wrists. "Get her down to the hide," he was shouting, "get her down to the—"

"Bub alert!" Merks bellowed. "Whoa, baby, way to go, she's got a pair of knockers!"

Of our group it was Karen who first cried out, cried, "Elvira! Elvira!" She was on ahead of me, enough sisterhood for all of the sisters, her pack bouncing on her back as she rushed toward the fray. My foot had fallen asleep and it took me a minute to get steady. Before I'd gotten my equilibrium, before I could catch up, Hecht and Merks were running away with Elvira, streaming down the lane to Bloody Pond. That body of water had been named not for menstruating women, but because so many soldiers bled there during the battle, turning the pond red. Let me say what I still believe: never has so much for our family turned on so little. Merks and Hecht had lifted my sister into a sitting position and were holding her camp style between them. I still claim, too, that the chain of events had happened quickly, and through the gloaming it was not possible to ascribe intent to anyone. The men crouched as they ran with Elvira so that they did resemble monkeys, but it is absolutely true that she rode like a queen on her litter, and with the scrap of her white shirt billowing in the dark she looked as if she were lit from inside. I couldn't exactly see my mother in the commotion, but she was somewhere close enough, I knew she was. She had surely gone to find my father, the man who could whistle with two fingers, stop the gang in their tracks should they get too rowdy. The rest of the men made for the pond, some sprinting, some stumbling, and I was there also. I used to love the games at camp, crawling with your heart ringing in your ears through the woods, not knowing if the boys behind the trees were your own team or the enemy. One of the officers had caught up with Merks and Hecht, and he had his arms raised to Elvie, running beside her. It was a corporal who was unraveling the rest of her binding—and so into the night fabric came fluttering into their wake.

Karen later repeated to me what the men were saying, were shouting, she said, but I remember the quietness, how light-footed the men must have been to run so softly through the grass. I remember the white binding floating behind them and the hush of their breathing, as if they were unnamed animals moving together in the wild toward a drink.

The pond is hardly more than a puddle with a collar of mud all the way around, and cannot be more than a few feet deep at its center. By the time Merks and Hecht reached the straggling grass at the water's edge, most of Elvira's clothing from the waist up had been stripped away. Karen, in a poem she wrote about the incident, described those men as a group of large birds gathering to pull apart and eat something half alive. But there is this: Elvira, for one, was not kicking or yelling or biting or pulling hair or remonstrating in any way. To me, in the moment, her stillness seemed just right and not at all strange.

When Hecht said, "Let's wash her up proper," the voices of the others, the cheers and the hoots, swelled into the air, as if they were celebrating, almost, I say almost, as if they were joyful. She was spread between the two of them, Hecht with her arms, Merks with her legs, and they were about to throw her into the pond—one, two, three—becoming boys again, boys with the one girl on a summer night. I'd swear if I had to that there was that sense of playfulness, and so I had little doubt that after the dunking we'd get back to the business of the evening, each according to his own. Elvira would shake herself off, I'd get her a blanket, she'd find her extra shirt. The men would continue to razz her, but someone would know to claim her as a mascot, the secret pride of the 28th Wisconsin. They'd figure that part out, I was sure of it. They were not so stupid, those men, and they'd quickly understand that she would set them apart, be their mystery jewel in the crown. No one would know about her, and yet she would make the 28th Wisconsin stand enviably tall. Elvira, their *je ne sais quoi*. Before that could happen, though, Merks and Hecht readied themselves to toss her, Karen knelt by the woods fishing in her bag, the men gathered around the pond, and I was still coming on, just about to get to the clearing.

As we were reaching our places, I heard something like a wail, a siren in the distance, I thought, the muffled sound of a far-off emergency. Not the noise Artemis made as she appeared on the scene to rescue Iphigenia from sacrifice, not the clarion call of a goddess come to do the over-the-top mission impossible. Mrs. Shaw had had enough foresight, I guess you'd call it, to stop at the fire and pick up the ten-inch carving knife Merks had brought along to slice the venison roast. She had not, after all, been hunting down my father. One minute I was about to catch up to the men and the next she was tearing in front of me, that kooky whine coming from yet another new place within her teeming self. Of course it stood to reason that she, with her bottled rage, would be the person to make a harpy noise in the woods, at night, when it was supposed to be quiet. She was pounding toward the pond waving that relatively short knife overhead, an instrument with a high-carbon stainless-steel blade, a weapon that had not had a place at the battle of Shiloh, a tool that did betray a certain farbishness on the part of Merks.

I have a fair amount of certainty that it was my mother, and only my mother, who determined the scene in which we found ourselves. If she could have seen herself charging those men, she would no doubt have been mortified. In the first place, she was amusingly puny in her shorts and T-shirt, hideously modern in her effects, and in the second, her eyes were bugged out, her curls had gone limp and were stuck to her face. The picture of delicacy, our Mrs. Shaw. I will say that she had strength of some kind; even if it was merely the lunatic's power to shock, to display our most primitive longings. I'm sure we all wanted to avert our eyes, as one does before the village idiot masturbating on the green. In her case she didn't raise her voice, didn't screech. It was more of a gibber, a continuous thin jabber. "Let go of her, let go right now, goddamn you, get your hands off her." She was babbling and waving that knife over her head in a way that was not at all safe.

"Mom," I called from behind. "Mom, hold on—"

She was running as hard as she could, hurling herself toward the crowd of men near the water. She wasn't going to stop, wasn't going to slow down, she was going to slice off their hands, their arms, cut through their hearts, whatever stood in her way, a regular Lizzie Borden, whack, whack, whack.

"What the fuck!"

"Jesus, lady!"

That silver blade whirred, the air streamed near the men's throats. Some of them jumped, parting the way, others stumbled backward. It was her pop eyes, the pitch of her whine, and her spastic propeller arm, as much as the knife, I think, that made them clear the path. She had been released from all of her personalities, from Mrs. Shaw, from Beth Gardener, from Liza38. She was perhaps as free as she had ever imagined herself, frothing at the mouth, swinging her blade. At the water's edge courage or righteous indignation failed even Hecht and Merks. Because they had not anticipated a force like my mother, in a few disjointed motions they dropped

Elvira. I can't say I blame them, under the circumstances. Merks ducked and Hecht scrambled to safety. Elvira, having been deposited in the sludge, dragged herself farther into the water and lay there, head submerged, as if she would prefer to drown than live through the following five minutes.

It's possible that the men, at that point, would have taken after my mother if she hadn't gone into the pond. I'm not saying that they wouldn't have harmed her. In ankle-deep water she seized Elvira under one arm and hauled her into a sitting position. Elvie sputtered a little, shook her head. Mrs. Shaw squatted and turned her daughter to her, in a sort of embrace, so that Elvira's naked back was to her friends. With this human shield in place Liza took one short breath, what she needed to settle her voice to the right raspy pitch. "If I do not kill you now, do you understand," she said, "I will have you killed."

Although not much surprised me anymore, it was news to me, that she was acquainted with hit men, that offing any one of the reenactors would require her only to snap her lily-white fingers.

Hecht said, "Listen, ma'am, Elvirnon—whatever her name is—"

"Leeeeave usss." That long *e*, followed by the hiss, sounded like a spell, a curse.

"Lady, you're way out of line here—"

My mother ordered them away again in her snaky tongue. They stood staring at her, those men who could conceivably have marched with Sherman through Georgia to the sea, burning and pillaging as they went. When one of them moved toward her, Hecht held him back and Liza lifted her knife. Brandished it, as we say in the trade. If I hadn't been more or less in shock, I might have laughed at her dramatic gesture, at the sheer nerve of an ordinarily weak person. It was Hecht who marshaled the troops, who told the men it was time to retreat. He once more showed dignity in his delivery, in his quiet demand that they return to the campfire, that they go eat their dinners. They did as he said, the good soldiers fading into the night, a few of them grumbling, as if against their own wills they'd been wished away.

I could see the white strips, the binding material in the grass, and I picked some of it up, and I went farther back to the torn vest, a shred of shirt. After all her effort my mother was breathing hard and coughing. When I heard her, I had to stop, had to ask myself what had happened. The men were gone and it was the three of us and the standard noises of a person in her own living room. What had just happened? Mrs. Shaw was sitting on the mucky edge of the pond, holding Elvira, meaning to protect her, I guess, against the chill air. More important, who was it, I wondered, who would actually know what had taken place? Elvie had her eyes closed, praying again, praying that she was only in a nightmare, that she'd soon wake up sitting next to Hecht at the fire. Karen was standing in the lane, her hands at her face, snapping pictures, I later learned, of the men as they returned to the venison roast.

I'm sure that I was still embarrassed for my mother. Not only had she been raving, she could have hurt someone pretty badly. What had she been thinking? She had been crazed enough to cut a jugular. She might have plunged that expensive carving knife into a man's gut. I think I started to shake, in the aftermath, not for myself, but for her, for what she seemed capable of doing. It was then, as my legs started to go, that she looked over at me, as if she knew I'd be right there, standing with bits of Elvira's uniform in my hands. She cleared her throat, she called to me, called, "Henry."

I went toward her, and before she told me to find Dad, before she gave her instruction, it seemed that for the first time in a year she was saying something real, talking in that old wordless way we used to have. I came near enough to see that she was actually looking at me, and I let everything I knew go as I held her gaze, as she said to me, in her silence, I leave this to you, Henry. You saw it all. You, in your quietness, you cobble together some kind of meaning.

Chapter Fifteen

Plenty of couples, at least in the world of make-believe, are brought together by calamity, the illness or death of a child, a debilitating accident or natural disaster, but who would have thought that a few men dicking around with Elvira would give the Shaws' marriage something akin to electric shock therapy? I sometimes wonder if Elvira actually had very little to do with the scene, if it was only the ways in which my parents responded to the situation that propelled them homeward. Who knows what crime or foolery any one person is capable of committing? Maybe my mother was also stoned at Bloody Pond and therefore in her dream state, acting from what seemed her purest impulses. The steps my father took in the aftermath were predictable, I suppose, and yet I have not found anyone, except Liza, who recognized how true he was to his own character, that his course of action was both implausible and wackily proper.

At the Pickwick Landing State Park Inn that night, by the pool, Karen and I got into an argument about the incident. My parents had gone together into my room with Elvira to try to console her, if in fact that's what she needed, and to try to figure out what had gone on. The squabble got started when I mentioned my mother's performance, her swashbuckling, I called it. Karen was standing on the cement steps of the pool, wading back and forth, but when I said the word "swashbuckling," probably in a sarcastic tone, she quit her pacing. She drew her skirts a little higher, and climbed out onto the deck.

"Your mother," she said, "was phenomenal." She was coming at me, toward my chair, in a stride and at a speed that seemed familiar. "She was completely stellar."

"I wouldn't go that far," I said.

She had reached me, was towering over me in a way that was not as friendly as you'd think a chum should be. "Did you hear that guy describing a Kotex? Did you?"

"I think so."

"He called it a sign of disease. A sign of pestilence, filth—he said filth."

"They were being dramatic," I said, meaning really that it was my mother who had been so. I tipped back in my chair, to try to preserve a modicum of my personal space. Customarily Karen would have sat me down and gently and firmly explained to me why she thought I was cuckoo. I was, however, already sitting. "No," she said. "They were not being dramatic." With her tight mitts she shook the folds of her black skirt. "Men take action because they mean it. They mean it. That—rape. The rape was not for show."

"Rape?"

She looked upon me as if she might take off my head with her hands or her teeth.

"Did I miss something?" I was stupid enough to ask. Did every woman have secret rage, the killer instinct?

"Did you miss something? Good question, Hank. Might you have missed the part where those men, the walking thesauruses, were saying, 'You can have her first, Mel,' and 'Show her your weapon, Mel,' and 'Shove it down her diesel dyke throat, Mel, and into her lesbo clam.' Did you miss that, Henry? Did you miss the part where they were yucking it up about her bubs, her maracas, about taking turns—"

"They weren't going to do any—"

"Of course not, they weren't going to as much as touch her. They were running toward the pond, drunk out of their minds, shouting about giving Elvie a little protein, a little sugar. But you're right, I'm sure they meant having tofu and carob bars for dinner." She was speaking in quite a loud voice herself in that chlorinated steam bath of a room. "When they were hollering about showing her their tools, they probably meant their Swiss Army knives, all the cool gadgets besides the blade."

"No," I said, remembering the choreography of the men, how gracefully they had moved around Elvie, and when they'd carried her, she'd been erect, as if she were the figure at the prow of a ship. She'd looked as if she were certain of her course. There had been a lightheartedness in the men and in the prank itself. "They weren't dangerous," I said to Karen. "And it was quiet. I could hear all of them breathing."

She moved closer to me, if that's possible. "You could hear them breathing and did not hear their obscenities—that's beautiful. That's perfect, that's really you, Henry. Where were you when they were about to throw her in the pond? As I recall you were there, watching. The men were discussing, at the top of their lungs, who should slam her first. For you it was quiet, oh my God. Why should I be surprised? You have not realized so many things, for so long." She started to cry, something I had never seen her do before.

"I—," I began.

She covered her closed eyes with her fingertips, recovering herself. "According to you," she said, looking down at me again in her contemptuous way, "according to Henry Shaw, those guys were going to throw Elvira into the pond, politely toss her into the shallow water, and then help her out, and if her neck wasn't broken, if she wasn't paralyzed, they were going to lend her their shirts and say what a good sport she'd been. Do I have that right?"

"It was a prank," I said, "a tease."

She backed away, as if she'd just realized I was a person she did not want to touch or be near. To continue in the spirit of high drama, she declared, "Your mother saved her. I'm sorry, you're not only a dimwit but you're also a pig, no better than the rest of them. Without your mother Elvira would be dead."

It was after she had left so abruptly that she began work, in the lobby, on "Shiloh Mist," a poem that won her the freshman literary prize at Yale a year later. The poem was about, among other things, the terrible moment when your best love reveals his weaknesses. While she was off documenting her feelings, I did not get busy, did not start immediately with pen and paper to narrate the event. Instead, I sat by the pool for a while empty-handed, trying to figure out what had happened, both at Bloody Pond and more recently with Karen. I thought I was painfully aware of my limitations, but if I was dim-witted, that would explain why I didn't know I was dim-witted. I could point out to her that I had gotten a slightly higher score on the math SATs, tied with her on the verbal, and what about the way she could pack away a man-size, husband-pleasing meal in a single sitting?

I replayed the scuffling that had taken place at the campfire, thought through it several times, and when that was done, I maintained that the men of the 28th Wisconsin would not ultimately have been hostile or dangerous to Elvira, that the intervention of Mrs. Shaw was unnecessary and served only to muddy the waters. I considered whether the men might have had more respect for Elvie's situation if she'd menstruated authentically, if she had used wads of cotton and taken the soiled clumps down to the Tennessee River, washed them out and laid them to dry on the rocks along the bank. As I said, there were scores of women who went to war, several hundred documented cases of females who dressed as men and took up arms. It could be said that in spite of the Pantiliner, Elvira was the most exaggeratedly authentic person on the field of battle that weekend—we all told her that afterward.

"Home from Tennessee," my mother wrote to Polloco, when we got back. "Exhausted." Too tired, no doubt, to tell the story, to try to explain what it meant to have a daughter like Elvira, to have the privilege of being the mother to such a spirited and courageous girl. Too weary to think critically through her part in the circus, to admit to Polloco that she was seething with rage, that it might pay to get a bulletproof vest or some kind of protection for his neck, in case she ever let it rip, up in Tribbey.

The night of the infamy I had been sent out by the warmonger herself, into the darkness, on a federal property that covers four thousand acres, to find my father. I was thankful to bump into him by Hurlbut's 4th Division Monument, not all that far from Bloody Pond.

"Elvira's been outed," I said.

"What!" he said. "Elvie?—Was it bad?"

"Ah," I said. Had it been bad or merely bizarre?

"She okay? Is she hurt?"

"She's fine. I—I think she's fine."

He and I quickly broke camp and carried the supplies to the idling van on the Hamburg-Savannah Road. We did not, incidentally, recover the buttons from the vest, those that had the much-sought-after Civil War patina. Liza had managed to get her stringy hair out of her face, and her eyes had settled back into her head, but her hands on the steering wheel were twitchy. Elvira lay in the way-back, wrapped in an army blanket. The men of the 28th Wisconsin were nowhere in sight, having taken off, Karen said with authority, to avoid arrest. My father tried to get the gist from Mrs. Shaw as we drove to the motel, but my mother snapped at him. "It isn't a story," she said.

"No, of course not, not yet," he said. "But something did happen."

All of that was so, but he could see that it was perhaps wise not to talk about it in front of Elvira. He'd patted the lump of blanket that was herself, hadn't gotten much out of her but a grunt. We drove the twenty-five minutes to the town of Counce without anyone saying a word. Later that night there was quite a bit of discussion between my parents about what action should be taken against Bernard Hecht and the others, and possibly the entire unit, on, at the least, a discrimination charge.

I missed some of the interchange while I was sitting by the pool with Karen, but from what I could gather my mother had been brief in her summary. I don't think she pointed out, as was her wont, that my father from the beginning was responsible for Elvira's present misery. She was general in her condemnation of the men, of their brutality and coarseness, and Kevin did not press her very hard for details. Once he was clear on the fact that there'd been no physical harm, he relaxed considerably. At about midnight, when Karen finally came in the room from the lobby, flushed from her creative outburst, she lay down on the cot the management had brought in and offered up her statement. "Nothing," she said, "nothing, despite the feminist movement, has really changed for women."

Liza did not take that opportunity to elaborate upon the Bloody Pond scene, to brag to Kevin that she had done her sex proud. She told him in vague terms that the three of us, Karen, Henry, and herself, had made enough of a fuss to repel the drunken louts. It was certainly generous of her to include us in her portrayal. In another misrepresentation, she claimed that Elvira was scared stiff, that she'd gone catatonic with fear.

My parents went around and around, trying to decide whether it would be better for Elvira to have a public airing of the violation, or if it was best that we gather our things and go without a word back to Chicago. Elvira didn't want to talk about any of it. I don't deny that she had been humiliated and maybe somewhat violated, but it was also true that she went about being dispirited in a grand manner. She lay in my room on my king-size bed with, for whatever reason, a warm washcloth over her eyes. I'm not sure why my mother needed to sleep on a rollaway beside her, keeping vigil, unless she thought Elvira might suddenly come down with cholera from the dormant plagues festering in the pond. Karen and my father and I were crammed into the smaller room, the one with twin beds and the cot. As it was late, it hardly mattered where we slept, and yet it was as surreal as any of the preceding incidents, Karen coming out of the bathroom in her flannel pajamas that had many many cows jumping over many many moons, while Dad and I were in the beds with the plaid covers pulled up to our chins.

Kevin turned off the light, and in the dark, into the muzzy darkness, I said, "Mom wanted to kill them all." I thought it was important to mention that detail, that he should know. "By the pond, she seemed willing to—"

"Uh-huh," Kevin said.

Karen sat up. "They deserved it."

"She was sort of flipped out," I said, turning toward my father's bed. "I don't know if anyone took her seriously, because she was hysterical."

"Yes, they did," Karen barked. "You damn well bet they did."

"She had a knife," I glided on. "I don't know, it seemed like she could have used it."

"If anyone could, she's the woman for the job," Kevin said, yawning. "She's the one," he said more distinctly, as if he were proud of her. Adequately protected, with the murderess right next door, he fell asleep. Wasn't that an interesting piece to learn about my father in the middle of the night? He condoned murder under certain circumstances, and he'd have scraped together bail money, stood by my mother if she'd stuck the knife down to the hilt into Hecht's bilious gut. What was wrong with these people? Karen, at the foot of the bed, on her cot, lay still and so did I, both of us acutely aware of each other, both of us, I'm sure, having an imaginary argument about Mrs. Shaw's posturing by Bloody Pond.

Karen's line: Your mother was brave and noble.

My part: Was not! She's a loony.

Brave!

Loony!

Brave!

Loony!

I think it was at the Pickwick Landing State Park Inn that I dreamed of Karen overtaking me, swallowing me, making me her love slave, pretty much against my wishes. In the dream I, the hero, was like a person standing on a beach when the tsunami hits. It was a short, exhausting night and I was not sorry to wake up.

Sunday morning my sister kept the shades down, the cloth in place on her face, and she insisted again on being left alone. Karen volunteered to sit in Elvira's bathroom, to keep an eye on her, while the rest of us continued our discussion in the lobby. To no one's amusement but my own I called Elvira's convalescence her Mary Todd Lincoln moment. Although none of us could of course see forward to any positive outcome, I think it's true that the experience at Shiloh gave Elvira additional steam that would hold her in good stead well past her schooling. There was a brief period at Jesse Layton when she threatened to apply to the Citadel, but already she was on the path to becoming a do-gooder, a rabble-rouser, volunteering for the AIDS project, teaching morris dancing to Hispanic fifth graders at Hull House, and going south to save the rain forest one summer. The year before she went to study social policy at Harvard, she worked as an advocate for migrant workers' children in California. She brought home in packs serious young women with heavy black-framed glasses and crew cuts, young women who were intent on changing the world, certain that it could be done. Kevin, for one, always enjoyed their company and got a kick out of sparring with them, giving them a run for their money. If Elvie bored us a little at holidays, ranting about the fine print in federal and state legislation, she was putting her rage to good use and I'm sure we admired her. All those years she'd pored over *The Official Records of the Union and Confederate Armies* had been great training for the future policy wonk.

Early on Saturday morning my parents drove back to the park, routed out the commanding officers of the 28th Wisconsin, and arranged for a meeting with the regiment at one o'clock, between the noon Field Medical Demonstration and the two P.M. Infantry Demonstration. There were a couple of bargaining chips my father used, tools that made him feel confident the men would make an appearance. First, he had all of their addresses. It would not be difficult to find any of them should he and my mother decide to prosecute. Second, there was evidence. Many exhibits of torn clothing, a partly singed Pantiliner, and as it turned out, photographs that Karen had taken at the scene of the crime. Always at the ready, from her backpack she had whipped out her twenty-five-millimeter Instamatic camera, loaded with general exposure film, and with the flash sparking up the scene, she had documented the huddle of men streaking through the night, my mother standing in the water in her John the Baptist pose, and the shreds of clothing cast off in the grass. There was no such thing as a one-hour developing joint anywhere near where we were, but my father was confident that the photographs would be usable, if need be. He spoke about them to the captain as if they were already printed in Technicolor.

It was in the Shiloh Methodist Church as the bell tolled the hour of one that the Shaws, minus Elvira, came before Captain Rigert, Lieutenant Hecht, the three sergeants, the six corporals, the adjunct, and a host of privates. The men had been camping for two nights, most of them without tents, and they were authentically disheveled and unwashed. There were forty or so of them, looking as if they'd been dragged to Sunday school, as if they had closed themselves off to the message and were putting in their time until they could get back outside to play.

David Merks was the only member who had ditched. Lieutenant Hecht sat in the front, next to the captain, the bad boy under supervision of the teacher. Elvira's friend Al was there, with his father, both of them looking surly. I could imagine that the captain, Lars Rigert, when he'd heard about it all, had ordered the men to show up. He might have told them that it was best to contain the damage, to hear the Shaws out, to accommodate them if possible. He was a librarian from Beaver Dam, Wisconsin, and he knew, from being in a school system for twenty-five years, how explosive a thing, even if it is a nonevent, can become.

My father came down the aisle and went up the stairs to the altar table with the flowers and the chalice. He was wearing his Illinois infantryman's long blue wool coat, a homespun checked shirt, the buff leather waist belt with the brass keeps and the standard belt plate, the gift Elvira had given him for Christmas several years earlier. He held his forage cap in his hands. What Kevin understood from two decades of teaching was the principle of elevation and dimension: to be an effective instructor, one should always appear larger than the audience.

"Thank you," he said finally. "Thank you for taking time out to listen." He was solemn, as the situation warranted, but he couldn't keep his nature, himself, from shining through. He smiled, just the right amount, a little sadly, as if this talk were the last thing in the world he wanted to do. Still, somebody had to do it; it was a job that could not go undone when you considered that a daughter was involved, and golly, if he wasn't the one who had somehow or other been chosen. He could communicate all of those sentiments without saying a word. By the tilt of his head, the hesitant grin, the folding of his hands at his breastbone. The atmosphere in the room lightened, and the men softened somewhat, in the pews. They could see that Kevin Shaw wasn't interested in nailing anyone in particular, but also, because there was a daughter involved, they might well have had the feeling that if he had to nail someone, he could make quick work of it. There is no question that in certain situations my father is a genius.

When he explained to the group what had happened, he left out the telltale item, and he didn't so much talk about the breach, the misdemeanors committed. He explained how Elvira felt, what she must have gone through as her cover was blown. How afraid she must have been, how heavyhearted it must have made her, that the era of Elvirnon was over. He described her passion for reenacting, and he reminded the men that they had embraced Elvirnon; they had held him up as a model recruit, touted him as the future of reenacting. They had been proud of him. "Men," he said, "she took it seriously, to the point—"

He needed a moment to gather himself. Mrs. Shaw and I were seated in the back, both of us, I think, wondering where he was going with his message. Kevin clasped his hands and nodded slightly, as if he were coming to an agreeable conclusion with himself. He could not have described Elvira more nobly if he'd been giving her eulogy, glossing over the fanatical aspects of her personality. "She took it seriously," he began again, "to the point that she believed in a past life. Her own past life. She sensed that she'd died here, at Shiloh, that she had been a drummer boy walking over these fields. She confided this to me, and I have never, before now, told it to anyone, including—" He looked out past the men, to my mother. "Including my wife. But I think it's appropriate to share this with you, so that you understand the profundity of her feelings for this endeavor."

All the Shaws not only with secrets but with secret previous lives!

What about Kevin? Where had he been in 1862 or 1492 or the first year of our Lord? Maybe we'd been tripping down the millenniums together since time immemorial, in various configurations, husbands and wives and children and lovers and slaves. Maybe Polloco had once upon a time been my brother or my son or my dog. Liza, in the latter-day Shiloh moment, was wearing a black sleeveless shirt and a long Lily-type skirt, not quite so frothy but flowered and flowing. She had been restored to her feminine non-butcher-knife-swinging state, although she, too, looked pale and wan, a little beaten down. She may have been worrying that the assault would push Elvira over the edge into lesbian mania. It occurred to me that Elvira might never have been a girl before this incarnation with the Shaw family. It's possible, I thought, that it takes a few lifetimes to adjust to womanhood, that you don't get the hang of it on the first go-around, that Elvira's discomfort with her own gender was born from nothing more than a lack of experience.

My father was explaining to the sinners that Elvira had had a vivid dream a few years back, a dream about dying in the Peach Orchard. Whether or not you believed in such things, he said, was immaterial. It was an act of bravery, was it not, on Elvira's part, to come and do a living history at a place of real or imagined past anguish?

"But in a larger sense—"

Oh God, no! He was going into his Lincoln spasm!

"In a larger sense, yesterday for Elvira was a test for someone so dedicated, someone who gave her full measure." My mother closed her eyes and grimaced. "That she should come here, to this field of battle, this hallowed ground, to understand her struggle and have then a different kind of death, a wounding of her spirit so grave that this love of hers cannot now long endure."

I glanced again at Mrs. Shaw. She was staring hard at me, as if to say Help!

"This love of hers has been crushed," he went on. "You, you men, have let her down. You have opened her eyes to evil." He said the word "evil" quietly, as if he didn't want to acknowledge it, didn't want to think about any kind of dark underside.

"What happened yesterday," he said, thankfully back to using his own syntax, "was criminal, something that could be punished by law. My wife and I have discussed calling in the police. We have weighed what that would mean for our daughter—exposure again, further humiliation. We have weighed that against the satisfaction of due punishment and retribution. Never have I seen men, capable, committed men such as yourselves, act in so uncivilized a manner. Nothing but time can ease the harm that has come to Elvira. Nothing but maturity can dull the keenness of her disillusionment. Even so, you must know that because she is at such an impressionable age, there will always be a scar, a trace of this injustice, that neither time nor maturity can take away. This incident will always be a part of Elvira."

I knew him well enough to realize that he was soon going to forgive them. He was using his darkest-hour-before-the-dawn approach. It was curious or perverse that my change of heart came right before his absolution. I thought suddenly of Elvira in her bed with the washcloth over her eyes, trying to blot out the image, the feel, of Merks's bald paws under her binding. You'd have to press firmly to find the rise of a breast under all that material, or else drive your hand up hard through the tight wrapping. *Elvira!* I wanted to be the one to shout it now, as if another person calling her name with the force of love could change the scene, take back whatever she'd suffered. I have more than once been blamed for not caring how other people feel, but that day I had a brief understanding of what it may have felt like to be Elvira at the campfire. I imagined Merks's ugly hands—for an instant I thought I knew how sweaty and pale and eager they were, sliding up Elvira's ribs. The sense of it faded almost as quickly as it had come, but I remembered long after that I'd felt the hands, that I'd had a physical understanding of what it was to be at someone's mercy. Whether or not Elvira experienced the sensations of a victim is still questionable, but at the Shiloh church that day I had what I thought was a stab of fellow feeling for her.

"Nothing can erase last night," my father was saying, "but I would ask you people for a couple of things that might serve to mitigate the blow."

"Stop him," I whispered to my mother.

"Number one," Kevin said, "I request that you who were in-volved, human beings my daughter admired, I request that you write her an apology. And number two, I ask that you consider what there is in you that allowed you to go after a girl who was only doing as you have done—pursued an interest, a passion, with an undying commitment."

Good old Kevin, appealing to those weather-beaten men to get out their stationery and compose a note to his daughter. He, like Pol-loco, believed in the power of the written word. In the next plot twist, in the next life, Richard and Kevin could run off together.

There was a moment of imperfect quiet, the uneasy shifting, the rustle of clothing, a cough or two. The captain stood and came to the altar, a step beneath my father, so that there was the affect of suppli-cation. It had come hard upon the unit, he said, that all along a young girl had been in their company, the fairer sex who had been listening to the conversations, the dreams, and yes, also the desires of the men who believed they could speak freely. That fact, the captain said, did not sit right with anyone in the regiment. He wasn't saying they were justified, certainly not; the actions they had taken were most regret-table. The offenders, he said, would be disciplined. They might even be court-martialed.

Bernard Hecht, head down, staring at the floor, was stoic, as al-ways, ready to meet his fate. If it had been 1862, Elvirnon would probably not have been treated like a lady. She might have been fucked up and down, backward and forward, by the lads who hadn't had a furlough in a while. I imagined that Hecht had those thoughts going through his head, that he would have liked to set the record straight, to inform the crowd that Elvirnon had gotten off easy. El-vira's friend Al scowled. They had dunked her, that was about it. More like, she'd dunked herself. They'd ripped her clothes some and dropped her by the water. And for that they'd nearly gotten their heads chopped off.

The men were grateful to my father, the captain said, for keeping the matter within rank, for not turning to the law of the larger land in these troubled times. It was his hope that Elvira would rejoin the war effort, that she'd stop by if she came to a reenactment, that she would come to forgiveness.

Someone in the back called, "She can leave the mother at home."

"Leave her in the kitchen, with her cleavers!"

Mrs. Shaw, do something! Lash out now!

The captain held up his hand, to silence the men. "Forgiveness," he said, "is what we all need to harbor in our breasts in this time of conflict."

Kiss my ass about forgiveness!

I turned to look at my mother one last time, trying to glower, to move her, to inspire her to a little insanity, a tad, a titch, a button-size piece of madness. Merks at the least should be jailed, should be hung; all of them should be made to march around at Elvira's bidding. Liza was watching the ceiling fan as if she were listening to an ordinary sermon. Funny, the times she chose to be inert. How could she stand by and let the captain treat the matter as if it were taking place in 1862? I got up, went the short distance to the entrance, stepped into the daylight, and slammed the door somewhat, in honor of Elvira. I told myself that my time with the Shaws would soon be done. In a week I'd find out if any college had accepted me. I was going to leave the lunacy, even if no school offered me a spot. I'd hop a train, work at the Gap, anything, anything to get away. My parents had stood by for the charade, for the playacting that had nothing whatsoever to do with a real apology for what had happened in real life. I still thought it probable that most of the men had been merely having a caper, some shenanigans, and yet I could not get past the image of Merks's hands on Elvira. He should be charged and booked for those beady hands alone.

Several minutes after my departure Mr. and Mrs. Shaw came out into the warm April morning. "Hi," my mother called, moving in light, dancing steps to the van. I was leaning against the locked door, my face to the sun. When she took me by the arm, she heaved a great big theatrical sigh. "Sometimes," she said, "you just take what you can get."

"Or sometimes," I said, "you take as much as you can get. *You* take as much as you can possibly get."

"Do I?" she asked, cocking her head. "I did the best I could, which is usually short of the ideal. But Dad—what a guy! He handled it beautifully. You never know when a certain kind of zaniness will come in handy. The captain said he'd had a magic moment, that Dad looked and spoke so much like Grant it was an honor to be in his presence."

"Grant? What are you talking about? Dad was in his Lincoln mode."

"He did have me worried there for a minute. I was just waiting for him to say that this girl, under God, was going to have a new birth of freedom." She shook her head, snorting, smiling, as if there were no one she had more affection for than her husband.

"Dad doesn't even look like Grant," I said, stuck on the captain's stupidity.

"The men will do as Dad asks, that's the main thing. They respect him. It's much better for Elvie this way, I know it is." She wrinkled her nose, in the manner of her daughter. "You take as much as you can get," she murmured, back to the start of our conversation. "I don't really think it's a matter of taking or getting. You've got to make what you have be enough. That's the trick, the awful trick."

"Awful," I said.

"It's true, too, that you have to be careful what you wish for. I never understood that, but you really do have to be sensible even when you're dreaming."

I think I laughed at that piece, at her hard-won wisdom.

"But the beauty of the system," she blathered on, "is that sometimes, when you're not looking for anything in particular, you're showered with riches. There's no sense to the world's workings, no sense at all."

It was definitely time for her to change careers, start writing greeting cards or drawing the misty flowers on Kleenex boxes. My father appeared on the other side of the car, and before he could speak, someone called to him, "Good job, Shaw!"

"Thanks, thanks a lot," my father said, waving as if he were a celeb at the stage door. Over the roof of the van he said to me, "I'm going to send the letter to the captain, that letter I wrote about Elvirnon being hurt at Shiloh, and he'll pass it around to the men. Pretty much just as we planned. There's a spirit to the story, and I can't help but think that's good. Elvira's going to be okay. She's going to be fine."

"No offense or anything, Dad," I said, "but I think you're all fucking crazy."

He nodded, as if he'd expected to hear that, as if I told him so every day.

"I mean you're both fucked," I said as fiercely as I could manage under my breath. My parents didn't hear me, and playing my own part, the disaffected teenager, I got into the van, put on my headsets, turned up the music as loud as it could go, all of that raw anger beating down past my ears and into my chest.

When we got back to the motel, the poet and Elvira were swimming in the pool. I'd gone to the church with the Shaws partly out of curiosity but in the main to try to impress Karen, to be the concerned brother seeing the incident to its end. I hoped she'd taken note of my efforts, that she would soon speak to me or even look in my direction. It was always surprising to see Elvira in her bathing suit, her shiny one-piece suit, to see the outlines of her girl's body. "I don't want to hear about it," she said, folding herself into the towel, heading back to the room she'd appropriated for herself.

Mustering my courage, I tried out my joke on Karen, the concept that had flopped with my parents. "Congratulations," I said, "for getting Ms. Mary Todd out of her chamber."

She did laugh and I was able then to make my next move, to tell her that it had taken a lot of time and energy for the dim-witted swine to come up with a punch line.

"You're doing very well," she said breezily. "Would you mind taking a look at this?" She pulled out her notebook from her tote bag, carrying on as if we'd had no argument. While she stood by dripping, I read her poem, fifty award-winning lines that, not surprisingly, glorify the girl victim and the woman warrior. The young man, the observer in her poem, is not drawn with much sympathy, is, in fact, pretty much a weenie. I hadn't exactly experienced what she'd described, but perhaps being sure, being insistent, are the best gifts of a real writer. It seemed to me that despite its subject matter and the brainless bystander, "Shiloh Mist" was a good poem. I said so. I said that I disliked the wimp but that the poem was great. My appreciation for her work and my newfound understanding of Elvira's pain allowed us to genuinely move past our quarrel, to go forward. Both the scene in the church and the event at Bloody Pond had an hallucinatory quality, but I was willing to say that no matter who did or did not do what, Elvira had suffered. I could not bring myself to call the violence rape, but in the moment I came to a compromise figure with Karen, settling on a solid 85 percent of the male population that should be castrated. Up from my initial offering of 75 percent and down from her inflated figure of worldwide eradication of the testicle. The temporary surge of love and protection for my sister, and hatred for just about everyone else, was no doubt similar to patriotic fervor, and I thoroughly enjoyed it for the nine hours it lasted.

"Shiloh did not live up to Elvira's expectation," my mother wrote to Jane. "Ultimately, probably a good thing."

We started home to Chicago that afternoon without saying much. Karen lent Elvira her Walkman, and Elvira, in the middle seat, listened through our stack of CDs with her eyes closed. Up front my parents talked softly. Near Champaign-Urbana, in the middle of the night, Karen started telling me jokes, some pretty vile, off-color jokes. We were worn out in the first place, and in the second, Karen is the last person you'd think would have an extensive repertoire of dead baby and Helen Keller jokes. That was something I had not known about her. I started laughing. My mother had woken and suggested to my father that she take her turn driving. Karen was telling joke after joke, straight, without cracking a smile. I was laughing so hard I was wheezing and coughing. After a vivid punch line involving a blender Elvira sat herself up and turned around to us in the back. She was groggy, rubbing her eyes. "You are so gross, Henry. I can't believe how totally rotten, how completely gaggy that is."

Overnight she had apparently become refined, turned into Miss Manners. "I'm just laughing," I managed. "I didn't write the book."

"Do you know what a dog burger you are?" She threw her head back, speaking to the ceiling, to all of us, or no one in particular. "Do you know what Henry said to me? Do you know what his definition of a joke is?"

It was Karen who said, "What, Elvie?"

"He told me this—joke—like it was supposed to be funny, about Mom having sex with Richard Polloco. That is the pukiest thing I ever heard. It's worse than a dead elephant joke. Only a megadork could come up with a joke that retarded."

She nestled back down into her blankets and was fast asleep. Karen knew enough to turn away and look out into the black night, the equivalent, in a car, of leaving the room. My mother put her hands to her face. It was as if I'd slapped her. I could feel it, my own hand having gone out to her cheek, the sting of it, and her motion to cover the place. It was as if she, in the front seat, and I, eight feet back, were the only people in the van, as if we were facing each other. She stayed like that, making an effort, probably, to live up to the heroic standard she'd set for herself at Shiloh.

It was not odd, under the circumstances, how long my father waited to speak. "Now, why," he said finally, "why would she want to do that? When, after all, she has me?"

Way to go, Dad! The million-dollar question!

My mother removed her hand from her cheek and put it on my father's shoulder. "Why don't you pull over," she said, "and I'll drive." She massaged him a little. "Kev," she said.

.　　.　　.

That closed-up sense of being in the car lingered after we'd gotten back to our house. My parents seemed always to be behind their bedroom door, inside their steady murmur. When I bumped into Mrs. Shaw in the kitchen, she treated me as if we were business associates who had the misfortune to share the same office. Elvira spent a lot of time up in her room, playing some of my music. She right away had one session with the school social worker and another with a recommended therapist, a renowned grief counselor. In the middle of the third session she excused herself to go to the bathroom, met my mother in the reception area, and said she didn't need to return. Whatever Beth may have learned over the year, she did not yet know enough to lay off Elvira. On the way home she lectured my sister about keeping appointments and being responsible. I heard them coming up the stairs, Elvira saying, "I told her everything. I couldn't think of anything else to say."

Mrs. Shaw had been going to a therapist named Pella. It seemed to be a novel idea, that Elvira might not want to rehash her injuries or discuss the issues she had with her sibling, her mother, her neighborhood, or herself. Liza and Pella were probably doing extensive dialoguing about Minty, about how Minty's death might allow Beth to be the kind of person she had always longed to be against all the constraints of her middle-class upbringing and Middle Western culture. It is frightening to imagine the character Beth Shaw could become by self-activation. Pella had also no doubt been advising Liza to do projects with her daughter, to try to bond with her on Elvira's terms. Consequently, Liza had asked Elvira to teach her to rollerblade. Those lessons, however, never got off the ground, because although Beth would sacrifice anything for her children, she did not want to risk breaking her wrists. But she and Elvira had gone to a few movies Mrs. Shaw would normally have never seen, they'd had dinner together at a steak house, and one weekend they took horrible Hilare to Minty's cabin in Michigan, to get it ready for summer.

I don't know that they all became best friends, but they seemed to have had an acceptable time, walking on the beach, airing the linens, playing cards, and eating crackers and Cheez Whiz.

Not so long after the trip to Shiloh, Elvira was knocking around in her room across the hall from me. It sounded over there as if she were throwing heavy things, books and stones, from great heights. When I went to look, she was standing on a stool, cleaning out her closet, tossing her old tools of the trade into large cardboard boxes. She didn't want any of her former prized possessions, not the Civil War tomes, her toy soldiers and cannons, the videos, the gear, the memorabilia from all the sites and museums we'd visited through the years. She intended to give her sword and her musket to my father, she said, but everything else was going.

I went through the predictable speech. She shouldn't let a couple of drunks determine her future. She was a good reenactor, possibly even a great one, and she owed it to Elvirnon to keep it up.

"Save your breath, Henry."

"I mean it."

"So you mean it. Big deal. I mean it too."

"I thought you had more starch," I said, thinking I'd try to insult her, see what came of that tack.

"That's a good one," she said, laughing in a har-har way and slapping her knee. "What do you know about starch?"

I wanted to wallop her. What did she know about discretion? *Rot in farb hell, Elvirnon.* It did seem that she was going to be all right, that she might not need my bleeding heart, that I might be better off saving my sympathy for someone else. "I don't know about anything in the starch department, Elvirnon," I said. "That's why I look to you. Why, for example, didn't you struggle when those guys were hauling you around? I thought you were pretty starchy, not to kick and scream."

"Yeah, well," she said, shrugging. "You're supposed to play dead when you meet a bear." She betrayed only the slightest quiver of coolness, but I knew she loved being able to say that sentence, that she'd been waiting for me to ask her how she'd kept her head at Bloody Pond.

"Still," I said, "those guys were strong. Weren't you afraid?"

She jumped down from her stool and she squatted by the box, picked up a bust of General Ambrose Burnside, stroked the head for a minute. You could hardly blame her for stalling, for trying to figure out how to explain herself. "I was afraid, and I wasn't," she said slowly, going, I felt sure, for the truth. "At first I was really embarrassed, when they started ripping my clothes. I hated that part."

I nodded, remembering that I'd been able to imagine the feeling.

"But then everything happened fast, and all of a sudden when I saw Mom with the saber, I was most afraid that she was just going to be so dopey. I wanted to die."

I admired Elvira very much at that moment, for heightening the scene, for turning Merks's kitchen knife into a saber. Picture little Liza with a saber, almost as long as she is tall, trying to whip it over her head.

"Elvirnon," I said, saluting, "you will receive the medal of honor in the mail very shortly. Look for a plain white envelope. You're the model of starch and val—"

"You are such a dweeb," she said, embarrassed all over again, at another family member's buffoonery.

It was shortly after my father had hauled some of the boxes to school, for classroom use, and others out to the trash, that a few letters arrived addressed to E. Shaw. My mother, I think, was hoping that Elvira might feel disposed to sit at the kitchen table and read the apologies out loud, as if they were Christmas cards. I never saw them, but they were apparently contrite enough, all of them written in the compact script of a soldier who had a small amount of paper to his name. I suspect that the men left out their own deeds, so as not to incriminate themselves in a court of law, that they were laudatory about Elvirnon's skills. They invited her to say hello when she was on the circuit again, not exactly a wholehearted invitation to rejoin the group. Still, the letters finished the job, as my father had requested.

We could only assume that the men had followed through on his second demand, that they had looked into their hearts and taken stock of their characters. Maybe they'd all gone to group therapy. The entire affair could have been nasty in someone else's hands, both sides digging in their heels, adding injury and making light where both were not warranted. The 28th Wisconsin could have gone after Mrs. Shaw, although certainly she would have gotten off with an insanity plea. The unit had understandably wanted to avoid modern-day legal battles and sexual harassment suits, and so enough of them had dutifully written their letters to satisfy my father.

Years later Elvira would tell me that she'd decided, right then at the Pickwick Landing State Park Inn, that she would never return to the life of the reenactor, not because she'd been humiliated, but for a selfless reason, for a principle. She could see ahead, to the men letting her back in, picking up Elvirnon where she'd left him, eating his venison and hardtack. Everyone, however, this time around, would know that she was a girl masquerading as a boy. Gawkers would try to make out the shape of her breasts beneath her uniform and marvel at her hairdo. The men around the campfire would have to be careful, restrained. One thing would lead to the next, and it wouldn't take long for girls, silly girls, vacant girls, to start joining regiments as drummer boys and junior infantrymen. They'd insist. Elvira had set the precedent, and there'd be strident girls everywhere, typical girls who would run around swinging sabers over their heads whenever anything made them mad. It would be the end of serious reenactment.

Not too long after we'd gotten back from Shiloh, I was accepted at a small private college in Vermont, a place I could very easily major in women's studies or the Hacky Sack or the political oratory of the 1860s, or any other subject I happened to dream up. Only after my parents had sent in the deposit did Liza ask me what I was thinking might be my major. She had not looked me in the eye since the family vacation. I told her that my real aspiration was to have been part of the Cambridge spy ring during the Cold War, to be Kim Philby. Seeing, however, as that was no longer possible, I supposed I'd major in history or English. Good old conventional Beth Gardener, daughter of Minty and Dwight, heaved a sigh of relief and went down to the kitchen to get herself a tall glass of cold milk.

For the summer I was going to be a pot washer at Silverpines, a job I'd thought of applying for when I learned that Lily had signed up to work in the kitchen. She'd asked me if I was interested. I'd get paid a little bit, be away from home, play the cello in the band at night if I felt like it, live in the worker ghetto down by the lake, see old friends come and go through the summer during the various sessions. There was English Dance Week, American Dance Week, Scottish Dance Week, Folk Music Week, and so on. At first I'd been thinking I'd shelve books at the branch library or, at the other end of the spectrum, be a lifeguard at the Fullerton Beach. It was hard to say what sort of summer job hell would be preferable. There had been two drive-by shootings near the library that spring, and the beach would undoubtedly bring me girls!girls!girls!, a blistered nose, and the pleasure of being keenly bored. Karen was going to be in Israel, and so she would not be romping along the surf in her nineteenth-century full-body bathing costume. The thought of being with Lily, seeing her day after day, held for me an exquisite terror. Day after day after day with her, and how were we going to get up every morning and work if we were also making love night after night? What if she grew tired of me in the first week, and I was stuck for the rest of the summer washing pots? Elvira would not be at camp to provide the comic relief that had been so helpful the first time around. There might be a college student, a stud, who swept Lily off her feet, and I'd be left not only with the pots but with the middle-aged camper women in their tennis shoes and peasant blouses. My parents wisely left the decision to me. If my mother had urged me away, I might have been tempted to stay home only to annoy her.

The end of our family life as I had known it was in sight. Shirana had been right about spring bringing change. Elvira's secret was out, and instead of going through a major depression, overall she seemed relieved. She claimed she didn't want to be around those types of reenactors anyway. They were jerks, was her official line. Morons. They'd always disgusted her; she'd barely been able to tolerate them. Yes, we didn't say, we remember how difficult it was to drag you to every single event. She had let her hair grow out to the downy fuzz stage, and she was starting once again to look attractive—adorable, even. There was about her the appeal of the gosling. Her pride had been wounded, but she seemed to understand that wounded pride was something a person could heal herself, and in fairly short order. In that understanding she was remarkably mature. It's possible that she had been preparing to move on for some time, knowing, as she must have, that she couldn't keep up the charade indefinitely. She was at loose ends for a few months, but in the following year she was anointed as one of the high priestesses of the Layton volleyball team. Mrs. Shaw became a volleyball fanatic, screaming at the top of her lungs at Elvira's games. The relative normality of having a jock for a daughter apparently inspired her to become Elvira's greatest champion, at least in the bleachers.

In spring there will be great change, Henry. Great change. "Home from Tennessee," Liza38 had written to Polloco after Shiloh. "Exhausted." I came to wonder if it was in the end too difficult, too much trouble, to describe what had happened to her there. She had lost her mind somewhat, going after the men with the carving knife, and although I have argued the point with Karen, I still think that the violence wasn't really so much about the rescue of Elvira, the fierce mother protecting her cub. It's more likely that she was waving the sword from a general despair: off with your head and yours and yours. She loved Polloco, but he had come to her in the wrong season of her life. They hadn't been able to be young and free together— that was the tragedy, or the illusion, anyway, of tragedy. She could leave my father, but she could not take away or replace the story that she had already lived, and neither could she remove Kevin from those years. She might start over, make an effort to erase nearly two decades, or she could pretend that without him she had as much access to her memory as she'd ever need. In odd, bitter moments she knew that it would take years before she appeared in Richard's drama as anything more than a ghost, a walk-on. She could never be part of so much of his turbulent history, his youthful adventures, where life had been deeply felt.

For Mrs. Shaw there was also the small matter of not being able to play the piano in the time of Polloco. She'd lost her focus, or was there something in him that had slowly leached from her the pool of feeling, the notion of her own self, the still place within, what she had drawn upon to make her music for all her life before she'd known him? She had thought for a while that it would be worth it for him, for their love, to give up everything, not to care, but she didn't know anymore. Give her back her loneliness! But first, off with your head! And yours too!

When she wrote to Polloco about Shiloh, how could she tell him that she'd saved Elvira by the pond, and yet in the most curious way it was something that she could not have managed by herself. She believed that she had delivered Elvira out of Merks's hands, but Kevin, it was Kevin who had used his gifts to negotiate, to soothe, to teach, to heal. They had both worked their charms to help their daughter; it was the two of them, together, only the two of them who could love Elvira as they did, whose love had lifted us out of the Shiloh National Military Park, and away, away! At the Shiloh church she had stared at the ceiling fan and she'd had an understanding, watching it go around. She had realized that she could not unlace Kevin and Beth, any more than she could undo the four of us, the Shaws.

After Shiloh she did not e-mail Polloco for many weeks because he was in Seattle working on a recording with old friends. I imagine they spoke on the phone on occasion, but there was trouble, I knew, because my mother's eyes were often rimmed with a briny red. She wore her slippers all day long, and when she wasn't scuffing around, she was either playing the piano or taking hot baths. She alternated playing with vengeance and with an elegiac lyricism that would have made even the most hardened listener want to weep. Polloco, at a safe remove, was doing an admirable job as the muse. Later, in the blistering heat of summer, after they'd broken it off for good, she'd drive through neighborhood after neighborhood crying out into the cool interior of the car, "Richard! Richard!" She'd play the two CDs he'd made, straining to hear beyond the music, straining toward his flesh. She used his brand of shampoo, his deodorant, soaking herself in what she could approximate of his smell, trying to bury her own short hair in her face so that she could feel surrounded by him. "Richard, oh God, Richard, where are you?"

In the fall she would walk along the lake calling his name still, searching the skyline for no sign, calling and searching, waiting for nothing, looking for nothing. Never again, never again would she know him in the way that had mattered so much to both of them. It would take time to learn that concept, never again. How is it, she asked herself every day, shaking her head, freshly shocked at the idea—how is it that we don't speak to each other? Time for her, she thought, was hateful, useless. She couldn't think what was worse: that with time she would eventually get over Richard or that he would get over her.

At college, reading a section of Hadrian's work, I came upon the lines the emperor had written to his dead lover in which he so plaintively refers to him as "the companion of my body and the guest of my heart." Not original lines, then, that Liza had written to Rpoll back in the winter, but the work of a homosexual Roman emperor. She had probably not ever read Hadrian, but perhaps my father had once upon a time recited the poem to her, and she had much later known fully what the words meant. The correspondence, hers and Polloco's, filled half a file drawer, and I have to admit I, too, found it strange, unthinkable, that there would not be another message to add to it, that there would never be another letter from him.

Soon after Shiloh my mother again took to borrowing some of my CDs, as if she thought the alienation of a band like Nine Inch Nails would help her through the youthful predicament of failed love. Or maybe after all the years I'd been interested in post-punk industrial rock, she figured she would earnestly listen to some of it. She might have hoped that it would give her an entry, some way to begin a conversation with me. One night that April she did come up to my room, and she did try.

"Henry," she said, looking straight at me, looking so deliberately it made my blood run cold. "I think we need to talk to each other. It's been sort of a difficult year, this year, and there are certain things I'd like you to understand."

I love it that parents can barge into your room and even think that you want to hear every facet of their emotional trauma. She was undoubtedly going to say the right words and phrases, what you're supposed to, that the troubles she and my father had been having had nothing to do with Elvira and me, that because of errors she'd made when she was very young, getting married too early, et cetera, she'd had to step out. She regretted that she'd gone about it backward, upside down, but it wasn't about blame, Henry. No one was to blame.

Before she could make her statement, I said firmly, "Mom." Saying her name like that made her close her mouth. I wanted her only not to go farther, not to begin. I wanted to hold her off at the pass indefinitely. "This may come as a surprise to you," I said, "and it's with all due respect and everything. It's just that, actually–ah, actually, I don't want to know one detail about this year. If you don't mind."

She was staring at me as if I'd caught her in the headlights, as if I had the power to run right through her.

"Whatever you did or didn't do," I hurried on, "you know, that's terrific, and I'd as soon take off and start my own life without some great big Anna Karenina jumps off the bridges of Madison County sort of thing, to haul around. If it isn't too much trouble. Because I don't think the truth, uh, the truth, is going to set me free or get me back to Kansas or bring me to Jesus–and I'm not sure, there's no guarantee, that telling would be a magical experience for you, either."

I don't believe she had yet blinked.

"What I mean," I said, "what I should say–the point is that I–I've had a pretty good childhood, very good, excellent overall. So the main thing is, thanks, thanks for the memories."

Up went her hand to her mouth, she shut her eyes.

"And we'll always, we'll always have Shiloh."

"Okay, Henry," she finally croaked. "God, oh God, what did I do to deserve such an incredible son?" She was at me, kissing my cheek and ear, fine, fine, fine I was saying, and then she got herself out of there. Moments later I, too, fled down the stairs, to the street and to the park, where I walked along the lake well past dark.

I know for a fact that she and Polloco had broken it off when she came in the house on a May evening, the kind of day when the green of the new season seems to be pulsing with an electrical force. It was he, I imagine, the strong one, who was finally decisive. It was his good sense that held sway: he would not keep on with a woman who was forever running back to the city, wracked with guilt. The tulips and daffodils in the neighborhood were up, window boxes filled with petunias, the magnolias in bloom. The whole street stunk and glowed. My mother came in the kitchen. There was a short conversation with my father, about how she was back, she'd taken a taxi from the station, the train had been late, the tracks were being repaired. She dropped her bag and headed into his chest and he put his arms around her. "I'm sorry," I think he said, and she nodded into his shirt.

It occurred to me that my father must have known about Richard Polloco for some time, perhaps even before the ride home from Shiloh in the van. Of all the unusual and embarrassing scenes I had witnessed and imagined, that one, my father embracing my mother in those final circumstances, was the most peculiar. Even now it is difficult for me to read through the file and determine what moved Kevin to stand by Beth and by waiting patiently help her out of her plight, a mess of her own making. The kinds of love I have felt for various women through the years would not have been sufficient to keep me at home and abiding. I occasionally wonder if my father held still ignobly, out of helplessness and fear. Certainly he would have been afraid of losing the life he knew and afraid of disrupting what he took for granted was his children's faith in goodness. I know that he was capable of great generosity, and so he may have acknowledged his share in Mrs. Shaw's unhappiness. I can picture him talking with her, asking her if they couldn't, with a few corrective measures, get their alliance back on course. I don't know how this is done, but perhaps his optimism was shattered just enough to make him tolerable. I leave it to anyone but myself to wonder if he could have treated with enthusiasm the tricks Liza had learned in Polloco's boudoir, the little something she might have brought home to the marriage bed. Or maybe through all of the year he did nothing more than wait with a simple understanding: he believed in Beth Shaw, believed in the forces that had made her and would hold her in place.

At the last book club meeting before summer the members met to discuss a novel that had to do with a young woman breaking up an older man's marriage. Marcia had her baby boy in her arms—oh how

I pitied that kid. He was going to be irredeemably pussy-whipped or insufferably precocious, or, least objectionable, grow up to be malevolent. The infant was suckling at her breast, getting his Marcia-fied nourishment, the intellectual mother's milk, milk, I'm sure, that like alphabet soup had in it letters and numbers.

When the discussion quickly opened into modern-day adultery, Glam Pam said, "Having sex outside of marriage is such a hassle. The rendezvous, the condoms, sneaking to the next motel—who needs it? I'm happy meeting my friend Peter at the coffee shop. We smoke cigarettes. We talk about books and movies. It's a secret from my husband only because I've never gotten around to telling him. I know it sounds tame, but the smoking and the conversations are as much naughtiness as I need, to keep me in balance."

"Sometimes," Mrs. Shaw said, sighing, "isn't it better to be lonely, to people your world in a dream, than to have the need these characters have for each other, nothing separating them but their own thin skins?"

Marcia said, "In your paradigm freedom is preferable to passion—is that what I hear you saying?"

"What she's saying," Glam Pam said, "is that intimacy can turn out to be excruciating. Women for so many years, on however many talk shows and in self-help books, are always yakking about intimacy, but quite frankly no one ever talks about being suffocated, about having so much intimacy you want to retch."

I believe the evening went into its brawl mode then, several members assaulting Pam about her beauty, about how she had a different set of problems than most of the women assembled. I went upstairs unnoticed, thinking about how the degree of intimacy Liza had had with Polloco, excruciating intimacy perhaps, was more than she'd bargained for when she wished for him at Carol and Jim Carodine's wedding. Without Richard's presence, and while Kevin unloaded groceries in the kitchen, she could sit at the piano and play to the idea of Polloco for the rest of her days. There was the paradox at work, the beautiful one, that by giving him up she could have him, she could keep him.

The first person in college I tried to talk to about my family, someone named Madeline, did not believe in my father's goodness. "What," she asked, "was his agenda?"

"His agenda?"

She was one of those hyperleftist types, for whom every gesture and act is a political statement. "You heard me," she said. "His agenda."

I began telling her, in that poisonously quiet and confiding way I have, about Buddha's Noble eight verses for training the mind, tenets that Karen and I had discussed over the years. Number four requires that you learn to cherish ill-natured beings. "Maybe," I said, "my father is the ultimate Buddhist, and my mother, the person who has spurned him the most, is his greatest spiritual guide."

"He sounds sick."

I did not go into a cheap meditation on unconditional love, didn't tell her that as a child I instinctively believed in such a thing. As a teenager I doubted. As a man, on rare occasions, I am willing, I think, to give it the benefit of the doubt. I like to imagine that I have seen its work. I have seen it personified, in Vermont town meetings, an older woman, usually it is, in the back row, unswerving, speaking without rancor against all the others, saying the truth, the sort of truth that will never work in our slow and cumbersome system of compromise and in a country of free enterprise.

But if that plain lackluster love does in fact exist, I learned about the substance of it first from my father. I can make the argument that he was afraid of losing his way of life, or he believed that Waspy Beth Shaw was going to stick around because of her heritage and their 401K plan. And yet, and yet, I sometimes can't help but think that what guided Kevin, what he trusted in himself, was the unreasonable love, the patient love, that he probably considered a nuisance at times. I stand in awe of it when I am not questioning the likelihood of it.

A few years ago, after my film school project and after failing again to tell someone the story of my mother's affair in any comprehensive and intelligible way—*what's wrong with this kid?*—I sat down and read all the messages, a task that took most of the night. I have to say that I always warm to Rpoll when I come, early on, to the opening that goes, "Hello my screech owl, my foghorn on a misty night," and so forth, that I can't help but feel that I am with an old friend. It was in my last reading of the file that I realized there was a coda to the story. I'd missed some vital information for years because I'd never really read the post-breakup messages to Jane, those messages that I'd printed only out of habit.

Mrs. Shaw, I learned, right as the relationship was ending, bought a piece of land in Tribbey, a stretch of marsh primarily, with a bit of prairie and woodland that abutted Miss Van Heusen's property. Using what must have been a sizable chunk of her inheritance, she paid for 160 acres that only the heron and the bullfrog can probably truly appreciate. Richard Polloco also loved that land and walked it frequently, listening to the peepers, the crickets, and the wood thrush. When it went up for sale, he raised the alarm. He, too, had plumbed the depth of dead Minty's pocketbook. The land was going to be tilled and filled, subdivided, and turned into a racetrack, a strip mall, a prison. My mother was going from bathtub to bedroom, weeping about this love of hers—for she believed in true love! Despite the real-life problems she had with Polloco, he was for her The One. She believed in the nineteenth-century idea that romantic love transforms a person, that she wasn't forever stuck with what had been her same old self, that that self had been touched with a great radiance. In her sadness the new and improved Mrs. Shaw heard Rpoll's call to save some wilderness. Rescuer that she was, she came to his aid—if nothing else, she might do this for him. She could think of him then, walking where they had roamed, where, on the prairie, they had lain together in the early spring, when it was barely warm enough. It was like a child, those acres, a beauty that in a sense they had made together, that was alive to the world and would always be known to them. She could say to herself, in her old-fashioned and deluded way, There is a thread between us, that will hold us, that will always hold us.

At Silverpines that summer after high school I washed pots for two hours, three times a day, in a steamy kitchen. Usually, in the evenings we, Lily and I, went to the dances, and it was in the hand-to-hand, glance-to-glance, down-the-line, where I realized that my parents' friends knew about Richard Polloco. It was not surprising, really, that word would have gotten around. The folk music community was a small one, and Rpoll and Liza from the start had had mutual friends. I understood that the affair was common knowledge, because the husbands asked after Mrs. Shaw and the wives did not. I understood because the girls my age came up to me in quiet moments to wonder how my year had been. "It was swell," I told them. "Sensational." The burden I felt was shame, what I had all along expected, although not for the reason I had originally anticipated. As it turned out, everyone in just about the world knew about Rpoll. Ha! Ha! The joke was on me. I had so carefully guarded the secret, given it safe harbor, protecting, I thought, those I loved best.

That summer the desire I felt for Lily kept renewing itself, and I half believed we would not ever outgrow each other. She had a simple grace and a happiness that for those months I did my best to believe in wholeheartedly. It hardly rained, we always went barefoot, in the heat of the day we rested in my narrow bed, and in the night we woke and slept and woke and slept. We were complete, we thought, and carefree, with our dirty pots and music and love. We both knew that in the faraway fall we would begin another life. We'd put our shoes back on, I'd head to Vermont, and she to Italy, where she was spending her senior year in high school. Despite her simplicity, she knew, more than I let myself admit, that everything for us would change, that even if we tried we would not be able to preserve our seventeen- and eighteen-year-old Silverpines selves. I suppose I realized that her sweetness would not ultimately be enough; and whatever her private opinion of me was—too dark, perhaps, too broody—she went off to Florence and later in the year fell in love with an Italian, a twenty-five-year-old painter.

The last time I saw her we were in my cabin at camp. Her parents had come for her. It was time to go, time for her to leave. We had the final kiss. We both shed tears, we clasped hands, pulled away, came

back for one more kiss, and another. When I drove off from Silverpines three hours later, desperation settled over me. As I turned onto
the main road, it was as if my time with Lily were sealing over behind
me; there was no way to reenter the summer, to get it back. That
is not to say that I didn't often, afterward, for a long period, call
her name when I thought myself alone. We managed not to see
each other the following summer, when I went to Costa Rica with
Elvie, and by the time Lily got to Kenyon College, I was involved
with someone else. She did, I guess, end up marrying, not the Italian,
but a geologist who plays the button accordion. I don't think about
her so much, not that much these days.

Shortly after camp, I departed from the Shaw household for
good, book club and all. I have sometimes thought, for the strength
of the story, that I should kill my mother. Or give my father, the pa-
tron saint of cuckolded men, a terminal disease. Even in fiction, as
every history must be, I do not have the heart to kill either one of
them, not for the sake of a poignant ending or my own wistfulness.
The Shaws are alive and seem well enough, in Chicago. Kevin, for
years now, has been the first sergeant of a reenactment unit that is
composed of Jesse Layton students, the 14th Illinois. Girls are welcome and the members take a pledge to keep the secret within the
regiment. He ran the marathon last fall, and he enjoyed the fact that
it nearly did him in. He's proud of the pictures that show him dragging over the finish line, right before he threw up and collapsed. My
mother has made several recordings with and without the Juice of
Barley. She is in demand for concerts and dances, and it seems there
are not many weekends when my parents are in the same county, the
same state.

After I left for college, the Shaws got a new computer, a new system, a new Internet provider, and Liza38 became BShaw, with a password I was not privy to. She hired the kid down the street, Max
Greenbaum, to come over and set her up, and so perhaps it is he who
knows, day by day, what goes on in her life. Max may know if Liza
later developed a friendship with Polloco, if their desire fell away as
mysteriously as it had begun, and they were able to be fond corre-

spondents. Or if Polloco found another woman, a wife even, if he became a father; if Liza took another lover, and another, another. All in all, despite the file I keep, this is my parents' history, and it is probably true that there is very little of it that I actually understand. Although I would possibly like to have children, that specific future is vague. I feel as if I am out in a boat in the middle of the water, that because of the fog I cannot see the shore where a small group, surely someone, is waiting. I expect, based on observation, that to have success in marriage, I'll have to commit blindly and remain blind. It is doubtful, I'd guess, that I'm going to enter into such a contract anytime soon.

When she dies, I like to think that it is I who will inherit the boggy and wooded remains of her love for Richard Polloco, the patch of land that has a conservation easement on it, so that it will remain undisturbed into perpetuity. I like to think that she will know that it is I who will most appreciate the bequeathment. I can't say if she has affection for the woman she was those years ago, foolish Beth, reckless Mrs. Shaw, out-of-control Liza. As I sit at my own keyboard, I picture my mother at hers, alone with her music, in the vapor of it. Each of us alone. Alone in this way, perhaps, in incarnation after incarnation. If I had told the story as it should have been told, it would have been about my father and it would have been shopworn on a different scale. It would have been an account just as old, though rare, out of date. I would hardly be in it; perhaps none of us would really have to be in it. We would see him on his horse, again and again, cantering toward the enemy line, waving his hat, getting shot and rising, getting shot and rising. But the only story I want to tell, the only one I seem to have in me, is this one. It is always about her.

Acknowledgments

Several books were especially helpful to me during the writing of this novel. I am indebted to Tony Horowitz for *Confederates in the Attic*; to Alan T. Nolan for *Lee Considered*; and to Janusz Bardach and Kathleen Gleeson for *Man Is Wolf to Man*. Thanks also to the John Stimson Archive, to Robert Cooper for the photograph of the two bad boys, and to the Bare Necessities for their music, for countless hours of pleasure. Last, thanks to Miles, brave and inspiring.